THE BEQUEST

B. E. BAKER

For Angela.
For Jenae.
For everyone who has lost a spouse.

It's never wrong to love again.

I promise.

1

ABIGAIL

In the week after my husband died, I said I was fine more than one hundred times. I didn't even start counting until the second day.

I was lying every single time, of course.

When Nate was first diagnosed with pancreatic cancer, I was not fine. During the next few weeks, while he underwent surgery and then every treatment they could throw at it, I was not fine. And even though I drew up every document that we might need and spent every possible moment with him before the end, after he died, I was not fine.

But now it's been a year, and with careful planning and a lot of hard work, I can actually tell the truth when someone asks how I'm doing.

"How's it going?" Robert Marwell's standing in my doorway, a half smile on his face. He's not a managing partner with Chase, Holden, and Park, but he probably will be in the next few years.

"I'm fine," I say. And I mean it.

He takes a few steps into my office and sits in one of the wingback chairs. One of the things I like best about

Robert is that even though I'm an associate and he's a partner, he doesn't summon me. He walks all the way down the hall to my office when he has something to discuss. "They're voting in early September," he says. "I know that feels like a long way off, but I think it's good timing."

In just four and a half months, they'll be voting on whether to add any new partners. "Why is it good?" It's not that I think it's bad, but I'd like to know his reasoning.

He glances back at the open doorway and drops his voice. "You've been at the firm for just as long as Nate and I, but other than your first two years, you've always been part time. If you were wanting to be Of Counsel or something, it would be a lock. But as it is. . ." He looks over his shoulder again.

Who's he worried might overhear?

His voice is barely a whisper now. "Lance isn't keen on adding you. Since you own Nate's share in a limited capacity, if we make you partner—"

"I'll be entitled to buy my own share when I'm voted in, and then I'd have double the ownership of anyone other than the named partners—which would give me twice the voting rights."

"I told them that didn't matter. How often do we disagree? When would your double share actually matter?" Robert shrugs. "You know Lance. It's less about what will really happen and more about his ego."

"But why is September good?" I press. "It's not like he gets happier and more easygoing over the summer." If anything, all the people taking vacation drives his blood pressure up.

Robert laughs. "No, but my other piece of news will help you understand."

I raise my eyebrows. "And?"

"The BenchMark case goes to trial in August." He leans forward. "I made sure you're on it, but when it comes time to try the case, I'll step back and let you take first chair."

A big win on something like that would go a long way toward reassuring the partners that I can perform when the stakes are high.

He crosses his arms. "If you win something like this, no one could justify voting against you, not even Lance."

I'm not even sure what to say. It's such a generous offer, and it's exactly the opportunity for which I've been hoping. With Robert in my corner, if this all goes as planned, my family will be back on track by the end of this year. "Thank you, so much."

He stands up and shakes his head. "Please. Nate would have done the same for me if our roles were reversed."

"Maybe not." I scrunch my nose. "I can't even imagine him handing a case to Maisie."

"You know what I mean," Robert says. "If I still had a wife and she needed his help, he would have given it." When he laughs, his eyes brighten and his perfect, white teeth flash. Even with a tiny streak of grey at his temples, Robert's a good-looking guy. "Nate certainly chose more wisely than I did. I'm just sorry that—" He swallows. "You know what I mean."

I do. Robert was nearly as upset as our family when Nate passed away. They'd been best friends since college. And I didn't meet the two of them until law school. I still remember the summer when the three of us had our first clerkship, together, at this very firm.

He pivots on his heel and walks to the doorway, pausing just before he leaves. "Do you have plans for lunch?"

I haven't gone out for lunch since Nate died. He must know that—he's certainly never asked me before. A warning bell goes off in the back of my brain. Is Robert asking me out? Surely not. First of all, he's one of my oldest friends—and Nate's. That alone would make it strange, but secondly, Nate's only been gone a year. Surely no one could expect me to date again so soon.

"It would be nice to have a little time away from the office to discuss the plans for the case. I obviously can't mention my full plans too loudly here." He looks surreptitiously up and down the hall one last time, like we're spies or something. "I have a deposition this afternoon, so if you want to hammer out some rough plans, lunch is probably our best bet." He tilts his head sideways. "I promise not to bite."

The case, duh. I'm such an idiot sometimes. Hopefully he didn't notice my hesitation. "Oh, sure."

My cell phone rings. Only my kids or their school call me on it, as Robert knows. "Take your call. I'll circle back around in half an hour."

Tension I didn't realize I was holding in my back releases the second he's gone, and I swipe to answer. "Hello?"

"Hey Mom, it's me."

"Gosh, I'm so glad you clarified, Ethan. One of these days I might even figure out how this phone thing works, and when I see your name, I'll know who's calling."

"I'm not holding my breath, boomer," he says.

"That's rude. I'm Gen Y, okay?"

"Barely."

"Everything okay?" He rarely calls me when I'm at work. Text messages are so much easier.

"Yeah, I'm fine. But look, Mom—I know you're busy, and I know your gut instinct is going to be to shut me down, but can you just listen?"

I suppress the giant sigh that's trying to claw its way out. "Is this about Dave's speakers again? Because we—"

"Mom, no, it's not about the speakers."

"What, then?"

"Just listen, right? Before you freak out or say no, you'll just hear me out?"

"I am listening," I say. "And I never freak out."

"You do say no a lot."

"What do you want?"

"Look, Riley's dad's competing in the Baja 1000 and they need some extra cash, so he's selling his brand new RZR XP turbo."

"Didn't Riley wreck it last week?"

"I mean, it got a little banged up, but it's nothing I can't fix. Seriously, Mom. Once it's repaired, it'll be worth thirty grand, easy, but Riley said he'd sell it to me for nineteen!"

I don't laugh. Or at least, I try not to laugh. "You don't want me to say no, and yet, you don't have the money to buy that. Please help me out. What am I supposed to say right now?"

"Mom!"

"Ethan!" I know he's struggling with his dad being gone. Spending time with Riley and his dad has been helpful, I think. But I don't have the time, and we don't have the money with only my (currently much lower) income, to buy huge things like fancy side-by-sides.

"How can you say I don't have the money? I have like eighty grand!"

"Are you talking about your college fund?" He's got to be kidding. All my sympathy for his cause just disappeared if he's really trying to convince me to sacrifice his future on some fun weekend plans. "I know you're not talking about spending your college fund on something this frivolous. And may I remind you, we would then need a trailer and a truck in order to even use that thing."

"Mom—"

"Ethan, I don't have time—"

"You didn't even listen to me," he says. "With the money I'd save getting this one—"

"The money you would *save*?" I can't help laughing this time. "You sound like a spoiled housewife. You aren't saving a single dollar—you're buying something that costs, what? Twenty-five times the amount you have personally saved?"

"I have a job now, Mom. And—"

My office phone rings.

Even Ethan knows what that means. "I know, I know. You have to answer that. But don't hang up. Hear me out at least. I'll wait."

I often wonder what God was thinking when he planned out the teenage years. They're emotionally miswired, they rage against the people who are helping them (who have nothing to gain, incidentally), and they're never satisfied with anything. Maybe it's not about the kids. Maybe these years were created to expand parents' patience. "Fine." I set my cell phone on the desk and pick up my office line.

"Hello?"

"Mrs. Brooks? Mrs. Nathaniel Brooks?"

I haven't been called Mrs. Nathaniel Brooks in nearly a year. It catches me by surprise and leaves me almost unable to speak.

"Hello?"

"Yes," I manage to say. "That's me." I clear my throat.

"Good." The man shuffles some papers. "My name is Karl Swift." Something about his voice, perhaps the wobbly timbre, makes me think that Karl is quite old.

"What can I help you with, Mr. Swift?"

"Er, well, it might be more correct for me to tell you what I think I can help you with."

He sounds like Bilbo Baggins at his birthday party. "Okay."

"I'm actually a lawyer as well—I found your name on your firm website from a simple search. I'm calling to notify you that last night, I read a will that had been posted in all the local papers and online."

"A will for whom?" I still have no idea why he called, and I'm beginning to think he was improperly named. Spit it out, Ol' Man River!

"Jedediah Brooks passed away almost two weeks ago."

Brooks. He's related to Nate, then. The name finally registers. "Nate's uncle?"

"Even so," Mr. Swift says.

"I'm very sorry to hear that he passed," I say, rotely. I didn't meet Nate's uncle more than a handful of times, and even then we barely exchanged a handful of words. He had a full head of white hair the first time we met, nearly twenty years ago at my wedding to Nate. He must have lived quite a long life.

"Thank you. His death was quite a shock, but at least it was quick. Jed always said he wanted it to be fast, not drawn out."

My hand trembles where it's holding the phone. Nate's wasn't quick at all—and it was so fast I could barely think straight. "Is that why you called? To let me know that he'd passed?"

"Not precisely," Mr. Swift says. "You see, as I understand it, both of Mr. Brooks' nephews, Nathaniel and Paul, predeceased him."

I murmur my assent. They were both so young. It still sounds so wrong to agree that they're both dead, even now.

"In that case, there is quite a substantial bequest made to your children, Mrs. Brooks."

"Excuse me?"

"Jed has a three thousand, two hundred and eleven acre cattle ranch out here, on the northern side of Utah. It's one of only six properties in the state that date back to the original land grant. In fact, portions of the property are actually in Wyoming, but it's mostly in a place called Daggett County."

"Are you saying that my children's great-uncle left them a three-thousand acre ranch?"

"Not entirely."

I wish Mr. Swift would cut to the chase. For a lawyer, he certainly lacks in clarity. "What does the will say, then?"

"Specifically, it provides that the ranch and all its appurtenances, including the home, a guest house, two large barns, an outbuilding for storage, and some three hundred and fifty head of cattle should be left to your children and the children of Nathaniel's brother, Paul, per stirpes."

I wonder what something like that is worth. Maybe Ethan could get his Razor after all. "Well, that's unexpected."

"However." Mr. Swift rustles more papers. "In order for the bequest to vest, the heirs or, in the case that they're minors, their appointed guardians, must adequately and actively operate the Birch Creek Ranch for a period of one full year."

Whoa. "A year?"

"Yes, that's correct."

"And if I hire someone?"

"I will, of course, send you the actual document so that you can read it yourself, but it was drawn up by a rather hot-shot lawyer in California. I doubt it will have any surprising loopholes."

"Does that mean I can't hire someone to run it for us?"

"I'm afraid the bequest stipulates that the heirs or their guardian must operate the ranch themselves and live on site for the full year. It allows no more than three ten day runs away from the ranch during that period."

And the Razor is back off the table. "My email address is listed on the same firm website," I say. "I would appreciate if you sent me a copy of that will."

"Of course," Mr. Swift says. "And I'm sorry it's not a simpler bequest."

"That's alright," I say. "I'm no stranger to the phrase, 'easy come, easy go.' I certainly didn't expect anything from dear Uncle Jedediah, so I won't be disappointed that nothing has materialized. My condolences, again."

"So you anticipate that you'll be turning down the offer?"

"I'm quite positive," I say. "If you'd like to send over whatever paperwork your office would like to keep on file, I'm happy to sign it."

"If none of his nephew's children accept the bequest, the ranch will be sold and the proceeds will be donated to the Institute of Research into Alien Life on Planet Earth."

The *what?* "That's certainly. . .interesting."

"The RALPE Institute received annual donations from Jed from the time he was doing well enough to make them. It's not everyone's thing, but that's what the will says. If that changes your mind, please do let me know."

"I wish them every bit of luck finding alien life." I'm proud of myself for keeping my voice steady.

"Do you happen to have a phone number on a Mrs. Paul Brooks?"

"Amanda?" I scroll through my contacts on Outlook. "Sure." I rattle off the phone number that I rarely use, and wish him a good day.

Robert pokes his head around the corner just as I hang up. "Ready?"

I'm about to stand when I remember that Ethan might still be on hold. "Almost."

"I'll go down and get the car. Meet you at the front?"

"Perfect, thanks." I press the phone to my ear. "Ethan? Are you still there?"

But he's not on the line anymore. I should have known. Teenagers aren't celebrated for their long attention spans. I'm sure he'll talk my ear off about all the reasons buying a wrecked Razor is the best idea he's ever had as soon as I get home from work.

Robert's waiting for me when I reach the ground level, his black BMW sleek and shiny. When he opens the door and stands up, my heart races. He can't possibly be planning to come around and open my door for me, right? That would be squarely in date territory.

I practically leap for the passenger door and open it myself, sliding inside as quickly as I can in four-inch heels and a fitted suit skirt.

"Where do you want to eat?" he asks.

I have no idea what's good around here. Before Nate died, I only came in for the morning, never staying for lunch, and since his death, I've been coming in at 7:15 after school drop off and leaving at 3:15, so I haven't had time to take a lunch and still work a full day.

"I'm fine with anything other than Chinese food," I say.

"You don't like Chinese?" He frowns. "Really?"

"I'll eat P.F. Changs or Pei Wei," I say. "Maybe it's the MSG, but all the other Chinese food I've tried gives me a headache."

"How about Thai food?"

"I like that."

"Great." He spends the rest of the drive and our entire meal discussing his plan for the case and my role in it.

I'm glad I brought a notepad along, because I fill two full pages with notes.

"You didn't have to write all of that down," he says. "I'd have been happy to clarify anything you forget."

"I don't like asking people to repeat themselves."

"Probably why everyone likes working with you."

When the waitress brings the check, Robert doesn't even glance at it. He just hands her his black American Express.

"You don't want to verify you were charged correctly?" I try not to let a note of censure enter my tone, but I'm not sure I succeed.

"You're such a lawyer." He laughs. "But the firm is paying—we worked every second. We both drank water, and we each only ordered one entree. I'm not sure how badly they could possibly screw it up."

I look at my hands as I smooth the napkin over my lap. "I do tend to worry about every little detail."

"It's what makes you a top notch litigator."

"And a giant pain in the rear." I don't look up, because I know it's true. I don't need to see the confirmation in his eyes.

"Abigail."

I swallow.

"Abby."

I finally look up.

His expression is soft. "You work harder than anyone I know. No one thinks you're a pain."

I am, however, terrible at accepting compliments with grace. "Well, thanks."

"I mean it. Not everyone wants to add another partner, but one hundred percent of the partners acknowledge that you're the highest caliber associate." He sighs.

"It actually may be part of the reason they don't want to promote you. You won't be available to make their lives easier if you're handling your own cases."

"I'm also the oldest associate." I didn't mind when Nate was earning money too, but I can't really catch up on the savings goals for our family on an associate's salary. I try not to think about the hit our savings took when we paid for the expensive treatments we threw at Nate's cancer, but I can't help it when I get the statements. It weighs on me.

"We aren't that old," Robert says.

"Bush was president when we were in law school," I say. "*Friends* was still on the air."

"You were so stunning in law school." He leans back in his chair, his head shaking slowly. "Everyone called you Elle, remember?"

"That pissed me off," I say.

"You did sort of decide to do law school on a whim," he says. "You didn't know the different types of law."

"I was nineteen years old. I didn't know gasoline came from crude oil and not natural gas." I laugh.

"You did."

"Fine, I was pretty smart for a teenager, but I still don't get it. It's not like that character started school young. She was just unmotivated and ditzy. She went for a guy. It was offensive."

"The women probably intended it as an insult, but none of the guys took it that way."

I huff. "I looked nothing like Reese Witherspoon in *Legally Blonde*."

He snorts. "Nothing like her? You were blonde, you were in great shape, and you dressed stylishly."

"I *was* blonde?" I pretend to be annoyed. "I pay a lot for this color."

"I'm so sorry," Robert says. "You were as blonde then

as you are now. Is that better?" He rolls his eyes. "Lawyers are the worst."

"They really are," I agree.

"Law students may be the only thing worse, but you showed them—top of the class." Robert looks down at the table. "I was pretty stupid as a law student too."

"Whoa," I say. "Are you finally admitting that your Birkenstocks were a crime against fashion?"

He meets my eyes, his gaze as intense as I've ever seen it. "You had just broken up with your college boyfriend when we started, remember?"

For some reason, mentioning my breakup with Shawn makes my heart race, which is crazy. That guy was a major loser. "I do, yeah. I was kind of wrecked."

"Nate and I had been roommates at UCLA and we both met you at orientation—you were wearing that yellow sundress. But I'm not sure you ever knew that we were both interested."

What? I've never heard this, not once.

"Nate insisted he was going to go after you right away. My sister told me that was idiotic—if you really like a girl, you wait for her to rebound first." He swallows. "I thought it was wise to play the 'friend' angle. Once Nate struck out, I figured you'd be ready for something real." He sighs. "Then you married Nate."

"Robert—"

"I know it's probably a shock, but I just need to get it out there. That's still the biggest mistake I've ever made, but I never let myself regret it. I loved both of you, and you were really happy. But now. . ."

Robert liked me? I had no idea. "But you and Maisie—"

"You mean the girl who was the closest I could find to a facsimile of you?" He snorts. "She wasn't nearly close enough, clearly. You know how miserable we were better than anyone."

Is he implying that if she'd been more like me, they'd have been happy? "I'm not sure—"

"Fool me once, shame on you. Fool me twice, shame on me, right? That's how the saying goes?"

He's hopping around so fast I can't keep up.

"Earlier today, I *was* asking you on a date, or at least I was trying to ask you. Then you looked like I'd stabbed a puppy, so I pretended it was a work lunch. I almost let it be, but I can't do that, not again, Abby. Because if I miss my chance a second time, I'll never be able to live with myself."

2

AMANDA

When I was growing up, my parents always gave us cash on our birthdays. The best part of the birthday experience was the luxury of a shopping trip to anywhere we chose. When I turned five, I spent $50 at the dollar store. My room was so full of trash, I could barely find my bed.

When I turned six, I spent $50 at the grocery store, buying enough candy to rot the teeth of the entire neighborhood.

On my seventh birthday, I spent $50 on stuffed animals. I hadn't yet discovered that they don't really love you back.

For my eighth birthday, however, my parents only had $13 to spare. My dad had just lost his job, and things were tight. I asked to go garage sale shopping that year, in the hopes of finding something worth far more than $13. We spent hours searching through old records and VHS tapes, mismatched and scuffed sneakers, and slightly abused toys. I didn't find anything truly valuable, even though we visited more than a dozen garage sales. But the anticipation when we walked into that thirteenth garage was still stupidly high.

After searching all day, my parents finally became exasperated and told me I just had to pick something. I ended up buying a pair of slightly-too-large ski boots that I never even wore. I'm not even sure why I bought them —I'd never been skiing and we had no plans to try it.

Hoping to find treasure among someone else's cast-offs was super dumb.

Online dating above 40 feels an awful lot like a never-ending sequence of garage sales. Except, unlike that thirteenth garage, my expectations are no longer very high. My naively optimistic hope is gone.

Which is why, even though Krystal swore this new dating app was better, even though she promised me that it was curated to ensure a professional man, I'm not even surprised when my date is essentially the male equivalent of those sad ski boots.

"Amanda." He holds out his hand enthusiastically. "So good to see you."

Roger recognizes me, you see, because my profile photo, unlike his, resembles my actual face. I force a smile. "Yes, I am Amanda."

"I was so happy when you swiped left!" Sweat has beaded across his forehead, and he swipes it away. Or, he tries to swipe it away. He manages to shove it to the side of his face, where it runs down his temple and pools near his double-chin, glistening.

"It's right," I say. "You swipe right if you're interested."

"And you did." He grins a little too broadly, making his jowls jiggle.

"Should we eat?" At least we're at one of my favorite restaurants, J.G. Melon. I always suggest it for a first date, because I love a good burger, and I usually can't justify eating one. But on a first date with a total stranger, I feel entitled to splurge on extra calories and saturated fat. Also, their cottage fries are absolutely to die for—they're the most delicious tiny little circles on planet Earth. They make most anything bearable.

Roger points to a booth in the corner. It's likely the only place in the entire restaurant where we can sit and talk as long as we want without being bothered. Darn him for noticing it. "I was surprised that you suggested this place."

"Why?" I ask. "You don't like burgers?"

"Well last time, you said—"

I'm not eating or drinking currently, and that's the only reason I don't choke, but I sure do splutter. "Did you just say the *last time,* implying that we've been on a date before this?"

He blinks. "What?"

"Have you taken me out before today, Roger?"

He frowns, and if possible, he looks even dopier.

That's when I remember. He had more hair, and he had a smaller mid-section, but it's definitely the same guy from two years ago. He asked me to watch a ballgame with him, and I learned never to commit an entire sporting event to an unknown.

"I'm so sorry I didn't remember." But mostly I feel sorry for myself.

"You never called me back, so I guess I should've known it was a mistake."

Heat rises in my cheeks. "If I'm being honest, I don't even select my own dates anymore. I don't have time. My assistant screens the guys and lines everything up for me." I call her my assistant, but it's actually my fifteen-year-old daughter who helps with work things and started setting me up for more dates. I'm going to have to strangle her later.

"Right, you're an influencer now," he says. "Champagne for cheap, right?"

I cringe. There's no way I'd ever use the word 'cheap' on my account. "Champagne for Less," I say. "Yep, that's me."

"Last time we went out, you weren't sure what you were going to do, I think."

"My account was doing fine already." But I had no idea whether I'd make rent in any given month. I still have rough spells now and then, but not nearly as often.

"Well, now that I know our date was a mistake, I'll give you this one chance to bow out."

I can't decide whether Roger's a decent guy, or whether he just has an unexpected amount of pride. "It's fine," I say. "I'm still happy to grab a burger." Not really, but what else can I say?

"It's not like I'll be wasting very much money, at least." His laugh is a little too loud, and a little too unbridled for a public restaurant, and his eyes roam far too much. It's definitely the pride thing.

My phone rings—and when I check the caller ID, it's Lololime. I've been waiting for them to call me for two days, ever since their rep informed that I was being considered for a permanent sponsorship spot. "I'm so sorry, Roger. I have to take this."

He waves. "Go ahead. I'll just get mine to go."

I ought to soothe his hurt feelings and reassure him that I'm not making excuses, but I don't have the time or the energy. "Hello?" I walk out the door and onto the somewhat busy street, but at least I'm clear of Roger and his passive aggressive moping.

"Mrs. Brooks?"

"Yes," I say. "But please call me Amanda."

"My name is Heather Hames, and I'm the director of social media marketing with Lololime. We've had our eye on you for a while, and I wanted to reach out and have a quick chat. Is this a bad time?"

I think about Roger, probably still moping. Eh, he can drown his sorrows with a plate of cottage fries. "Not at all. In fact, you just saved me from a *second* first date with a very boring guy."

"Wait, what?"

By the time I explain what happened, Heather's laughing. "But you missed out on the burger. I work out of our Seattle office, but to hear you describe it, that's a true travesty."

"Don't worry," I say. "If this call takes a little longer, he'll duck out and I can grab my burger anyway."

"That's one of the things we like best about you," Heather says. "Your feed is always fresh, witty, and engaging. I'm sure that's why your stats are as good as they are. It's hard not to feel an instant connection with the little tidbits of real you toss among the glitter and confetti of a normal glamorous living page."

"Thank you," I say. "I do try."

"As you probably already know, before we select a brand ambassador, we assemble a short list of contenders, and then we choose from among them. You're my pick, so I'd love to make it more likely you're chosen."

More likely? What does that mean? "Okay."

"I wanted to mention the one area where we worry your page might need a little. . .bolstering, and please keep in mind that this doesn't mean we don't already love what you're doing."

Sure it doesn't.

"As you know, Lololime has been working hard to expand its market share. We began as clothing designed for pilates workout programs, but we quickly expanded to yoga, running, and racquetball."

"I really love the new running line," I say. "Especially the running shorts."

"The images you post from your runs are one of the things that attracted us to you in the first place," Heather says. "But we are now expanding into a whole new realm of activewear. We'll be targeting people in all walks of life, and hopefully bringing a little sophistication and glamour to everyday people. Not just people in New York, Chicago, and Los Angeles, but also in small towns all over America through our internet sales line. We've redesigned our entire website to be more accessible and give more price point options."

"Really?"

"Until now, we've focused on high quality, moving lower quantity of product with a higher markup. We plan to keep that model, but the reason we're searching for new sponsorships of the highest category, in the amounts we mentioned in our initial email, is that we'd like to find ambassadors who can carry us into new and more expansive markets."

New markets? Lower quality and lower markup, but higher volume?

My image is high end. It's New York glam on a budget, sort of. But the 'budget' is still more than three times what the average American makes. "I'm not sure—"

"We think you're bright, you're at the perfect age for our target demographic, and you have children. That's what we're looking for—clothing for the entire family. Bring some class to the everyday, for everyone at home."

Class to the everyday? What part of my life is everyday? "My girls go to private schools," I say. "And I—"

"Yes, and we know that's going to be a limitation on your success in this area. It's the reason I'm calling. My boss wants to simply strike you from the list, but I think you can add some depth and dimension to your current posts and expand your following to bring in the 'every woman' even a little more than you already do. Think of it like this. Right now, a lot of normal people watch your account like it's a window into a life they can't ever have. I'm hoping you can open that window and invite them in a bit more."

Uh. Okay.

"How about you focus on trying that for the next, I don't know, thirty days or so, and I'll check back in with you as you do."

"Sure," I say.

But when she hangs up, I realize that I have no idea what she means. Of course, I immediately call my closest influencer friend, GlamBamThankYouMan. "Zoey!"

"Did they call?" Her voice is way too high pitched, which means she's prepped to celebrate. I need to redirect or I'll hear nothing but shrieking.

"It wasn't a great conversation," I say. "It left me confused." I explain what Heather said. "I just don't know what that means, add *dimension*."

"They want you to do more normal things."

I think about yesterday's post, where I took Maren and Emery to get facials. "Instead of taking the girls to the spa, maybe we get burgers and fries?"

"Sure," Zoey says. "That's a good start."

"But is that enough?" I sigh. "I wish I didn't need to change things."

"Two hundred thousand dollars a year to do three posts a week." Zoey whistles. "I'd jump through a lot of hoops for a contract that promised me that kind of money—for two years."

She's right, clearly, but. . . "I'm just not sure that burgers and fries are going to be good enough to make us look more accessible." I think for a moment. "Maybe I should, I don't know, paint my own bathroom." That sounds terribly messy, and it would probably take a really long time. "Or I could take the girls ice skating. That's something everyone does, right?"

"Everyone goes ice skating?" I can practically hear Zoey's eye roll through the phone. "Girl, let me think about it and I'll call you back with some ideas. They can't be worse than yours."

By the time I walk back to J. G. Melon's, Roger's already gone. That's a relief—I order three burgers and plenty of cottage fries to go. The girls will be thrilled. Now if I can think of a way to photograph that and stay on brand somehow. Maybe if we're sitting in front of Central Park?

Of course, by the time I get everything arranged, the burgers will probably taste disgusting. I check my watch. I was nervous to set up such a late lunch—worried I'd be late to pick up Emery, but this works out perfectly. They call my name, and I grab my bag and scoot out the door. I almost don't realize that my phone is buzzing.

It can't be Lololime again, right? I whip my phone out, careful to keep the bag full of greasy food away from my new silk blouse. I don't recognize the area code, much less the number. "Hello?"

"Mrs. Brooks?"

"Yes?"

"Mrs. Paul Brooks?"

People almost never call me that anymore, not after three and a half years. "Uh, sure. That's me." It's probably a telemarketer. I almost tell him that I don't even own a car, much less need an extended warranty, but something holds me back.

"My name is Mr. Swift, Mrs. Brooks. I'm calling with some sad news."

Of course he is. No one ever calls with good news anymore. Whatever happened to the huge checks that one guy brought to your door? Not that anyone I knew ever got one, but it was nice to know the possibility was out there. Now it's just bad news, terrible news, and gosh awful news. "Okay, well, you may as well share it. We aren't getting any younger."

"Ain't that the truth?" He chuckles.

I shouldn't have made a joke. It's only encouraging him to draw this out. I chomp down on an exasperated huff.

"Your late husband's uncle, Jedediah Brooks, has passed away. Your sister-in-law, Abigail Brooks, gave me your number. I'm calling to let you know that your daughters were mentioned in his will."

Jedediah, Jedediah. I wrack my brain for any memory of a person named Jededi—"Is that the uncle who lived on a huge ranch?" My hopes soar. If the girls have inherited a ranch. . .Maybe I won't even need more *dimension.* Maybe our fortune, that Paul's death wrecked, might improve through good luck instead of bad.

"It is, indeed. Your husband spent every summer on his uncle's ranch until he turned eighteen. I'm sure he shared many fond memories with you about that time."

"Uh, yes." I vaguely remember a few anecdotes about poison oak and stepping in cow pies. "So what exactly did he leave my girls?" If it's even half of what we lost. . .Paul might have been a monumentally lousy husband, but he was a financial genius. I can still barely think about how he put all our money into brilliant options. . .that unfortunately expired without being exercised after he died.

I didn't even really know what an option was until one of his co-workers explained that he'd invested heavily in a brilliant portfolio of options that should have yielded close to a hundred million. But options have to be exercised or they expire.

And when they expire. . .they're worthless.

Which is how we wound up penniless, the one good thing about Paul rendered useless by his unexpected death.

For some reason, Mr. Swift has a lot of papers to shuffle. "Well, I was hoping that perhaps your sister-in-law might have already filled you in."

"Abigail?"

"She is your sister-in-law," he says. "Is she not?"

"We aren't very close." The understatement of the year. The first year or two after Paul died, we exchanged Christmas gifts and birthday cards. But since Nate's death, I haven't been sure what to send, much less what words to say. She actually loved her husband, unlike me. I'm sure that made things much harder. "Did she say she was going to call?"

"No, she didn't." Mr. Swift clucks. "Well, your late husband's uncle left a generous bequest to his nephews, or if they predeceased him, which of course they did, to their children. It's essentially his entire estate. All cash, all holdings, the property, the land, and of course, all the cattle."

I can barely breathe. It's all my fondest dreams, finally coming true. Financial stability. An end to my desperate fear that everyone will discover I'm a total fraud and my income will drop to zero. "I'm so sorry for his death, but—"

"However." He clears his throat. "There is a stipulation."

"A what?" It's something to do with contracts, that much I know. Sometimes I really envy Abigail. Her parents taught her to focus on things that matter, instead of frilly outfits and tiaras made of paste. She must have immediately understood whatever thing Mr. Swift is saying.

"The girls will only receive their equal share of his

substantial estate if they relocate to Daggett County, Utah, and live on the ranch for one full calendar year. They're also required to actively work the ranch for that entire year."

"Wait. In order to get Uncle Jed's ranch and cows and whatnot, we'd have to move to where?"

"Daggett County, Utah," Mr. Swift says. "It's just south of the Wyoming border. In fact, a portion of the three thousand, five hundred acres that comprise Birch Creek Ranch are actually located in Wyoming."

Lololime is sounding better all the time. "I know less than nothing about ranching," I say. "And my girls are in school."

"I don't think it's possible to know less than nothing," Mr. Swift says. "And I imagine the school year is nearly concluded. I hear that Manila has excellent schools."

How excellent can they possibly be? I groan. "Well, I guess I have a lot to think about."

"You certainly do," he says. "How much time do you need?"

"What happens if we don't come work the ranch?"

"If none of the heirs opt to work the ranch, it will be sold, along with all other property, at auction, and the proceeds will fund Mr. Jedediah Brooks' passion—research into extraterrestrial beings."

"Aliens?"

"Even so, Mrs. Brooks. Alien research."

That's ridiculous. "There must be some way to fight this," I say. "I can't possibly pull my kids out of school here. They're at one of the finest schools in America. I'm sure Manila is. . .fine, but it can't compare to the education I'm providing in New York. I have no idea how they'd ever catch up if we left, even just for one year."

"I'll certainly be happy to send you a will, and you can have your lawyer take a look."

“Fine.” I share my email address.

“I’ll send it over this evening.”

“Thank you,” I say. “And Mr. Swift?”

“Yes?”

“What did Abigail say? Did she turn it down, or are they going?”

“She told me emphatically that she plans to decline.”

Of course she did. The only thing that might actually make me want to go would be watching *Abigail*, queen of the corporate world, Miss Composure herself, trying to ride a horse, tie up a calf, and pull eggs out from under a clucking chicken. “I think I’ll probably do the same.”

As much as I love the impractical dream of lucking into a huge windfall of cash, it’s not reality—Lololime’s sponsorship is. A two-year contract for regular posts, as many free clothes as I can wear, and the security of knowing that I’ll make rent every single month—that’s all within my grasp. Or it will be, once I figure out how to add dimension and depth to my posts.

I can’t possibly pull the girls out of school in order to chase rainbows.

3

ABIGAIL

My heart lurches in my stomach. I'm no doctor, but I'm pretty sure it shouldn't be there. "Robert—"

"See? That's enough, right there. The way you just said my name?" He shakes his head. "I want nothing to do with making you feel like that. So I'm just going to say this once, and then I'll never bring it up again."

My stomach twists and cramps and I finally understand the expression 'I'm tied up in knots.'

"Since I've already completely destroyed this entire lunch, I'll tell you my deepest, darkest secret." A muscle in his square jaw works. "I feel like I owe it to Nate—you should know that I loved him like a brother. I had never done a single disloyal thing to him in my entire life."

He runs his hand over his jaw. If he didn't have such a defined jawline, his beautiful eyes, his perfectly shaped nose, and his flawless skin, combined with movie star hair, would probably make him look too beautiful. As it is, he's always been the best looking man I've known.

"A small part of me was happy when I heard that Nate passed." He wads his napkin in his hand. "I know that makes me a terrible person. At first, I thought my penance for that sentiment would be never, ever acting on my feelings, never confessing the truth. But it's been a year, and I know that's not long, but I also think that if you could ask him, Nate would want you to be with someone like me. Someone who cares about your kids. Someone who cares about you."

"Robert—"

"There you go again with the mournful *Roberts*," he says. "Look, I just wanted you to know how I feel. I think you're the most incredible, the most brilliant, the most organized, the most capable, and the most stunningly beautiful woman I've ever met. No one else compares. No one else has ever come close. If you *ever* feel differently than you do right now. . ." He stands up. "Like I said, I couldn't do nothing, not again. But I value our friendship too, more than you probably know, so I'll never say another word. I'll never so much as glance at you sideways. Things with me will be one hundred percent work and friendship from here on out. . .unless you change your mind." His half smile is at once the most handsome and the most gut-wrenching thing I've ever seen.

Oh Nate, why did you leave me?

I can't even blame Robert for how he feels or even how he felt when Nate died. I've certainly spent my share of time angry at Nate for leaving me to handle everything alone. "I'm not even close to being ready to move on, Robert."

"Or at least, not with me." His smile breaks my heart. "Don't worry. I'll be fine."

I'm terrified things will be unbearably awkward between us, but that fear, at least, appears to be unfounded. On the drive back to the office, Robert slides right back into talking about work like nothing ever happened. In fact, the drive back feels the same as the ride over felt. It's not until I'm pulling out my office chair to sit down and get back to work that I realize why.

He's felt this way for a very long time, which means he's had a lot of practice at pretending that everything is fine.

By now, Robert's probably a master at suppressing his feelings. I'm not sure whether that's sweet or tragic. "Oh, Nate. I wish you were here right now. You'd know what I should do."

It's probably not strictly sane for me to talk to my dead husband out loud, but it makes me feel better. I've done a lot of things I never thought I'd do in the past year.

Like Pizza Mondays. Before Nate got sick, I'd never have agreed that my kids should gorge themselves on pizza and breadsticks every Monday, but the take-out guy at Il Primo knows me by name now. "Abigail. I have your pizzas ready. Extra parmesan?"

No matter how many times I've told him no, and it's got to be close to fifty at this point, he always offers. "Thanks, Teo, but I'm good."

Am I good, though? A friend of nearly twenty years just told me he'd like to take me on a date. I set the pizza boxes in the passenger seat and before I can put the car in gear, tears well up in my eyes. It's not that Robert's a bad person, no matter what he said. He's one of the best guys I know. If Nate hadn't asked me out first, who knows? But he did.

And the only reason Robert could ask me at all is that he's gone.

Forever.

So maybe I do still lie sometimes when I say I'm fine, but at least I have the hope that it will one day be true. That's something.

When I get home, Ethan's mixing up a salad, Izzy's

slicing a cantaloupe, and Gabe's setting the table. Whitney, as usual, is playing the piano. She's my only musically inclined child, and I'm delighted to have one.

"What's all this for?" I set the pizza on the table and pull out a stack of plates.

"I figured it had probably been a long day," Ethan says. "It is a Monday."

He's such a liar. "I appreciate the help," I say. "But I'm on to you."

Ethan's grin is far too charming, and his hair falls into his face roguishly. No mother, no matter what she says, is really delighted when her teenage son turns out to be ridiculously handsome. It makes me incredibly nervous. I wish he'd waited to grow into his good looks until, say, college. Or maybe grad school. "I know, I know, I can't get the RZR. I know that money's for college, and I shouldn't have asked."

I didn't expect him to surrender so smoothly. "What did everyone do today? Anything fun?"

"Not today," Gabe says, already reaching for pizza, "but tomorrow is field day! Can you come?"

I hate that the schools wait until it's so hot in Houston before doing field day. "Uh, well—"

"Mom has a lot of work to do, runt," Izzy says. "I'm sure she'll make it if she can."

"I did get assigned a new case today."

Whitney groans. "Another one? Why didn't you tell them no?"

I laugh. "I want to be on this case. Uncle Robert helped me get it." I lean forward. "You all know that your father had just been made partner. . ."

"When he died?" Gabe's voice is still just a little too loud at the wrong times. Hazard of being seven.

I don't flinch. That's progress. "Yes, and when you're a partner, you make more money. Thanks to this case, I'll be more likely to be made partner sooner. The extra work will be hard, but the extra money would be good for all of us."

"You know what else might be good for all of us?" Ethan asks.

"What?" If he says a Razor, I'm going to explode.

"I hear Utah is nice," he says casually, like he's telling me that it's going to rain tomorrow.

It takes a moment for me to process what he's saying. He was on the phone waiting for me when Mr. Swift called—what exactly would he have been able to hear from his end? I open my mouth and close it again. As their guardian, I don't technically have to tell them anything about the bequest. It's my decision to make—whether to turn it down or move to Utah. Thank goodness for that.

But if Ethan already knows. . .

"Let's say grace so we can eat," I say.

The kids bow their heads and I pray—I don't want to deal with anyone whining for being chosen. Once the prayer is over, they all dive in, stuffing their faces. It bought me a few moments to think about what Ethan likely heard and how I want to approach it. "Your Great Uncle Jedediah passed away," I say. "I found out today."

"What made him so great?" Whitney asks.

Ethan laughs. "No, she's not saying he's great. She's saying he's Dad's uncle, which makes him our 'great' uncle, like a grandpa, only an uncle."

"Oh." Whitney looks just as confused as before.

"The great part is that he left us his ranch in his will," Ethan says. "It's almost four thousand acres."

Clearly he heard enough, but not the right parts. "He left it to the four of you, and to your cousins, Maren and Emery, as well."

Izzy, predictably, is bouncing up and down. "I bet

there are horses. Are there horses?" She's been taking riding lessons for two years. You'd think that would be enough, but the girl is the same as I used to be. She can never get enough time around them.

"It's a cattle ranch," Ethan says, his tone utterly confident, as always. "Of *course* there are horses. Probably loads of them."

"Ethan." My tone is too sharp. I bite my tongue.

Izzy's voice escalates into squeal territory.

Whitney, as usual, is looking from Ethan to me and back again, trying to figure out why I'm not excited, and why Ethan's so interested. She's always been the keenest observer of all my children. Gabe's shouting and jumping because someone else is. Seven-year-olds can always be relied upon to mirror any strong emotion they witness.

"Guys," I finally say.

Izzy stops leaping and turns to me. "Why aren't you happy? You love horses too."

"We have a home here," I say. "Do you really want to *move* to Utah? It snows there. A lot."

"Exactly." Ethan flips his hair back with his hand in a move so familiar I almost don't notice it. "Heard of snowboarding, Mom? It slaps."

Heaven help me, but I almost can't handle teenage slang. "Yes, I've heard of it, thanks."

"Are there really horses?" Izzy asks in the same way Cinderella asked if the pumpkin carriage and glass slippers were real.

I lean forward, bracing my elbows on the table. "It's been a year and three weeks since Dad passed away. We took the day off to talk about him at the one year mark." Even now, my throat still closes off at the thought. "His uncle passed away a week after that anniversary, and as Ethan so helpfully mentioned, he left you a share of his ranch. I'm sure there are horses, because it's a working cattle ranch with three hundred and fifty cows."

Gabe's eyes widen. "Wow."

"It is pretty neat. However, the stipulation to taking under the will is that we can't simply go visit. We can't put someone else in charge of it. If we want to keep our share of the ranch, we need to relocate there and actually work the ranch ourselves for at least a year."

"Awesome," Izzy says.

"Right?" Ethan's grinning at her, his hair again blocking my view of his sky blue eyes.

"I am being considered, after a year of very hard full-time work and many years of part-time work, for partnership, just as your dad was considered before."

"But I hate having you gone all the time," Whitney says. "Why do we need more money?"

I don't grit my teeth. I won't grit my teeth. She's simply expressing that she likes to be around me, and that's a good thing. She doesn't understand finances and the fact that without a full time income, we'd need to live in an apartment. "They don't pay me very much when I don't work very much, sweetheart. If you want to go to college some day and live in a nice house like this one, you'll have to work hard too."

"You're not even considering it?" Ethan's nostrils flare and his hands flatten against the dinner table. "You've just decided for us, without even asking us?"

"You can't go anyway," I say. "You start college in the fall."

"Actually, I don't." One eyebrow lifts and his lips compress into a tight line.

"You'd rather work a ranch than get a college degree?"

Ethan stands up, tossing his hair back again. "I would rather do that, but that's not what I'm saying, *counselor*."

I hate when he calls me counselor. He doesn't like

when I press with leading questions, but what else can you do with teenagers? They willfully ignore you otherwise. With his mood, we clearly need to continue this conversation without an audience. "Alright, time to get ready for bed. Whitney, help Gabe brush his teeth—"

"I can brush my own teeth!" Gabe runs from the room.

"If you let Whitney check and make sure you did a good job, I'll let you watch an episode of *Pokémon* before bed."

That always works. "And Isabel—"

"I know," Izzy says. "Do the dishes and clean up after dinner." She mutters under her breath. "Because you don't want me to listen in to whatever you're saying."

Sometimes she's a little too smart for her own good. "Ethan." I point at my office, and he follows me without argument. I close the door behind us, and circle the desk to sit in Nate's wingback leather chair. Ethan takes a seat in one of the upright chairs across from me. "What is your point?"

"I won't be going to college this fall, no matter what you decide for us about the ranch, because I didn't get in anywhere."

His words make no sense. "What do you mean, you didn't get in? You had a great SAT score, and your grades aren't perfect, but they're respectable. I'm sure that, even if your letters haven't come yet—"

"Mom." Ethan slams his hands down on the table so hard that it shakes. "No letters are coming. I didn't *apply* anywhere."

He didn't *apply*? "I wrote your personal statement. I helped fill out the applications."

"I'm not like you and Dad," he says. "I don't want to work in an office all day. I want to use my hands. I'm really good at fixing things and putting stuff together, and I like to be outside."

He's spouting utter nonsense. "Honey, do you think I *want* to sit in an office all day? Do you think I *want* to stare at a screen? Until I was ten years old, I told everyone who asked that I wanted to be a rock star. I really thought I might be one day. Your grandparents taught me that I could do or be anything at all." I pause to make sure he's listening. "That tripe is the reason so many kids wind up working at McDonald's and loafing in their parents' basement."

"We don't have a basement."

"You've noticed," I say. "Take that as your sign. Work is rarely *fun* or *fulfilling*. It sucks most of the time—that's why they pay you."

"But Mom—"

"Ethan, you're seventeen. You've been cared for and raised in a very nice home. You've been given everything, so pardon me when I correct your understandable delusions—delusions I probably created. I know that right now, anything feels possible. I've nurtured you and nudged you to the very edge of the nest. You're ready to take flight. I would be remiss if I didn't tell you that, with your current flight plan, you're going to go splat." I still can't quite wrap my brain around the fact that he didn't even send in the applications I spent so many hours perfecting. He's talking again, something about how he won't crash, because he can always work on cars or something, but I can't listen to any more. "Did you throw the applications in the trash? What exactly did you do with them?"

Ethan's mouth hangs open for a moment.

Good. He's realizing how big a mistake he has made. And now it's time to figure out some kind of solution. It's taken me a moment, but the gears in my brain start working again. I may not have been a perfect wife. I may not be a perfect lawyer. I may not be a perfect mother either. Clearly I'm not.

But I am perfect in times of crisis.

"The good news is that, in spite of your catastrophic lapse in judgment, we can still fix this," I say. "Or at least, you may not have your choice of any school, but I'll call my friend Gus. He was my best friend at Harvard, and now he's the provost in charge of the admissions department at Rice, which means—"

"Mom." Ethan looks disapproving. "I don't *want* you to fix anything. I don't want to go to college at all."

"You're being ridiculous."

"And you're not listening. I've never wanted to go. That's your dream for my future, but I'll be eighteen soon, and no matter how much you poke and prod, no matter who you call, you can't make me go."

I failed him—I had no idea how much losing his dad has wrecked his view of the future. "Sweetheart, you just don't realize how severely not going to college will limit your future. It's hard to see now, but—"

He crosses his arms and takes a step backward, and I realize that if he really won't go, there's nothing I can do.

"Don't sign anything saying we don't want the ranch," he says. "Because I do."

It's like he's speaking Greek. It's like I don't know my own son. But there's a solution to this, I know there must be. "You can't have the ranch," I say. "You're a minor."

"Which means you can sign away my right to it," he says. "Believe me, I know. It's your leverage."

How could such a smart kid not want to go to college? "What do you want, then?" I can't believe I'm negotiating with my son to keep him from ruining his own life.

"How about this? If you'll agree to come with me for the summer to work the ranch, I'll agree to go to any school you can get me into for a full year and give it my all."

Go to Utah for the whole summer? Has he lost his mind? "I have a job."

He shrugs. "That's my offer. I get an entire summer out there with you to convince you that college isn't my path. And if I can't do it, then I go to college, just like you want."

"But it's pointless," I say. "You turn eighteen on September 2. College classes start at the end of August. Even if we spend the entire summer there, I won't change my mind. You'll still have to go."

"That's a risk I'm willing to take."

There couldn't be a worse time for me to walk away from my job, but if I have to choose between what my son needs and what my career demands. . .well, there's no contest.

I call the other kids. "Do you guys want to spend the summer at that cattle ranch?"

The resounding chorus of yeses decides it. "I guess I need to call my friend Gus, and I should call Robert, too, right away." And then I need to pray for a miracle, because there's no way I'll make partner this fall.

I'll be lucky if I still have a job by then.

4

AMANDA

Maren's giggle sounds a little too diabolical for my tastes.

"What's the rule about being on our phones while we eat?" I hold out my hand.

"Mom, we're sitting in the park." Maren slides her phone into her purse. "I'm fifteen. It's not like I'm a little kid anymore. I deserve some autonomy."

"I'm happy to hear SAT words being put to use." Even if I'm not 100% sure what autonomy means. I assume it's independence or freedom or something along those lines. "But you still owe me the phone."

Emery's sly smile is my confirmation that I'm making the right call. I struggle as a parent pretty much every day. Am I doing the right thing? Am I being too firm? Not firm enough?

For a second, I worry that Maren's going to throw a fit in the middle of Central Park and refuse to give me her phone, but when I really turn up the heat on my glare, she hands it over. The whole interchange has me thinking. . .I haven't checked their social media accounts lately. I imagine Maren's due. Instead of slipping her phone into my pocket, I start swiping.

"Hey," she objects. "That's private."

"No, it's not," I say. "In fact, it's all public. That's kind of the point."

Her sulking confirms my suspicion that I'll find something I don't want to see.

"Twitter," Emery coughs.

Maren's head whips around like a twenty-something on the scent of a pop-up sample sale.

Twitter it is.

It doesn't take me long to realize why Emery pointed me that way, but the more I scroll and the more comments I digest, the more alarmed I become.

Maybe if you can't think for yourself.

In your dreams, loser. He wouldn't go out with you if someone paid him, not that your family even could.

As if anyone would care what you think.

Do us all a favor—never comment again. Actually, don't talk or type again in any form.

Someone needs to call the police, because that's worse than a simple crime. That's a violation of the laws of nature.

It would be bad enough if those comments had been made in response to things Maren had said. I'd be genuinely concerned, but my anger would be directed at terrible kids.

But my concern right now is for my own child. Maren said those things herself.

By the time I finally slide the phone into my purse, my hands are shaking. "Maren."

Her soft pink lips are compressed into a hard line, and her eyes shift downward, avoiding mine.

"What do you think I found on Twitter?" Other than the fact that I haven't been paying enough attention to my own daughter. She's turning into a little monster. Her account certainly doesn't show depth or dimension. Only cruelty.

Where is she learning it?

"Maren, I'm waiting for an answer."

"You have no idea what school is like." Her hands clench the bench tightly, her half-eaten burger forgotten on the paper in her lap.

"You're right. It's been quite some time since I was in high school myself, and I've never been to yours as a student." Actually, I don't go to her school nearly often enough as a parent. I'm not really the kind of mom who joins the PTA. "But I know enough to be positive that *this* isn't who we want to be."

She swallows.

"I'm not sure why you would say such cruel things, to anyone, but you're certainly done doing it."

"This is how you have to act to succeed. The world is kill or be killed, Mom. Dad knew it, and it's only gotten worse—"

Her dad did know it, but I don't want her to act like he did. It's miserable for everyone around them. "Don't get all defensive when you should be apologetic. Have you learned *that* word yet?"

"Mom!"

"There are a lot of people on this thread that are going to be getting a call from you."

She holds out her hand. "Fine. Give me back my phone and I'll message them."

"I'm not sure you are going to get your phone back. . .ever."

Her eyes widen and her mouth dangles open for a moment, and then she rolls her eyes. "Be real, Mom."

Something very close to rage floods my body. "You think I'm not being *real*?" I stand up, only vaguely aware that I'm now shouting at my teenage daughter in the middle of a busy park. "It may seem like these are just words, but there's a person on the other side of them. You have been afforded every chance at success, and—"

"Just like every kid whose posts I have commented on." One eyebrow quirks up. "It's not like I'm insulting poor little scholarship students."

People all over the park are staring. I sit down and lower my voice. "I need to think about what to do here."

"Great." She crosses her arms, the edge of her hand knocking her hamburger off her lap. It rolls until the eaten part reaches the ground, and then the contents splay outward into a fan. Toasted bun, lettuce, meat, pickles, bun.

A boisterous goldendoodle jogging alongside his owner snaps up the meat and keeps on moving. His dark-haired owner turns around, eyes wide. "I'm so sorry," he says, starting to slow down.

I wave him on. "No big deal. It was our fault."

"That's what you might call an apology," Emery says. "In case you just didn't know what it was."

Sweet little Emery has never sounded snarkier. "What in the world?"

"While you're taking people's phones," Maren says, "maybe you should steal hers too."

All the energy in my body suddenly feels spent. My eyes lock with my darling twelve-year-old. "What am I going to find on yours?"

Emery digs her Mary Janes into the thick grass in front of us and shrugs.

"Em?"

"Same thing as you found on mine, I imagine," Maren says.

"No!" Emery's face is entirely white.

Why would Emery tell me about Maren's bullying if she's doing the same thing? "Emery Celeste Brooks."

When she looks up, her eyes are full of unshed tears.

"What's wrong?"

Her small, skinny arms slide around my waist and her head presses against my chest. I know she's twelve, but sometimes it feels like she's still much younger.

"People say the same kind of stuff to her," Maren says. "All the time."

Realization finally dawns. "You're saying mean things to Emery?" My hand is suddenly itching to slap my eldest. How did I not notice any of the comments were on *Emery's* page?

Maren rolls her eyes again. "Of course not. I'm not the devil."

How am I lost again?

"Hate to break it to you, Mom, but Em's kind of a loser at school." She pulls her hair back into a high ponytail. "It was watching her get torn apart that made me realize I never wanted to be picked on—so I went on the defensive. Scare them before they can bully you."

I brush the hair out of Emery's eyes. "Is that true? Have you been picked on. . .for a long time?"

She burrows her face closer, turning toward my shoulder. I take her phone too, preparing myself to deal with it later. The whole thing makes me sick. "Let's head home. We'll sort all this out later."

"Unless you're pulling Emery out and enrolling her somewhere else, I doubt you can do much." Maren's tone is so flippant that even knowing she didn't have a hand in tormenting her own sister, I want to slap some sense into her.

"You should consider that the people you're ridiculing are someone else's sister. They're just like Emery."

"I should?" Maren says. "I'm just doing what you do." Her mouth turns up in a half grin. "Looking out for myself."

I can barely make sense of what she's saying. Since Paul died, I've done everything I can to make money for our family. I couldn't even contemplate going back home to live, so I spent hours on ideas, and even longer preparing cute photos and scouring the internet for things to post that would build my particular brand. I pored over contracts that made no sense, and I connected with other people who did the same thing as me. But in all that time, I can't even think of an instance when I belittled or hurt another human being, especially not on purpose.

Normally we'd take the subway, but I'm too tired to deal with it and I hail a cab. Emery curls against my side on the trip home, and Maren presses her nose to the glass. Sometimes I wonder how I ended up with two such opposite daughters. Other times, I wonder whether it's my fault. After all, Paul was nothing like me.

He crushed people in the business world on the regular, and he enjoyed doing it.

I actually really admired that about him. He went out into the world and he slayed whatever dragons, financial or otherwise, threatened us. It was one of the only things I still liked about him after the first year or so we were married. I suppose Maren's actions could be likened to Paul's. Am I holding her to a double standard because she's a girl?

It's times like these that I desperately miss having someone else pulling on my team. Paul didn't listen very well or very consistently, but when I cornered him he gave me opinions. It was something.

I'm tired of being utterly alone.

But is my only alternative really someone like sleazy, passive-aggressive Roger? Blech.

When we get home, I expect that the girls will quietly do their homework and get ready for bed. After all, they must surely be as drained as I am. I'm digging through poor Emery's social media, discovering it might even be worse than I thought, when Maren taps on the door to my bedroom.

"Yeah?"

"Can I have my phone back yet? I'm really sorry I was so mean. I clearly got carried away. From now on, I promise that I'll be more careful about what I say."

It feels like she found some kind of template for an apology online and is regurgitating the words back to me. "No." I set Emery's phone down and lean back in my bed, reclining against the ten carefully arranged throw pillows. "I told you. I'm not sure I'll be returning it."

"You've got to be kidding me right now." The simultaneous eye roll and dramatic sigh is actually fairly impressive. If there was an award for successfully expressing utter disgust, she'd be waving it in my face right now.

"I'm not making a joke." I sit up straight, having had a stroke of inspiration. "In fact, I should warn you. I found out today that your father's uncle, Jedediah, who lived in the literal middle of nowhere, died not long ago."

She blinks. "What does that have to do with *anything*?"

Her attitude is appalling—someone *died*. Granted, he's not someone she knows, but how can she be so rude about someone's death? And possibly more concerning, how did I not notice she was this awful before now? "If you could be polite for long enough, I'd explain." I wait.

Her shoulders finally droop.

It's not much, but I'll take it. "A lawyer called to let us know that your great uncle left his cattle ranch to the two of you in his will."

Her eyes widen. "Is something like that worth a lot of money?"

I can't fault her for wondering—I had the same question. "I'm not sure, but probably."

"That's amazing! Why didn't you tell us that before?"

"Tell us what?" Emery's standing in the doorway, her hand wrapped around a toothbrush, toothpaste dripping down her chin.

"Dad's uncle left us his cattle ranch on the Utah-Wyoming border. . .but we can't just sell it. We only get the ranch if we move there and work it for a full year."

"That's so cool!" Emery says.

"Oh my G—"

"Don't say that," I snap. "Obviously I told him that we won't be moving there."

Emery's face falls, her toothbrush sliding out of her mouth, a shoestring of white slobber following it.

"Don't give me a heart attack like that again," Maren says. "Geez, Mom."

"I might go there if you can't fix your attitude. Maybe a year of forced isolation and manual labor is exactly what you need." I arch one eyebrow in a way I hope is imperious.

Maren looks like a runway model trying to calculate the tip on a check, so I'm guessing I succeeded.

"I probably don't get a vote," Emery says softly, "but if I did, I'd say yes."

My heart contracts a bit. Of course she would. If you were being attacked by wolves, you'd run literally anywhere to get away, even the badlands. "Darling, we'll fix this. I promise."

She jams her toothbrush back into her mouth, wipes her slobbery hand on her Hello Kitty pajama pants, and shuffles back down the hall.

I really hope I didn't just lie to her. It's awfully hard to 'fix' people being mean to someone. Their habits and their opinions don't change overnight. I remind myself that she's got adorable and expensive clothing, a brilliant mind, and a stunningly beautiful face, even during what is typically an awkward phase in adolescence. I'm sure everything will be fine.

Or I really, really hope it will, anyway.

The next week feels like a mad dash, between researching methods to stop cyber-bullying, defending Maren's phone from Maren's very demanding self, and thinking up clever and hopefully multi-dimensional posts each day for my insta account.

I'm surprised when I get a text from Abigail. DID YOU HEAR FROM THE LAWYER?

It's ironic that she's texting, since the paperwork from Mr. Swift is right in front of me. I even signed it already. It'll go out with tomorrow's mail. I DID.

ARE YOU PASSING?

OF COURSE, I text back. LIVE IN THE MIDDLE OF NOWHERE? DEFINITELY NOT.

She responds with five laughing emojis. I always forget how many emojis she uses. She's not a laid back person, but she texts like a teenage girl.

Of course she doesn't ask how the girls are doing, so I don't volunteer. I'm contemplating whether I ought to tell her that Maren's doing cheer and Emery made team for gymnastics when my phone rings. I nearly drop it.

It's Heather, from Lololime. I swipe immediately and then wonder whether I ought to have let it ring once or twice. Does answering this fast seem desperate? "Hello?"

"Amanda?"

"Yes, it's me."

"I'm glad I caught you. We had a management team meeting today, and I had some notes I wanted to share." My stomach clenches hard.

Of course, Emery and Maren choose this moment to burst into my room. I throw my hand up in the air with my fingers splayed. I mouth the word, "Lololime!" Maren freezes and beams, throwing me thumbs ups. She does not, however, leave the room. Neither does Emery.

I try to ignore them so I can focus.

"—with the images from the museum, but that's not exactly what we meant."

"Okay."

"The burgers were cute too, and a little closer to what I was trying to say, but it still felt like. . .I don't know. Almost like, if Kim Kardashian was trying to slum."

What does that even mean?

"Your image is so perfect, so untouchable, that while a lot of people like to watch your feed, I think it's hurting your interaction and engagement."

She means my sales. "But people have been buying—"

"Yes, I'm sure sales on hair extensions and face cream have been stellar, but our product is different."

It feels like the world's caving in around me. Hair extensions and face cream and boutique dresses and sandals do earn consistent money, but it's so exhausting always trying to coordinate everything without feeling like I'm doing infomercials. I was really looking forward to—no, if I'm being honest, I was desperate for—a real job. A company I'd be a spokesperson for.

It feels like she's calling to let me down easy.

The security I've longed for is slipping through my fingers, like it always does. Like when Paul died, and I found out our money was just—poof—gone.

"Did you tell her about the ranch yet?" Emery shouts. She's holding the paperwork and waving it at me like a red flag in front of a bull. "About how we'll be leaving New York and going to live on a cattle ranch?"

What in the world is she saying?

"What's that?" Heather asks. "Who was just talking?"

"Sorry, that's my twelve-year-old daughter. I'm sure you've seen her on my feed."

"Emery, right?" she asks.

"Right. Don't mind her—kids. They're always yelling."

"Did she say you're moving to a cattle ranch?"

Why would she say that? She knows we aren't going. "Well, she did, but only because—"

"Are you serious? That sounds amazing! We have an entire Western wear inspired line we're planning on testing in the Midwest in the spring. I can't wait to show it to you. In fact, I think adding you to the product test might be an excellent way to see whether you'd be a good addition to our permanent team."

I can barely breathe. "You think what?"

"Oh, Amanda, you have no idea how exciting this is! I wish you'd mentioned it earlier. Were you worried I might think it's off brand for you?" Heather makes a hmm sound. "I mean, it *is* a pretty big departure from your typical posts, but it's a huge branch off for us, too, and I think it might be exactly what we both need." She makes a clicking sound with something—maybe a pen. "Let me talk to my boss. How soon will you be going to this ranch?"

"Um—" My voice cracks. Honest to goodness, I sound like a teenage boy. I clear my throat. "How soon did you need us there? My girls won't be done with school for a week and a half."

"If you flew out right after that, you could be doing themed posts in the next two weeks." She mutters into the phone. "We could delay the decision, especially if we could divert funds from the Howdy line." She pauses. "Yes, that would work great. Could you be there by the first week of June?"

I mean. Could I?

Emery's bobbing her head. How much of my conversation can she hear? I need to turn my speaker volume down, clearly. "I think I could, sure."

"I still can't believe how well this worked out," Heather says. "I love your feed, but I was actually supposed to call you and tell you we had decided to go another direction. But now. . ."

My hands are shaking, I'm so agitated. She said they wouldn't decide for a month. Were my new posts that bad?

"This is an opposite world for you, and I think your followers are going to love it." She squeals. "Heck, *I'm* going to love it. Think how amazing you'd look in a cowboy hat. Or do they call them cowgirl hats? You should reach out and find some other vendors to make some money while you're testing for us. I mean, this could be really big."

I'm jotting down notes on the side of a to-go bag from the nearby deli. *Cowboy hats. Western wear. Howdy line. Start new themes June 1.*

"You could post about the scenery and the people, and think of all the activities you could do! You'll be experiencing something so different from your normal routine, and we'll all be invited to tag along without the hassle or the stress. Followers in big cities will be curious, and small town people will probably love seeing how you can brighten up the things they're surrounded by in their mundane, everyday lives."

I keep waiting for her to say she's kidding, that this is all a joke.

But she just keeps talking about ideas and themes and the audience it would attract.

When she finally hangs up, and the axe that was dangling over my head has been delayed, Emery says, "You're welcome."

I'm tired and overwhelmed and the gears in my brain

are spinning a hundred miles an hour, but I'm truly grateful. "Thank you, Em. I have no idea how you knew she'd go for that, but. . .just, thank you."

Maren holds out her hand. "How about you thank me by returning my phone, since now I'm stuck going to the sticks?"

It's been a week—that's probably long enough. I hand it over. After all, I have a lot of things to plan. I can't get all of it done with her nagging me incessantly. "But *be nice*. Have I been clear on that?"

"Crystal," she says.

The second Maren leaves, Emery swoops in. "Did I hear that right? Are we actually moving?"

"Just a quick vacation for a week or so, darling. Don't stress."

The enormous smile that spreads across her face is the first genuine smile I've seen from her in weeks. "I can't believe it."

"Remember how happy you are right now when we're hot and surrounded by cow poop." I frown.

"It won't be that bad," Emery says. "Plus, I looked it up online. It's supposed to be really beautiful up there."

"We aren't going for the beauty," I say, "or for the animals or the clean air."

Emery tilts her head. "We aren't?"

This is probably a good learning opportunity. I imagine that if, on the off-chance he made it to heaven, Paul's up there right now listening to us, he'll be delighted that I'm sharing this principle with his child. "Your dad talked about a lot of things I didn't understand, but one thing I do remember him saying is that he always hedged his bets. That's how people with his job got the name 'hedge fund manager.' He would try and secure one investment, but set up another in case the first one failed."

Emery's mouth is dangling open.

"That's what I'm doing right now—whatever I have to do to keep Lololime happy. And on the off chance that my plan falls apart, we'll be learning a little about another opportunity." Not that I really have any intention of running a ranch, but maybe we could sort of manage it a bit and let someone else do the work. "If I snag the Lololime account quickly while we're out there in bumpkin-ville, then we can all come home right away."

"So there's no chance that we'll work the ranch for a whole year? And stay?"

I imagine myself petting a cow on the head, and try to think of anything else I might need to do. Carry hay to them? Feed the babies out of bottles? I can't imagine very many people are less equipped to run a cattle ranch than I am. I shake my head. "It's very, very doubtful we will be there more than a week or two, but it can't hurt to learn more about the option."

5

ABIGAIL

"It's not hot!" Gabe's spinning round and round, his arms spread out, his face turned upward, his backpack swinging out behind him.

"Why isn't it hot?" Whitney asks. "Isn't it summer here?"

I chuckle. "Summer isn't quite the same in the northern part of the country." It's been hot in Texas since late March. "Tomorrow's June, and I think around here, that's the start of summer, but this probably already feels summery to them."

"They are spoiled," Izzy says. "I am so excited for this summer, but do you think Cody will remember me when I get back home?"

Her lesson horse Cody 'remembers' anyone who has a treat in their hand. "I'm sure he'll welcome you back with an eager mouth," I say.

Izzy scowls. "What if I forget everything?"

"I'm sure you'll improve a lot, with all the riding we'll be doing on a ranch," I say. "Don't worry." I press the button on the key fob the rental car company gave me.

For what I'm paying to rent it for the summer, this car better make us dinner and wash the dishes, too.

The navy blue Toyota Sienna chimes and the headlights flash.

"A minivan?" Ethan groans like I asked him to buy me tampons at the store. "For the whole summer?"

I can't quite help my smile. "It was the cheapest option."

"Liar. You got it to torture me."

"Gabe needs a DVD player," I reason. "It makes sense."

"Well, it won't change anything. I'm still going to love everything about the next three months. You'll see."

I hope he does, as long as he also comes around on the college thing. My kids haven't had much fun in the past year, and they seem to desperately need this change of pace. I check my watch. "If we leave right now, we should arrive just in time for dinner."

"Whoa," Ethan says. "The drive from here takes that long?"

"My cell phone map says it's about three hours away," I say. "We'll be driving through Wyoming for a big chunk of the way."

"At least it should be a gorgeous drive," Izzy says. "Did you know that Flaming Gorge is right by the ranch? People travel from all over to see it."

"I can't wait to take a quad out there," Ethan says.

"We don't even have one, and that's not why we're here." Does he think running a ranch will leave him lots of time for playing around on ATVs? "Stop being ridiculous."

"Uncle Jed may have had one," Ethan says. "And if he did, then now we do, too!"

He's entirely too excited. "Alright, in the car, everybody."

We're supposed to be here for three months, but you'd think we were moving for years by the way everyone packed. Thank goodness it's summer, or we'd need a U-Haul just for the winter clothing my little Texas honeys would need.

Even I have to admit the drive out is picturesque. It's not like I've never traveled around the United States before, but this is my first time in Utah, and now that I'm here, surrounded by mountains and crisp, clean air, I feel like it might have been an oversight.

"What's a Scone Cutter?" Whitney asks, staring at a sign for a restaurant.

No idea. "Do you guys want to find out?"

After a chorus of affirmations, I pull into the drive-thru line. As it turns out, it's basically a long rectangular dinner roll they slice and stuff with honey butter, or cinnamon butter, or a dozen other options. Except I think the dinner roll may be fried.

"I love these," Ethan says.

I know that my usually contrary boy is not intentionally loving everything just to irritate me, so I shove my irritation down and try to enjoy his happiness. Still, I can't keep from pointing out the obvious. "My old sneaker would taste good if I put that much butter on it."

Ethan shrugs. "You'd better not leave those things lying around." He winks. "You might be looking for new shoes."

The other kids are just as energized. I wish my job was even a quarter as enthusiastic about this plan as the kids. Robert was shocked, but he understood my reasons and went to bat for me immediately. Unfortunately, Lance was looking for an excuse to show everyone that I'm not committed, and he didn't have to look hard with me bailing for the summer.

"He couldn't call off the vote," Robert said, "but I wish we could delay it. He's already grumbling."

"I will do every single thing I would have done if I'd been in the office," I promised.

"I know you will," Robert said.

But we both know working remotely won't be the same, and there are sure to be communication issues and time change issues and a whole host of other problems. Not to mention, I can hardly schmooze the partners who are on the fence about bringing me in. . .from Utah.

I shove my concerns out of my mind, because there's absolutely nothing I can do about any of it. I put together two motions and a list of deposition questions on the plane and emailed them to Robert the second we landed.

Take that, naysayers. I'm working on a Sunday, while traveling. So much for saying I won't get anything done.

Of course, we haven't even reached the ranch yet, and I have no idea how much time we're really talking about spending on running it.

As if he can sense my reservations, Ethan says, "It's going to be fun, Mom, I swear."

I'm not worried that the kids won't have a good time, but I don't tell him that. It will hardly be helpful. The other three are watching *The Jetsons* on the DVD player. Score one point for the minivan. "I'm so lucky to have an expert at working mountainous cattle ranches in the car."

"I know you think I won't be able to do anything," he says, "but I'm actually really good at mechanical stuff."

"You are." He always has been. He started by fixing the other kids' broken toys as a child, and graduated by junior high to working on project cars with his dad. In the past few years, he's only improved on a talent that was clearly intuitive from the start. "But sweetheart, your mechanical skill is an extension of your real genius—math."

His incredulous look is quite familiar.

"You don't think so?"

"What does math have to do with working on mechanical stuff?"

"It's the same part of your brain that does both things. Trust me, I know you're great with engines, but one day you may wish you'd done the legwork with a formal education that will let you apply that same strength to more lucrative things."

"And by then, it will be too late. The apocalypse will have wiped out all institutions of higher education, rendering self improvement and mental development impossible, a thing of the past, a relic."

I roll my eyes.

"Then, when the zombies begin their march to decimate the world population, I'll be unable to stop them, because I won't understand the finer points of differential equations." He shakes his head. "Oh boy, will I be sorry then."

"Very funny," I say. "Let me know if you still think it's funny when you're eating soup from a can—"

"Down by the river?" I've missed his crooked smile.

And I miss his dad, from whom he stole that smile. If Nate were here, he'd know how to get through to him. It feels like I'm banging my head against a brick wall. A dimpled, blue-eyed, fairly athletic brick wall, with beautiful, albeit too long, hair.

Once we hit the easy-to-navigate state highways, I trade places with him and get back to work.

"Do you really need to do that today?" Ethan asks. "It's a Sunday."

"It is," I say. "But I have no idea how much work we'll be doing the rest of the week, or when I'll have time. I promised I'd still bill fifty hours a week, even from the ranch. It's going to be really hard to do that while watching four children and doing whatever else is required."

I don't mention that our take-out options will be nonexistent, which means we'll be cooking a lot more. Or that I have no idea whether this place will have a dishwasher, or trash service, or even how consistent the internet will be. That's my biggest fear, right there. What if there's no broadband? Reviewing all the documents the file clerks scan in without decent internet will easily take me twice as long.

Just as I'm finishing up a memo for Jim, my phone rings. "I'm surprised I have service out here." I'm not sure I recognize the number, but with all the details I rushed to finalize, I can't really screen my calls. "Hello?"

"Abby?"

"Hey! Long time, Gus! How are you doing?" He's finally called me back, hallelujah. I walk him through our problem, including how Ethan flipped out and threw his applications away in his grief. I forge ahead, even when Ethan stiffens. He has no one to blame but himself. He did freak out, and I'm positive it's because of what happened to Nate.

"Wow, I can't believe he. . . I'm so sorry. I had no idea."

"I swear that's the only reason I'm asking for a favor—extenuating circumstances. Obviously I know that he's way past the deadline for admission."

"The thing is, I'm not sure I can really help," Gus says. "I mean, I could probably get him on the waitlist, if his test scores and GPA are good enough."

"He got a 1490 on the SAT," I say. "He had a perfect score on the math, and he has mostly As. He did end up with a few Bs, but they're all in honors classes at least. His one C was in sophomore English."

"That teacher hated me," Ethan grumbles.

"Losing his dad was rough, Gus. I'm not going to lie. I

didn't support him as well as I should have, either. If there is *anything* you can do, I'd be eternally grateful."

"Like I said, I can't promise anything, but send me his stuff and I'll do my best."

Better than I hoped for, honestly. I'd practically resigned myself to the fact that he'd be starting his post-secondary education at a community college. "Thanks."

I'm not sure whether he hangs up, or whether our reception cuts out, but either way, it was the call I'd been hoping to receive. It's the reason we're on our way here—to try and improve the future for my child, to get his motivation back. I'd do most anything, adjust most any plan, repair issues on the fly, and work into the wee hours of the night to do that.

But with the packing for a long trip last minute, and with the time it took to prepare to leave the office for months, I didn't sleep much last night. I suppose that's why I fall asleep. When Ethan nudges me awake, the sun is already low in the sky. I rub my eyes and look around.

"Manila town limits," a sign reads. "Population 365."

"Whoa," Gabe says. "That's a lot."

I suppress my laugh.

"It's a lot if you're talking about days," Ethan says. "It would be a lot of Skittles. But as far as people living in a town go, three hundred and sixty-five is pretty small, buddy."

He's right. It is small. Smaller than I realized.

But I can do anything for one summer, right?

"I'm hungry," Gabe says. "Are we almost there?"

"We're close," I say. "Really close." Although, I'm not sure what kind of dining options there will be at the actual farmhouse—since it's been uninhabited for three weeks. When Mr. Swift overnighted me the key, I didn't think to check in with him on the state of the premises. It all happened too quickly for better planning.

The word 'market' catches my eye and I point. "We should probably try and buy some groceries. At least some milk and cereal and bread."

"Where?" Ethan glances over at me like I've lost my mind.

"Pull in there." I'm already pointing, but I wiggle my hand around so he notices.

"Mom, you're clearly still tired. That's a hardware store." Ethan scoffs. "See? True Value."

"And it says 'market' below it." I slug him on the shoulder. "That's their grocery store, I'd bet money on it. A town of under 400 wouldn't support a bigger one."

His skepticism remains, but he does as I ask and parks in front.

All the kids pour out of the car. It's times like this, when we've been cooped up inside a moving vehicle for three hours, that it feels like I have more than four children. "Guys, I'm going to pick up some stuff I think we may need." I drop my voice, but make sure Izzy and Ethan are listening. "Why don't you see if there's a bathroom and make sure the little ones go?" The best thing in my life is having older children. It makes caring for the younger ones so much more manageable.

Ethan and Izzy nod, far less peppy than they were three hours ago, which makes sense, as it's eight-thirty in Houston, and we all woke up at five this morning.

"Mom," Izzy says. "Don't go crazy. That car's already packed like Gabe's lunch box."

My kids pack their own lunches for school, and Gabe has a tendency to get carried away. Like, most mornings he almost can't close his zipper. "I'll be mindful." But in a new place, with four kids to care for, I'd be remiss if I didn't get enough for us to eat. My phone says we're still twenty minutes away. It's not going to be a quick jaunt into town, even for groceries from a hardware store.

There's a surprisingly robust selection of food options, thankfully. I mean, all the aisles could fit into the clothing section of an H-E-B, but so could a lot of full grocery stores. By the time I reach the checkout, my cart's almost full.

"Mom." Ethan probably says my name more than anyone else, but he has at least a dozen different inflections. This one means, *You have lost your mind. Again.*

"You'll be thanking me when we get there and there's nothing to eat except the squashed fruit snacks at the bottom of Gabe's bag." I just hope there's a functioning refrigerator, or we're going to be eating a lot of frozen pizzas and toaster strudel in the next few hours.

"I'm not holding all that on my lap," Ethan says.

"Always the gentleman," Izzy quips.

Sometimes I'm really proud of her for roasting him. It hasn't been easy to come after him in the family order—he's not always the most considerate brother. He loves her, but he's a little abrasive.

"What I mean is, of course I'll hold it on my lap, unless you want me to drive," Ethan says.

And that's when I'm the most proud of him. He says what he thinks, all the time, but often, once he hears the words out loud, he amends his declarations. Not everyone can do that. His dad was like that—he'd admit when he was wrong and acknowledge it publicly.

I pay, and we're out the door. It takes almost five minutes to get all the kids and all the groceries squeezed into the car, but with the sun setting, I'd rather not try and find a place to buy dinner. Ethan lets me pile him up with stuff, including a rather precarious stack of produce. At least no one argues with me or begs for McDonald's. With four kids and more than fourteen hours of travel under our belts, it's a small miracle.

"I'll hurry," I promise.

The sun has lit the entire sky an orangey pink by the time we're cruising down the street off which the ranch is set. Ethan's so excited that we're close that he's belting "On Top of the World" by Imagine Dragons. It's making it hard to think, much less hear *The Jetsons* in the back.

"Cut it out," Izzy says.

He ignores her.

"We're almost there," I say.

"Shut up, Ethan!" Whitney throws something—not sure what—that knocks the bag of apples sideways. They roll off Ethan's lap and spill all over the center console. One rolls down into the floorboard.

"Guys!"

"Sorry, Mom!" Whitney says. "But Ethan won't shut up and I can't hear."

I slow way down so that I can grab the apple. It's totally unsafe to have anything anywhere near the pedals on the car. I finally end up stopping in the middle of the road while I rummage around for it. I'm lucky this road has no traffic on it.

My hand finally wraps around the shiny, smooth skin. "Ha, ha!" After I sit up again, I look around to make sure it's clear for me to drive.

There aren't any other cars, but there is a tall, shirtless man mowing the front lawn of a small white farmhouse. It may not be that warm outside, but his body still glistens with sweat. I can't look away from the defined pecs, the bunched biceps, and the washboard stomach. Ohmygoodness, I'm too old to go entirely blank when I see someone who's magazine centerfold hot. I'm sure he's young enough to be—

But then he looks up, and I realize he's not young at all. He's close to my age. And he's staring right at me staring back at him, and he has no idea that I wasn't staring at him the entire time we were stopped. My foot slams against the gas pedal and we shoot forward, but he waves in spite of my quick departure. I wonder whether this man, who must be a relatively close neighbor, could see through the window and might recognize my face. I really hope not.

The sun has dropped so low that there's barely a golden glow when we crest the ridge and turn into the driveway my map is bleating at me to take, and my heart has finally settled down to a sustainable rate. "I think this is it, guys."

All four kids sit up and turn toward the ranch. Someone even pauses the stupid Jetsons and eliminates the infernal and obnoxious noise. None of them say a word.

I don't blame them. Bathed in golden sunset, with a backdrop of some of the prettiest, pine-ringed mountains I've ever seen, the whole thing is like a scene right out of a movie. There's a sprawling farmhouse at the top of the drive, with a smaller, more modest house a few dozen yards to the left of it. Beyond the house, there's a large brown barn. It looks fifty years old, but I'm sure the harsh winters weather the wood quickly out here. It's not dilapidated or falling down, so that's good. Past the barn are two more outbuildings, one of which is a smaller red barn with white trim, and one that looks in this lighting like a metal building. That's probably the storage building mentioned in the will description.

"Wow," Whitney says. "It's so pretty."

"Yeah, I like that red barn. I call it," Gabe says.

Ethan laughs. "You can't call a barn, buddy. Sorry."

"Why not?" He doesn't even wait for a reply before asking, "Can I call the animals inside it?"

Izzy rolls her eyes. "You can't call any of that."

"What about the little house? No one else will even want that." Gabe's voice grows whinier by the minute once we pass seven o'clock. . .Texas time. He's probably almost at maximum capacity by now.

Uncle Jed must have lived in the nicer house, which means that smaller one probably hasn't been cared for or cleaned or maintained. "We'll have to check it out later," I say. "If it's as big a mess as I'm worried it might be, no one will want it."

His little face falls, and it's so pathetic.

"I'm sorry, bud, but when we get inside, you can call a room. How's that?"

"Fine." He presses his nose against the glass, and it's cooled down enough outside that it fogs up from his breath.

I park in the circular drive that loops right in front of the maroon farmhouse. The maroon paint looks fine, but the white trim is peeling. "That trim would look so much nicer if it were repainted—maybe in navy blue."

"There's a chimney," Izzy says. "I wonder if it'll be cold enough for a fire."

"It's cold enough now," Whitney says. "Look at the glass." She points at where Gabe's breath has fogged it up.

"I doubt it's cold enough for a fire," I say.

"Let's find out." Ethan opens the door, and cooler air rushes in.

But not cold. Definitely not fire weather.

"Maybe we could light a fire outside," Ethan says. "Roast some hotdogs and marshmallows."

"I didn't buy any of that," I say. "But we have a whole summer ahead of us. I'm sure we can do it soon enough."

"This is awesome." Whitney opens the door.

Gabe shoves past her, knocking two boxes of cereal and a bunch of bananas to the caliche-rock ground. "Sorry." But he doesn't slow down. He has a room to claim, after all.

I grab two gallons of milk and my purse and march up

the porch steps. I stop dead in my tracks when I hear an unfamiliar low noise.

"Everyone stop," I say.

The kids freeze, thankfully.

They notice it too. "It's a dog," Whitney says.

"A border collie," I say. "Or at least, I think it is. It's black and white. I suppose it could be an Australian Shepherd."

"Is it Uncle Jed's dog?" Ethan asks.

"Mr. Swift didn't mention a dog," I say. "But he didn't say much about animals other than the cows."

I set both gallons of already-sweating milk down and rummage around for my key. It takes me a moment to find the large golden key, but now that I have it, it's time to approach the very unfriendly looking dog.

"I thought Border Collies were nice," Izzy says. "They're really common farm dogs."

"Assume every dog is a threat until you know it," Ethan says.

"Does anyone have the sandwich meat?" I look around.

Izzy nods. "I think I do. Hang on." She shifts a few things and then digs in her bags. "Yes." She tosses it to me.

The dog's head whips up at the movement, its eyes finally looking interested.

"Is it sick?" Whitney asks. "Why is it just lying there and growling?"

"Maybe it's sad," Gabe says. "If it's Uncle Jed's dog."

It took a seven-year-old to figure that out. Now that he's mentioned it, I'm positive he's right. "I wonder if anyone has been feeding it." I crouch down and approach slowly, extending my hand with a few pieces of turkey in it.

The dog begins to growl again.

I pause.

It relaxes and I move closer again.

"Maybe we should get a hotel," Ethan says. "We can call Mr. Swift in the morning."

"Let's see," I say. "We just need to show it that we're not scary." I shift a little closer. "Here you go boy, or girl. We're the nice family that has come for the summer."

It lifts its head a little and whimpers. The sound kind of presses on my heart. That's how I felt after Nate died.

"You're okay, boy. I swear you are." I toss the turkey and he snaps it up. "See? Nothing will fix it, but food helps." In my scariest move yet, I reach out and pat his fluffy head. He whines again, this time for longer. "I'm going to move you over, okay? So that we can go inside."

He whimpers, but doesn't object when I shift him over and slide the key into the lock. It turns smoothly, and we're in. Every single one of my kids crouches down and pats the dog on the head, but he simply drops his face back down over his paws and closes his eyes.

"Is he okay?" Gabe asks.

"I think he's just sad," I say. "I'll make sure to grab some food for him tomorrow. He doesn't look emaciated, so I bet someone is feeding him, but it can't hurt."

Once we've determined nothing can be done for the dog this moment, the kids' enthusiasm about the new place returns. Ethan jogs through the door. "First one in the house!"

Gabe shoots past him like a cockroach fleeing the light. "I call the best room. The best one!"

"You can't do that," Whitney says. "It's not specific enough. You have to see the room, and be standing inside of it, and then say 'I call this room.'"

In the time we spent on the dog, the sun set and now it's pitch black. It feels like an eternity of fumbling around with the flashlights on our phones before Izzy finds a light switch, but once it's on, the children all disappear. Except, instead of hiding, they're searching. The rest of them may be too old to insist as obnoxiously as Gabe, but picking the best room matters to all of them.

They can't call the master, because they'll lose it, but they need to suss out which of the remaining rooms is the best faster than everyone else, or they'll be stuck. "There are six bedrooms, and only five of us, so don't stress. You'll all have a place."

Luckily the fridge works fine, although judging from the fusty smell, I did not buy nearly enough baking soda. It's not the only thing that needs to be cleaned, either. The once-cream linoleum counters probably weren't ever works of art, but now it's hard to tell what's stained with dirt that can be removed, and what's age-stained. I find rags in a drawer near the sink, and the water is on, luckily. I put away the groceries in the mostly bare cabinets, wipe down the counters, and locate the very vintage plates and bowls and utensils. They're dusty, but once I rinse them off, serviceable.

"Guys, let's bring our things inside and then eat something." I preheat the oven. One thing everyone will always eat is frozen pizza. I've never had the brand they sold at the hardware store, but how different can frozen pizza really be?

"I want the room with the big bay window," Izzy says.

"You know what a bay window is?" I'm shocked.

"When I stayed at Elizabeth's last month, her mom took us to see some model homes."

"Are they moving?"

Izzy shrugs. "I don't think so, but her mom loves to look at shiny, new houses."

"She'd hate this one." I laugh.

"I love it," Gabe says. "Look what I found!" He hoists

a dead mouse up in the air. "It's like the coolest stuffed animal I've ever seen."

"Drop that right now," I say.

"Oh no!" Whitney shrieks. "It's a mouse! It's dead!"

Ethan, out of nowhere, slaps it with his hand and sends it flying across the room. My heart feels like it's going to pound its way out of my chest, and I keep shivering involuntarily, but at least it's not alive.

Although, where there are dead mice. . .

I make everyone wash their hands, and then we clear the other rooms one by one to ensure no other dead rodents are hiding, waiting to be played with. My appetite's gone, but everyone else seems perfectly happy to dig into the pizza, which is finally ready. This oven probably needs to be replaced. It's green inside, which was my first clue, but it takes almost twice as long as the box said it should to cook the pizza, which means it's probably not heating properly. At least everyone eats it.

And in spite of the depressed dog and the dead mouse, they're all in good spirits. After dinner, we spend twenty minutes and finally succeed in luring the dog inside.

"What if he's not housebroken?" Izzy asks.

"I suppose we'll lure him out the same way." He's still lying on the ground, more like a rug than a dog.

"Good thing you got those groceries, Mom," Ethan says.

He doesn't often praise me for doing simple things. It feels nice.

"Thanks for dinner," Whitney says. "I liked the pizza. It tasted like crackers with pizza sauce and cheese."

I pick up a piece of cold pizza and take a bite. She's not wrong. The crust does remind me of saltine crackers. "I'm glad you liked it."

Once the kids have all unpacked their things into

blessedly empty dressers, they brush their teeth and head for bed. Not even Ethan argues with me—the beauty of the time change, I suppose. We're all tired. I'm locking the front door when I see headlights. You'd think the dog would be barking, but he just lies there. "You're kind of useless," I mutter.

I peer out the window at the approaching car, watching as it parks in front of the small house. The lights shut off, leaving everything dark, but I'm positive that it's two men who climb out. My heart's racing, but I can't go to sleep knowing there are two intruders right outside.

Who are they, why are they here, and how do I get them to leave?

I consider waking Ethan, because at least he looks like an adult male, but I can't do it. He's only seventeen—still a baby. If there's danger, I won't send my minor son out to face it. I fumble around on the counter in the dark until I find my cell phone. It only has one bar, and I'm not even sure who I'd call out here. Does 911 work when you're in the middle of nowhere? What if I lose reception entirely? Every cell in my body screams for me to run and hide, but the mother inside of me keeps me moving.

I force myself to unlock the front door and debate about turning on the porch light. In the end, I decide it's better to see what I'm dealing with than to try and sneak up on them. After all, what would I do if I *did* surprise them? Try and punch them?

They'd probably laugh.

When the light flips on, both men swear. They look. . .shocked to see me. If I had to guess, I'd say they're both in their mid twenties, or possibly early thirties.

I make my voice as loud and as self-assured as I can muster. "I know this place has been vacant, but it's not any more. I'm going to have to ask you to leave."

"Leave?" one of them asks.

The taller of the two says, "But we live here."

"Not anymore, you don't," I say. "I'm sorry if this is inconvenient, but we're Jedediah's relatives and we're going to be staying here for a while."

"You don't want us to help with the ranch anymore?" the tall one asks.

Uh. "You're ranch hands?" Is that what they're called? What if that's an offensive term? "You work here?"

"I'm Kevin," the taller one says.

"And I'm Kevin's better-looking brother, Jeff." The shorter one lifts his hand up to his forehead in some kind of cowboy salute.

"Oh, I'm so sorry," I say. "I didn't realize." Mr. Swift said we couldn't hire someone to run it for us, but he failed to mention there was already (hopefully) competent help on the premises. "I'll rest much easier knowing you're here, actually. Please, carry on. I'm sorry I came out here and fussed."

"We'll likely be up before sunrise in the morning to rotate the water and move the cows, but as soon as you're awake, come find us," Kevin says. "We'll be done by lunch time, and happy to show you around a bit."

What a relief. "Do you know if the dog we found is Jed's?"

"Roscoe?" Jeff asks. "Yeah, he's not doing too well."

He could say that again. "He barely seems to move."

"We keep putting food out, but he hardly eats it." He spits. Gross.

"He did eat some turkey from our hands," I say.

"Maybe he'll perk up, now that you're here," Kevin says. "That'd be great."

Oh good. Another thing to worry about. "Let's hope." I wave. "Sorry for being a little hostile. Have a great night."

"See you tomorrow."

As I turn out the porch light and lock up again, I feel pretty foolish. I should've known someone would be here. It's not like three hundred and fifty cows would be fine all by themselves on a ranch for weeks. All in all, this isn't my dream setup, but at least we have a big old house to ourselves. Five people sharing two bathrooms will be tight, but we'll survive. We might even look back on it and find it's just what we needed. I keep seeing little Roscoe in my mind and wondering if that's how we've looked to the rest of the world.

Maybe it's time for all of us to sit up and start living again.

6

AMANDA

My first thought, in terms of adding a real world angle, was to road trip from New York to this cattle ranch. However, when I put it into a map online, it said it would take about thirty-two hours. That's without figuring in detours and bathroom breaks, etc.

When I imagined what the rental car, not to mention my hips, would look like after thirty-two hours of gas station donuts and Pringles. . . I booked us tickets to Salt Lake City. It's not a place I thought I'd ever go. I'm not a big skier or hiker, so what's the point?

When Mr. Swift told me that my husband apparently spent every summer in Manila, Utah, population under 400, I almost didn't believe him. It's not like I could call his parents to ask—they passed away the year before I met Paul, when his younger brother Nate was just starting law school.

No matter how hard I try, I cannot see Paul on a ranch, tending cows, or whatever you do with them. Are they like sheep? Do you stand around watching them with a staff? The extent of my knowledge about ranching comes from a handful of Hallmark movies where a character goes to a ranch. Usually the person who travels there has to carry a heavy grain bag and ends up spilling it somewhere. Bucolic creatures come over to eat it, and there's always poop on the main character's shoe. Eventually a developer always shows up, sniffing around, trying to buy up the land to fill it with GAPs and Starbucks stores. (In the middle of nowhere, yes.)

Wouldn't that be nice?

But we couldn't even sell it for a whole year, not if we want to keep the proceeds.

Ugh.

At least I pack smarter than the idiots on those Hallmark movies. I packed two pairs of boots, two pairs of sneakers, one of them quite old and worn out, and several pairs of my tiredest looking jeans. I even found a flannel shirt in the back of my closet. When I inevitably have to haul a heavy bag of pig food, I'll be sure to put it on.

I booked a nonstop flight, but thanks to some lousy weather over our planned flight path, or so they say, it takes two flights, with a miserable two-hour layover in Denver, before we reach Salt Lake. At least it's not hot or muggy when we deplane. And thank heavens for phones —my girls spent both flights doing who knows what on their tiny screens.

I came up with a whole list of possible promotional photo ideas with the images Heather sent me. It's hard to tell exactly how the product will look from a picture, of course, so they're subject to change. Heather assured me that the actual clothing pieces would arrive at the ranch in the next few days. In the meantime, I've got a half dozen things I had promised to push back until June, so I can start with them. It'll be a little bit hard to mention the newest dating app way out here, but maybe I can turn it into kind of a joke that highlights what a remote place I'm in.

"Are we close?" Maren asks. "Because my battery's almost dead."

"It's quite a drive from here," I admit. "But I have the rental car booked, and I'm sure you can charge it in the car."

Maren blinks. "Really?"

It's not her fault—we've never had a car. It's not as if the subway makes recharging simple.

"I bet it's a pretty drive," Emery says. "I'm excited."

Maren mutters something under her breath that makes Emery wilt. I wish she'd stop doing that. It's not a crime to be an optimist. "Let's go grab our bags."

We're only planning to stay for a few weeks, but you'd never know it from the volume of luggage. Part of that is my fault—I have no idea what to expect, and when I don't know, I over prepare. Even with one of the pay-for-use-carts, it's hard to pile all of our things up in a way that we can easily navigate. And by the time we reach the rental car kiosk, the line of people waiting is already quite long.

Maren's phone dies, and I really wish I'd thought to bring one of those power banks. If they weren't so heavy, I would have.

"We'll be headed back way before my cheer camp, right?" Maren spears me with one of her most obnoxious looks. "Because Greta's going to the Hamptons every weekend and I promised her that—"

"Don't worry," I say. "We'll be back with plenty of time for you to do cheer camp and waste time with your friends."

"How long are we planning to stay?" Emery asks.

I can't imagine we'll last more than two weeks. "A week or two at most."

"Thank goodness." Maren looks up at the ceiling. "If Greta stops inviting me to things and becomes friends with Lark instead because we stay too long, I'll never talk to you again."

It might do Maren a little good to find some new friends, but I don't bother suggesting that. Finally it's our turn.

"How can you not have any SUVs left? I reserved one last week. I have the confirmation right here."

"We had a mechanical issue with a Tahoe," the lady behind the counter says. "And then our Expedition wasn't returned on time."

"What am I supposed to do, then?"

"Well, we have a full-size van—"

Maren groans.

"Or we can offer you a sedan."

"I paid a premium for the SUV," I say.

"Which we will absolutely refund you for." Her perky smile is not improving my mood.

I glance back at our monumentally large pile of suitcases and bags. "Do you think all of that will fit in a sedan?"

The woman's face tells me what I need to know.

"You don't have anything else, other than a full-size van?"

She shakes her head slowly.

A full-size van, like the mom from the Brady Bunch probably had to drive. I sigh. "Fine. I guess give me the van."

"Make sure it's not in any of the photos." Maren's cackle isn't very attractive.

"Look, girls, sometimes things don't go as you planned, and you just have to roll with it."

"Nice pun, Mom," Emery says.

"Oh my gosh," Maren says. "Are you kidding?"

But fifteen minutes later, I'm bouncing around in the driver seat of the van, my hands wrapped around the enormous steering wheel at ten and two, wondering if I'll really be alright, driving this for three hours. I should've arranged a shuttle or something.

"How long has it been since you drove something?" Maren's right eyebrow's hoisted almost to her hairline. "Because you don't look very. . .competent."

"It's fine." It takes me a few miles to settle in, but I only clip one curb, and the tire doesn't even go flat.

"We're going to die," Maren says. "And no one will even know where we are. They'll never find our bodies."

"Stop being such a drama queen," Emery says. "There's no one out here to hear you anyway."

I don't snort, but I want to. I love when Emery shows a little bit of fire.

It takes us nearly four hours to reach Manila, which only reassures me that a road trip would have been a terrible mistake. What's worse is that we only stopped once and it still took me that long. I've forgotten how to drive—I'm a nervous wreck, being passed the whole way. "Finally," I say. "We're only twenty minutes away."

"If you didn't drive like a grandma, we'd have been here an hour ago." Maren yawns.

Is it bad that I want to spank my fifteen-year-old daughter on the first day of our trip? Probably. "Your grandmother drives like a maniac, which is precisely why *I* drive so safely."

"Safely, huh? Or. . ." Maren coughs. "Slowly."

"Same thing," I say. "And if you ever learn to drive, I'll be sure to teach you to copy me."

"Not a chance."

We breeze past downtown Manila in thirty seconds, even going twenty-five miles an hour. "Wow, that's a small town."

"It's cute, though," Emery says.

She has always been my cheerful child, but the flip side to the highest highs is that she usually has the lowest lows, too. It's nice to see her in such a happy mood. Looks like this trip might be great for more than just me. Now if I could only get Maren to stop grumping about every single thing. . . That would be a miracle.

The GPS on my phone bings to tell me that we've arrived, but we're at the end of what appears to be a long driveway. It's not dirt—it's covered in small, packed white rocks, at least, but they're not very smooth. The van bounces and jostles and whumps so badly that I finally slow to a crawl. Up ahead, there's a very old Corolla parked in front of a tiny house.

I sincerely hope that's not the 'generous farmhouse' Mr. Swift indicated was part of the property.

The car must be something Uncle Jed left behind—I wonder whether it even runs. I'm not sure whether it would be worse for me to drive that old tin can around town, or this enormous school bus. I slowly creep around it, and as I do, I see a much larger, almost sprawling farmhouse at the top of the rise, thank goodness. Beyond the farmhouse are a large brown barn, a huge metal building, and a cute little red barn with *chickens* scratching around on the ground beside it.

The breathtaking mountains that rise up on either side in the background almost make this whole drive worth it. I put the car in park and hop out, unwilling to miss the chance to snap some photos of this view. I frame up the larger, maroon farmhouse with the wrap around front porch, with the sun behind it. I snap a handful of shots from two angles, one of them disguising the badly peeling trim paint, and hop back into the car. I can't help editing them quickly while the car idles. I'm delighted to notice there's a bright red chicken on the front porch, and another white one off to the side of the house that really frame up the whole thing.

"Mom, really? You can edit those later. We're going to be here for a week, at least."

"I'm surprised you even noticed we stopped," Emery says.

"The cell reception here sucks," Maren says.

"Now I get it." Emery's smile is adorable, especially when she's making fun of Maren.

I climb back in. "Alright, you two, I'm going to park and get this house unlocked, and then we'll look around and see what we've gotten ourselves into."

"Are we going to eat?" Maren asks. "Because I'm starving."

"Of course we will," I say. "Let's get our stuff inside, and then we'll find someplace that makes something in town."

"Another twenty minutes away?" Maren's whining is starting to grate on me, badly.

"Just grab your stuff," I snap. "And stop complaining every single second."

Her eyes widen, but she listens. Thankfully.

"The air is so nice," Emery says. "It smells like. . ."

"Mountains," Maren says.

Then the wind shifts and it smells like. . .manure. Ugh.

I sling my laptop bag over my shoulder and heft both my huge suitcases to the ground. Ideally, I'd haul them both in, but with the front porch steps, that's unlikely to end well. I settle for grabbing just one. The heavy base whams on every single stair, but eventually I reach the top. My purse is stuck under my laptop bag, and the key Mr. Swift overnighted is in the front pocket of my purse. I try sliding my hand around the laptop bag to pull it out, but everything gets all jumbled and I end up dropping it and nearly falling on my face. The rental car agreement gets jostled and flies out, and the wind takes things from there. It's halfway across the porch and still moving.

Emery stomps on it.

That sequence of bizarre happenings is probably why I didn't notice the minivan pulling up the drive, but it's hard to miss when it stops right behind our monstrously large white passenger van. Who on earth could be—

It's Abigail.

I think back to our text conversation. I told her I was passing. Didn't she say she wasn't coming either? So what's she doing here? Mr. Swift didn't mention anyone else was coming. I worry that the old Corolla belongs to yet another relative.

Abby's hair falls in beautiful, darkening layers over her shoulders as she opens the door of the minivan and steps out. Of course she's wearing a perfectly pressed pant suit and smiling at me, as though my presence here is a mystery and not the other way around.

"Amanda?" When her eyebrows pull together, a tiny crease forms between them. "I thought you said you were passing."

"I got the impression from all your laughing emojis that you were, too," I say.

Her laugh is just as loud and unbridled as I recall. "Well, I certainly wanted to, but apparently my kids had other plans."

It must be Ethan who climbs out of the sliding door on the minivan, but he looks like he's twenty-something, not seventeen. His hair's longish and dark blond, and it falls naturally across his ridiculously handsome face. His sky blue eyes, his golden tan, and his dimpled smile are a powerful combination—he looks like a California surfer. He couldn't be more out of place here, in the middle of the wilderness.

I almost feel sorry for Abby. He looks as charismatic

as Paul, which means he's bound to be just as self-centered. I imagine she hasn't had an easy time dealing with him since Nate died.

"How long are you planning to stay?" I ask.

"The entire summer," she says. "We arrived last night."

"We're only here for a week or two," Maren says. "Thank goodness." Her exhalation of air puffs her hair up around her face.

More kids are pouring out of the minivan. I'm always a little stressed out when Abby's around. Her kids are very polite, for children, but there are so many of them. "Maren!" Izzy is so much taller. If she didn't have the same shock of short blonde hair that she had at Paul's funeral, I might not recognize her at all. She races around Ethan and barrels toward Maren.

My daughter's eyes widen in something close to mortification. Good for Izzy. Maren could use a good slap, but maybe some excited normal adolescent behavior will help. When Izzy plows into her, knocking Maren's phone out of her hands and sending it clattering against the wood slats of the porch, Emery snickers.

"Wait, Emery?" Abby asks. "You've become so stunningly beautiful! You got your braces off and your teeth look amazing." She climbs the steps and hugs a delighted Emery.

Meanwhile, Whitney and Gabe are pushing past Ethan on their way to hug us too. I forgot how touchy-feely their entire family is. I brace myself seconds before Whitney hugs me around the waist. I hope her hands aren't sticky.

"Aunt Mandy," Whitney says. "It's so nice to see you." She certainly hasn't gotten braces yet. Her teeth look like a jumbled deck of cards, with several pointing at odd angles.

"It's nice to see you too." I pat her back, trying my

best not to be awkward. I don't even hug my own daughters very often—whenever someone grabs me and hugs me without asking, it always feels like a violation. Why do kids get a pass?

Gabe, unlike his sisters, hangs back, hovering near the bottom step. "Aunt Mandy?"

"She married Dad's brother," Ethan says.

Gabe blinks. "Dad's brother was named Uncle Paul." If I hadn't heard him try to speak as a toddler, I might not notice, but the careful way he forms his words reminds me that he was severely speech delayed. He's made excellent progress. "But Uncle Paul is dead. So she's not actually related to us?"

Ethan cringes. "No, Gabe, don't say—"

"It's alright," I say. "Don't worry about it. You and I aren't blood related, no, but my children are your first cousins." I can't quite bring myself to say that I love him the same as if he was part of *my* family. I've never been very good at lying convincingly.

Gabe nods as if he's weighing my words. He's a strange seven-year-old. "It's nice to meet you, Aunt Mandy."

"It's good to see you too, Gabriel."

That earns me a smile, and it actually makes me smile in return. He's odd, but he's also pretty cute with his mussed, wheaten hair and angelic blue eyes.

"Have you seen the chickens yet?" Whitney asks.

Izzy hops up and down on the balls of her feet. "Or the goats?"

"There are goats?" Emery's eyes light up.

"Why am I not surprised there are *goats?*" Maren asks. "Can we go inside already? I really need to charge my phone. The car charger wasn't working right. It kept kicking on and off."

"You may not be very happy with the cell phone reception," Abby says. "It's pretty spotty."

"Have you tried connecting to the WiFi?" I ask. "Enabling WiFi calling did wonders for us when we were staying in Brussels—"

"There isn't any WiFi." Abby's lips compress tightly and her nostrils flare, like she's telling me the entire world is suffering from typhoid fever.

"No WiFi?" Maren sounds like she can't believe it either.

A tall man on the side of the porch clears his throat. "Reception is rough in this entire area, but there's a pretty decent spot up on the top of the hill." He points. "Old Jed jokingly called it his office."

"This is Kevin," Abby says. "He's one of the two ranch hands who've been running things for a while, now."

"I started here four years ago," Kevin says. "Jeff's my brother—he started a year before me. He's finishing up with moving the water, but he'll be back in a few."

"That's a relief," Maren says. "I thought we were going to have to do the farm work ourselves."

"We will," Ethan says, "if we want to fulfill the requirements of the bequest."

"How do you know?" Maren asks.

"I read the will," Ethan says, "and I intend to fulfill every single one."

Oh, yeah. He's going to give Abby a lot of headaches. "Well, that's wonderful," I say.

But in reality, it kind of pisses me off. I mean, I don't want to stay here any longer than I must, and I don't really care whether it gets sold to fund alien research. But I hate the idea that Abby's family will inherit the entire thing. It's probably my mom's fault. If she hadn't put me in all those stupid beauty pageants as a kid, I wouldn't have such a stubbornly competitive streak.

"What would we have to do?" Emery asks. "If we want to help?"

"Uncle Jed appointed three men to supervise, and at least two out of three have to agree that we've assisted with each of the specified ranch activities," Abby says. "They're his friends, or at least people he trusted."

"Presumably," I say.

"Well, I don't know any of them, obviously, but I asked Kevin and Jeff about them."

"I know them all," Kevin says. "This is a pretty small area, so most everybody knows everybody else."

"Are they nice? Are they good people?" I'm not sure why I'm asking. There's no chance we'll actually stick around to complete any of the assignment that insane old man set for us.

"The first guy's named Steve Archer. He's a horse trainer who broke most of the horses out in the barn." Kevin tosses his head, sending his shaggy hair rippling.

"Who's the second?" Maren's paying a little too much attention.

Probably because, even though he's got to be twenty-something, Kevin's relatively good-looking in a country kind of way. "Eddy Dutton, the local vet. Everyone loves Eddy. And then the last one is Jed's best friend, Vernon Ellingson."

"Who's that, again?" Abby asks. "He's the one I don't remember."

"You don't remember him because he had a stroke," a man I assume is Jeff says from a ways off. His voice is rougher than Kevin's, and he's not nearly as handsome. I like him much better.

"Wait, if he had a stroke, then—"

Jeff spits. "Mr. Swift told me his son Patrick would be filling in." He doesn't look very impressed, or maybe I'm misreading him. It's hard to tell what someone's thinking when they're busy wiping their mouth on the sleeve of their shirt.

"And Patrick?" Ethan asks. "You've said something about everyone. Is he not cool?"

Jeff laughs.

Kevin smirks. "I doubt you'd call Patrick *cool*, no. And I hear he wants to buy Birch Creek."

Whoa. That's a plot twist.

"It hardly seems fair if one of the people deciding whether we've complied with the terms is self interested," Abby says.

"Nice, Mom." Ethan grins. "Slide right into lawyer mode and get that sucker kicked out."

She rolls her eyes. "Good try, but you already know it's not going to matter."

Ethan's brow furrows. "Oh, come on. You swore you'd at least consider it—try to make sure we meet all the requirements for the summer. That was the deal."

"I did agree to come," Abby says, "but I didn't agree that I'd spend a single second contesting will terms or arguing with the people appointed to run things."

Ethan jogs up the steps and slides a key into the lock. "If this guy ends up being a real pain, and you don't—"

Maren dashes past him and through the door, but then she screams.

"What's wrong?" I drop my luggage and leap toward the door.

"It's just Roscoe," Ethan says. "He doesn't know Maren yet, and he didn't like her racing in like that."

Abby walks past me, clearly not worried about the dog. "Come on in, Amanda. We'll reconfigure and find you and your girls somewhere to stay this week."

Reconfigure? "Wait, you guys are staying here, in the same house as us?"

She pauses in the doorway. "Of course we are—there isn't anywhere else. The guest house is occupied." She tosses her head at the two guys still standing on the porch outside. "I just went and had a few extra keys made at the local hardware store, which is why Ethan has one."

"And we got a lot more food." Whitney's grin is huge as she carries grocery bags into the kitchen and sets them on the table. Once she gets close, Roscoe quiets down. "Now that we know the fridge works, it's safe to stock up."

I ditch my suitcases and follow Whitney inside.

"How big is this place, exactly?" Maren's still standing a few feet from the doorway, her eyes fixed on the black and white dog that's lying under the kitchen table.

"Really, don't worry about him," Ethan says. "He's had a hard run, with his master dying, but he's all growl and no bite."

"I'm less worried about us not having enough space and more concerned about the lack of WiFi," Abby says. "But don't worry. I already put in a call."

"Or three." Ethan coughs.

"Or three," Abby agrees, "to the only local provider—Union Wireless."

"That's smart," Jeff says from the porch. "Now you'll be at the top of their list when they come to Manila."

"Wait." Abby pivots and steps back onto the porch. "Come to Manila?"

Jeff frowns. "Right."

"What does that mean?"

It's like watching a train wreck happen.

Kevin scratches his head. "I think they'll be here in July. Or is it August? And when they come, they'll probably do you first or second, since you're calling them now."

"Do me?" Abby's tone is the aural equivalent of someone holding a trash bag away from her body with two fingers. "They'll. . .do what for me? Install the broadband they advertise. . .in *July or August?*" Her hand is shaking a bit, and her face looks flushed.

"They usually come twice a year," Kevin says from behind Jeff. "So you're lucky it's so close." He actually looks delighted.

Meanwhile, Abby's coming unglued. Her face falls. Her lips are moving without any sound being created.

"That's a long time to go without internet," I say. "You sure you'll be staying here all summer?"

"I. . ." Abby closes her eyes and runs her hand over her face. "I need internet every single day. It's the only way I can work remotely."

"Mom, we'll figure something out, I promise. Don't freak out." Ethan's jogged out and come back, his arms full of groceries and his eyes genuinely concerned. Maybe he's not as selfish as I remembered.

"This is your fault," Abby spits out, before she turns and ducks back out.

Her other three kids, including little Gabe, all trudge from the trunk of her minivan, where they're loading up with bags of stuff, to the kitchen. I usually have most everything delivered to our place on the East Side, but if I had to haul groceries in, I wonder whether either of my girls would lift a finger without being shouted at first.

"Can I help you with your bags?" Ethan asks on his way back out. "Aunt Amanda?"

"Right," I say. "Sure."

He lugs them both in, his muscles straining, but he never complains. Something about that small gesture makes my eyes mist up. Paul might have been a self-centered jerk, but I do miss having someone to help out with the unwieldy things. It's pathetic that I'm this emotional over something so stupid. I wipe at my eyes when no one's watching.

"There are six bedrooms," Gabe says. "I got the best

one, because there's a little passageway that connects my closet to Ethan's." He looks like he really means it.

"Oh, well, that is cool."

"Can your girls share a room?" Abby asks. "If so, I can put Whitney and Izzy together. You can have the Master, and I'll take whichever room your girls don't want."

"I am definitely not sharing with Emery," Maren says. "She talks in her sleep."

Abby looks at me like I'm supposed to be doing or saying something.

"I do," Emery says. "I'm sorry."

"Oh." Abby's mouth dangles open stupidly.

"I think if there are six rooms, three and three is an even split."

"There are two bathrooms," Gabe says. "And a kitchen, and a living room, and another family room that's full of books. But there's not a very big pantry."

"Two bathrooms?" I exhale slowly.

"They're big ones," Ethan says.

"I suppose we'll each take a bathroom?" I can't keep the pained note out of my voice.

"If that's what you want," Abby says.

"It's what's fair," I say. It's not my fault she decided to have *four* kids. We shouldn't be inconvenienced because of her decisions.

"Oh no! Do I have to share with Ethan?" Gabe moans. "But there's only one bed in there."

"I'm not super excited either, little guy, but maybe the girls will take that room."

"Mine has bunk beds," Gabe says.

"And a terrible view," Ethan says. "Any chance you guys want the nice, big bed in mine?" He clasps his hands in front of him like he's praying.

"Whitney kicks," Izzy says.

"Kids," Abby says.

"Fine," Izzy says. "But I want an extra pillow as a buffer."

They grumble a bit as they put the groceries away, but just like that, they all go along with it. Because Abby said the word 'kids' in a reproving tone. I need some of her super special mom potion or whatever has her kids being so *nice* to each other and so compliant with her.

Abby and her kids vacate faster than I thought possible, and I'm putting my clothes away when I realize what a fast one she pulled. Since I took the Master bedroom, that means that every single time my kids need to use the bathroom, they'll be traipsing through my room to do it. This is exactly the reason I've always struggled to deal with her. She acts all friendly and kind to your face, but somehow, she always seems to get the better deal while I always get the shaft.

7
ABIGAIL

When I was in grade school, I learned that a human can live three weeks without food, three days without water, and three minutes without air. I've since learned that's not precisely true, but it's also not ridiculously far off.

Internet access is oxygen to me—at least with regards to working remotely.

I've been without it for two days now.

And I am not okay.

It took me four tries on my cell phone to get one SMS message through to Robert. NO WIFI IN THE LAND TIME FORGOT. I'M SCREWED.

I have no idea how long it took him to message me back, but I don't receive his reply for almost half an hour.

YOU'LL FIGURE SOMETHING OUT. YOU ALWAYS DO. TRY NOT TO STRESS. NO HARD AND FAST DEADLINES THIS WEEK.

He's trying to calm me down—what else can he really do? But I know as well as he does that the final round of depositions happens over the next few weeks. Thanks to the fallout from the dumb pandemic, they allow us to do them remotely in most instances, but I need to have the documents reviewed and indexed, and I need the questions prepped and ready.

The internet company may say they won't come until July or August, but every company is made up of people, and people can make exceptions. Maybe I can convince them to come sooner. But until then, I need to figure out some sort of workaround.

A tap at my door distracts me. I drop my laptop on the pink polka dot and gold floral quilt that covers the old, creaky twin bed in my summer bedroom. My eyes don't appreciate the decor, and my old back is still complaining that I gave up the king bed that had a mattress made this century. "Yeah?"

The door swings open a foot or so. "Hey, Mom." Ethan's standing in the doorway, wearing the unsure look on his face that means he needs to ask for help.

"What's wrong?"

"Nothing's wrong. Why do you always ask me that?"

I suppress my laugh. "What do you need?"

"I was hoping we could go over this list and make a plan." He inhales sharply. "You're really good at plans."

My heart swells. Apparently I really needed to hear that he liked something about me, even if he no longer trusts my advice on his education or my guidance for his future. "Alright."

"I bet the girls would want to be involved, and maybe Aunt Mandy—"

No way. I'm doing my level best to keep things cordial, but if she sticks around more than a week, I'm going to lose it. "She won't be here very long." I stand up and take the list from him. It's a printout of the list of tasks, plus a more thorough list of daily tasks he's added, presumably with Jeff's and Kevin's input. I'm kind of impressed with his initiative. "We shouldn't bother her with this stuff."

"I know Uncle Paul died a few years before Dad, but she still looks really sad to me," Ethan says.

Oh, no, now I'm crying. I'm such a bad person—worrying only about myself and making my life easier. At least my kids are decent most of the time, and insightful, and kind. Maybe I'll get bonus points in heaven for doing a moderately good job at making them better than I am myself.

"Mom." Ethan's arms wrap around me a little stiffly, but I press my face against his broad chest. Sometimes, even with his height, it's easy to forget how young he is. His frame is still spare—he lacks the bulk his dad had—but he's also gotten so big.

"It's okay to be sad," I say. "And I think you're right. I think Aunt Mandy is probably still pretty sad. Maybe this week will be good for her."

"But keep Maren away from me," Ethan says. "Because I swear I'm about an inch away from punching that brat."

I push backward, wiping my eyes. "Ethan Elijah Brooks."

He rolls his eyes. "Oh, please, Mom. I won't actually do it." He mutters under his breath. "Probably."

"If you ever hit a girl, your father would—"

"Are you sure she's a girl?" His lopsided grin widens. "I think she might be a cyborg who's in a committed relationship with her phone."

I slug him on the arm. "She's a teenager growing up at a private school in New York City."

He sighs. "She never had a chance, I guess."

Not at being a normal person who can relate with the ordinary world. "She might be less prickly if you tried making friends. You could talk to her about something that matters to her."

"Like what?"

"I don't know—social media?" None of my kids have accounts—I barely get on myself—but he could ask her about hers.

"Talk to her about. . .oh wait, hang on." Ethan turns his head like he's listening to something outside, when I know very well that there's no one calling for him. "Whoops, I think that's Kevin. I better go see what he needs. There's probably a tractor that needs repairs." He's out the door before I can even laugh. He may have a good heart, but he's not Dr. Phil.

Apparently escaping my attempts to force bonding with cousins was more important than making a plan.

I pull the will out of my briefcase and grab a legal pad. There's a calendar of major events and phases of ranch life, but I focus on the things listed for June and July. The main tasks, on the will list and per the information Ethan added, are driving the cows out to the Forestry land for the summer, prepping the meadows for hay, irrigating each of the hay meadows, and harvesting them in July and September for the alfalfa, and starting in August for the grass. Apparently that task goes into September, right until the cows return.

The most nerve-wracking task we must certify as having done is driving all the cattle onto the Forest Service land. Mr. Swift mentioned something about coordinating with Ranger Dutton. I type a quick email to Mr. Swift on outlook on my phone asking for details on how to reach out to him, but the message won't send until I find a place with better reception. The battery on my phone is already down to half—constantly scanning for service isn't helping.

How did Uncle Jed manage here without internet?

Why didn't Jeff and Kevin insist he bring in broadband? I was mostly kidding about this being the land time forgot, but my joke might have been painfully accurate. My current plan involves pinning Jeff and Kevin down so I can figure out exactly what we need to do to prepare for driving the cattle to the Forestry Land, and what we need to do in order to prep for hay and irrigate.

But the top of the list is finding a place with internet I can steal until we can get it installed for ourselves.

When I finally leave my room, Maren's poking haphazardly at her phone, which is attached to a charger.

No other kids are around, but I know Ethan went outside. When I duck out there, I see Emery, Whitney, and Izzy, with Gabe trotting along behind them, on their way to the barn. "Be careful around the horses," I say.

"Mom, we know," Izzy says.

She's had two years of English horseback lessons once a week, and she thinks she's going to be the next rodeo queen.

"Does she like horses?"

I startle at the voice, but when I look for the speaker, I don't see anyone nearby.

Kevin stands up, and I realize he was behind a metal water trough that's turned on its side. "They all seem pretty excited about the animals, and our horses are pretty good, but they're still twelve hundred pound animals."

"She's taken lessons for a few years."

"Which one?"

"The blonde with the bob," I say. "Whitney, the one with the longer, darker hair, has had a year or so of lessons. She knows the basics of horse care, but she's not as confident in the saddle. Gabe comes with us to the lessons, so he knows the rules, like not walking behind them or making loud noises that could spook them."

"What about that other little girl?"

"I have no idea. Emery's my niece, but we don't see them much."

"Someone should make sure she's clear on safety rules at least." He harrumphs. "Never mind. Looks like Jeff's on it."

Sure enough, he is. The kids are standing in front of him in a half-circle, like they're at school, heads bobbing as he talks. "That's a relief. But speaking of horses and whatnot, what would the cattle drive to the forest involve? Apparently we have to participate."

"I can't imagine anyone expects all them to come." He bobs his head at Whitney and the other kids.

"That's a relief, but I imagine Ethan will insist, and Izzy and I should be capable, maybe. What exactly does it involve?"

"We all get on the horses and we use them to push the cows up into the mountains." He shrugs. "Most of them have been before and they know what to do. They're eager to get up there—even now they're testing the fences."

"Why not take them now?"

"Forestry Service rules," he says. "Gotta wait until they give the all clear."

"I imagine Whitney will insist on going if Izzy does. They're both pretty excited about their cattle ranch adventure."

His smile is kind. "The best person to decide if they're safe is Steve Archer."

"The horse trainer?"

Kevin scrunches his nose. "Everybody calls him the Horse Doc."

"That's cute," I say.

"I'll give you his number. We drive the cows in a little

over two weeks, though. So I'd call him quick. If you all need some help, you wanna have time for it."

"Thanks." I type in the numbers he rattles off.

"But Steve don't usually answer his phone," Kevin says.

"What?"

"He's usually on a horse, plus, the reception's not great."

Don't I know it. "What do you suggest I do if he doesn't answer?"

"I'd just drive out there. It's real close."

"Great. Speaking of small town life—you don't happen to know anyone at the internet company, do you?"

He chuckles. "Sorry, that's over in Green River."

Drat. "Do you know anyone around here who's on the friendly side who might be willing to let me do some work at their office or home until we get our broadband working?"

"Huh." He sucks his teeth, presumably while he's thinking. "Well, only person I know who definitely got it last time was Steve."

"The Horse Doc? That Steve Archer?"

"Yep. I imagine the vet's got it, and maybe the Ellingsons. They always get the newfangled stuff."

The internet's apparently a 'newfangled' thing. You can't make this stuff up. "Great, well, I'll start with Steve." Two birds and all. "Directions?"

"Turn out of the drive and drive straight. It's the white farmhouse a few miles down the road with the big barns behind it."

"To the left?"

"Nah, turn right, toward town. The house above us is Amanda Saddler's place, and past that is Wilde Ranch."

Which does not help me at all.

"Steve's probably four miles from here, toward town."

He points as if I can't even figure out which direction the town is located.

"I appreciate it."

"Jeff and I are taking your boy out to help us work on the tractor. We got a few meadows left to clear sticks from and drag. I figure that's something he can prolly do."

"Right," I say. "Great idea."

When he turns back to work on what I think is a hole in the bottom of the metal trough, I try calling Steve. As he predicted I would, I get voicemail. Twice. On the third time, my phone won't even dial. I don't swear under my breath—I'm proud of that.

Five minutes later, I've left Izzy in charge, notified Amanda that I'm headed to a neighbor's house, and packed my laptop and bag of case files. I just hope this Horse Doc is home and friendly. *Please be like Kevin, but with internet I can borrow.*

The directions were spot on—just like Kevin said, there's a tiny white farmhouse with an enormous red barn behind it. The barn is beautiful, as if it cost three times what the house did. It's even got white trim, including big white Xs over the doors. It looks just like the barns in my kids' animal picture books. There's a rundown little green barn next to it, but by the looks of things, it's full of hay and shavings.

There's a circular drive in front of the house, but there's a large gravel area in front of the barn that looks like a parking lot. I park the minivan there. Kevin insisted, if Steve was home, he'd be in the barn. I look around and I listen carefully, but I don't see anyone. It feels a little rude to just walk in, but I'm not sure what else to do. Three horse heads appear as I draw close, one of them whinnying loudly.

"Hello?" Still no answer. I try a little louder. "Hello? Mr. Archer?"

Still no response.

Unless I count another loud call from the same horse who started whinnying earlier. He's a big, well-muscled, shiny chestnut with a white stripe down the middle of his big, round-cheeked face. "You're the only one here, huh? Where's your trainer, fella?"

Is he a fella? I approach the stall to get a closer look, but the toe of my boot hits something that clinks. It smashes into something else and makes a terrible shattering noise. My pulse is pounding in my ears. I've come into this man's barn and broken something. What is it? I look around frantically, shocked to discover it's more than a half dozen empty bottles of *beer*, and I broke two of them.

Who on earth drinks in a barn? It's the middle of the day, for heaven's sake. It takes me almost five minutes to locate a broom, and I can't find a dustpan. I'm stuck using a metal muck shovel as a makeshift dustpan, because I can't leave glass all over the floor. The big black trashcan is near a towering stack of hay bales, and I bump it too hard and knock the lid off entirely. It makes a big wham when it hits the ground.

I'm a little past trying to be quiet, so I dump the broken glass and the other bottles as well, into the can and pick the lid up, slamming it back down.

"Huh? What?" A man's voice from somewhere behind me startles me.

I spin around just as he shoves into a sitting position, hay poking up at odd angles from very unkempt hair. He was clearly asleep on a bale of hay. He's broad across the chest, like really broad. His t-shirt stretches as he does, and I wonder how tall he is. Which I should not be doing. What kind of person sleeps in a barn, on hay no less? I think about the beer, and I have a bit better idea what kind of person might be sleeping here in the middle of the day. "Mr. Archer, I presume?"

The man blinks and squints, trying to focus on me. It's probably harder because I'm backlit and he's hungover. But it's then that I realize I've seen him before.

He was mowing his lawn Sunday evening.

Shirtless. Glistening.

And now I can't get that image out of my head. My mouth goes instantly dry. My hands shake so I stuff them in my pockets.

"Who are you?" He sounds as bleary as he looks.

"My name's Abigail Brooks. I'm living just down the road for the summer, at Jedediah Brooks' ranch."

"Brooks. Brooks. Staying at Jed's." He slaps his face twice in quick succession and sits up straighter, brushing hay off his old, beat-up jeans and blinking repeatedly. "Are you Nate's wife?"

I flinch, but I don't think he noticed. "Yes, Nate was my husband."

"Was?"

"Did Mr. Swift not inform you of the terms of Jedediah's will?"

Mr. Archer leans back against the hay bales behind him, stacked nearly to the ceiling. "He did mention that it was possible some of Jed's great-nephews and nieces might come work the ranch and have to prove they'd done it. Is that you guys? Why didn't he just leave it to Nate?"

I sigh. Aside from being a drunk, Mr. Archer is apparently also a bit dim. "Nate died, Mr. Archer. More than a year ago."

His jaw drops. "He *died*?"

"I take it you weren't very close?"

He snorts. "Not lately, no." Mr. Archer shoves to his feet—he is tall. At least eight inches taller than I am.

Maybe more than that. "Steve Archer. Part time horse trainer." He extends his hand.

I take it reluctantly. He has a more impressive grip than I expected from such a mess—his hands are both large and strong. I suppose that's to be expected for someone who works with animals all day. I kind of like that he admits he's only working part time. "I heard you're called the Horse Doc."

He shifts a bit, and I'm shocked. He smells—but not like body odor, alcohol, or manure like I'd expect. He smells. . .good. Really good. What kind of drunk wears cologne in the barn? "That's just a local joke."

"Well, I think I'll stick with calling you Mr. Archer."

"Please," he says. "Call me Steve at least. I've stuck my foot right in my mouth, and I'm sorry. I'm a little slow to wake up all the way when things are busy."

Busy? I'm the only person here, other than a few horses. I don't laugh, but it's hard. "I'm sure it's difficult when—" I realize I'd been about to chastise him for the day drinking. I certainly don't know him well enough for censure like that. "When you have such a comfortable bed." I glance at the hay bale, which looks miserably poky.

He laughs. "Well, I've slept in less comfortable places."

I'm sure he has. One of the hazards of being a drunk, I assume. "I'll get right to the point. I'd hate to waste your time. I've heard you're the person to teach horseback basics. I have four children, and at least two of them, as well as myself, need to learn how to ride for a cattle drive in a hurry. The will requires us to participate in driving the cows into the forest."

"In two weeks?" His eyes widen.

I nod.

"What's your past experience with horses?" He looks

me over like I'd eye a contract sheet, detached and clinical.

My appearance is fine—for someone in her late thirties, I'm in reasonably good shape. But I'm sure I don't look like someone who knows how to ride. "I took a riding class in college, two semesters. I learned a few basics. I've been on a few trail rides on a cruise, where the horse tucks its nose into the bum of the one in front of it. And I've taken a couple of months of lessons here and there. I won't fall off unless I'm pretty badly bucked, and I won't abuse a horse's mouth, but I'm not as confident as I'd like to be."

"That sounds like a fair assessment."

"I'm not sure about my son—he's more of a four-wheeler rider—but I have two daughters, twelve and ten, who have been taking lessons for a while. Unfortunately for this circumstance, they've been doing English."

He shrugs. "Usually they learn a little cleaner form that way. Doubt it'll hurt. Mostly horses need to be asked politely to do their job and then allowed to do it."

"Would you have time to help?"

"I assume you'd rather learn on your own horses?"

Do I have horses? He must mean Uncle Jed's horses. "Since those are presumably the horses we'll be riding in two weeks, that would probably be best."

"I think Jed has ten or twelve horses that are still rideable." He taps his lips, and I notice how full they are. Something I should not be noticing, especially after ogling him before. And now I'm imagining him with his shirt off. Again. "A few are used regularly by Kevin and Jeff, but I imagine some of them have been a bit neglected."

"Is that bad?"

"Might need a reminder of their job, that's all. When can you start? This afternoon?"

"Sure." I don't really want to ask him whether he's sober enough to teach, but I'm worried he's not. "Will that work for you? You aren't too. . .tired?"

"Mrs. Brooks, I'm always tired."

I bet he is. "Alright, well, if that works for you—"

"I can come over in about two hours. Make sure whoever needs a lesson is ready to go."

Hopefully he'll sober up in that time. "I'll do it."

"And Mrs. Brooks?"

"Yeah?"

"I'm very sorry for your loss. Nate and I didn't always agree, but he was a good man. I'd have behaved better if I'd been fully awake when we first met."

I nod and turn to go. I'm a dozen paces away when I remember the internet. Steve has already picked something up—a bridle maybe? He's tugging on some part of it. "One more thing."

When he looks up and our eyes meet, I realize something I didn't even notice before, probably because of the image of him shirtless. He has brilliant blue eyes, and they're deep like the ocean. If I didn't know better, I'd have said they were also intelligent. "Yes?"

"I'm here this summer for my children. They need this time, but I'm trying very hard to keep my job while working remotely from here. When I arrived, I discovered that Uncle Jed doesn't have internet service to his place."

Steve laughs, and his entire face brightens. He rubs his hand across his five o'clock shadow, the bristles from his beard scritching loudly. "What were you hoping I might do about it?"

"I know this is a real imposition, but is there any chance you have broadband? If I could borrow your WiFi connection for a bit, I could review the files that are urgent. If I can't find internet somewhere, I'll be forced to boost off my cell phone signal. Kevin and Jeff have informed me that the only reliable place for that near Birch Creek Ranch is at the top of the hill overlooking the east meadow."

"Jed was an odd one." He points at the white house. "You're welcome to—"

"I won't go inside," I say. "If you can just tell me the WiFi info."

"Network is the only one that shows up," he says. "And the password is bananassuck, run together, all lowercase."

"Bananas?" I ask. "Actually, never mind." It's not like we're going to be friends. "Thanks. A lot."

He grunts by way of reply, which seems about right.

Luckily, he has a swing on his front porch. I set my bag down and pull out my laptop. It's a little embarrassing, but having fast internet feels like coming up for air after a long swim. I answer a dozen emails, and then dive into the pile of discovery documents that have come in since yesterday. Mondays always suck, but when the opposing counsel is dumping batches of unnecessary paperwork to bury the stuff that matters? That always pisses me off.

I'm nearly done, but it's also been an hour and a half. I take a break to call Izzy. She doesn't answer, but by some stroke of luck, Ethan does.

"Mom?"

"I'm at the Horse Doc's house, and blessedly, he's letting me use his internet. I sent an email to Union Wireless offering to act as a surrogate mother for their demon child, if only they'll come do our internet in the next week. Hopefully they have a need for something like that."

"You're so weird, Mom."

"I'm taking that as a compliment."

"You're proving my point."

"Do you want to learn to ride a horse?"

"Sure."

"Wait, you do?"

"If I'm going to be living on a ranch, I ought to learn."

"In about half an hour, Mr. Archer will be coming over to teach us our first lesson."

"Oh, great."

"Make sure that's alright with Jeff and Kevin and ask Whitney and Izzy to be ready."

"Can he teach four of us at once?"

I didn't think about that. I suppose we'll find out soon enough. "Let's assume he can." A beep tells me someone's calling on the other line. I check—it's work. "Hon, I better take this. Can you get everyone ready?"

"Sure. See you."

I click to the other line. "Hello?"

"You're alive," Robert says. "Thank goodness."

I groan. "It's good to hear your voice. I wish I could pull myself through the phone and back to reality."

"Is it that bad? I figured it might be kind of nice not to have internet."

"What kind of place doesn't have WiFi?" I ask. "It's insane. And apparently they come twice *a year* to install it out here. Twice a *year*, Robert."

"Certainly a little different than what you're used to."

"A little?" I start to gather my files. "It's like I'm in an episode of *Survivor*."

Robert chuckles. "Definitely do whatever it takes. Met anyone interesting?"

"Thankfully we have two ranch hands who can help. Speaking of, I've actually got to get going. This drunk cowboy's going to teach us all some basic horseback lessons so we don't fall off when we help drive the cattle out to the forest in two weeks."

"You're making that up," Robert says.

I laugh. "I wish I was."

"He's really a drunk?"

I drop my voice. "He was asleep on a stack of hay when I got here, and the barn was full of empty beer bottles. I could barely take a step without knocking them over."

"Just come back home, Abby."

"I can't. Ethan's so excited. I haven't seen him like this. . .well, not since his dad died."

"I miss you, and you've only been gone a day."

"Am I going to lose my job?" I close my eyes. "If I can't get internet for a month and it makes me late on things. . . I'm really worried."

"I'll do your work myself if I have to—you won't lose your job just because you're a phenomenal mother."

"Thank you, Robert. I mean it. I owe you."

"You'll never owe me a thing."

"I better go."

"Call when you can."

"I will." I hang up and stand. Steve Archer's staring at me. I jump. "Oh. I didn't realize you were right there." Listening to every word I said. I wonder how long he's been there.

"Sorry," he says.

It's not like I can be upset—I have no expectation of privacy at *his* house. "It's the first place I've had decent cell reception in days and my boss had a lot of questions for me."

"You were talking to your boss?" He lifts one eyebrow.

Heat rises in my face. "Yes. Why?"

He shrugs. "Didn't sound like the way I'd talk to my boss."

"Isn't your boss a horse?"

He laughs. "Probably the horse's owner—that's who usually pays me."

I wrack my brain, trying to remember what I'd said. I get hung up on how I'd laughed at Steve, calling him a drunk. The guy who let me spend the last hour and forty-five minutes on his porch. The same man who's giving us last-minute, emergency horse lessons. "You're ready to go?" I can't bring myself to meet his eyes.

"Yep. You?"

"You won't mind if I camp out here on your porch for the next month, will you?"

His lips part, and his brows draw together.

"I'm kidding." Sort of.

"Oh." Even his forced laugh is kind of charming.

What's wrong with me? "I'm a little worried about getting my work done, that's all."

"Doesn't sound like your boss is going to fire you, at least."

I really wish I knew what he'd heard. "Not yet, anyway." The whole drive back to Uncle Jed's ranch, I keep seeing Steve's face when he smiled. His face when he thought I really meant to live on his porch. His deep blue eyes. His dark hair, a little too long, his clean-shaven face.

Clean-shaven? When did he shave? I know he didn't go into his house. I was camped out in front of it.

Unless he has a back door, obviously. My brain's not working right today.

The girls are dressed in jeans and boots when we arrive, standing in front of the barn and waving wildly. At least they're excited. I'm doing this for them, I remind myself. A change of pace. A summer spent in a place their dad used to come. A chance for Ethan to imagine that changes of plan can be fresh and fun.

I just hope he'll realize that it's not always the right move to do something different.

"I see your kids over there?" Steve asks.

I point out which child goes with which name and tell him their riding experience.

"And you're coming too?" When Steve looks me up and down this time, he's not analyzing. He's *looking*. He notices that I noticed, and he shrugs and smiles, as if to say, *I am a man.*

My eyes dart to his left hand—clean of any rings—and a wave of guilt washes over me. Something about him has made me lose my mind. I'm acting like an insane person. "I better run and change my clothes."

"That's an awfully nice pantsuit to wear around horses," he agrees. "By the way—is that navy blue minivan yours?" His expression is a mix of curious and. . . mischievous.

Oh, no. He must have noticed the blue minivan stopped in front of his house yesterday. While he was mowing. Did he see my face? I feel the heat rise in my cheeks. "It's a rental."

"I see." He shrugs and starts toward the barn. Hopefully that means he didn't realize I was staring at him. This is awkward enough without him thinking I'm attracted to him. Which I most definitely am not.

By the time I've changed into jeans and boots so new that the bottoms are still slick, Steve's standing outside the back of the barn. He's holding the reins to a horse—which seems awfully fast. How long did it take me to change? Whitney and Izzy are both standing beside a horse.

Ethan's nowhere to be seen.

I jog over to where they are, slowing down to figure out how to open the gate, and then again to close it. "Where's your brother?" I ask Izzy once I'm close enough that she'll hear me.

"He's really slow at grooming," she says with a superior air.

Of course he is.

"He spent the whole time picking Ollie's hooves." Whitney's smirk is classic.

Ethan hates to be bad at something, so he's scowling when he finally walks out, his horse saddled, but still in a halter.

Steve hands me the reins to the dark brown and white paint gelding he's holding and crosses to check Ollie's saddle and girth. "Nice work, Ethan. You lined it up just like I said, and it's almost tight enough." He tugs on the girth one more time, with a practiced hand, and tucks the ends into a slit on the saddle. "You have the bridle?"

Ethan takes it off his shoulder and passes it to Steve.

I stink at bridling. After about the third time I banged the horse's teeth in my college course, one of my instructors just took over doing it for me. It's a stroke of luck that he got my horse ready while I was changing, but I'm worried about the next time we ride.

"Alright, let me show you how to get on." He loops the reins over Ollie's head. "If you're tall enough, you can just swing up like this." He sticks his toe in the stirrup and his leg moves up and over smoothly. He makes it look absurdly easy.

"What if you're short?" Whitney asks.

"I'll give you a boost," Steve says. "Just let me make sure Ollie remembers his job first." He shifts the reins slightly and Ollie swings in a small circle. He backs up. He leaps forward, and Steve clucks. "Just a moment."

It's fascinating to watch him work. He doesn't look the least bit tipsy, which is a relief. Ollie tosses his head a few times, his lighter, almost blonde mane flying up in the air, but after a moment, he settles in, head down, and moves quickly, lightly, and smoothly. "There you go." He swings off and hands the reins to Ethan. "Need help getting on?"

"I don't think so."

To Steve's credit, he stands patiently and assists Ethan. My big boy is clearly a little stiffer and lot less coordinated than he'd like to be, but he's young and he manages. Steve's so matter-of-fact about everything that even Ethan relaxes.

"Ollie will stand patiently for you—he's a cutting horse. They do their job, but they'll wait until it's time."

True to his word, Ollie stands, shiny brown head down, quiet and calm.

"It helps a lot to have horses that know what's expected," Steve says. "I trained all these myself, so you don't have to worry about them having bad manners. They all aced kindergarten."

"What's mine called?" I ask.

Steve pats my paint on the neck. "This is Snoopy."

I smile. "Snoopy? He was almost all white, and he was a dog."

He shrugs. "I didn't name him."

I don't ask who did. It seems like something he'd offer if he wanted to share.

"Alright, do you need a hand?" His eyes are steady on mine. He must not have overheard much of my call, or he'd be angry with me, probably. I think.

"I'll be alright."

He stays close anyway, which is good. My boot gets caught on something and I nearly reverse directions and head back down. Only Steve's hand on my hip keeps me from complete embarrassment. "There you go."

Neither of the girls need help, which is promising, but also a little irritating. Like Ethan, I don't love looking silly. "Alright," he says. "Follow me over here. We'll head into this empty meadow that Jeff and Kevin already cleared. The ground will be a little hard, but these guys are used to it."

"What's your horse named?" I ask.

"This is Kronk," Whitney says.

"And mine is Maggie," Izzy says.

One mare and three geldings. I did hear that there are two men to every woman up here. I can't help smiling at my own internal joke. "Glad you're having fun," Steve says.

He's not really wrong.

But about half an hour later, I'm not smiling. My lesson, and even Izzy's, has been fine, but Ethan's struggling, and Whitney's on the verge of a meltdown.

"You can't yank on him like that," Steve snaps. "How'd you feel if I stuck a metal bar in your mouth and popped you in the face with it?" He shakes his head. "If you do it again, I'll pull you off."

"I'm sorry." Whitney's eyes fill with tears.

"And Ethan, use your feet. They aren't supposed to dangle, and they should never bump into him unless you mean them to. If you can't get him to turn, press on him with your foot with purpose."

"Which foot?" Ethan's not usually this patient or calm. I'm proud of him.

"Off," Steve says, but he's not looking at Ethan. He's staring right at Whitney.

She sits back in her saddle like he taught us at the beginning, and Kronk stops dead. Tears are running down her face. "I'm sorry." Her words are barely louder than a whisper. If I weren't right behind her, I wouldn't have heard them at all.

"I told you if you did it again, it was time to get off."

She slides off, pulling Kronk out of the small pasture. I swing off Snoopy as well and walk alongside her. "It's alright, sweetheart."

She shakes her head.

"Look at me."

When she does, the hurt in her eyes fills me with fury. Steve is still teaching Ethan and Izzy as if nothing happened. I'd like to throttle him. Wasn't he listening when I said Whitney had only been taking lessons for a year? She's ten, for heaven's sake.

"I'm going to—"

"Please don't say anything, Mom." Her eyes plead with me.

"Fine." But I need to kick something. Hard.

After we cool the horses down by walking around the barn a dozen times, and after we tack them down, I'm still simmering.

"Go into the house and check on Gabe, will you?"

Whitney nods and walks toward the house, still dragging. She went from so happy to so upset, all because of how awful Steve was.

They're just finishing, it seems. "You know how to tack down?" Steve asks.

"I can help him," Izzy says. "You don't have to babysit us."

He gives them a few extra directions. "I think we should try to do another lesson tomorrow. If you're going to ride out in two weeks, we'll need to meet pretty often."

"Thanks," Ethan says.

"Yeah, thank you so much." Izzy smiles.

"Let me write you a check," I say.

He shakes his head. "My fee is $120 per group lesson, but you can just write me one check at the end of the week."

I fall into step next to him. "Are you sure?"

Once we're far enough away that Ethan and Izzy can't hear us, he stops. "Are you sure you want another one?"

I wasn't expecting him to ask that.

"You look pretty upset." He crosses his arms. "Do you have something to say?"

"She's only ten." I'm a little deflated by him bringing it up head on.

"If you want that ten-year-old to go out on a trail ride for several days, I can't treat her differently."

I look upward, searching for patience. "You can't mean that."

He frowns. "You disagree?"

"It's my job to build my children up, Mr. Archer, not to tear them down. Yelling at her? Kicking her out of the lesson? That's hardly helpful."

"Your hands were quiet." He holds his left hand in front of him like he's holding the reins. "Your seat isn't perfect, but it's natural enough, and you listened. Whitney's hands were bouncing around already, but when I asked her to tell Kronk to turn, she did this." He pops his hands back. "If I let her keep doing that, if I don't yell, what do you imagine will happen?"

"I'm not sure."

"Nothing the first time. Probably nothing the first twenty times." He leans closer, and his smell washes over me again. "But I'm sure that by the twenty-first, or the twenty-second, it's going to be ugly. This is literally my job. That horse is a patient, hard worker and that's why I chose him for your ten-year-old. But even sweet Kronk will get sick of being abused eventually and buck her off."

I swallow. "Okay."

He softens. "I don't want to make your sweet little girl cry, but I do want to make sure she doesn't break her neck. If she can't control her hands, she can't ride. It's not safe."

I still don't like his methods, but I suppose I can't argue with his reasoning. "You'll let me know when we're closer to it whether she needs to be left at home?"

"Of course."

"Alright. Are you available tomorrow?"

"I am if you can do afternoon again, but it needs to be at my place. I won't have time to come here."

I nod, still upset.

"And Mrs. Brooks?" He's got quite a confident stare, for a drunk layabout.

"Yeah?"

"Feel free to use my front porch anytime you want."

And he's back to nice again. I cannot figure him out, but once we get past this dumb cattle drive, hopefully I won't need to anymore.

8

AMANDA

When we first drove up, I loved that there were chickens scratching around in the front yard. They really add to the whole country feel.

I am not, however, enamored of the chicken poop I just stepped in on our front porch. I stumble backward and bump into the black and white dog. I nearly land on my butt.

"Roscoe? Is that your name?" His head bobs, which must be a coincidence. "Can you keep the chickens off this porch? Their poop is disgusting."

He sits down and tilts his head.

I point at the chickens and I swear he follows my finger. "No-no chickens here." I point at the porch. I sound like a crazy person. There's no way a dog is more likely to understand if I talk to him like a toddler or someone with broken English. I do pat his head. He leans into my hand, so I scratch his ears.

When my phone rings, he brings his ears forward. He looks like a completely different dog when his ears are up. He's actually really pretty. "Hello?"

"Morning." Miraculously, Heather's voice is clear and crisp through my cell phone speaker.

"We may have a problem," I say. "I don't see a package anywhere. Are you sure it shows that it was delivered?"

"That's what my tracking shows," Heather says. "It's pretty large. It weighs more than thirty pounds. I sent another one today that should be there by Friday. The fact that the first one isn't there worries me."

Me too, because I want to get my photos done and get out of here. "Alright, well, I'll talk to the ranch hands and see if there's somewhere else it might be."

Heather's saying something, but her voice is so distorted that all I can make out is, "...until then... having... beautiful."

Gah! Why does the cell reception suck so badly? I hang up and text her. It takes three tries for it to even go through. It took me almost an hour last night to post the image I snapped of the farmhouse. I haven't even been able to see how the engagement has been.

When I come around the corner, Emery and Whitney are giggling while playing with baby goats.

In the mud.

I'm happy that Em is getting some cousin time, but her designer shoes are absolutely *ruined*.

A dozen or so choice words come to mind, but it's not like I can change things now. And I got the shoes for free, since they're a brand I push. I force myself to breathe in and out, and then I have an idea. Isn't this why I'm here?

I snap a half dozen photos of the girls before they notice I'm there.

"Hey, Mom! Look at this one! Kevin and Jeff said only the mom has a name—Bonkers, which doesn't seem very nice—but the good news is, that means we can name the rest!"

If I hadn't already calmed down, this would have

helped. Emery so seldom seems truly happy. "Wonderful. What did you name the little chocolate brown one?"

"I named him Hershey," Emery says.

Perfect name, actually. I expected something terrible, like chocolate chip or brownie.

"This one's Spot—I named him." Whitney points at the white baby with a big brown blotch over his left eye. They both have floppy ears and dopey looking faces. I'm not really someone who loves animals or mud, but even I can't help smiling.

"I took some cute photos," I say.

Emery immediately looks down at her Gucci Screener sneakers. "Um, about the shoes, I'm going to clean them off, I promise."

There isn't enough soap in the world to fix them, but I don't bother pointing that out. "I'm sure you will," I say. "Now where was the place the guys said had decent reception?"

They point to a hill that looks like it's nearly a mile away. I don't manage to suppress my groan.

"I can drive you over." Jeff's coming out of the big red barn on a two-seat four-wheeler that has a big bed in the back. He stops it near the entrance and unloads a large shovel and some other muddy stuff.

I hope the seat is cleaner than the rest of it. "That would be great, thanks." I start walking toward him, Roscoe trotting alongside me, but he drives to my side before I've gone very far.

"I'm sorry about the internet," Jeff says. "I know the rest of the world kind of needs it. Jed wasn't ever too worried about that kind of thing." He pats the seat.

When I climb up next to him, Roscoe hops into the now-empty back bed and lies down.

"Whoa," Jeff says. "That's new."

"Is he not allowed back there?" I turn around and shake my head. "No, no."

Roscoe hops out, but he looks mournful.

"Aw, I feel bad."

"Oh, he's allowed into the back," Jeff says. "He always rode along behind Jed."

"He did?"

"Since he died, he hasn't left the front porch except to eat a bite or two of food and drink a cup of water."

"This is good, then?" I pat the empty bed again. "Here, boy. Come along."

Roscoe hops right back up.

"It's really good," Jeff says. "I think he really likes you."

Pets never like me. Or maybe it's that I don't like them much and they can sense it. "Weird."

"Very." Jeff turns around to pat Roscoe's head and he shifts away from him.

"Is he aggressive?"

Jeff shakes his head. "Only to things that might attack the chickens. Skunks, weasels, raccoons. That kind of thing."

Huh. "Oh, I almost forgot. There was supposed to have been a package delivered for me. Tracking shows it arrived."

"You didn't see it on the porch?" Jeff frowns. "That's usually where packages get dropped."

I shake my head. "Nothing but a rocking bench and chicken poop."

He laughs. "No shortage of chicken poop. Make sure the girls don't ever feed them on or near the porch or it will get way worse."

I'll definitely warn them against that. "Do we need to feed the chickens?" I hadn't even thought about it.

"Kevin and I do most everything," he says. "But I'll be sure to show you how we feed and water them. We also get way more eggs than the two of us can eat. If your kids want to be more involved, they might like gathering them."

Fresh eggs? There might be a photo opportunity there, as long as I can keep poop out of it. "I'd like that. Thanks."

"About the package." He sighs. "It's possible it wound up one house over. Sometimes our postal lady don't see too good. Your name's Amanda, right?"

I nod.

"The woman who lives up the road at the top of the hill is named Amanda Saddler. Pauline might have just seen Amanda and not paid attention to the numbers."

Wonderful. "How would I go about retrieving it, if it was misdelivered?"

Jeff tilts his head, clearly doubting my intelligence. "Just drive up and knock."

Right.

"We're here." He points. "I'll be clearing branches in the far pasture, but if you're still here when I get back, I'll be happy to pick you up."

Clearing branches? I don't even ask. "Thanks."

"Your nephew Ethan's a hard worker. He seems real excited to be here. I hope your girls have half as much fun as he is."

Me too.

As soon as I hop out, Roscoe does too, his tongue lolling. "Uh, I guess he'll stay here with me?"

"That's the darnedest thing," Jeff says.

The second his cart thing lurches away, I whip out my phone. Before I even allow myself to look at the last few posts I've made, I edit and upload the photo of Em with the goat. I tag #buytowear, #cowgirl, #countrylife, #goats, and #babygoat, along with #Gucci and #GucciScreeners. I don't owe them a post right now, but I hope it generates some attention anyway.

Being multi-dimensional is exhausting.

After I sit down, I allow myself to see how the post with the farmhouse is doing.

More than 100k likes, and over a thousand comments. That's great, even for me. Maybe Heather was right. Maybe I needed to shake things up a bit. I go through and reply to comments with the most interaction, or the ones that are made by instagrammers I know.

A lot of them are asking how long we're here, why, and where. Plenty of others are commenting that this is exciting and new for me. Those are the ones I hope Heather's noticing. I spend the next hour responding to texts and answering emails, with Roscoe curled up right next to me. Zoey calls me just as I'm almost ready to begin the trek to the house. Why's everything so spread out?

"Hey girl! Are you alive?"

"All evidence to the contrary," I say. "How long were you going to give me before you called the police?"

Zoey laughs. "Less than two more hours. What the heck is going on? Why has your phone been off?"

"It hasn't been off," I say. "I'm in the boondocks. There's terrible cell reception and no internet at all."

"I must have misunderstood you. It sounded like you said there's no internet."

"It's gorgeous, though."

"I saw your post with the goat. I suppose some people might find that beautiful."

"Not the animals, Z. The mountains. The big blue sky. The pine trees and the birds and the fresh air." At least, up here, it's fresh. When we were driving up to the top of this hill, I smelled cows pretty strongly.

"Well, yeah, but I can see photos of that."

It's not quite the same as feeling it, or seeing it in a 360-degree panorama, but I don't bother explaining. She'll think I've gone mad. "It's only for a week."

"We'll see," she says.

"What does that mean?"

"If your posts up there keep exploding, do you think Lololime's going to be welcoming you back to New York with a parade?"

"What does that mean?"

"Check your insta, dummy."

I put her on speaker and check. The post on the goat is blowing up, and when I pull up my engagements, they're five times what they usually are. What's going on? "Why do people like the goat so much?"

"I'm not sure it's the goat. I think it's because the photo's so different than what Gucci's kids' line usually sees."

When I refresh my email, I've got a message from a rep at Tide, asking to send me detergent to clean the shoes. They're offering three grand just to push their cleaner in affiliation with the dirty shoes, but they want to include a rider that keeps me from posting if it doesn't remove all the mud. In that instance, if I don't post at all, I'll only be paid half the fee.

Fifteen hundred dollars for washing my kid's shoes on the gamble that they'll come clean? I'm okay with that.

"Still mad about the internet?" Zoey asks.

I am, but not nearly *as* mad. "I think I can work with it. Now if I can just get down the road to recover my package from Lololime. . ."

"What does that mean?"

"Apparently some old lady who lives down the road is named Amanda too, and the ranch hands figure my package was probably taken there."

"So that place may be different in nearly every way,

but the postal service is the same." Zoey laughs. "Speaking of—if you decide to stay for more than a month, I'd love to sublet your place."

Is she kidding? "You live in Los Angeles."

"I know, but I've been thinking that a little travel and a new round of guys to date couldn't hurt my brand, either."

For the love. . . "I'll definitely let you know, but don't hold your breath. This is the kind of place that works to boost interest as a short-term gimmick. Not for an entire summer."

I'm halfway back to the house, the little dog bouncing along beside me, when Jeff comes rumbling by and picks us up. Not a minute too soon—I've already got a blister forming on my left heel.

"You may want to get a different pair of shoes, if you decide to stick around. I know Roscoe's hoping you'll stick around."

What's with everyone asking me whether I'm going to stay? Does it really look likely? "Thanks."

I swing off the utility wagon thing and head for my car, Roscoe still trailing me like a furry bodyguard, but I'm stopped before I reach it. "Mom, they're all getting horseback lessons again this afternoon," Emery says. "What about us?"

"Horses are the kind of thing that takes months and months to learn," I say.

"They're riding out in two weeks to drive the cattle up into the forest." Emery's eyes plead with me.

"Why would they take the cows to the forest?" I shake my head. "That sounds insane."

"They go up there for a few months so that we can grow hay here," Jeff says.

Now he's just annoying me. "Yes, well, I hardly think—"

"Please, Mom? Can I take lessons?"

"I'm not sure even Steve can teach more than four beginners at once," Jeff says. Thankfully, after lobbing that perfect excuse my way, he parks the cart by the smaller house and wanders off toward the barn.

"Exactly," I say. "Now come with me. We'll head up the road to look for my missing package, and then I need to go into town to buy some Tide."

"I can pick some up." Abby's standing in the doorway of the house, her purse slung over her shoulder. "I'm going to try and find someone, anyone, who will talk to me about installing the internet."

Pretty much no hope it'll come before we leave, so I don't care much. "It has to be a very specific kind," I say.

She shrugs. "Write it down. If the hardware store has it, I'll bring it back."

If not, there's always Amazon, assuming I ever get any packages. Oh my word, what if even Amazon can't subdue the wilderness? "Alright. Thanks."

Abby calls her kids over. "Izzy, Whitney, listen. I'm going to be gone for a bit. I've got another round of documents to review today, and I need to send a brief I drafted this morning."

"Okay," Izzy says. "That's fine."

"I need you guys to make lunch and watch Gabe—and I mean you really have to watch him. There are a lot of animals around here, and I can't have him getting stepped on or kicked."

"We will," Whitney says.

"Where's Ethan?" I ask.

"He went with Kevin to move the water, whatever that means," Abby says.

"What about Maren?" I haven't seen her yet today.

"She was still asleep, last I checked." Abby jogs down

the porch steps, avoiding the fresh chicken poop like a pro, and opens the door to her minivan.

"It's nearly noon."

Abby shrugs. "I wasn't sure if she knew what your rules were during the summer."

"We're going to learn how to feed all the animals," Izzy says.

"And how to muck stalls," Whitney says.

"Wait," I say. "I'm not sure—"

"Emery definitely doesn't need to," Abby says, "but Jeff offered to teach mine after he finished with clearing the far pasture."

Jeff's apparently still within hearing distance, because he shouts back after mention of his name. "I'll drag it tomorrow, but I figured a break to train some helpers wouldn't be a bad thing." He gestures toward the barn.

"Where's Gabe?" Abby asks.

"He's watching *Charlotte's Web* on the television," Izzy says. "Ethan said it's called a VHS tape. The sound and picture aren't very good, but he doesn't seem to care. I told him to come find us in the barn when it's done."

"Great. Well, use the house phone to call me if you have questions or problems," Abby says. "Once I'm on Steve's porch, I should have reception. I did yesterday, anyway."

"The horse guy?" I ask.

"He said I can use his porch and boost off his WiFi as long as I need it," Abby says. "He might have been kidding, but I'm pretending he was serious."

How has she already met people? More than that, she's already got people offering to do her favors. It's irritating.

I open the door of my ridiculous van. "Emery, go wake up Maren and tell her she needs to help muck stalls." That'll teach her to sleep until noon.

"Are you serious?" Emery asks.

"Yes. Tell her if she doesn't, I'll. . ." I can't actually think of anything worse than mucking stalls. "I'll think of something terrible."

Emery drops her voice. "Hey, Mom, if you meet someone who teaches horse stuff, can you hire them for me? I really do want to learn, too."

Her earnest tone and her pleading eyes pull at my heartstrings. "I'll try and find someone."

Watching her skip off to catch up to her cousins, I wonder whether we ought to stay more than a week. If Abby can work her magic and get us internet, a few more weeks might not be that bad.

When I walk to the van, Roscoe follows me again. He tries to hop up when I climb in.

"No, boy. You can't come."

He looks reproachful, I swear.

When I close the door, he drags himself one slow step at a time onto the porch and drops in front of the door like a sad sack. I actually feel guilty when I leave. I drive up the road until I notice a gravel side road. I nearly miss it, my tires skidding as I swerve to make the last-minute turn. This van is much taller than anything I've ever driven and for a split second, the tires on the right side actually lift off the ground.

My heart feels as if it might give out for a moment, but after the wheels drop back down, it starts beating again. I crawl my way up the drive, terrified of any other driving mishaps. It takes what feels like forever, but finally I round the bend and see a rundown wooden farmhouse. You can tell it was gorgeous once, with stunning hunter green trim on a caramel-colored house. The two front windows are stained glass, and they look like they were made by a master craftsman.

But the lawn is overgrown, and one of the shutters is

hanging askew. It makes it look sad, unloved even. I'm not positive this is the right place—Jeff was hardly specific—but I park the car out front and walk to the door.

The house looks even worse up close. The paint on the front porch is peeling, the wood clearly rotting in a handful of places. The glass on one of the front porch lights has a bird's nest in it, and a bright red bird squawks loudly as I draw close. When I press the doorbell, it makes a fzzt sound, as if the electrical isn't working quite right.

I knock instead, as hard as I can.

If this woman really is old, she may be hard of hearing.

"Coming," a female voice shouts.

A moment later, the door flies open, and a very short woman squints at me. "Who are you?"

"I—well, my name is Amanda—"

"My name's Amanda."

"Right, that's actually why I'm here. I'm Amanda *Brooks*, and I'm staying next door, at Jedediah Brooks' ranch."

She frowns. "Alright."

"I think a package of mine might have inadvertently. . ." I notice she's wearing a puffy, Lololime vest. "Uh, I was supposed to get quite a large package yesterday, and it never came, even though the tracking shows that it was delivered."

She stares at me blankly for a moment, and then cackles. "You were, huh?"

I nod.

"Well, I imagine there was a mix-up, and it's my fault too, for not checking the label. I have a very eager niece, you see, and she's always sending me things. I figured this was a strange sort of care package though, even from her."

A strange sort of shuffling sound draws my attention

and I look behind Mrs. Amanda Saddler at a black and white pig. It's wearing a hot pink Lololime scarf around its neck.

Oh, my.

"I'm afraid I've scattered most of the things hither and yon," she says. "Let me see what I can find."

I follow her around the house as she hands things to me. Some of it's western style, but a lot of it looks like it's from their new line. "There was something else I put somewhere. . ."

Before I can point out the scarf on the pig or the vest she's wearing, she throws her hands into the air and runs out the back door. I'm left scrambling after her, my arms full of pants, capris, shirts, and headbands. I notice the latest backpack near the back door and snatch it to stuff everything into. Once we reach the back yard, I'm completely shocked.

The front yard was neglected, but it appears to be due to the amount of time she spends back here. There's a beautiful garden coming in, and there's a pristine line on which dozens of pieces of clothing are hung. I wasn't aware anyone hung their clothes to dry anymore.

"I'm so sorry, again." She's moving toward the center of the garden, her pig trotting along behind her, the fringe on the end of the pink scarf dragging in the dirt, and I finally see why.

The scarecrow's decked out in exclusively Lololime, from his pants, to his shirt, to his bright, lime green hat. I should jog over and help her take things off, but I can't help myself. I whip out my phone instead, and I snap a few photos, careful to include the pig.

By the time I reach her, she's almost halfway done. I help her extricate the straw stuffed arms from the shirt, tearing a tiny hole in the back. Or maybe a bird pecked that hole. Who knows? When she pulls the bandana from the scarecrow's neck, I almost stop her, but then I realize it's part of their new line, the bandana texture incorporating the recognizable Lololime logo. "Thanks."

"I really am so sorry," she says.

I think about asking for the vest and the scarf, but I decide that if a pig will wear a scarf like that, it should keep it. "Don't worry about it. I'm sure it's been a while since there's been another Amanda living out here."

"Never happened before, far as I know," she says. "Glad to have you in the neighborhood, so to speak."

"Do you happen to know how we could get internet service more quickly?" I ask.

She rolls her eyes. "That Jed. Why didn't he get the broadband installed? He's always been such a pig-headed fool."

Seems like a strange insult for someone who has a pet pig, but I don't argue. "I do wish he'd already done it." Wait. "Do you have internet?"

She leans a little closer. "I love Netflix."

My smile's involuntary. "Do you, now?"

"Don't tell anyone I told you this, but I've watched *Bridgerton* a dozen times." She cackles again, and I think I may love her.

"Well, I'm happy to hear that you've got a way to get in touch with the outside world."

"Now don't you go condescending to me." Her eyebrows pull together.

"I would never—"

"I'm an old lady, I know, believe me. I've been living here for eighty-one years, and I may make it eighty-one more, you just wait and see."

Now I know I love her. "I hope you do."

"And if you have time, please come by again." She squints at me again. "You got kids?"

I nod. "Two girls."

"Well, if they like Netflix, bring them over, any night. We don't have to watch *Bridgerton*. They got all kinds of good shows, and they're always adding more. You can watch them any time you want. There's one called *Crash Landing on You* that I loved, but it's in another language. You can watch all the episodes close together, or you can just do one a day. Whatever you want. This particular show's got subtitles, but you get used to them. Think your girls would be willing to do that?"

She's explaining how Netflix works. I want to keep her. "How about I write down my phone number," I say. "And you can call me when you have a free night."

She makes a cooing sound, high-pitched and almost shrill. "When I have a free night?" She slaps her knees. "You're hilarious. I'm always free. But I'll take your number anyway."

She won't let me leave until she's loaded me up with peas, broccoli, and spinach. I'd have a carload of radishes, too, but I lied and said I was allergic. No matter how cool a lady she is, I'm not eating radishes. I'm turning over the engine when I realize that I haven't gotten permission to post a photo of her.

By the time I reach the door again, that bird is cawing and she's already swinging it open. "My cardinal always tells me when I've got company." She squints at him. "That's enough, Arizona."

"Arizona?"

"Not a sports fan, clearly." She quirks one eyebrow and I feel judged.

"Uh, no, not really."

"Ah, I forgot to give you the vest!" She's fumbling with the zipper. "You must have thought I was trying to rip you off."

I shake my head and wave her off. "Not at all. Keep it, please."

Her hands stop sliding the zipper. "Really?"

"Absolutely. But I do have a favor to ask. Two, actually."

"What's that?"

"I took a great photo of you in front of the scarecrow. I can show you, if you'd like. I wanted to know whether I had your permission to post it on my social media feed, with the hashtag #trendynewneighbor."

"A hash what?"

I explain the basics of what a hashtag is.

"If you think anyone will want to see an old lady and her pig, you go right ahead. Any young men leave positive comments, you send them my way." She winks. "But what was the other favor?"

"Is there any chance I could use your WiFi to post it?"

"Of course! And you can come over any time you need to post something, or if your girls need their internet fix."

I might hold her to that. "Thank you so much!"

The photo is cuter than I even realized, with the pig looking back at me, the Lololime tag showing clearly on its shoulder. I explain in the text that my closest neighbor, a few miles away, shares my name, and that the postal worker got confused. "Now I feel bad that I didn't let her keep it all." Then I use the hashtag I mentioned and a dozen more.

Before I've even pulled out of the drive, my #loveyourneighbors post is already blowing up.

And I get a text from Heather. THIS IS EXACTLY WHAT I WANTED. THAT SHOT OF THE NEIGHBOR IS SHEER BRILLIANCE. I'LL SEND YOU A NEW BOX. LET HER KEEP IT ALL.

9
ABIGAIL

These lessons are a mistake.

Much like this entire summer plan.

We have no business being on a ranch, much less working it. And this man does not have the patience to teach children.

"No, Whitney. Stop." Steve's voice isn't irritated, but it is firm.

I trot my horse, a beautiful palomino gelding I'm borrowing from him, toward that side of the large, beautiful, covered arena. He does have a nice setup, I'll give him that much. But before I can say anything, I notice Whitney's face. She's not crying. She doesn't look sad or even angry.

She looks determined.

"You're not yanking this time," he says, "but your hands are holding him too tightly while you're asking him to go. That's why he keeps stopping—mixed signals."

Whitney nods.

"Can you try again?"

She nods again, this time keeping her hands down low, above the end of her chestnut's mane. He trots nice and slow, just as Steve said he would. "Great. Now, you're used to turning your horse like his head is a pulley. We're not that precise, and we're not that severe in Western."

"Okay."

"Are you two listening?" He turns toward Ethan and Izzy, who are working on doing big, loopy circles at a trot on the other side.

They both stop.

"You don't need to stop to listen," he says.

They start trotting again.

"I know it gets boring trotting all the time. We won't start cantering until next week, when I'm sure you can handle it while maintaining control. The only reason you even need to be able to canter on a cattle drive is to either catch up with an errant cow, or to control the horse if he spooks. We're going to focus this week on basic control with one hand. Who knows why using just one hand matters?"

Izzy raises her free hand.

"Yeah, Izzy?"

"So you can use the other hand for something else, like roping a cow." She looks so proud of herself.

"That's right." Steve's smile is transformative. He goes from a stern, almost scary cowboy to the star of a Western. John Wayne would be jealous of that smile.

After a terrible start in which I lost my bridling privileges, and Izzy was forced to redo her saddle girth twice, we actually make decent progress. Ethan's struggling more than anyone near the end, which is good. Whitney manages to get her hands figured out and move her chestnut right along. Her circles are even fairly well done.

Most of my frustration is gone.

But my thighs are screaming. I wince as I swing down and out of the saddle.

"Sore?" Steve sees *everything.*

It's obnoxious.

I shrug. "I haven't done any riding in a long time."

"I'm convinced those muscles aren't used for anything else in the world," he says. "You miss a few weeks and you're back to square one."

Why's he suddenly being so nice?

"Should we give them any treats?" Whitney asks.

"I think the bucket may be empty." He points at the tack room. "But there's a fridge in there. Grab them each a carrot."

Whitney clearly can't find the carrots, so I duck inside to help her. I can't help noticing the pack of Guinness beer, right next to the bag of carrots. Ugh. Just right out in the open in the barn. He can't even keep it in the house, like a normal person.

Maybe he needs to have beer close by at all times. Geez.

After the horses have been dealt with, all of them given at least one carrot, and the tack is put away, the kids head for the minivan. "Thanks again," I say. "I think we made some good progress today."

"You'll be surprised how quickly they improve with lessons each day. Most kids forget half of what they learn in the six days in between with weekly lessons."

I'd never thought of that, but it might be true. "I hope so, because I can't help thinking this is all a huge mistake."

He leans against the wall of a stall. "If you think it's a mistake, why are you here?" He's not accusatory, but he doesn't exactly sound supportive.

"You didn't know what I was talking about yesterday. It seems like you're better informed today."

"I called Mr. Swift, and then I heard from Patrick Ellingson."

"He's one of the other three people who are supposed to decide whether we fulfill the will's requirements."

"He is," Steve says. "And our families have been friends for a long time."

"Well, don't worry too much. I have to make a show of doing everything I can in order to fulfill the requirements, but we have no intention of staying past the end of summer."

"Why come at all?"

I consider telling him it's none of his business, because it really isn't. But something about the earnest way he asks makes me *want* to confide in him. "It's Ethan." I drop my voice, but the kids are all in the car. It helps that 'hot' in Utah is apparently in the 70s. That's cool weather in Texas. "He hasn't taken his dad's death very well, and he decided not to apply to any colleges at all."

"He just graduated?"

I nod.

"But what does that have—"

"He's a minor until September 2," I say. "Which means I can make the decision about the ranch. Starting this fall, though, he gets to make all his own decisions, and I want him in college."

"You made some kind of deal?" His eyebrows shoot up.

"That's exactly what I did." I cross my arms. I don't care if he disapproves. "I told him we would do our very best to fulfill the requirements while we're here, but by the end of the summer—the kids start school again on August 23—if he hasn't convinced me that staying here and working the ranch is the right move, he'll surrender peaceably and go to college."

"But you said he didn't apply," Steve reasonably points out. "He can't just show up."

"That's true," I admit. "But I don't give up easily. My friend's a provost at Rice University, and I sent Ethan's excellent test scores and GPA over to him. He's been put on the waitlist."

"What if he doesn't get bumped up?" Steve asks. "What then?"

I'm sure the distaste is plain on my face. "Community college, I suppose."

"So there's no part of you that's really considering letting him work this ranch?" He purses his lips.

I shake my head.

"Patrick demanded that I make this offer, and I wish he hadn't, but here goes." He sighs. "He's willing to pay you, outside of the terms of the will, to walk away and let this go."

"Why would he do that?" I'm instantly suspicious.

"It's nothing nefarious. First, we both think it's pretty lousy that Jed left nothing to his own kin. But second, he doesn't want to wait until the end of the summer to buy the ranch. He'd rather buy it from the estate now, as is."

He doesn't say he'd prefer that we not screw things up, but his implication is clear as day. "I've promised my son that I would be here all summer to let him learn and try to convince me, and I know you don't know me, but I keep my promises. Always."

"I just told him I'd mention it," Steve says. "It saves his family money to wait, so once I explain it, I'm sure he'll be pleased to wait."

"We're not here to snatch money from a relative we didn't even know. We're not here to try and insert ourselves into your small town, either. We're just passing through, and once Ethan has seen that I care enough to do this for him, once he believes that I listen to him, he'll realize that he's the one being unreasonable, and we'll all go home."

"If you say so."

His know-it-all, nonchalant tone pisses me off. "I do say so."

"Alright." He smiles.

This time, it doesn't remind me of John Wayne. It makes me want to punch him. "You're so condescending."

His eyes widen. "Excuse me?"

"Do you have kids?"

His nostrils flare. His hands clench into balls at his side. His face flushes red. But he doesn't respond.

"I'll take that as a no."

His eyes narrow.

"Let me tell you this. People without children are often critical of parenting decisions. They frequently think that they know better." I lean forward. "But until you have a child, and unless that child is *my* child—"

"Whoa, until I have a child that's your child?"

I choke. That is what I said, but it's not—

"I think you're a nice lady," he says. "But it feels a little premature to start making plans to have children."

He is the most irritating man I have ever met. I inhale and exhale slowly. What about him makes me so angry? "It's been a long week, and I should not have been yelling at you. I'm immensely grateful you've been willing to help us."

He should be prickly. He should be incensed. But he looks. . .happy. "I get it. If I had traveled to a strange, isolated place, surrounded by strangers, and everything was new, and I was trying to work remotely and parent. . .I might get a little growly, too."

Growly? I'll show him—I'm doing it again. *Stand down, Abby. You're trying to show him you're* not *crazy.* Not prove that you *are*. "What time tomorrow? And here again? Or back at our place?"

"I think the setup is better here, but I'd like you to

learn on your horses." He taps his lip. "Which do you prefer?"

"You're the professional. I leave it entirely up to you."

This time, I feel like I earned his half-smile. "Alright, let's do it here for the next few afternoons. I'm sorry about the time, but it's the only time—"

"It's great. Ethan's moving water and helping feed cows in the morning, and the other kids are feeding animals and mucking stalls. Please don't apologize for doing us a favor."

"Great, well tomorrow, ask Jeff and Kevin to send you with some rope. We'll practice holding it and maybe even throwing it from horseback. Then next week, we'll start riding your animals every day. If I have any extra time, I'll come by and ride them a few times, too. Should make for a smoother trip all around."

He's probably a drunk who sleeps until noon every day, and he's abrupt, and his friend is obnoxious, trying to force us to sell now, but he's a hard worker, and he seems to mean well. I suppose for a summer horse trainer, that's more than enough. "I appreciate your help."

"Did you use my porch today?"

My cheeks flush. "I did. I hope that you were serious. No police officers showed up to escort me from the premises, so I assume you were."

"You can still come anytime you want," he says.

"Thanks. It's a life saver, actually."

"I'm glad."

When I walk past the front porch, I notice there's a throw pillow on the swing. I can't help turning around, but I don't expect Steve to be staring at me.

"Your kids are lucky to have you," he says.

I have no idea how to respond to that, so I don't. I simply smile. The kids talk about nothing but horses in the car on the way back.

"I hope Maren kept Gabe alive," I say.

"Actually, Kevin offered to take him out. He was going to clean the chicken coop."

Poor Kevin. I imagine Gabe has talked his ear off, but at least I won't owe Amanda a favor. As much as I'm looking forward to the end of the summer, I'm more desperate for the end of the week. The six-bedroom farmhouse, as it turns out, feels far too small for our combined baggage.

"Hey, Mom?" Izzy asks.

"Yeah, sweetie?"

"I think there's been a miracle."

The road is straight enough for me to turn sideways and look her in the eye. "What?"

She holds up my phone. "A text message came through on your phone."

It might not be a miracle, but it's a surprise. The text's from Robert, which is not surprising at all. CALL WHEN YOU CAN.

"You need to head up to the office?" Ethan asks.

"Huh?"

"That spot on the hill where there's good cell reception," Izzy says. "The spot near those three pine trees all in a row?"

"I guess I do."

"I'll show you how to work the Polaris," Ethan says. "It's super easy." The gleam in his eyes gives him away. He loves anything with a motor.

Fifteen minutes later, I'm finally dialing Robert's number. "Hey," I say when he answers. "Did you get the interrogatories? Their responses were infuriating."

"I did, but your replies were great and I already sent them."

"What's wrong, then?"

He's silent for a moment. "It's a hassle for you to call me, isn't it?"

I laugh. "I had to learn how to drive a Polaris utility cart thing in order to drive up to the top of a hill, which is the only place on this ranch with decent cell service."

Robert swears under his breath. "I'm so sorry. I'm a jerk. I just wanted to hear your voice, I guess. Find out how you were doing. I miss having you in the office."

Last week, saying any of that would have freaked me out. Maybe it's because I'm so far away. Maybe it's because I'm standing on top of a hill, not accessible by any stretch of the imagination. Maybe it's because, in spite of my miserable remote work, Robert's still supporting me 110%. But for whatever the reason, it warms my heart instead. "I'm happy to hear your voice too."

"You are?"

"It's been a rough few days," I admit. "Exhausting, actually." My voice cracks on the end of that word, and a surge of emotion washes through me.

"Abs, are you okay?"

I inhale deeply to keep the sobs that are threatening to break free at bay. "I'll be fine. This is the kind of thing you do as a mother. But there's this long list of tasks we're supposed to accomplish, and none of it's anything I know a thing about."

"Like what?"

"Well, I already told you that in a little over two weeks we have to drive three hundred and fifty cattle into the forest that abuts the ranch."

"I don't understand why. That sounds insane."

"They're all branded, I've been assured, and they're dying to go up there since they go every year. Apparently even with all the acreage we have, the usable meadows need to be watered and tended so that they can grow enough hay to be baled and preserved for the winter. For a very small fee, the Forestry service lets us run the cattle up there over the summer, as long as we keep them in designated areas."

"How are you supposed to do that?"

"Well, again, we ride our horses up there and like, ride around, herding them as needed."

"Do you even know how to ride well enough for that to be safe?"

"Most of what I remember has come back, thankfully, but the kids are having a rough time."

"That's too bad," Robert says. "But how did the old drunk guy do? Is he helpful at all?"

"He's not old," I say. "And we had a second lesson today. I might have been too critical before." I drop my voice out of habit. "I actually feel pretty bad. I think he heard me talking to you, maybe about him. I'm worried he heard me say he was a drunk."

"How old is he, then?" Robert asks. "Twenty?"

"No, he's our age, probably," I say. "Maybe a few years younger or older. He knew Nate, apparently."

"Oh."

"What's that 'oh' for?"

"Is he married?" Robert asks.

"I don't see how—"

"Maybe his wife can help you figure some of the other stuff out."

"He doesn't have a wife." It feels like he's worried about Steve being my age. "Seriously, Robert, what's wrong?"

"Your opinion of him sure does seem to have improved."

Now I'm sure that he's jealous. . .of a drunk cowboy. "Robert, this Steve Archer guy—"

"I don't like him. I've been listening, and I've tried to stay out of it, but I don't like him at all."

"Don't be worried." I decide to wade out into the deep and muddy waters between us. After all, I'm a million miles away, standing on the side of a mountain. Surely if I'm ever going to be honest, now's the time. "He's unpolished, he's abrupt, and we've butted heads on how he treats the kids twice now."

"He's not very bright, then. No one should *ever* question your parenting. Now, your cooking? Maybe."

"If I had something to throw at you right now—"

"Then I'd never have been brave enough to say it," he says, but he still sounds nervous.

"Listen, Robert, this horse trainer? He's also best pals with the guy who wants to buy the ranch. He actually suggested that his friend pay us some kind of bribe money to walk away."

"Are you kidding?" Robert's level of indignation seems a little disproportionate to Steve's crime, but I appreciate his loyalty. "If I were there right now, I would teach him a few lessons on manners."

I try to imagine Robert punching Steve—but it only makes me chuckle.

"Are you laughing?"

"No," I say. "I was just imagining how you'd bludgeon that cowboy where it hurts—with a nice restraining order."

"I'm not just a lawyer," Robert says. "I've got a decent right hook."

Even so, one hundred times out of a hundred, my money would be on Steve. Not that I'd ever admit it.

10

AMANDA

YOU NEED MORE THAN A WEEK. WHY NOT STAY FOR THE SUMMER?

I haven't been able to think about anything else since seven a.m. when Heather's text came through. My posts have been doing well, sure, but my posts always do well.

Not usually this well. Even I have to admit that.

I've gained nearly ten thousand followers since coming out here, and my engagement is up by 30%. That makes for happy advertisers, and that means more money. Which means stability, and that has been in short supply since Paul died.

I close my eyes and try to go back to sleep.

"Amanda?" Abby must be outside my door.

"Yeah?"

"I'm so sorry for waking you up, but I have a favor to ask."

Of course she does.

"I have a hearing today, a preliminary one on an important motion, and I really need to be there."

"Okay."

"Can I open the door? It's weird talking about this through solid wood."

I rub my eyes and sit up, but I don't try to disguise the annoyance in my tone. "Sure."

The door opens slowly, and of course Abby's already wearing a business suit, with her hair done, and bright, outlined, eye-shadow-ed and mascara-ed eyes. "I really am sorry to ask this, but when I called, his office person said we're supposed to pay same day by check."

Pay for what? I still have no idea what she's asking me to do.

"I've left plenty of food, and Izzy can watch Gabe, even if Ethan's busy moving water, or helping with the vet most of the day."

"The vet?"

"He's coming this morning to finish vaccinating the rest of the calves."

The sound of clicking on the wooden floors draws my attention downward. Roscoe has pushed past Abby and walked to my bed. He's now licking my hand. I snatch it away. Why do dogs always lick everything? His eyes are so hurt that I reluctantly shift it back and let him lick. Ugh.

I'm not sure what to say to Abby. "Can't one of the ranch workers do whatever you want me to do?"

Abby looks put out. "Look, I know you're only going to be here a few days, but it's not like I'm asking you to refinish the porch or something."

"I actually may stay the entire summer." The prospect filled me with dread five minutes ago, but it suddenly seems more appealing. After all, if we leave and Abby sticks around, she and her kids could inherit the entire thing. That would be infuriating.

"Wait, how long are you staying?" Now she's the one who looks pained.

I shrug. "I haven't decided for sure."

"I'm not here for a photo op, Amanda. I'm actually here for my kids—we're committed to helping out and seeing what it would be like to run a ranch."

"So are we," I lie. I almost wish it was true when a look of pure horror spreads across her face. "Are you really that desperate to get rid of us?" I shift, which Roscoe takes as an invitation to hop up on the bed. "Whoa, what are you doing?" I shake my head. "No, no, no." He immediately hops back off, shoulders hunched, face cast downward. Now I feel like a bad person, and I let him lick me. Why is it never enough with dogs?

Abby glances at her watch as if Roscoe's interruption was some kind of ploy on my part to delay her. "Can you write the check or not?"

Write a check? "Why do I have to pay—"

"Neither of us is paying." Abby casts her eyes upward. "Did you read any of the emails from Mr. Swift?"

I have no idea what she's talking about.

"He left a new checkbook in the drawer to the left of the dishwasher. It draws on the ranch account, the one connected to the estate. He created it in our names and for our use while we're here. It's only to be used for ranch expenses."

"Can't you just leave a check for him?"

"We won't know how much it will cost until the vet's done. If it's too big of a hassle for you to write one check, I'm sure I can drive down to his office and drop it off after I get back."

"No need for that," I say. "I'm sure I'll be capable of doing it."

Her smile is 100% fake. "Perfect. Thank you *so much*."

There's no way I can stay here more than a week. Before I have time to lose my resolve, I text Heather back. NOT A GOOD IDEA. I'M NOT MADE FOR COUNTRY LIFE.

The second I hit send, Heather calls me. I'm sure I won't have good enough reception to answer. . .but miracle of miracles, I have two bars. Why do I have reception the one time I'd rather communicate via text? I consider not answering. It's not like she'll know.

But that's not very professional, and this is a big deal. I hit talk, and hope for the best. "Hello? Can you hear me?"

"You sound like one of those cell phone commercials," Heather says.

It's not a very original joke, but I fake a laugh anyway. "That's what I feel like up here, every single day. And fair warning. I have no idea how long my reception will last. It's never been this good."

"I'll be quick then. You were kind of a dark horse candidate for the last slot in our lineup, and I was the one who was really pulling for you. Your competition has more than twenty-five percent again as many followers, and slightly higher engagement. I just think you have more potential for growth, and to be frank, I like your posts more."

Ouch. I mean, it's good that she likes me, but she basically just told me I don't have a prayer.

"But since your trip, my boss is actually paying attention. She and I were talking, and we had the same thought at the same time."

Uh.

"Your brand is sort of a glamorous living showcased through the real life of a beautiful and graceful widow. You're pretty open about failed dates, about frustrations with your kids and their school and activities, and even with your shopping experiences. It's why people trust you."

That all makes sense. "Okay."

"But when we analyzed the data, you have ten to forty

percent more interaction on posts about your love life than about any other topic."

"That's been pretty dry lately."

"Which is why I'm calling. We want you to find a cowboy to date. Or more precisely, my boss mentioned that it's too bad you haven't met a hot cowboy. She sort of indicated that if you did, and if your engagement and followers increased yet again, it would be the evidence she needs to sign a contract with someone who's still expanding. And you'd improve our trust in the fact that you'd be open to our guidance and direction."

'Still expanding' must be code for crappy. "A hot cowboy?" Where exactly am I supposed to find one of those? "Manila is a town of less than four hundred people."

"You're saying there's not one hot, single cowboy, out of those 400 people?"

"I did hear the two ranch hands talking about a big local rodeo, but that's not until July 4."

"Wait, did you say ranch hands?"

Oh my gosh. "They're both in their early twenties. I'm forty-one, Heather."

"Still."

I can't believe I'm even having this conversation. "They're closer in age to my daughter, Maren." That's a horrifying thought in and of itself.

"Or, if you can't find a cowboy immediately, then at least stick around until the July 4th rodeo and snap some cute photos. What guy's going to care if you just cozy up next to him for a few pictures?"

I have clearly made poor life choices, if this is my new goal in life. Snap pictures with fake love interests to increase the number of people who will click on my posts. "Okay."

"Okay? As in you'll do it?"

"I'll stick around through the rodeo." I can't believe I'm even agreeing to this. "And if I see any hot cowboys who are close to my age, I promise to flirt with them."

"Thank you!" Heather squeals. "I knew my girl would come through."

My girl? "What are you talking about?"

"Oh, nothing."

"Heather?"

"Things are a little competitive here at corporate, and I may have a friendly bet going with a few co-workers of mine that our boss will pick the person we nominated. The New York office *always* wins, and I'm sick of it. That's all."

She's betting on me, at least. That's something.

"The odds on you were ridiculous. I really hope this works, because I could really use a new car."

She's betting on me precisely because it's unlikely I'll land the contract. Fabulous. "Listen, I had an idea—"

Her voice, when she cuts me off, is garbled. "Mandy? I can't hear you."

Of course she can't. Thanks for nothing, stupid Birch Creek. "I better go search for a hot cowboy." I doubt she could hear the sarcasm in my voice before I hung up. I planned to wear my rattiest pair of jeans and an old t-shirt, but if I'm supposed to be finding a hot cowboy, I better up my game. I dress in the bandana print sundress I packed on a lark. The only shoes I have that will go with it are strappy sandals. I'll have to really keep an eye out for chicken poop.

I wake Maren and make us both eggs for breakfast, but the yolks are so orange that I worry there's something wrong with them. Luckily, my phone data works well enough to pull up a webpage that explains one great thing about fresh eggs is their bright orange color. "Apparently color indicates that they're rich in vitamins." I almost feel bad about giving half my eggs to Roscoe. Almost, but not quite.

"Huh?" Maren's leaning against one arm, still half asleep.

"How late were you up last night?"

She scowls. "I was reading, if you must know. That dumb book *you* gave me for Christmas. The super long one."

"You stayed up all night?" I'm not sure I believe my own ears.

"You said the author called you once, with questions about a book she's writing."

"Oh, right. She's a lawyer friend of my sister-in-law who stopped doing legal work and started writing."

"She writes siblings pretty well."

"She should. She has a ton of kids. She writes women's fiction and romance, which I love, but I thought you might like the fantasy books."

"Did you like it?"

Maren shrugs. "Eh."

It must have been good if she stayed up all night reading it.

"The next one's about the villain from the first book, and I can't figure out why. I don't want to read that."

I sigh. "Well, if you liked the first, maybe you need to show her a little trust."

"Maybe."

When I walk outside, almost tripping over the dog, I catch myself staring appraisingly at Kevin. He's way too young, and flirting with him would be terribly awkward, not to mention possibly actionable since I'm in a position to run the ranch. Would that kind of make me his boss?

Maybe I could pay him to pose for me. If we were careful with angles, it might not be obvious how young he is. . .

He isn't bad looking. His face is a little goofy, like a young Harry Connick, Jr., but some people like that. Not me, but a lot of people. "He's way too young. It would never work."

"What would never work?" Ethan asks from behind me.

I jump.

"Sorry if I startled you." He's sanding down the porch, which looks like it's been freshly sprayed with a hose.

"What are you doing?"

Ethan smiles. "I thought we had to move the water this morning, but apparently we can't go over a certain amount of usage each week, and we're a little too close. Closing off the main intake was quick, so I figured I'd start working on fixing up the trim and porch paint."

"Fixing it up?"

"I'm sanding so I can repaint," he says. "Mom said the house looks nice, and that it looks like the paint on it has been done recently, but the trim kind of just disappears."

"You're only here for the summer, right?" I don't understand why he'd manufacture work for himself.

"Dad used to always do stuff like this." Ethan stops. "You know, Mom would make a comment, and he'd work hard to do little things to surprise her. I figured since he's not here, I could sand the trim and get it prepped and one day when she's out all day, I can paint it, as a surprise."

I can't breathe. I'm about to break down and sob.

In the fifteen years I was married to Paul, he never once surprised me with anything. I bought my own birthday and Christmas presents—Valentine's Day too. I'm not sure it ever occurred to him that it might mean more if he picked something. When I asked for something, he'd say, "Sure. Merry Christmas." Even if it was April.

After spending one day with them, I'm already drowning in reminders that I married the wrong brother. And now her son is trying to do the same thing—surprises that his dad's not here to provide. "That's nice of you."

"You think she'll like it?" Ethan's face brightens. "Maybe you can help pick which color of navy paint I should use. I'm not great at stuff like that."

"Oh, I don't know—"

"Mom said you're leaving in a few days, and I'm not sure if they have paint in town. But Green River isn't too far. Maybe one day we could go out there? Or if you don't have time, can I borrow your van? I can give you money for gas."

How can I tell him no? "I'm sure we can come up with something. But as it turns out, we're going to stay a little longer."

"Really?" His brow furrows. "When are you leaving?"

"We'll be here until at least the Fourth of July."

"We will?" Emery was coming toward the house from the barn at just the right time, of course. She starts whooping.

"What's going on?" Maren sticks her head out the window. "Some of us are trying to go back to sleep."

Ethan snorts. "Only one of us."

"We're staying a whole *month*!" Emery says.

Maren's hands clench the windowsill. "You're a liar."

"Now, Maren," I say. "Don't say that kind of thing to Emery. She's repeating what she just heard me say. We've decided to stay a little longer."

"Mom!" Her mouth opens and she's huffing louder than I've ever heard before. "You promised!"

Oh good grief. "Look—"

"Just fly me home. I'll stay with Erin."

"I'm not going to fly you home," I say. "And we'll still make it back in time for the school cheer camp."

"What about the Prism Elite one?"

Probably not that one. "That one's optional," I say. "It's not even put on by the school."

"But my whole team is going, and they'll get better than me!" She's wailing now, so loudly that I'm sure the neighbors can hear. "Why are you doing this?"

A large white SUV rolls up, which must be the vet. Unfortunately, the impending presence of outsiders doesn't even make a dent in Maren's emotional upheaval. Her head disappears, and I breathe a sigh of relief.

But then her entire body, still clad in plaid pajama pants and one of Paul's old shirts, shoots out onto the front porch. "Mom. You can't really mean to keep us here. We aren't prisoners. I want to go home."

"Actually, we're all minors," Ethan says. "Since she's your mom, that's exactly what she can do."

"Shut up, Ethan. You're the worst part of this nightmare."

"Right back at you." He winks, which only infuriates her more.

"Don't even bother arguing with her," Emery says. "It won't help. Maren hates everything but her phone and her friends."

Maren freezes. "That's not true."

"If it wasn't true, you'd have come outside already," Emery says. "There are baby goats, and kittens, and chickens, and horses, and cows. Lots of cows."

"Believe me," Maren says. "I can smell them all, even from inside."

Emery frowns. "Maybe Mom should send you back home. You'll only ruin things for everyone else." She turns on her heel and runs back to the barn, Gabe, Izzy, and Whitney on her heels.

For the first time in a long time, I actually feel sorry for Maren. It's her own fault, but she's totally alone. I know exactly how that feels. Even if you have no one else to blame, it's still miserable.

"Mrs. Brooks?" The vet must be standing behind us. His voice is deep and throaty, but still somehow smooth.

"I'm Mrs. Brooks." I turn around, and this time, I'm the one who freezes. I expected the vet to be, I don't know, rough. Dirty. I hoped, at his best, he might look like the horse trainer I saw from across the yard.

But this man looks nothing like that.

His hair is longish. His features are perfectly symmetrical, with a sloped jaw, a defined, sharp nose, and an angled brow. His eyes, though, they command my attention.

Maren had a section on genetics in science last year, and I discovered that less than two percent of the population has green eyes. His are grass green, which perfectly offsets the lighter shades of dark blonde that highlight his russet hair.

He's ungodly good-looking in his crisp, button-down shirt, faded jeans, and cowboy boots. He even has a little bit of scruff, like he didn't have time to shave—the cowboy Heather told me I needed to find. I can't help glancing at his left hand, sure it will have a ring encircling the third finger.

But it's bare.

"Abigail Brooks?" He narrows his eyes at me.

Probably because after saying I was Mrs. Brooks, I haven't spoken a single word. I'm like the heroine in a 1980s teen romance, unable to speak at all when I first meet the high school quarterback. Now all I need is a bad perm and some glasses so my best friends can do a makeover.

"Abigail Brooks is my mom," Ethan says. "This is my Aunt Mandy."

The vet starts chatting with Ethan, probably having decided I'm slow. "I've got the checkbook, whenever you need it."

Both men stop talking and turn toward me. "The checkbook?" Ethan asks.

"Why would I need your checkbook?" the super hot vet asks.

"Uh, Abby told me that since she had to work, I was supposed to pay when you're done."

"Right," he says. "I'm Eddy Dutton. Nice to meet you." He jogs up two steps and holds out his hand.

I should be saying whatever stupid and polite things people say. Like my full name. It's not like the vet will call me Aunt Mandy. But I can't seem to think straight when I'm looking at his face.

"Her kids are fighting and it's clearly distracting her—they were supposed to be going home in a few days, but they've decided to stay a whole month."

Bless Ethan. He's always been my favorite. "That's me," I say. "Amanda Brooks."

"Nice to meet you, Amanda. I'll come let you know when we're done." He turns toward Jeff and Kevin, clearly ending our brief conversation. "Where are the calves?"

"Farthest meadow," Jeff grimaces. "Sorry."

"It's fine," Eddy says. "I know the drill. Are the other meadows all prepped for hay?"

"Finished clearing the last one yesterday—Ethan's a hard worker," Jeff says. "Having him around helped."

"Glad to hear it," Eddy says. "You guys ready?"

"Actually, I'm coming too," I say.

All four guys turn toward me slowly, like from a scene in a movie.

"You are?" Ethan pauses, his expression completely confused. "Why?"

"It's not like there's anything else going on." I shrug. "Is that alright?"

"Of course," Kevin says. "Happy to see you taking an interest." He doesn't sound happy, but he's too polite to tell me no.

"Are you planning to go in that?" Eddy lifts one eyebrow as he scans over my handkerchief dress and open-toe sandals.

"I probably ought to change."

"Why don't you and Jeff go set up pens," Eddy says to Kevin. "I'll bring Aunt Mandy and Ethan in my truck. Ground's dry. Should be fine."

Kevin and Jeff, who don't seem to care at all, disappear immediately.

"You gonna take more photos?" Ethan asks.

"Are you a photographer?" Eddy asks.

"It's her job," Ethan says, before I can respond.

"My cousin does that," Eddy says. "She mostly does studio work, though. Graduation shots, senior photos, that kind of stuff."

"I take a lot of candid shots," I say. "And I'm supposed to get some of cowboys. You won't mind if I take some?"

Eddy shrugs. "Snap away."

I probably ought to explain that I'm an influencer, but any time I tell normal people what I do, I get a lot of confused questions and disbelieving looks. "I'll be right out."

I duck inside, but I still hear Eddy's next statement. "She doesn't seem like someone who'd make a good rancher."

I need to go change, but I can't quite drag myself away before listening to Ethan's response.

"I heard she just broke up with someone. He didn't

take it well, so she had to get out of the city for a while. Since we were coming here for the summer. . ." He drops his voice, as if he's talking to a co-conspirator, instead of a vet he's never before met. "I think she just needed something different."

As he says the words, I realize that, other than the stalker, he's right. I did need something different. I hate not being connected to the rest of the world. . .but I needed the break. It's not healthy to be completely tied to social media all day long.

"She's hiding from a stalker?" Eddy asks. "Well, this is a good place to do it. Thanks to Jed's stubbornness, there isn't even any internet."

I have no idea where Ethan heard that story, but it makes me sound super desirable instead of like an older woman who's met every single man in New York and is now repeating them without realizing it. I finally jog to my room and slide into the scruffy jeans and t-shirt I'd been planning to wear. It's ironic that my "cowboy catching" outfit was utterly unsuited for spending any time with an actual cowboy.

When I finally emerge, they're still talking.

"Actually, I haven't finished sanding yet," Ethan says. "I'm trying to prep and paint this porch and the house trim as a surprise for my mom. I've got to do the prep work while she's working, and if I only do half, she'll immediately notice. Can I come out in an hour? It's only a twenty-minute walk, and I don't mind meeting you."

"You're a good kid," Eddy says.

I can't disagree with him.

"Thanks." Ethan picks up the sander.

"You ready?" When Eddy's full attention fixes on me, my brain shorts again. And we're about to be alone in his SUV. This is not good.

"Yes," I finally manage to say. *Get it together, stupid.*

Luckily, it's a quick drive, and once we reach the field, Eddy's so busy we don't do much talking. I follow his simple instructions and hand him the things he needs. Calves don't like vaccinations much more than kids do, but no one cares when they cry, and you can tie their legs.

I do find the time to snap a few photos of Eddy while he's working. He really does make cowboy look good, as much from the back as the front. Talk about making my job easy. Now to find out how old he is—he barely looks older than Jeff and Kevin, but he's a vet. He seems like a competent vet. He must be at least thirty, right? Unless he's the Doogie Howser of the vet world.

"Have you always known you wanted to do this?" I ask. "Like in high school." I do my best cheerleader impression and shout, "*Class of 1999!*" I pause. Was that too obvious? Just weird? "Did you know when you graduated?" It's hard not to cringe.

He squints up at me from where he's crouched on the ground. I wish I could snap a photo right now, but it would be too obvious. "Class of 1999? How old do I look?"

"Ouch," I say. "I was class of 1999."

"Really?" He winces. "Rough."

"What class were you?" Kevin asks.

"Two thousand," Eddy says. "A completely different *millennium*."

I laugh. "You really had me going there."

"Did I?"

I shrug. "You look twenty-five."

He already looks like a movie star, but when he grins? Forget it. What is someone this good-looking doing in the middle of nowhere? And how is he single? Women should be throwing themselves at him. Or maybe he *is* married, but doesn't wear a ring because of the dirty, messy work he does?

Or maybe he's a real jerk.

Actually, that must be true. It's not like there are a bunch of great guys my age, just wandering around, unattached. The forty-something singles scene is like shopping at a Nordstrom Rack. There may be some treasure hidden in there, but it's buried under piles of returned and damaged merchandise and things so odd no one ever bought them.

Once they've finally caught and stuck the last calf, the guys start taking the pen apart. Eddy's chatting while they work, until a piece gets stuck. He leans over a little to pull it out, his arms flexing, and I see my window.

I snap one last shot.

With the way the sun backlights the whole thing, it looks like a scene out of a movie. You can tell he's really good-looking and in great shape, but you can't really see his face.

I ought to ask if it's okay for me to post the image, but I'm too afraid he'll say no. I fall in love with it while editing, and I can't face the prospect that he might refuse.

"You ready?" he asks.

I nearly drop my phone. "Yes. Let's go."

"Longer and more boring than you thought?" He's smiling, but there's an undercurrent to his question—almost like he's nervous that I've been miserable.

I'd probably muck stalls, if he was doing it.

"It wasn't too bad," I say. "Other than the occasional smell of poo, the air was fresh, the weather was perfect, and the company wasn't awful either."

His smile broadens. "If you liked that, you should come with me the next time I get a call about a dental abscess."

I must make a face, because he laughs.

"Or maybe I should call you when I'm done with work

one day," he says. "We could do something less smelly and more fun."

Did he just ask me out?

It occurs to me for the first time that in a town of 400, his options are probably even more limited than mine back home. "I'm not sure," I say.

He shrugs. "Can't fault a guy for trying."

"It's just that. . ." I may not be the best cook. I may not be great at faking emotion. I may be terrible and useless at anything to do with animals.

But I know how to hook a guy.

"What?" He stops only a few feet away from his SUV.

I sigh so forcefully it blows my hair away from my face. "You're so much younger than I am." I smirk. "With such a large age gap, I don't see where this could ever go."

A lot of women would say that the way to draw a guy's attention is with a rocking body. Or great food. Or flirting outrageously.

I think they're wrong. It's making sure he laughs when he's around you.

Judging by his laugh, I'm on the right track.

"Is that a no, then?" he asks. "Because you should know, Kevin and Jeff both owe me favors. I could come out here every day for the next week, if that's what it takes."

I put my hands on my hips. "For what?"

"Do you know how many animals there are at Birch Creek?" He shrugs. "Could be anything. Colic. Bumble foot. Eye infection. You name it. I could have you writing checks all week long."

"This account isn't my money," I say. "It wouldn't cost me a dime."

He steps closer. "But think of the animals. Would you really put them through all those senseless farm calls?"

My heart rate picks up and my hands feel clammy. I

haven't been around a guy who made my hands feel clammy in a very long time. "Alright."

"Alright, you'll let me take you out?"

I shake my head. "I'll give you my number. If you play your cards right, it *could* be a date."

"Oh, if there's one thing I'm good at, it's playing the odds."

He hands me his phone, presumably to put my number in, and opens the door for me.

"Do guys still do that here?"

He frowns. "Do they not open doors in New York?"

"No one really has a car, but I've never had anyone open a cab door for me."

"I guess I'm old-fashioned."

While he's walking around to his side, I scroll through his contacts a little to see how many girl-sounding names are saved.

There are a lot. Which shouldn't bother me. Neither of us are young. So he knows a lot of women? So what? I enter my number, typing in 'You Wish' instead of my name. Just as I click save, he has an incoming call from someone named Claire.

I hand his phone back.

He declines the call, and swipes through a few things. He's frowning when he looks up at me. "You didn't save your number?"

"Oh, I did, just not under Amanda. If you want to ask me out, you'll have to figure out what name I saved it under and then also remember my name without it being typed into your phone. I'm sure with all the women's names and numbers you've got, that's unlikely to happen."

He rolls his eyes. "Oh, come on."

"You don't appreciate things you don't work for, Dr. Dutton. Didn't anyone ever tell you that?"

"I suppose you have a lot to teach me."

"You have no idea."

While he totals up the number of calves he treated and works up the invoice, I stare as much as I want, which is quite a lot. I sort of figured that, up close, upon longer acquaintance, I'd notice something annoying.

A mole.

An underbite.

Nearsightedness that makes him squint.

Anything.

But the longer I stare, the more I want to stare.

When I write the check, and he thanks me and climbs back in his SUV, I'm actually sad. He waves as he drives away, and I can't stop looking at that dimple that shows up even from a half smile.

It takes me almost an hour to get reception for long enough to post, but it's worth it. The photo of him, muscles straining, sunlight streaming past his silhouette? #HotCowboy #DownandDirty #GiddyUp #VetCheck-MePlease There's no way Heather's not going to be delighted about this.

Let's hope my followers are, too.

When I check later that night, it turns out, they are. I tell myself that's why I'm so excited.

Now if only I believed it. . .

❧ 11 ❧

ABIGAIL

After alternating between good cop and bad cop, I then freaked out on about five different people from Union Wireless. The last lady I spoke to told me she understood my urgency, and even though the crews weren't set to be here until July, she would get them out early for me.

So when I see *Union Wireless* as a sender in my inbox, my adrenaline spikes.

I click on the email.

Abigail:

As promised, we're going to come out to your location early! Congrats. The install typically takes 1-3 business days, depending on your location and the difficulty for the crews in running the line to your desired location.

Your install is scheduled for:

June 26, between the hours of 8 am and 4 pm.

Thanks for your patience,

Rebecca Johnson

. . .

June *twenty-sixth*? A measly four days early!? I groan. I've spent every morning this week over at Steve's and as far as I can tell, he's been asleep every single time. He has been reliable for our lessons, but I can't say I'm impressed by how little he seems to work. Sleeping all day, one horseback lesson, then up all night. . .doing what?

Not that what Steve Archer does is any of my business.

Luckily, he said we should take the weekend off from lessons. It's a good thing, because instead of getting used to riding, my legs only seem to get progressively more sore. And my roping skills are laughably bad. Jeff says that's fine—I hope he's right.

Apparently the cattle drive doesn't really require much roping. That's mostly for dealing with injured ones. It's a relief to me that Kevin and Jeff will be there with us the entire time. If we weren't here, they could handle things themselves, but they'd break the cows into two groups. With an extra few people, they can manage the whole bunch of cows at once.

Or so Kevin insists.

I hope he's right. Ethan's a better rider than I expected—mostly because he's pretty athletic and can manage most things. My riding has improved, but I've always been somewhat competent. I'm still worried that Ethan and I are going to be worse than useless when we're actually out for a ride, trying to force cows to move where we want.

Izzy's English skills have transferred to Western remarkably well, so that's something.

The most improved, by far, is clearly Whitney, but the verdict is still out on whether she'll be good enough to be safely surrounded by cows in unfamiliar terrain.

A text from Robert comes in right after breakfast. I

PROMISED THE REVISED CONTRACTS TO NEWTON MONDAY. ARE THEY DONE? I DON'T SEE THEM, BUT MAYBE YOU SAVED THEM SOMEWHERE ELSE?

I forgot about the stupid Newton contracts. If I'd been at work, I'd have remembered. I put files in order of when they were promised to the clients and work my way methodically through them. If I was running late, I'd take a file home and work on it after Gabriel went to bed.

Here, my miniscule closet is full of Parcheesi, Backgammon, Clue, and Monopoly. The dresser in this room is clear full of tablecloths, linen napkins, and sheets with prints so loud they'd make the 1970s blush. My few actual documents are stacked up on top of the nightstand, which is already cluttered with a lamp and an old clock that never shows the right time.

Between trying to feed kids and bathe kids and wash clothes and make nice with another family and do my work on a rocking porch bench. . .I feel close to a complete breakdown. I do not have the time for a breakdown, and too many people rely on me. Besides, Abby doesn't break down. Abby doesn't cry. Abby doesn't fall apart. She makes a plan, and she gets things done. And when problems arise or I miss something, I do whatever it takes to get back on track. So that's what I'm going to do right now.

Steve Archer told me I could come over to use his internet any time. He isn't doing lessons today, which tells me he may be busy, but I'm not sure what else to do. At least I'll be quick. In and out fast. Maybe he won't even notice I'm there.

Ethan's already gone when I leave, moving water. I really should go with him at some point and find out what exactly it means to shovel sod in order to block one ditch and then open another, but that day will not be today.

Whitney and Izzy and Emery are playing their favorite game—Uno. Because it's best with four players, they let Gabe play too.

Maren's still sleeping, but all she does when she's awake is read, anyway. I wonder what she's going to do when the supply of books she brought runs out. Probably start burning ants with a magnifying glass. Or pulling legs off beetles to show her mom that being here really is making her slowly go insane.

"I'm going to run over to—"

"Do some work," Whitney says.

"We know," Izzy says.

I didn't think I could feel any worse. I was wrong.

"Mom," Gabe says.

I'm breathing in and out as deeply as I can, trying not to cry. It feels like, sometimes, in the middle of making plans and executing them, and then changing things to account for errors and miscalculations, that I'm drowning. I'm missing things that matter in my desperate attempt to do things we *need*. "Yeah, baby? What?"

"Thank you for working." His grin fills his entire face. "I miss when you hardly worked, but I know that now you gotta do all Dad's work and all yours."

"I'm sorry about it too," Whitney says.

"Yeah, thanks," Izzy says. "I know it sucks."

I'm extremely blessed to have the children I have. "I never regret working for you guys, but sometimes I wish I was around more. I think your dad probably felt the same way." *Way to make them all sad, Abby.* I am such a downer. "Don't worry about me today. I just have a few contracts to review and then I'll be back to join the fun."

"Promise?" Gabe says.

"I do."

"Okay, because you *have* to watch *Charlotte's Web.*"

I don't tell him that I've already seen it. "When I get back, we'll do it."

"Deal," he says. Seven is a fun age.

I feel like I could drive to Steve Archer's place with a blindfold on at this point. The road curves right, then left, then right again. I hang a left, and then make a quick right and I'm there. Less than five minutes. I'm lucky that I found someone with WiFi and a house small enough that I can boost it from his porch. And I'm lucky that we're in Utah, not Texas, where I'd be *baking* outside every day. So far, the high has been 75 degrees. With a breeze and the shade from the porch, it's been a much more beautiful place to work than I'm used to, with far fewer distractions.

Only this time, when I park, there's someone sitting on my swing.

Or rather, his swing. Steve Archer's holding a mug of coffee and looking at me in confusion.

I probably look almost as shocked. I've never seen him awake before noon. Most days, he hasn't woken by the time I leave at two or three in the afternoon. Since when do functioning alcoholics change their behavior patterns for weekends?

"Morning," Steve says.

"Uh, yeah, good morning," I say. "I didn't expect you to be awake."

He frowns. "How did you know I was sleeping?"

I could hear his white noise machine playing ocean sounds, but I'm not about to say that. It's not polite to draw attention to how small someone's house is. I've been careful not to talk on the phone while he's asleep. When I absolutely had to do a zoom call or talk via phone, I'd walk a dozen paces away and rest my computer on his birdbath. It's not exactly ideal, but it's the farthest I could get from the house and still have a decent signal. I figure, if I can hear his white noise machine, he could hear me talking. "Just a guess."

He grunts.

"I'm sorry, I know it's the weekend. I can find someplace else. Kevin said he thinks maybe the—"

He stands up. "It's fine. I can have my coffee out in the barn. It's just that I have this one cat, Bungo, who loves coffee and he won't leave me alone."

Plus, it's so nice here in the morning. "I'm certainly not going to kick someone off their own porch swing. I can download the contracts and then drive back later to upload the revised versions. It won't take more than five minutes each time." Crisis averted.

Steve shakes his head. "Please. If you think it won't bother you for me to be here, get your work done. We can share the bench. Might be nice to have another human on the property for a bit."

I've seen someone here, lending a hand with the horses, but I suppose that's not quite the same as company.

Not that I'm going to be any better. I'm probably worse, since I know he wants to get rid of me. I still get a little irritated when I think about the fact that two of the three people Uncle Jed appointed to determine whether we've complied with the conditions want us gone. If we *did* want to stay, it feels like we wouldn't have much of a chance.

Awkward or not, I have to get these done, so I force myself to sit down on the far left of the swing. "Thanks."

The contracts download quickly, and luckily they're much cleaner than I feared they'd be. It takes me a few minutes to work out the issues with the first, and the second is a mirror of it. I whip up an analysis and attach the analysis and the redline to Mr. Newton and copy

Robert. Once the email goes through, I lean back and release a sigh of relief.

"Done?"

"I'll get out of your hair. Thanks so much for letting me come work here. Not just today—this whole week. You've been a lifesaver."

He shrugs. "It hasn't bothered me at all. It's not like I pay for usage on the internet."

"Well, it's never nice to have someone invading your space, but you've been pretty decent about it." I'm not sure whether I'm talking about the internet or our presence in the area. Either way, I suppose my statement's true.

"It's not that I don't want you here," he says. "I think when we spoke before, I didn't explain very well."

I slide my laptop into my bag. "I probably overreacted. We don't have an interest in staying anyway, so there's no conflict."

"But I've had a week to watch you with three of your children."

"What do you think about Whitney?"

He bobs his head. "She's coming along faster than I thought. Her handling has improved, but let's see how she does on your horses next week."

"Jed's horses, you mean?"

He shrugs. "I guess that's what I mean."

"I'd think you'd be relieved that we're leaving. Your friend Patrick can buy his precious land the second we're gone."

"Patrick's inheriting his dad's ranch. It's his sister who actually wants to buy it. Patrick just offered to pay you to vacate earlier."

His sister? "Oh. That's. . .alright." Not that I care who buys it.

"Patrick's a lousy human being in a lot of ways, with

his bribes and his manipulation, but his sister Donna's a really good person. She's probably the person I admire most in town."

Inexplicably, a hot flash of jealousy shoots through me. Which is absurd. I don't know Donna, and I don't care if she's Steve Archer's favorite person in the entire world. In the entire universe. I hope they get married and have ten children.

"Actually, it might be better for her to buy in a few months anyway."

It's utterly irrational, but for some reason I do not want to hear any more about Donna. "Alright," I say. "Well, I'm always happy to help." I stand up.

Steve Archer does, too. He sets his empty mug on the seat of the swing. "Listen, I think maybe we got off on the wrong foot. I know you're busy, but if you ever want some adult time, I'd be happy to take you to dinner. Manila's finest, or we could take a little drive and head over to Green River. I can show you the feed store, the actual grocery store, and even the middle school."

"Why would I want to see a middle school?"

He smiles. "There isn't one in Manila. Dutch John, Flaming Gorge, and Manila only have two schools between them—both located in Manila. One's an elementary school that runs through sixth grade. The other is a high school that picks up with seventh grade. So Green River's quite the impressive metropolis, as evidenced by the existence of a middle school."

"Sometimes I feel like you can't throw a rock in the Houston area without hitting a school."

"Sounds nice."

I shrug. "Pros and cons to everything, I suppose."

"How about it?" he asks. "Any interest in a tour led by a local?"

Wait, is he asking me on a date?

"If mornings are better, the Gorge Reel and Grill isn't bad." He smiles. "It may not sound like it, but it has decent French toast and killer waffles."

"Would you be able to wake up that early in the morning?"

He tilts his head. "What does that mean?"

"Never mind." I toss my head back toward my car. "I doubt it's a good idea for us to have dinner together, or any meal, really."

"I'm not handsome enough." He shrugs. "C'est la vie."

"No, it's not about that. You're teaching us horseback lessons, and you're my only source of internet until June 26. Without that, I'll lose my job. So no matter how good-looking you are, it's a bad idea."

His eyebrows shoot up. "How good-looking am I?"

What is wrong with me today? "Look, the point is that, I'm happy to start over." I force a smile. "But I think we should be friendly neighbors, nothing more."

He frowns. "I was asking to show you around as a friendly neighbor. What did *you* think I was doing?"

"You said you weren't handsome enough, and surely that implies—"

"That you didn't want to be seen with a scruffy old tour guide?" He tilts his head.

"Oh. Well."

He holds out his hand. "But don't worry. No pressure from me. I'm happy just to be friends."

"Friendly neighbors," I reiterate. But I take his hand to shake.

The second our fingers touch, a shiver runs up my arm and pulses through me. His hand is so big, and so strong, and calloused in a way I've never experienced. I'm suddenly very aware that this is a man who uses his entire body in a very precise and calculated way. He controls animals that weigh more than a thousand pounds. He breaks green horses and trains the broken ones.

It's been years since I've really touched any man but my husband, who had very smooth, very refined hands.

They were nothing at all like Steve's. Who is supposed to be a trainer and one of the people involved in determining whether we're complying with will terms. I definitely shouldn't let him take me on a 'friendly neighborhood tour.' It's a terrible idea that will just confuse things.

Me.

It will confuse me.

And I'm still holding his hand, like some kind of halfwit.

I snatch my fingers away, but it does nothing to stop his knowing grin. "Did you say you'll be getting internet on the 26th of June?"

He changes gears fast. "Uh, yeah."

"And we'll be done with the cattle drive by then."

"We?" I ask. "You mean Kevin and Jeff and I and Izzy will be done."

"I bet Whitney can go too, as long as you have someone along who knows what they're doing. If anything did happen and I was there, I could talk her through it. Or I could trade horses with her, if it came to trouble."

I love the idea of him coming, which should set off all kinds of warning bells.

"And on June 27th, you'll no longer need to make use of my porch swing," he says slowly. "Then if I wanted to show you around, you'd be out of excuses."

I wait for the anxiety I felt when Robert mentioned liking me, and all the fear and crippling guilt I've felt whenever any man has brought up the possibility of anything even somewhat related to a date. . .

But it never comes.

Probably because nothing here this summer is *real.* It's like make-believe. That might make a friendly neighborhood tour with a random, possibly drunk, horse trainer who makes my skin itch and my heart pump faster, an alright idea. With no expectations for either of us, how bad could it be?

"I would probably be out of excuses," I agree. "I might even say yes—to a neighborhood tour. It would be rude to turn down the guy who has helped us out so much."

He grins. "I'll mark my calendar."

12
AMANDA

Dr. Dutton doesn't call. He doesn't even text.

Which is totally fine.

It's not like I really wanted to date a vet in the middle of nowhere.

I'm only disappointed because the post I made with his photo has done so remarkably well. And because Heather keeps asking about him. "I could send some things he could wear," she suggests for the fifth time. "Maybe an athletic shirt? Or a backpack. He could use that—you said he's a vet, right?"

"I already told you," I say. "We aren't dating. I barely met him. There's nothing between us. I certainly can't show up on his doorstep and hand him a shirt and bag and ask him to use them for me."

"Tell him if he puts it on, that you'll stay to watch him take it off."

"I'm hanging up now," I say.

"Think about it!" She's relentless.

I wish I could ignore her—I'd like to stop thinking about it, please and thank you. And every time I do imagine him, I remember that even though I flirted shamelessly, and lobbed my best moves at him, he still hasn't called.

Ugh.

"Amanda?" Abby's climbing the hill to my office. It's so unfair. She's made friends with the horse trainer, so she disappears for hours, sitting on his front porch, probably flirting. Meanwhile, if I want to post something or call my soon-to-be-boss, I hope, I have to hike up to the top of a stupidly tall hill. And even up here, I apparently still can't get any peace and quiet.

"Yeah?"

"Oh good." She holds her hand over her eyes. "You are up here. With you sitting on the far end, I couldn't really see you from the house."

Which was exactly the point.

"It's a good thing Maren knew where you were."

That little traitor. "What did you need?"

Abby sits down next to me and plucks a lavender wildflower from the bushy weed growing near my feet. "These are nice. I wonder what they are."

"You walked all the way out here for wildflowers?"

"You're sure crabby." She drops the flower and pets Roscoe's head. That traitor scoots away from me and closer to her. "I heard you're staying until after the Fourth of July now?" Is her voice strained? Is she mad about it?

"Uh, yeah, turns out, Lololime really likes the change of pace of posts out here, and they want me to stick around a little longer." I don't mention that they also want me dating. Although, if I did, I could find out how she feels about me flirting with the horse trainer she can't seem to decide whether she likes. He's not nearly as beautiful as Eddy, but he's around a lot more. Plus, he looks absurdly good in a saddle.

"Great." She forces a smile that never reaches her eyes. "Well, on the good news front, for the last week you're here, we should have internet. After haranguing everyone from here to the coast, they finally agreed to come early."

"That's great!"

"Only four days early," she grumbles. "But I'm taking every win, no matter how small."

"Since they said they were coming in July, we could have been put at the end of their list. I think that's a pretty big win."

"But on the bad news front." She grimaces.

What now?

"I just talked to Kevin and Jeff. Apparently they're going to a family reunion that happens once every five years, and there's no way for them to get out of it. They're glad we'll be here, so they can go."

"What does that mean?"

"They'll be gone for a week, leaving right after we drive the cows up to the forest property, apparently."

"That's horrifying," I say.

"I agree. We need to pay a lot more attention to what they've been doing so that we can do it in their absence."

"You don't really expect *me* to do any of it, right?"

"No," she says. "I didn't, but I figured you may have changed your mind. You seem to be doing that a lot." She stands up and brushes off her jeans. "Well, I won't keep you. I'm headed inside to read the Bible with the kids for a while."

"There's a big church building in Manila," I say. "You could go there." And give us a break from your self-righteous, know-it-all attitude.

"We're not big on organized sermons," Abby says. "But thanks for the suggestion." She starts walking toward the house, which annoys me. How does she know I have nothing else to say?

I pop up and jog to catch up with her, nearly tripping

over Roscoe, who races after me dutifully. "Are you upset we're staying longer?"

Abigail's lips compress and her nostrils flare, but only for a moment. "Of course not."

"Are you sure?" I can't help digging at her a bit.

"It's been great for the kids to spend time with your girls." She clears her throat. "Or at least, one of your girls."

"What does that mean?"

She shrugs. "Nothing."

"Just say what you want to say."

Her arms swing as she walks even faster. "Maren doesn't seem to be very happy to be here, and it shows."

"She'll get over it. She's a team player."

This time, she doesn't even bother hiding her snort.

"What's your problem with her?"

"I don't have a problem with her," she says. "But she's causing issues with all my children, and they get along with almost everyone."

"Yes, your kids are such an unbelievable delight. How could anyone not love them?" I actually feel a little bad as I say that ironically, because her kids are pretty good. Ethan's a little obnoxious sometimes, but he generally means well. And Izzy is capable and patient with Whitney, Emery, and Gabe. She makes lunch almost every day, and she never excludes Emery for not being her family.

"I know my children aren't perfect," Abigail says, huffing a bit from her quick walk and all this talking. "But they have tried to forge some kind of relationship with Maren, and they've been consistently rebuffed. Actually, they've been rudely rebuffed."

"Why do they need to forge anything at all?"

"I suppose they don't need to," she says, "but I thought it would be nice for them to know their cousins, and they've all been through something pretty similar."

"Maren's not a fan of the ranch, so it's not like being here will bond her—"

We're almost back to the ranch house, and Abigail stops, pivoting on her heel to face me. "Not the ranch, Amanda. I'm talking about losing their fathers."

Oh. "Mine are over it," I say. "Paul died three and a half years ago." Plus, he wasn't the best dad to begin with.

The pity and condescension on Abigail's face makes me want to slap her. "You think Maren's fine? You think Emery is? You don't recover from losing your dad in three years. They may not recover in their *lifetime*. He won't be there to threaten whatever guy takes them on their first date. He won't be there for prom, or their wedding day. He won't be there to complain to when you annoy them, or when they think you've gotten things all wrong."

"Yours are lucky then." I cross my arms. Roscoe whines and lies down by my feet, putting a paw over his face. I wish I could do that.

"Why are they lucky?"

"Because you never get things wrong." I can't quite help my smirk.

She half smiles. "I said when the kids think their mom has gotten things wrong. I didn't say either of us were ever wrong."

I laugh. "You're such a lawyer."

"I'm sorry if I hurt your feelings about Maren. I don't always approach things the right way, but I've been worried about her. And now that you're staying longer, I think we need to do something."

All the tension that I dissipated with my joke returns with full force. "*We* need to do something about *my* daughter?"

"She's being terribly mean to Gabe, and when Whitney defends him, she's pretty rude to her as well. You've done nothing about it, so consider this your formal notice that if you don't take steps to curb her attitude and behavior, I will."

How dare she criticize not only my daughter, but my parenting? "You haven't even been here—how could you possibly know what she's done?"

"My children actually talk to me." That's a low blow.

"Mine talk to me, too. I'm also here to see what happens, as opposed to you—you're always gone, flirting with that horse trainer for all I know."

Abigail's hand tightens into a ball at her side, and for a moment I worry that she'll actually punch me. Color floods her cheeks and her lips twist. "It must be nice," she says.

Although it really feels like a setup, I can't help myself. "What must be nice?"

"Not having to do any real work. First Paul supported you while you did nothing but shop, and now you post a few photos a week and people pay you for it. I'm sorry if my *job* has inconvenienced you, but some of us are forced to use our brains to earn a living, and that takes time."

She's right, of course. And that's the gist of my problem with her. She's a Harvard lawyer. . .and I'm a nobody who relies on the fickle attention of scads of unknown followers, all of whom could realize that I'm a fraud at any time. And I certainly can't fall back on my brain. Two years of college does not even a degree make, much less any marketable skills.

I never should have argued about Maren in the first place. I've never felt less secure in my own parenting skills—even with a handful of hours a day spent with her children, Abigail is killing it, whereas my sullen daughter has done nothing but read in her room and complain. She hates the smell of cows, the food is terrible, the bed is uncomfortable, she can't talk to her friends, and there's nothing to watch on television. I've wanted to smack her myself at least a dozen times, but I have no idea how to make her behave more like Abigail's kids. I should be asking her for help, not bawling her out for being a negligent mother.

"I—"

Abigail drops her face in her hands. "I'm sorry, Amanda. I'm so sorry." When she moves her hands, it's clear that she's crying. "It has been so hard since Nate died. I don't know how you've survived. I should not have lashed out like that—but what you said." More tears well up and run down her face. "It's exactly what I've been afraid of. I'm trying to parent *and* provide and I'm failing at both. All the time."

What must it feel like for her? To lose an actual partner, someone she loved and respected, someone she wanted by her side for the next fifty years? Jealousy pulses through me. I know she lost Nate and it's wildly inappropriate for me to be jealous of her, but I never had what she's wrestling with missing so deeply. I've never been a great parent, and I've never been a happy wife.

Even now that's Nate's gone, I'm still jealous of her on both fronts.

"I'll talk to Maren," I say. "Maybe—"

"Mom!!" Whitney's voice is shrill, followed immediately by shouts from the others.

Abigail turns and takes off like a shot for the barn. I follow quickly behind her, all details of our argument dropped the second a kid needs us.

This is my first time in the barn, so I'm a little overwhelmed. There's hay in big stacks, an open door full of saddles and junk, and rows of stalls. Several horse heads hang out, and I instinctively shy away from them. Enormous, murderous creatures. I shudder and move on.

The kids are all inside of a large open pen of some kind with big rectangular metal tubs along one side.

There are buckets and strange, oddly-shaped rake looking things scattered all over, as well as a dirty, white-looking roundish thing.

"Who's hurt?" Abigail asks.

"Me," Whitney sobs.

Abigail drops down on her knee, heedless of the mud she's getting all over her jeans. "Come here, baby, let me see."

While Abigail's examining Whitney, I scan for my kids to make sure they're fine. Emery looks concerned, as she should, but Maren's jaw is jutting out, and her eyes are flinty.

That's not good.

I edge my way around the pen to where she's standing. "What happened?"

"Nothing," she says. "I mean, it should have been nothing, but Gabe's always such a baby."

Was Abigail right? Am I a terrible parent? Did Maren hurt Whitney? "Tell me what happened," I say as calmly as I can. Even so, a note of frustration definitely works its way in.

Maren, predictably, reacts by huffing and shaking her head. "I didn't even want to play with them, but when we were doing relays they needed even teams and then they moved on to this dumb game and I was already out here."

"What game?"

"An idiotic version of duck duck goose," she says. "You sit in a circle, and one person is it, but they call it horse horse goat."

It sounds kind of cute, actually. My insta page would love it. I wish I'd gotten a video. "Okay, so you run around and round, with one person trying to tag someone. Presumably they say 'goat,' and that person has to run?"

"Right."

"What are the buckets and rakes for?"

"Oh my gosh, Mom, even I know more than you. Those aren't rakes. They're scoopers, for mucking stalls."

It takes me a second, but I realize they're oddly shaped so they can scoop poop. Gross. "What were you using them for, though?"

"Since we're horses, we don't just run in a circle, we have to jump over the obstacles." She compresses her lips.

I am surprised they convinced her to play. "I bet you were good at it, since you jump so much for cheer."

"I was good."

"But how did Whitney get hurt?"

"Everyone lets Gabe win," she says. "Every single time. He's super slow, and he whines constantly, and he can't catch anyone. So whoever's closest to him just lets him tag them. Even Emery did it."

"He's seven."

"You sound exactly like them—like his age explains everything. I was seven once, too."

I am a bad mom. I've raised a total brat.

"It's wrong to let people win. It sends the wrong message, that they don't need to try hard. So when he said 'goat' to me, he chased me and chased me and lost and had to go again."

"And?"

She shrugs. "It happened a few times. People got mad because they're dumb."

"Whitney tripped her the next time she wouldn't let Gabe catch her," Emery says.

"That was a terrible thing to do," Abigail says. "Why would you do that?"

Whitney's face is blotchy from crying. "I'm so sorry, Mom. I did apologize. Gabe was so sad, but I knew it was wrong."

"I still don't understand how Whitney was injured." I can tell there's something wrong with her arm.

"After she tripped me, I shoved her," Maren says. "She got my shirt all muddy."

"Whitney fell and landed on the water trough," Izzy says. "I think her arm's broken."

"I'm going to run up the hill,'" Ethan says. "I'll check the map on my phone to see where the closest emergency room is."

Abigail nods. "Thanks."

"We're coming too," I say. "I'm so sorry, Abigail."

"I don't want her there," Whitney says.

Of course she doesn't. "We're all sorry." I tap Maren's hand, and when she still says nothing, I kick her.

"Yeah. Sorry."

My daughter is a monster. I just wish I had some idea of how to fix it.

13
ABIGAIL

The closest ER is forty-five minutes away, in Green River, Wyoming. I'm too upset to leave any of my kids with Maren, and they're all worried about Whitney, whose arm is already swollen, so everyone piles into my car.

"Maybe we can go out to eat after," Whitney says.

She's the cutest kid, always looking for something good in every situation.

"I just wish Emery could have come."

"Aunt Mandy has some things to talk to her kids about," Izzy says.

"Emery doesn't need to hear it," Gabe says. "She's already nice."

She is one of the sweetest kids I've met. I wonder what happened with Maren. I suppose every child reacts to grief and trauma in their own way. Clearly, high school has been hard on Maren.

Apparently, Sunday night is a busy time at the Castle Rock Medical Center. After waiting for over an hour, I finally send Ethan to get fast food. "Anything you can find." I press cash into his hand. "Be careful with the rental car. You're not covered."

"Alright little munchkins. What do you want? McDonald's? Taco Time? Subway? Or we could try a place called the Arctic Circle." He fakes shivering. "Could be great, but it's risky."

"Whoa, there are so many restaurants here," Gabe says.

I suppress my laugh. Compared to home, this town is barely a blip, but compared to Manila, it may as well be New York City. "I vote for Taco Time. We've only been gone for a week and I already miss Mexican food."

"Sure," Izzy says.

"I like tacos," Whitney says. "As long as they're not super spicy."

I laugh. "Mild everything."

Ethan shakes his head. "You girls are so weak sauce."

Of course, because it's the way these things work, they finally take us back two minutes after he leaves. "Maybe we'll be done by the time he's back," Whitney says.

"What happened to you?" The doc's looking at a chart as he walks in. When he looks up, a smile on his face, I drop my purse.

Because the doctor is none other than Steve Archer, our horse trainer.

Obviously, there's been some kind of mix-up.

"Is this a joke?" I ask.

He freezes, his eyes shifting slowly around the room, starting on Whitney and stopping on me. "Abigail." The friendly, 'I'm a cool guy' doctor smile is gone, replaced with an expression I can't read at all.

"Whitney got shoved against a water trough. I think her arm's broken," I say. "We need to see a doctor to get some X-rays."

"You're in luck, then," he says. "Since I happen to be a doctor."

I swallow.

"Whoa, you're a horse trainer *and* a doctor?" Izzy whistles. "That's so cool. I wanna be a horse trainer doctor, too."

"I'd say that I'm a part-time horse trainer these days," he says. "Mostly I help people with problems and break a few horses a year for fun."

"But you're really a people doctor, right?" Gabe asks. "Not a horse doctor who's, like, filling in because it's such a small place?"

He laughs. "I'm really a people doctor. Went to medical school and everything."

How could I not know?

It hits me then, his nickname. The Horse Doc. I thought it was because he fixed up horses with problems, or as he says, helps horses with their people problems. As if he doesn't know what to say either, he takes two more steps and reaches Whitney's side. "Let me see that arm, kiddo."

She flinches when he reaches for her.

"This won't hurt," he says. "It may be a little sore, but it won't hurt, I promise."

I'm surprised to see her visibly relax. Probably spending five hours in the last week listening to him bark orders helps her trust him here, too.

He holds her arm firmly but gently and tugs it one way, then the other. He asks her to squeeze his hand, and lift. "I think you're right," he finally says. "I think she's broken her radius, likely a green stick, but we'll know once we get the X-rays."

I exhale. "Okay."

He meets my eyes. "It's going to be fine. Kids heal really fast."

"Thanks."

He's utterly and completely professional—which isn't really a surprise. He's exactly the same way during lessons. Calm while managing several people and animals at the same time. Even-handed, attentive, bright. But how can he hold down this job while drinking so much? And sleeping until two in the afternoon? The horses don't mind, but I assume the people do.

"Oh." It hits me then—he's an ER doc. He might have been sleeping, not because he was up drinking, but because he was working all night.

"What?"

"Did you work night shifts last week?"

He shrugs.

"That's why you slept all day."

"You were paying attention to when I was asleep?"

"I could hear your white noise machine," I confess.

He smacks his head. "How embarrassing."

"Why didn't you tell me you're a doctor?"

"People act different around doctors," he says. "I wouldn't have mentioned it until sometime after June 27, if I had my way." His smile's just for me, and it feels like the whole world drops away.

Then his words register. June 27th. That's the day after I get my internet. He's saying he didn't mean to tell me what he does for a job. . . until after we went on a date.

After the long wait to be seen, I almost get whiplash with how quickly they do the X-rays, read the results, and return to wrap her arm in a cast. "The good news is that it is just a greenstick fracture," he says. "They heal quickly and don't require surgery or pins."

"That's a relief," I say.

"I doubt she'll have any trouble from this more than six weeks down the road."

"But can I still ride in the cattle drive?" Whitney's face is so eager.

Steve ruffles her hair. "Not this one, kiddo, but don't worry. You're only ten. You'll have a chance at some point, I'm sure."

Whitney frowns. "We're going home at the end of the summer, and the ranch is getting sold to aliens."

Steve snorts. "Aliens?"

"That's what the will says."

"I thought it was a charity?"

"This would be a nonprofit." I shrug. "It was a passion of Uncle Jed's, apparently."

"Bizarre," he says.

I can't argue. A few moments later, I sign some forms and we're ready to go. Ethan, predictably, shows up just as we're leaving. "Good thing you're here," I say. "I was worried we'd have to walk home."

"I come with food. Tacos for everyone." Ethan starts handing out tacos and does a double take when he sees Steve. "What are you doing here?"

"He works here," I say.

"Yeah, right." But even as Ethan scoffs, his eyes widen as he takes in Steve's scrubs and white coat. "Whoa, really? That's crazy."

"Can you spare a moment?" Steve asks.

Ethan answers for me. "We'll eat. Take as much time as you want."

The waiting room has cleared out, which is probably a relief to Steve. "Is anything wrong?" I ask. "If our insurance won't cover everything, we've got an HSA."

"No, not about that." He waves his hand in the air as if money stuff is boring. I suppose it is. "Look, I just wanted to make sure that you're alright."

"Kids fall, sometimes. I mean, in this case, she was pushed, but. . ."

He chuckles. "Not about Whitney either. I wanted to make sure *we're* alright."

"Oh. I'm fine—there isn't a 'we' here, that I know of."

"I'm sorry I didn't mention I was a doctor. I figured it was better for you to think that I'm—"

"A drunk?"

His jaw drops. "A what?"

I shrug. "Empty beer bottles in the barn and full ones in the tack room fridge. Sleeping all day. . ."

He laughs. "You didn't think that."

"What was I supposed to think?"

He can't seem to stop laughing.

"You don't drink, I take it?"

He stops laughing, finally, and wipes his eyes. "I'll have a drink now and then, but never enough to make me sleep late. Certainly not enough to need alcohol in the tack room."

"You fell asleep on a bale of hay," I point out. "And I saw the beer in the tack room fridge myself."

"The day we met was right after my first night shift. One day prior, I'd taken in a new horse." He runs his hand over his face. "Denver—I think you met him."

"New horses make you day drink?" Oh! "Or maybe you needed something to help you sleep?"

"Woman! You talk so much you don't let anyone get in a word."

I snap my mouth shut.

"Denver came up North because he stopped sweating. It's something that happens in hot and humid places like New Orleans. A buddy of mine sent him to me. Usually the second they leave the humid, boggy places, they start sweating again, but Denver didn't."

I am still so confused.

"A very particular kind of beer, Guinness, will kick start their system and make them sweat again. It took a few days for Denver, but it worked. Only that morning, I was probably too tired to toss the bottles, and I was so exhausted while watching him drink his beer, that I sat down on a hay bale. . ."

So he's a doctor, and I'm an idiot who jumps to conclusions.

"You can talk now," he says playfully.

"I don't know what to say."

"Say you're looking forward to June 27th."

I was, but for some reason, I'm not anymore. "I never lie."

He blinks. "Lie?"

"The more I think about it, I don't think us touring the area is a good plan. I'm only here for the summer, and you clearly have a very full plate."

"I can't believe it."

"What?"

"You've got to be the only woman in America who doesn't want to spend any time with me once you find out I have a respectable job."

"It's not the job—I'd have come to the same conclusion either way."

He stares at me for a long time, as if he's weighing my words.

"Dr. Archer," a nurse says. "The patient in room 6 is complaining of nausea."

He waves at her. "Coming." But he turns back when he's only a few steps away. "We still on for a morning lesson at your place tomorrow?"

I nod.

"Alright. See you then."

All the way home, I think about his shock. Most women probably would be more excited about a handsome, rugged, doctor than they are about a handsome, rugged horse trainer. But a doctor feels *real* to me. I knew nothing could happen with a horse trainer. After all, when I go home, it's not like a horse trainer would sell his barn and move to Houston.

But a doctor could.

Which means this might be more than a palate-cleansing fling.

This suddenly feels very, very real. And real is too much for me right now. Maybe ever. Which means that I already know what I'll say, no matter how many times he asks me out.

No.

Always no.

14
AMANDA

Another package has gone missing. It probably doesn't help that the mailbox on the street is overflowing with letters. I haul them all in, dropping one every two feet. It takes me forever with all the leaning over and picking up, and reconfiguring, and dropping another, but eventually I reach the house. I dump them unceremoniously on the counter.

"What's all that?" Abby asks.

"This is the mail—which specifically did not include a package that I was supposed to have received already from Ariat."

"What are they sending you?" she asks.

"Boots," I say. "They reached out to say that they like my recent posts and asked if I'd be interested in some area appropriate clothing and shoes." I shrug. "Since we've got a few more weeks, I said why not? But. . .the package is nowhere."

Abby's now flipping through the mail of a dead man. She just can't let anything go. "Mhmm," she says. "That's nice. I have to pay for all my clothing."

"But you also get to choose it."

Abby's now opening letters and sorting them.

"What are you doing?"

She looks up. "You do actually manage your own life, right?"

Oh my word, she's such a snot. "Of course I do."

"I'm ashamed to admit that I've looked at living here a bit like a vacation. A terrible vacation in which I'm both working on a farm and also doing my job, but still. Since we're here, we're supposed to be managing things. Like paying the power bill." She points at the light above our heads. "If we don't do things like that, they tend to cut the power off. Then no internet will feel like less of an urgency, I promise."

She's a brat, but she's probably also right. I turn to help her, filtering out the spammy mailers and chucking them, while handing the reputable-looking mail to her. "National Forestry Service?" I toss it onto the spam file.

"Wait." Abby lunges for it.

"You think we need that?"

"That's where the cows run," she says. "Remember?"

"I thought it was Bureau of Land Management."

"Kevin says out here that land is all desert. He said the forestry service land is way better—and cheaper too."

Huh. I suppose I ought to be paying more attention, but it's hard to care when I've only got a few weeks.

When Abby opens the letter, her hands tighten on the edges of it, and the color drains from her face.

"Not great news, I take it?"

"It says that because we didn't file for a renewal of our permit, we can't take *any* cows up to the forest this year."

"Perfect," I say. "Geez, why didn't we do that to begin with? Now they can just stay here, and you won't have to spend all day herding them up there."

Abby grits her teeth, but I try not to let it annoy me. "Amanda, I know that you're not here to participate, but have you heard anything Kevin and Jeff have said?"

Not really.

"The cows *need* to go up there," she says. "If they don't, we won't be able to grow enough hay to feed them through the winter. If that happens, and we're forced to buy hay for hundreds of cows, then we'll lose any profit we might have otherwise made."

I lean forward, bracing my hands on the table. "Abigail, correct me if I'm wrong, but in a few weeks, your son Ethan is going to college." I lift my eyebrows and wait for an answer.

She blinks. "That's right."

"And this entire ranch, as well as the cows, will presumably be sold."

She nods.

"None of that money comes to us, right?"

"Right."

I lean even closer. "So why do you care?"

She releases the letter and it flutters to the table. "Well, I guess. . ."

For someone who insists this isn't a real option, she sure acts like it *is*.

"So what if the cows stay here? So what if there's not enough hay for the winter?" I shrug. "Let the new owners deal with that."

Abigail looks a bit like a kite whose strings were cut. She collapses into a chair and leans back into it. "It's been such a mad dash of one emergency after another since Nate died."

I sit next to her. I remember that feeling. I have PTSD from that feeling, really. For more than a year, I had no idea whether we'd be evicted. I pulled out a cash advance on a credit card to pay rent once, and ouch, that was hard to repay. "You're only here for Ethan, so—"

"Ethan will know if I don't take it seriously, and he'll blame me." Her brow furrows. "I told him that we'd try. That we'd make sure we succeeded at every task, and that I would give the entire enterprise a fair shake."

"But what can you do at this point?" I shrug. "I mean, you've done what you could do, right?"

"I guess." A moment later, she ducks out the door for another riding lesson—which might actually halt. I mean, if there's no cattle drive, there's no desperate urgency to learn how to ride and rope, either, and Emery will lay off about it. Hallelujah.

I've walked all the way to the 'office' on the hill, and I'm filing a complaint with the US Postal service for the lost package when Ethan comes pounding toward me on his big brown horse. "Aunt Mandy!"

In forty years, I doubt I've ever stood up quite so fast, and Roscoe flings himself in front of me, his fur on end, growling. "Ethan, watch out."

But his horse slides to a stop just in time, grass and dirt flying, a half dozen yards in front of me and the dog. "You talked to Dr. Dutton, right?"

"What?" Where did that come from?

"In the middle of our lesson, Mr. Archer asked Mom why she was upset. I didn't even know she *was* upset. That guy's smart. But she said that the Forestry Service didn't approve a renewal of our permit, because we didn't file the right forms, or rather, Uncle Jed didn't."

"Okay."

"Mr. Steve said it's too bad we don't know Eddy, because the only person Ranger Dutton listens to is his son."

"Are you saying the park ranger in charge of the permits is Eddy-the-vet's dad?"

Ethan nods. "You seemed to have a nice chat with him the other day. Could you possibly ask him for a favor?"

The guy who flirted outrageously, but never called me? The guy with the prettiest face I've ever seen? The guy whom my followers are still asking about? Yes, why don't I just call him up and ask him for a favor?

I'd rather *eat* my lost boots than beg him for a favor. "Ethan, the thing is—"

"Please, Aunt Mandy?" He may be seventeen, but Ethan's still got the little boy puppy dog eyes down pat.

I open my mouth to shut him down, but instead, for some reason, I say, "I'll call, but I can't promise you that it'll help."

Ethan closes his eyes and mutters, "Yes." For once, I feel like a rock star. It's nice to be the one people are grateful for, the one that people are excited to have on their side.

"Don't get your hopes up. I gave him my number," I say. "But he never called."

"Are you sure he didn't call?" Ethan asks. "I mean, more often than not, we have no reception."

Why didn't *I* think of that? "You're brilliant, young man. Now go, and let me call the guy."

"Remind him that Jed died and that we *just* got here." He makes prayer hands, but that jostles his horse, who tosses his head and starts to trot toward me. Ethan swings him around and they take off.

My hands feel jittery as I search for a listing for a vet in Manila. Only one pops up. Edward Dutton. Before I have time to think it through, I hit talk.

"Dr. Dutton's office," a woman says.

"Oh." I clear my throat. I'm not sure why I didn't expect a woman. "Uh, is Dr. Dutton there? I was hoping to talk to him. About calf stuff."

"Calf stuff?" I hate the sound of suppressed laughter in her tone.

"Well, I have some cows, and I have some questions about the cows."

"Cows?" she asks. "Or calves?"

"Is he there?"

She laughs. "Here he is."

Was he listening that whole time, while she mocked a paying customer?

His tone is light and happy when he answers, which makes me think he was. "Hello, this is Eddy."

"Dr. Dutton," I say. That's as far as I get. I can't think what else to say. I want to ask why he didn't call. I want to ask if he did call, but he only ever got my voicemail, and if that's the case, why didn't he leave me a message? Instead, I sit here stupidly, thinking of his grin.

"Are you there?" His voice is smooth, like a whipped coffee.

"Sorry," I say. "I know you're busy."

"Is this Amanda?"

My heart stops dead in my chest.

"Amanda Brooks?"

"Uh, yes," I say. "That's me."

His voice is bemused. "You have a cow question for me?"

"More of a calf one," I joke. If they're laughing at you already, you may as well show them it doesn't bother you.

"Then shoot."

I think that means to tell him, not that he think something's gone wrong. "I bet you remember that Jed died not that long ago."

"Yes, I hadn't forgotten that."

I'm not sure I can do this over the phone. Asking a favor's kind of an art, and it's not something you just call and blob out, especially with someone you barely know.

Someone who didn't call when they said they would.

"I tried to call you, you know."

Can he read my mind? "Sure you did," I say.

"No, really. I even tried the home line for Jed's house a few times, but once it rang and rang, and once a little kid picked up. No matter how many times I asked him to get Amanda, he just made farting noises."

I can guess which kid that was. Maren may not be doing very well, but she's not a maker of crude sounds. Gabe, on the other hand, is at the age where he thinks anything related to poop is uproariously funny. "I'm sorry about that, but why didn't you call my cell?"

"You didn't give me your number."

I thought he was smarter than that. "I saved it under —" Saying *You Wish* sounds so conceited. "Under another name."

"You told me, that but I couldn't find it anywhere."

"It was under *You Wish*," I finally say. "I guess it wasn't worth the effort of wading through the 9,657 other girls' numbers to find the one that wasn't a real name." I'm trying to turn it into a joke, but it actually makes me sad he didn't search diligently enough.

"You're on speaker phone now, and I think my sister Krystal can back me up here. There's no number saved for anyone named *You Wish*."

"There really isn't anything there," Krystal says. "Is there any chance that you somehow didn't save it?"

That's when it hits me. "He had an incoming call—Claire someone—when I hit save. Maybe it didn't go through as a result."

"You're saying I searched through his phone three times for no reason? Amanda, I had to wash my hands in industrial strength bleach and spray my eyes with Windex after being in such close proximity to his high-tech little black book." She squawks. "Ow."

I hear Eddy mutter, "I said back me up, not stab me in the back."

They're kind of funny. It makes me wish I was close to one of my brothers. "Well, I'm not saying that I believe you—"

"How about you grab coffee with him right now," Krystal says. "I mean, it's not like he has anything else going on." There's some kind of scuffle, and she mutters again. "Hey, I'm helping you, loser."

"Sorry about that," he says, his voice clearly coming directly from the microphone—no more speakerphone reverb. "Sometimes I trust my family a little too much, apparently. She's kidding, of course."

I'm not sure what to say.

"Unless you wanted to get coffee. Then she was serious."

"About you calling? Or about you having nothing to do?"

"Most of today was blocked off for reviewing files, but I'd rather eat my own toenails."

I snort, and then cover my mouth with my hand. What is happening to me? I haven't snorted since I was a teenager.

"Amanda?"

"I'm still here. Sorry, we have awful reception out here." Yes, blame the cell company, good one Mandy. I clear my throat. "Actually, coffee sounds nice."

"Does it?"

"Mhmm."

"Hey, that's great. The thing is, Manila's so small that there aren't dedicated coffee shops. But, I can pick you up and bring you some coffee. I have a great blend—"

"I'll come to you," I say.

"Are you sure?"

"I'm sure."

From the outside, his vet clinic looks nicer than I expected for a town of this size. I suppose that when most people are ranchers or living on property, there's plenty of work for a vet year round. It's a newish, large brick building, with a beautifully carved wooden sign that reads: Dutton Animals.

I've barely parked and opened my van door when Eddy shoots out the front of his building, two cups of coffee in his hands.

"Wow," he says. "Nice ride."

"You didn't notice this baby last time?" I wiggle my eyebrows. "It's pretty impressive. If things get rough, it's good to know I could take side jobs kidnapping small children."

"Nah," he says. "Your van has windows."

"Well dang. This was all the rental agency had—no windowless ones at all." I grimace. "I tried telling them that I have two kids, not twenty."

He laughs. "It takes a pretty confident woman to make a full-size van look good, but you manage it fairly well." He hands me a cup.

"How did you know I was craving. . ." I sniff the coffee. "Flat black coffee?"

"O ye of little faith." He sets his cup on my hood and whips a handful of things out of his pocket. "Sugar, creamer, and for the grand finale." He tosses some pocket lint on the ground and brandishes a piece of striped hard candy. "Peppermint, to offer the taste of Christmas all year round."

He's ridiculous. "One creamer and three sugars."

"She likes it sweet, folks."

"I hate to tell you this because you seem like the kind of guy who likes an audience," I whisper, "but there's no one else here."

"Downtown Manila on a Monday." He half bows. "Very impressive, I know."

"Hey Eddy," an older woman with grey hair hollers from across the street. "Keep it down."

He laughs, and I join him.

"Do you want to go for a walk?" he asks. "Or sit and whisper in the car?"

"Who's that?" I ask.

"That's Dolores Jenkins. She has a huge flower garden, and she insists that her plants hate the sound of my voice. If I speak louder than a murmur outside of my office, she becomes. . .agitated."

"You're kidding."

He shakes his head solemnly.

"Walk?"

"Right answer." He helps me dump my sugars in and stir them, picks up his coffee, and takes my arm.

"You take yours black?"

He shrugs. "I'm lazy and not very organized. I kind of got used to it by default."

I shouldn't care, but for some reason, drinking his coffee black makes him seem even more manly. Stupid, I know. "So where are we walking?" I'm speaking at barely above a whisper.

"You don't have to keep your voice low," he says.

"But you still are," I point out.

"Apparently it's only my 'strident tone' that agitates her John Cabot roses. You could probably screech like a banshee and she wouldn't mind."

"Terribly grating voice." I pretend to write a note on something. "I'll have to remember that." I scribble again. "Kills plants."

He bumps me with his hip.

"Whoa," I say. "Don't make me spill. This town may have a vet, but the closest human doctor is forty-five miles away, apparently."

"Nah, Steve's right around the corner."

I stop walking. "So you knew he was a doctor?"

Eddy frowns. "Everyone knows that. They call him the Horse Doc, as in, even though he's a doc, he still loves horses more."

"Yes, that was very clear from the name." I roll my eyes.

"I guess I didn't think much about it—I'll strive to be more clear. I'm a vet, which is short for veterinarian. That's like a doctor, but for animals."

"And you're also the local comedian, I take it."

"Sadly, most people don't find me very funny."

"Do you tell them you'll call and then *not*?" I arch one eyebrow.

He slows down. "I did call."

"You know what I mean." I sigh. "But I actually had an ulterior motive in calling you today. Normally I wouldn't have dreamed of calling some guy who didn't call me."

"An ulterior motive?" His eyes look almost hurt.

"My nephew begged me," I say, and this time I'm speaking softly because it's hard to admit.

"I'm glad he did."

"Here's the thing," I say. "We got a letter, almost ten days ago, but we're just now checking the mail. It hadn't really occurred to us that we were in charge of that sort of thing."

"Okay."

"It looks like a computer-generated notice, but it basically said that our permit was canceled, and now we can't send any cows up to the Forest Service land."

"And good old doctor Steve told you to ask for my help." Eddy frowns. "I don't know whether to punch him or thank him."

"Why would you thank him?"

"Isn't that obvious?" He locks eyes with me and I

forget my own name. "But I hate when people use me to get to my dad."

"It's strange that you say 'people,' as in, this has happened before. Lots of people have used you to get to your dad, the park ranger?"

"It's a cow town," he says. "I remember the very first time it happened. I was sitting in the cafeteria in third grade, eating a very dry, very gross peanut butter sandwich my mom had made, and a kid showed up with a cup of noodles, piping hot. It smelled so good."

"You're kidding."

He shakes his head. "His parents had clearly made it and rushed it to the school. The kid, someone I'd known for my entire life, handed it to me, and then he asked me if I would talk to my dad about increasing their permitted numbers by twenty."

"Did you?"

Eddy grimaces. "I'm an idiot who was paid with a contraband cup of noodles, so of course I did."

"It didn't work?"

He shakes his head. "I got a whipping for it, but otherwise, no."

I'm not loving his dad. "Really?"

"Dad's a real stickler."

"But in this case, the person who should have applied *died*, and we weren't even here yet. That letter was postmarked the day before Abigail even arrived. Surely there's some kind of exception for, I don't know? Death and clerical errors or something." I narrow my eyes. "And in case I haven't yet mentioned this, I make a mean cup of noodles."

He shakes his head. "Alright. I'll ask."

"You will?" Something occurs to me. "But you said the last time you tried to help, you got a whipping and they didn't get the approval."

"Oh, that was the first time, not the last time. I'm quite a bit smarter about it now. I never tell my dad I got paid to ask." He winks, and then he pulls out his phone.

"Whoa, are you going to call him right now?"

He tilts his head. "Did you want me to call him, say, in a month? Or perhaps a year?"

"Don't you think this might be better done in person?"

"Well." He leans in closer and presses a finger to my nose. "When you're as beautiful as you, yes. But when you're a son asking his dad for a favor? The phone is just as good. Maybe even better, as long as the dad doesn't hear the voice of, say, a gorgeous woman prompting him. I'd hate for him to know there's something far better than a cup of noodles involved."

I swat his arm as he presses talk. At first he wanders away—a dozen yards or so. He's kicking anthills while talking, and it's so cute that I can't help snapping a few photos. I'm shocked that there's actually reception here, so I edit one and upload it.

'Still a kid at heart,' is my caption. I tag it with #KickingAntHills #GiddyUp #AlwaysABoyInside #SweetCowboy #StirringUpTrouble and #MyHotCowboy. With his phone obscuring his face, you can't see anything clearly but his hair: a little tousled, a little overgrown, and perfectly shiny in the morning sun.

"Okay." He slides his phone into his pocket. "Do you want the good news or the bad news?"

"What does that mean?"

He smacks his forehead. "I almost forgot the subject of payment," he says. "I can't possibly tell you how it went until we've worked that out. You might stiff me."

"Payment?"

"Obviously my fee has gone up since the cup of

noodles incident, and I want more than a walking coffee date." He grins.

Oh.

"I was thinking two dinners and a hike."

"A hike?"

"You drive a hard bargain, Mrs. Brooks." He shoves his hands in his pockets. "I would be willing to nix the hike."

"What if you're awful and I hate you?" I shake my head. "One dinner."

"Done."

"That was fast," I say.

"You got taken." He bites his lip. "I'd have settled for just this walking coffee date."

I roll my eyes. "Just tell me what he said." I'm surprised by how badly I want to be the hero back home.

"The good news is that he's going to renew the permit."

I whoop a few times before I realize we aren't *that* far from the scowling gardener.

"The bad news is that it had nothing to do with my call."

"Nothing? Really? Why did he renew it, then?"

"Apparently some horrifyingly scary woman called and cited a dozen regulations and then sent a follow-up email that included an applicable exception to the rule, and the penalties for not granting a renewal after the death of a permit holder."

Abigail.

Of course.

It's always Abigail who does everything.

"I'm not obligated—"

"Ah, ah, ah," he says. "Not how it works. A cup of noodles was offered, a cup of noodles will be paid."

I huff. "I'm not sure—"

He sidles closer, and my heart races. “Now, Miss Amanda, I’d hate to think you weren’t a lady of your word.”

I back up a step, but he keeps coming, his scuffed boots grinding against the gravel.

“My father was called, and I groveled, just as I said I would. You even got what you wanted. The fact that it wasn’t because of me—”

I’ve bumped into a large tree, and I can’t really get around it—there’s an entire forest of pine trees behind me. I hold out my hand to keep him from running right into me, and as he moves toward me, my palm flattens against his chest.

And his clearly defined, rather large pecs.

Really nice muscles on a man may be my biggest turn on. “Well.”

His bright green eyes never leave mine. “You’re not backing out, are you?”

I swallow. “I suppose not.”

He exhales gustily. “Oh, good.”

“But I do have one question.”

“Shoot.”

“With all that talk earlier, I just want to be sure.”

He lifts his eyebrows.

“We’re not actually having instant noodles for dinner, right?”

His laughter is one of the most beautiful sounds I’ve ever heard.

15
ABIGAIL

I survived five terribly awkward horseback lessons with Steve, including one where he showed me how to toss a rope. I insisted I didn't need to know—Jeff and Kevin would be there—but if the kids were learning, he said I should learn too.

With his arms around me, it was really hard to remember that I didn't want him to show me around Manila.

But as soon as he left, my resolve strengthened. Being shown around by a ridiculously attractive, age appropriate, exceptionally skilled horse whisperer would have been exciting.

Having a man who's an expert at managing dangerous situations, a man who's used to getting everything he wants, a man who's probably the most eligible bachelor in three counties show me around?

Hard pass.

It's everything I can't handle, and everything I don't want. It's too much, and the risk of injury is far too high. Every time I forget, I see Whitney's cast and I remember. When you do something risky, you can get hurt. Badly.

I've already endured about all the hurt I can handle this decade.

"You ready, Mom?" Ethan's been up for half an hour—I heard him rummaging around. That's the curse of living here. I hear every little noise that any of my children make, including Gabe complaining that Ethan's too loud and it's too early.

Of course, in the months after Nate died, I would wake up most nights because of a nightmare that one of the kids was dead. Our house is so large and spacious that my children feel far away. So it's been a blessing too, this close-quarters living.

Most things in life are like that: the things I love are also the things that make me bonkers.

The one good thing that has come from Nate's passing is that I have a little more patience for the things that make me insane, because I have a greater appreciation for my blessings now that one is gone.

"Mom?" Ethan's voice outside my door is both eager and nervous.

"I'm ready," I say.

When he pushes the door open, he has his hands over his eyes, but one finger is cracked so he can kind of see.

"If I was naked, how would that help?"

"Shut up." He tosses something fairly large at me, but I dodge and it lands on my bed.

"What's that?"

"I made a little pack for everyone." He shrugs. "Gatorade, water, jerky, granola bars, and nuts."

"Look at you, Martha Stewart."

"You think Whitney and Gabe will be fine?"

I sigh. "Amanda will be—"

"You think she's going to pay attention to them?"

"I think she will, yes," I say. "And Maren has been different this week."

"I hadn't noticed." Ethan's eyes harden, and his tone darkens.

"She's been trying," I say. "Ever since Whitney's arm—"

"Great," he says. "Well, I'll be sure to remember that when I want to punch her in the nose the very next time we talk."

I roll my eyes. Ethan's always so melodramatic, but he rarely means what he says. It's almost all talk, like the tiny dog that barks incessantly, or the cat that hisses but curls up at your side the second you sit down. "Is Izzy ready?"

"She's already in the barn, feeding the horses."

"Isn't it early for that?"

"Feeding," he says. "Not grooming or tacking up."

"I'll be out soon."

"Are you nervous?"

"Of course I am," I say. "There are mountain lions, and holes, and bugs."

Ethan's dimpled grin has made me smile since the day he was born, but it has so much of Nate in it that now I sometimes feel a bit desperate to see it. "You say those three things as though they're the same risk level."

"To me, maybe they are."

He's shaking his head as he walks out the door.

I don't believe in stupid things like personal affirmations or vision boards. That's the kind of hokum that people with no real plan cling to, but I have prepared to the best of my abilities, and a little prayer here or there can't hurt. So when I pray this morning, I ask God to send my love to Nate, as always, and then I ask him to keep me and my kids safe, and let us move the cows smoothly to the designated area on the map.

By the time I finally make my way outside, Ethan's snack bag slung over my shoulder, Ethan and Izzy *are* already grooming their horses, and Snoopy's already in the cross ties. It's early and I'm still a little loopy, but it looks like Kevin's currying him for me.

Until Kevin turns around, and I realize it's not him. It's Steve.

"Oh." I freeze.

"Morning." He says it casually, like he's supposed to be here.

"I didn't know—why are you here?"

"That's rude, Mom. He's been over here every day, helping us for two weeks." Ethan shakes his head. "Some people's mothers never taught them any manners. Geez."

"Teenagers are the worst," Izzy says. "Leave the adults alone."

"It's a good thing I have two moms." Ethan ducks into the tack room to grab his saddle.

Steve walks toward me. His voice is low, probably in the hopes that both kids won't keep jumping into the conversation. I can relate to that sentiment. "Is it okay that I'm here?"

"I didn't think you'd be here, since Whitney—"

He brushes my hair back and tucks it behind my ear. "She's not my only student."

It feels like my ear is burning where his finger brushed it. "No, I guess not."

When his eyes meet mine, they look lighter than usual, almost a sky blue. "If you want me to leave, I will."

I should tell him to go. "I've taken up too much of your time already."

"You didn't come to my porch at all this week."

"I didn't have any document review to do, so it was easier to just boost the reception from my phone at the 'office.'"

"You hiked out to that hill to avoid me."

"I saw you every day."

He steps closer still. "With a three-child buffer."

When I inhale, his sweet, fresh-smelling cologne fills my nose. My heart flips. "There are two kids with us right now."

"I want to spend the day with you." He reaches for me, but at the last minute, his hand pushes past me and drops the currycomb into the grooming box. He's slow at grabbing the brush. Too slow. It has to be intentional. "Excuse me."

"You're riding Snoopy?" I ask.

He shakes his head. "I figured you might not want to start the day covered with dust and dirt. Just trying to be neighborly."

Again, with the heart flip. "Thanks."

"It won't help for long. Drives are dusty."

"I bet they are."

He leans against the wall right next to me. "So do my good deeds buy me permission to come?"

"I'd be stupid to turn you down," I say.

His boots scuff the floor of the barn when he pivots, but he's not fast enough. I see his huge grin.

I should've said no. He's going to take my anxiety about our first cattle drive as encouragement, and my feelings haven't changed. I do like the idea of having him with us if anything goes wrong. I'll have to deal with the fallout later.

"If you keep helping with my saddle, I'll never get fast at doing it myself," I say.

He shrugs. "If you're only here through August, it won't matter."

"She may fall in love with the ranch life," Ethan says. "You never know. We could be here for the next fifty years."

I bite my tongue—I promised Ethan I would consider it, so I have to try to be open-minded.

The sun's peeking out over the horizon by the time we're all tacked and ready.

"You're lucky that Birch Creek is right at the bottom of Birch Creek Canyon," Steve says. "Most of the other ranchers using Forestry Service land have a much longer drive."

"And look—the cattle are raring to go," Kevin says.

I don't know much about cows, but he certainly seems right. The teeming mass of mooing, lowing cattle, all of them red or black, shift and stomp.

"At least they won't be banging on the fences anymore," Jeff says.

"What does that mean?" Ethan asks.

"This time of year, the cattle are ready to go up into the hills," Kevin says. "They test out the fencing anywhere they can to try and get through."

"Why don't we take them sooner?" I ask. "It's been summer for weeks."

"That's the Forestry Service's fault," Jeff says. "They only allow June 20 through September 20." His eyes brighten. "Hey, maybe you can take that up with them for us."

I laugh. "Yes, I'm sure they'd love to hear from me again."

"I loved hearing you go off on them," Jeff says. "I had no idea what you were talking about, but I've never heard of Ranger Dutton changing his mind so quick. There are some advantages to being a scary, big city lawyer."

"I'm hardly scary."

Kevin clears his throat, and Jeff snorts.

"Where are the bulls?" I scan the cattle, but don't see any with horns. "Do they go up later?"

"There's one." Steve points at a cow that's a little bigger than the others.

"And there's another." Jeff points at one that's pretty close. "They're out there. You really can't spot them?"

I can tell a slight difference, but. . . "None of them have horns."

Steve, Jeff, and Kevin share a look, and then all three of them start laughing.

"What's so funny?" Clearly I'm an idiot, but I'd like to know why.

"Angus are naturally polled," Steve says. "It means they're born without horns. It's one of the reasons Jed picked them. He hated removing horns in the spring."

"Removing the horns?" Izzy looks stricken.

"I know, it gets bad press," Jeff said, "but it's better all around to remove them if they have big horns. They can injure themselves and others, and if there's something dumb cattle can do—"

Kevin jumps in. "They'll do it."

"Alright," Jeff says. "The sun's nearly up, so let's review our jobs. It should be manageable, since we've got a dominant steer, Handsome Rob, there, as we call him. You can see that he's already waiting at the front of the herd. The others are used to following him, as we'd always shepherd him through first from one pasture to the next. Iz, you and Ethan will be my swing riders. You need to try and stay about a third of the way back. You should always be able to see me, and if you have questions, holler. I'll come see what you need."

Ethan and Izzy nod.

"Abigail and Steve—thanks for coming by the way—will be my flank riders, and you'll try and stay about two-thirds of the way back. Your job is to keep the cows together, and keep them moving. You won't be able to see me most of the time, but you'll see Kevin at the back, because he's won the big prize."

Steve laughs, and Kevin scowls.

"It's your turn," Jeff says. "I was the tail last year."

"The tail?" I ask.

"It gets pretty dusty by the end," Steve says. "It's not always a comfortable place to ride, and his job is to encourage the cattle who don't want to move any more. It's not bad at first, but it'll get progressively more exhausting."

"Now that the sun's up. . ." Jeff moves his horse, a big red gelding, toward the gate.

"Time to go." Kevin's riding a grey, and it takes off with the slightest nudge, shoving past a few cows to head for the back of the herd.

"You take things nice and slow, Miss Isabel," Steve says.

"I will." Her eyes are bright, her cheeks rosy. She's not often included in things like this, since she's only twelve. Actually, no one in my family is ever included in things like this. She's probably about as nervous as the rest of us.

"I hope she's ready."

Steve drops his voice. "There's a reason we tied the donkey to her."

"Wait, what reason?"

"She's on Maggie, and she's already a very steady, dependable mount. Her lessons have been on her for the past week, and they know each other. But Donk is slow and annoying, and having him trailing along should keep her from being one of the riders expected to deal with problems."

"It won't get in her way?"

Steve shrugs. "There are only three hundred and fifty cows. If we were trying to run five hundred, or even a thousand, we'd need more people, but often Jed only had four guys to move his herd."

"You've been on drives before?" I ask. "You don't have any cattle, so I wasn't sure."

"But I grew up here," he says, as if that explains everything.

"I hope you're not trying to redirect because you *haven't* been on one, and you're just acting like you know everything."

He rolls his eyes. "Woman, please."

"*Woman*?"

"Oh, I'm sorry. Are you actually a man?"

I sigh. "You're lucky we're riding horses right now."

"Would you punch me, if we weren't?"

"Probably," I say. "Or light you on fire."

"A violent woman." He grins. "I like my mares fiery. Did I mention that?"

Before I can say anything else, he kicks his horse, whose name I don't even know, and takes off. The cows are spreading ahead of me on one side, but Ethan handles it pretty well. I'm glad I'm not the person stuck in the dust cloud at the back—although when I turn around it doesn't look that bad. There's plenty of grass here, so not much dirt to fly up. And the cows presumably don't *want* to be left. Hopefully Kevin won't really have a terrible time of it.

The first time I try to herd cows back into the main group, they break off further and start running the wrong way. I swear under my breath and spin poor Snoopy around. Before I can get Snoopy cantering after them, Steve's already there, hollering and redirecting the recalcitrant bunch back toward the main group. I watch Izzy and Ethan, noticing what works and what doesn't, and I improve.

I don't approach them wrong or head-on again, and my job gets easier. Having Steve help is kind of like having two extra guys. He never seems tired, and he rides effortlessly. I watched him in the ER not long ago, and he looked capable, confident, and at ease. I thought then that I'd likely seen him doing the thing he was best at.

But watching him ride is different.

His mare, which I discovered is named Farrah, moves like an extension of his body. He doesn't bounce, or shake, and he hardly even moves his hands. She transitions from a slow and easy walk to a dead sprint at a simple kissing noise. He's probably shifting his body, too, but I can't see it. I honestly can't understand how his upper body stays so still, even when she runs.

Meanwhile, I'm doing my best impression of a sack of potatoes bouncing around atop poor Snoopy.

The next few hours aren't too bad—Jeff and Kevin know where we're going, and the cows want to go there. But it gets hotter as the day goes on, and the cows lose a lot of their steam, especially the calves. Izzy and Ethan begin to flag, have one cola, and are off again, like wind-up toys that have been rewound. But as the calves slow, we have to work harder to keep them going, and that's rough because. . .

I'm running out of energy, too.

Steve notices, of course.

"You alright?"

"I think I've probably permanently bruised Snoopy's back."

"He'll be fine. He looks like he's having fun. You hardly weigh anything, so he pulled the long straw. But you're going to be sore tomorrow, I imagine."

I hardly weigh anything? I almost laugh at that absurd statement. I've never been one of those waify girls. "Oh, I'm sore already."

He laughs. "The good news is, we're almost there. Just one last hurdle to clear."

"Hurdle?" For some reason, his use of that word alarms me.

"The Forestry Service doesn't like having cows in the parks, near any roads, or around any major water sources."

"That's right." Kevin lopes up alongside us. "Our allotment has a specific area we're supposed to start the cows in."

"Are we close?"

"We are," Steve says. "But."

"But what?"

"We're nearly there," Kevin says. "I was coming up to tell you to keep them moving."

"Will do," Steve says.

Kevin's already headed back, and I notice that Jeff's talking to Ethan and Izzy.

"Should I be worried?"

"Not at all," Steve says. "This is the fun part."

"What *is* this part?"

"We're almost to the first open meadow that will likely be fully grassed."

"Isn't that good news?"

"They won't want to move past it," he says. "So we need to keep them moving. If they stop and start grazing, it could take us hours to get them to move along."

Ah.

"Prepare to hoot, holler, and run, if necessary." He doesn't look like he's warning me—he looks like a little boy on Christmas Eve.

"You really do like this part."

"It's the whole reason I came." His eyes light up, and I wonder whether that's true. Did he really come along to spend time with me? Or to race around on Farrah in the open wilderness, shouting and being rowdy?

I'm a little nervous that Ethan, Izzy, and I won't be up to the task. What if we let them stop, and then we're stuck here all day with no recourse? Jeff and Kevin both pull whips off their belts.

"Do we need those?"

Steve shakes his head. "No, you'll be fine."

"Okay."

He stops then, his face turning toward mine. "Abigail."

"What?" I meet his eyes.

"Are you alright?"

I must take too long to respond.

"Don't worry—this part will be fine. For all your jokes about Snoopy's back, you've been moving really well. You look like a natural out there."

Uh-huh.

Farrah sidesteps closer, so he's almost right next to me. Snoopy, good man that he is, doesn't even stomp or whuffle at her invading his space. Steve lowers his voice. "Whitney probably would've been fine, but I wasn't 100% positive, so I held her back. I *was* entirely sure that you and Ethan and Izzy would be fine, so trust my judgement. When we're past the meadow and on our way to the first spot on that map, you'll be invigorated. You'll say, 'Steve, you were right. You're a brilliant man and a stand-up horse trainer.'"

"I already know that," I say. "Anyone with eyeballs can see it."

"Well, I have a critical horseman's eye, and I'm telling you not to worry. You'll do great."

I nod.

It's a good thing his pep talk's over, because Jeff cracks his whip and the cattle pick up the pace a bit. Once we round the bend, I see what they mean. A long, wide, beautiful meadow with a lovely sprinkling of wildflowers covering it stretches out in front of us.

"We're going to spread," Steve says. "I'll circle to the far side, and you stay here. If I shout 'now,' I want you to move toward me, shouting as loud as you can. It's a wedge movement and it'll get them moving straight ahead. Got it?"

"Yeah."

"And hey, Snoopy has done this dozens of times. If you're not sure what to do, loosen the reins a bit and he'll go after them. He's got amazing cow sense."

It's a good thing one of us does.

Handsome Rob definitely picks up the pace at first, but once he hits the flat, broad meadow, he frolics a bit and his head goes down.

He's eating.

But Jeff's all over that, moving him along quickly, before he gets more than one mouthful. The other cows all try to follow his lead, but Ethan shouts and Izzy shrieks. When a large black cow tries to duck around the back of Izzy, Donk kicks at her. The cow's so shocked that she pivots too fast and knocks right into the side of another one, sending them both careening forward. They look a little like bumper cars.

When our part of the herd reaches the meadow, I can't watch Izzy and Ethan anymore, but I'm not worried. Steve's right. None of us can rope very well, but we're pretty good at shouting and racing around until the cows change direction. And Snoopy does the hard part himself. There's a definite benefit to having horses that already know what to do.

Since Jeff and Ethan and Izzy have done such a good job, our cows keep moving, generally speaking, which is great. But a group of six breaks hard toward Steve and he's busy circling around them and driving them back when a big bull decides he wants some of the purple flowers. He pushes past two cows and darts through a gap, running in front of me.

I peel off, Snoopy moving more quickly than he has before, loping fast on the even, grassy ground to cut the bull off. He snorts, and he paws at the ground, and for a moment I wonder if he'll charge me. But instead he merely drops his head and starts munching.

Which is exactly what I can't have him doing.

A few other cows have already started to turn our direction. I can't let the only real issue we've had be my fault, but even when I turn Snoopy right at him and shout, he ignores me. Do I ram him? I don't have a whip.

Then I have an idea. When my kids wouldn't look at the camera, I'd make a really strange sound, an off-putting sound. Every human in the room would always whip their head right toward me when I made it—it always grabbed attention quick. That was, after all, the point. I have no idea how he'll react, but I swing Snoopy around again and I race at that dumb bull, and as we draw near, I make the chirping, dolphin sound at the loudest volume I've ever used.

The bull jumps, all four hooves going outward as he drops a few inches. His eyes practically roll back in his head, and I swear, he leaps almost 180 degrees and bolts back for the herd, the dumb cows that were following him circling around to get into line as well.

"What in the world was that noise?" Steve asks.

"I have a few tricks up my sleeve," I say. "And don't you forget it." I urge Snoopy forward and leave Steve behind for once.

My arms are a little shaky and my butt is definitely bruised by the time we make it through the meadow, but it was fun. At least, it's fun in retrospect, now that we're walking and all the cows are past. Steve ambles poor, sweaty Farrah over to me with a bemused look on his face.

"You'll have to teach it to me later," Steve says.

"I don't think it can be taught," I say. "It's an innate skill. You either have it or you don't."

He tries, but it's awful. "That sounds like the warbling of a seagull in pain." I laugh. "I'm afraid you don't got it, Steve."

"How do you know it can't be taught? I have faith in you."

"You shouldn't. You don't know me at all."

"I feel like I know you pretty well."

"Oh you do?" This should be good. "Why don't you tell me what you know?"

He cocks one eyebrow. "Are you sure you want that? I'm a great judge of people."

"Is that from taking care of so many patients in the ER?"

"Nah, it's because of the horses. They don't lie, and they never dissemble. It makes it easier to see the false things—the lies humans tell themselves."

I hardly think that being around horses makes someone more intuitive with people, but I don't bother arguing.

"Right now, for instance, you're thinking I'm an idiot. How could spending all day with four-hooved creatures possibly give me insight into the human heart?"

How did he do that?

"Alright, alright, my first party trick is done. Pick your jaw back up, and tell me if you really want to hear what I've learned about you."

How can I say no now? I'd look like a coward. But I am a little afraid. "Once, I had a guy draw a caricature of me—it was in eighth grade, I think."

"Yeah?"

I nod. "I had these glasses that I thought looked pretty nice. In my defense, my prior pair had been hugely round, made from pink plastic, and the side bars attached down at the bottom, like a librarian."

"I would pay good money to see a photo of those."

"I'm pretty sure I've destroyed every photo my mother ever took. I still blame her for being stuck with those—she should have stopped me from picking them."

"But the caricature?"

"Right. So, I was delighted when the caricature artist who visited our class chose me to draw as a demonstration. I thought it was quite the honor, but I think he chose me because he knew that it would be easy to make mine funny." I forgot how upsetting it was at the time. "He drew me with huge, face-eating glasses, fluffy, puffy hair, and a lopsided smile full of brackets and wires."

"Your smile is perfectly symmetrical," he says.

"Maybe so, but no one noticed the shape—the braces were all they saw. And I realized then that our own image of ourselves is rarely very honest."

"Is that your way of saying you don't want to hear what I think?"

"Maybe, because it was painful. But that caricature helped me to see what others saw, which was helpful too. I got my braces off quickly thereafter, and I begged my mom for contacts. The puffy hair took a little longer to tame, but eventually I got that under control as well."

"And you blended in with the rest of the sheep?"

I bleat.

He laughs.

"I've never been very good at blending in," I say. "But I didn't stand out quite so much."

"Well, if you don't care what I think, that's fine."

Now I have to know. "Just tell me."

"You face things head on, but you always arm yourself to deal with them. When you talked to me about the Forestry Service letter, you weren't crying, and you weren't upset. You'd already checked out the webpage and you were asking my advice as a courtesy."

"It ended up helping," I say. "I think Amanda, surprisingly, came through as well."

"But you're the one who scared poor Ranger Dutton into doing the right thing."

"I suppose."

"I can't speak to what you were like in grade school or high school, but now you're independent, you take action competently and forcefully, and you're fierce."

This isn't nearly as bad as I thought it would be.

"But as with most things, our best traits are also our worst."

There it is. The sting in the tail.

"You can't ask for help—you insist on paying or otherwise dislodging guilt from any favors you receive. It's probably to make sure you're never justly asked to do anything for anyone else. It makes sense—you have to safeguard your time as there's not much to go around. You only acknowledge a weakness or flaw so that you can tighten up your armor, not because you're okay with not being the best at every single thing."

"I know I'm not—"

"And you talk more than anyone I've ever met. You have something to say about everything under the sun, most of it well-crafted and sound."

That didn't sound mean.

"It makes it almost impossible to know when you're out of your depth. You sound equally expert in all instances."

"I sound like a real pain."

"You parent your children like you approach life. You're everything to them, and you beat yourself up for any misstep, no matter how slight."

I can't help my frown.

"But it makes you an excellent mother, and your children are some of the most balanced, empathetic, and bright that I've ever met."

It's almost harder accepting the compliments than the criticisms. "Well—"

"I'm not quite done."

"No?"

He stops Farrah, and Snoopy stops, too.

"It nearly broke you when your husband died. You clearly loved him a great deal."

His words are a slap in the face.

"You're probably not ready to date anyone. I'd be shocked if you were—that kind of love is hard to follow."

My hands tighten on the reins.

"But you'll never actually be ready to move on. It's not in your nature. You loved him like you love your children, absolutely and completely."

"Then why—"

As if she can sense his desires, Farrah shuffles forward until he's within a foot of me. "But you need to do it anyway. Someone like you can't hide. Someone like you needs to live fully. You were ready to let me take you out. . .when you thought I was a loser."

"I don't think horse trainers are losers," I protest.

He grins. "What about drunken horse trainers who barely function?"

He's got me there.

"You thought I was a drunken horse trainer with a rocking bod, but still a mess."

Wait, did he know it was me, that day he was mowing? "You never mentioned that you even saw me."

"There's exactly one navy blue minivan in Manila," Steve says. "But once you found out I was a doctor, and that I wasn't a drunk, you suddenly clammed up. You shut me out, and I think it's because I became higher risk. If

I'm a viable option, I'll never get the green light. Dating me is too dangerous."

"It's not—"

"I bet there's even someone back home, someone suitable, and part of the reason you came here, to a place you didn't want to be, was to get away from a guy who wanted to take you out." He shrugs. "He would have been a real option too, and that's not okay, not for Abby Brooks. It could wreck her life, and her vision of herself, to love someone else after losing her perfect husband."

"You think you know everything," I say. "But you have no idea."

"Alright, then if I'm wrong, let me take you out."

I kick Snoopy and he takes off, which would have been a lot more impactful if we hadn't just reached the end of the line.

At least I'm not worried about being sore on the long ride back—I'm too busy making sure I'm never alone with Steve again. I wish it wasn't totally obvious what I was doing, but his knowing smile haunts me the whole way home.

16

AMANDA

"You'll turn off the water? Because it's supposed to rain. We don't want to use up our allotment if we don't need it, and without Jeff or Kevin here, I'm worried things will slip through the cracks." Abby's going to get wrinkles if she doesn't calm down.

"I said I'd close it off, Mom. I don't need them to handle the water. I did all this even when they were here, remember?"

"And you fed the horses?" Abby asks.

"I did," Izzy says. "And I scooped the stalls before putting them out."

"Before you ask, I refilled the chicken food and water," Whitney says.

Gabe extends two energetic thumbs up. "And I fed the goats and gave them water."

We're the loafs, I suppose. We've done nothing but make cookies and brownies, watch movies, play games, and wander around watching the animals. And I did go up and visit Ms. Saddler—twice. She loves brownies, like *loves* loves them. I've never had someone squeal quite that much.

"I unloaded the dishwasher," Maren says.

Everyone turns her way. That's probably the first chore she's done since we arrived. "Nice work."

"I'll load it today, too. I think maybe from now on, I should do the dishes."

See? Abby thought I needed to talk to her, but I knew that when Whitney got hurt, she'd realize she had gone too far. Maren's always been like that. She self adjusts. If I'd sat down and tried to tell her what to do, she'd just have gotten mad and things would have been worse all around.

"I can make dinner," Emery says. "Izzy showed me how to make that thing from last week."

"Chicken crescent rolls," Izzy says. "Yeah, she helped me make them. Mom, do we have the stuff?"

"I think so." Abby opens the fridge and then bobs her head. "I've got to run—meeting in twenty minutes—but I'll be back later to help with—"

"Mom," Ethan says, "we know. It's fine."

"It's alright for me to be stressed," she says. "You can't even call me with problems unless you run to the hill first."

"I'm here," I say. "If there's a problem, yo, I'll fix it."

Abby stares at me blankly.

"From that song," I say. "Check out the mike, while the DJ performs it."

"Um, that is not how it goes," Ethan says. "It's actually—"

"I have to go." Abby looks at me. "Thank you."

I haven't done anything yet, but it's nice to be recognized. I have been the one adult who has been home this whole time. Her kids hardly ever need anything, but that's not the point.

"Are you going to be at the 'office'?"

Abby cringes. "Ideally I would be—I like the open

air." She's still pretending that she's not avoiding Steve. "But with the rain. . ."

So she'll be at Steve's, I presume. He must be working or she'd be freaking out way more.

"Internet comes in Friday," I say.

A round of cheers from the kids reminds me that we've all been counting down the days. Although, one part of me is a little sad. My job is a constant ding and ding and ding, usually, but for once, I've been pretty free. I've read books—trying to catch up to Maren on the series my friend recommended so we can talk about it. It's better than I expected. I've played games with the kids. I've made so many cookies that we've taken to freezing them so they're ready whenever anyone has a craving. The lack of easy takeout or delivery options has made that a necessity.

"Maybe we should go to Green River today," I say.

As if my words prompted the storm, thunder peals and lightning crackles. And the rain starts to pour.

Ethan groans, but he heads outside. Can't leave the meter running—this whole ranch thing is an even bigger headache than I'd guessed it would be. On our second game of Clue, Emery finally screws up the nerve to ask me what she's been angling toward since yesterday.

"So, Mom. I've given this a lot of thought." I can tell she has. "And I really do think you should let me take horseback riding lessons."

I frown. "I thought the lessons were over. They did the cattle drive."

"We have to go up into the hills two or three times a week to check the calves," Izzy says. "And we'll have to take more salt."

"And they have to make sure they're in the right place," Gabe says. "Kevin says they roam sometimes."

"How fun," I say. "But I think you're too young—"

"I'm twelve, and Izzy's twelve." She folds her arms.

Which just makes me think about those tiny, bony arms, broken and bent after a wild horse bucks her off. "Izzy has been riding for years."

"Whitney's ten." She presses her lips together. "And she's going to go as soon as she gets her cast off."

"Maybe before," Whitney helpfully adds. "Mr. Steve says that once it's had a week or two to heal, the bones will be set and with the cast to protect me, it's probably fine."

"You know," Maren says. "That guy gets money going and coming."

"How so?" I ask.

"Well, he gets paid to teach people to ride, and when the horse throws them off and they break their leg, they have to pay him to fix it."

I laugh.

"That's not how I broke my bone," Whitney says. "It had nothing to do with a horse." She glares at Maren, who falls entirely silent.

More thunder booms outside.

"So, how about it?" I've successfully put her off a few times, now, but it feels like this time, Emery's not going to let it go.

"Mr. Steve's a great teacher," Whitney says. "For real."

"I'm not sure he'd have the room—"

"Mom's not taking lessons anymore," Izzy says. "I asked if he could teach Emery and he said that was up to you."

We're only going to be here another two weeks. What could a few lessons hurt? "Fine. Not more than twice a week."

"That's all we get now, anyway," Whitney says. "Woohoo!" The girls all hop up and dance around.

"Watch out," Maren says. "Don't look at my cards."

"Oh please," Izzy says. "Like I need to cheat to beat you."

But Maren actually wins the second round. She's been quieter and more reserved since Whitney's injury, and she needed the win. I can tell.

After lunch, the rain finally slacks off. That's when I begin to wonder where Ethan went. It shouldn't take him too long to close off the main water release. How long has he been gone?

As if my thoughts magicked him into being, he bursts through the door, sopping wet. "A tree fell down." He wheezes. "And it knocked the fence over. The horses are all loose. I tried to catch them, but I only got Snoopy and Captain. The others bolted in a big bunch. I put those two in the barn."

"Oh no," I say. "What do we do?"

He shakes his head. "I'm not sure."

"How far could they get?" I ask. "It's not like there's only one fence on the property.

"It was the back pasture," he says. "It backs to the Forestry land."

Izzy starts to cry.

"It's fine. It's going to be fine." I text Abby, but it doesn't go through. I try four more times.

"I don't have any service either."

"Maybe I should go to Steve's." I tap my lip.

"Yes," Ethan says. "He'll know just what to do."

"I bet he's working," I say. "Or your mom wouldn't—" The kids stare at me blankly. I don't want to explain what I'm saying, so I change tracks. "If he's gone, your mom will still have some ideas."

"She's got that deposition, though," Ethan says. "That's the appointment. We're not supposed to interrupt her unless—"

"But Maggie could be dying!" Izzy really is frantic.

"I'll go right now," I say. "If she can't come, well, we'll think of something else." It's barely raining anymore, so thankfully I don't get too wet on my way to the van. I'm just about to pull out onto the main road when a truck stops and turns on its flashers. The driver rolls down the passenger window.

I roll down my window too, but even so, I can barely hear Eddy. "Amanda?"

"Yeah."

"Are you alright?"

"I'm fine," I say. "But a tree knocked a fence down and the horses ran away."

"They'll probably find their way back," he says.

"The kids are freaking out." My voice feels hoarse from all the yelling. "I'm going to get Abby."

"Is she working?"

"Yeah."

He shuts off his blinkers and turns into the driveway, moving past me. He waves at me with his hand. What does he want me to do? Turn around?

He parks in between the two houses, in the place closest to the barn. It takes me some time in this beast, but I turn around and park next to him. By the time I open my door, he's standing right outside. "I can help."

His deep voice, his rain-soaked hair—it sends a shiver from my head down to my toes.

"Are you cold?"

"The rain," I say.

He wraps an arm around me. "I'm sure they didn't go far. It was probably a combination of the tree limb startling them and the thunder, but if the kids are nervous, we can ride out and check on them."

"We?"

He laughs. "I can ride out."

"I'll go with you," Ethan says from the porch.

Eddy drops his arm like I burned him. "Great." Then he frowns. "Do we have horses? Because the Polaris is going to be a disaster in all this mud."

"Yeah, I caught Snoopy and Captain."

"The paint, right?"

"That's Snoopy," Ethan says. "He's the one Mom usually rides."

"He'll be perfect for you."

"What about you?" I ask.

He shrugs. "I can ride anything."

How hot is that? I shiver again.

"You should go inside and dry off. I'd hate for you to get sick."

I run inside to grab a jacket to support my cover story, which feels dumb. It's like seventy degrees. But I can't just lounge around while they're riding off into the woods, so I jog out to the barn. They're still getting the saddles and stuff on, so I wasn't too late.

"Is there anything I can do?"

"I'm telling you, I know it's nerve-wracking, but it's not like they broke to the road. They're wandering around in the middle of nothing, and they'll be easy to find."

"Abby said we lose cows every year to mountain lions and bears."

Ethan frowns.

"That's why I grabbed this." Eddy pats a rifle strapped to his saddle. "But honestly, Amanda, don't worry. They usually stay somewhere dry for a while after a big storm."

His words make me feel better, but I'm still anxious as the two of them ride off, the mountains looming large behind them, the fallen tree marking the place where the fence is down. They're still close enough to make out their forms and a little of their faces. I whip out my phone and snap a few photos. In my favorite one, Ethan and Eddy are talking, and Eddy's clearly smiling. It's only a side profile, but I love it.

And the best part? The rain has stopped, and there's a rainbow behind them.

It doesn't even surprise me that I have a single bar of reception. I upload the photo real quick. "Downed fence let the horses out—but we'll catch them thanks to a little help." Then I tag it #MyHero #GiddyUp #HeroesRide-Horses #HotCowboy and #RideItLikeYouMeanIt.

This has certainly been a weird trip—entirely different than the last twenty years of my life, almost all spent in New York City, but there's more beauty than I expected, too. And it doesn't feel half as lonely as I thought. Partly because of Abby and her kids, who are always everywhere and who take up a lot of space. But also because of Eddy, who seems to show up just when I need him.

He may insist that he's not doing anything helpful. After all, Abby scared his dad into behaving. And he says the horses would come home on their own. Even so, having a vet who rides a horse as well as any trainer, willing to ride out with your nephew to make you rest easier, isn't too bad. Judging by the preliminary comments on my post, my followers agree.

Just marry him already and have gorgeous cowboy kids.

So frigging dreamy!

My ovaries just contracted.

I'm not sure ovaries can contract, and I want nothing to do with anything that makes my ovaries do *anything,* but I understand the sentiment. I take the rare opportunity, with decent reception, to answer a few emails. I'm just telling Tide that I'd be happy to do a repeat post about their new stain stick when my phone rings.

I'm completely surprised that my reception is *that* good.

"Hey Heather," I say.

"Girl." She whistles low and long. "Please tell me that's the vet."

"It is," I say.

"I swear he gets hotter with every photo you post."

"He's just a friend," I say.

"Then move over." She laughs. "I'm booking a flight."

"I'm not sure how long I'll have reception, so. . ."

"You don't have WiFi yet? Geez." She sighs. "Look, I wanted to tell you that my boss loves the new cowboy posts, like even more than I do. She likes the small-town life angle, the neighbor, and the way you finally seem connected to real people around you."

"That's great."

"She'd love a few more posts with people like that elderly neighbor. Quirky people whom you're obviously meeting and connecting with."

"I can do that," I say.

"And I think I speak for all women when I say, the more of that vet, the better."

I laugh. "Got it."

"And one last thing. We're going to be making final decisions about the contract at the very beginning of July, but if we choose you, my boss wants to make sure you'll stay put, at least for the rest of the summer. Is that a problem?"

I would have said that Maren would lose it and that I'd go crazy too. I would have refused if she'd asked me a week or two ago. But now, I keep thinking of Eddy putting his arm around me. Eddy riding off into the forest to help me.

No one has cared much about my life or my struggles in a really long time. I'm clearly not the kind of person who's destined to be with a vet in a town of four hundred, but it's fun to play pretend sometimes. I can allow myself a few more weeks. "Sure."

"Perfect."

I'm beginning to think that it kind of is.

17
ABIGAIL

I've been counting down the days to June 26 for a very long time. The closer it gets, the more I worry that it won't really happen. I never in my life felt like having internet was really a big blessing. . .until I didn't have it. If I were truly a rancher, or if I were a dance instructor, or if I were a nurse, it wouldn't matter that much.

But as a lawyer who's working remotely, I need to be able to get online.

Robert has been patient, but even he has his limits.

So when, in the middle of watching a horseback lesson, the Union Wireless van rolls up the driveway, three days before our install date, I panic. Are they here to tell me that we can't get internet after all? Is there something wrong with the area or with the house itself? Are they delaying their plans to work here? I don't dare to hope they're bringing good news.

I practically race to the front porch, where there's a man in a bright blue and green polo shirt knocking on the door, and nearly faceplant when I trip on the top step.

Luckily I catch the rail, but I swear the internet guy is chuckling when I right myself.

"You're from Union Wireless?" I'm panting like a dog that's been playing fetch too long.

"I'm Joe," he says. "Are you Mrs. Brooks?"

Amanda opens the door. "Hello?" Her eyes swivel from Joe down to me, where I'm still leaning on the rail. "Abby? What's going on?"

I shake my head. "I came over to find out." I try to keep the desperation out of my voice, but I'm not sure I succeed. "Is there a problem?"

"Well, our work dried up sooner than we thought over in Dutch John, so we thought we'd see if we could start early—"

"Yes!" I clear my throat. "Of course you can. That would be great."

And Jeff and Kevin come back in two days. This is shaping up to be the best week ever.

"Great," he says. "Can we get started now?"

Amanda's beaming. "Of course. What do you need?"

"Just a signature here." He holds out a clipboard, but then waffles, unsure which of us to hand it to.

I snatch it and scrawl my name across the bottom. I'd sign it in blood, if I had to. Amanda's just as excited as I am, and when she turns back to the house and tells Maren, her shriek startles the internet guy pretty badly. Which is hilarious to me for some reason. I'm a few paces away when I hear Gabe exclaim, "Wait, will we have Netflix?"

I'm beaming when I get back over to the pasture where Steve's teaching the kids a lesson. He's got Emery on the lunge line, but she seems to be doing well. If she weighed a little more, she might not flop around quite so much, but it's not like I can force donuts and cheese sticks down her throat.

"What's going on?" he asks. "You look happy."

"That's the internet company," I say. "If this all goes like it should, you're about to have your porch back."

He doesn't scowl, but he hardly looks happy.

"You should be excited for us," I say. "This is going to make life so much easier."

"Well, if your kids are ever too rowdy, or if you just want to enjoy the great outdoors—"

I know it's mean, but I can't help myself. "That's a brilliant idea. I should buy a porch swing. Once I figure out how to keep the chickens away, it'll be perfect."

He does frown this time, and he maintains his sour look through the rest of the lesson. I should feel bad, but it only puts me in a better mood. Not because he's going to miss me, but because I'll suddenly be free again—free to live the life I thought I'd be living when I agreed to come. I'll have access to the internet whenever, and I'll be able to call people through WiFi calling, and my kids will be able to call me.

If I'm being honest, I may be a *little* bit happy that he's sad, too. I mean, it's always nice to be wanted. But that's not the *main* reason I'm ecstatic. Once the lesson is done, and the kids are tacking down, Izzy and Whitney gleefully and somewhat officiously helping Emery, I walk Steve to his car.

"Thanks for taking on Emery. I know it's probably annoying to—"

"I like teaching people to ride. I love seeing them improve."

"Oh, well, then I take my gratitude back. Don't want to waste it."

He rolls his eyes. "Congrats on your internet."

"Don't count my chickens yet," I say. "They may yet hit a snag or an underground blockade. The sky may actually fall. But if it doesn't." I rub my hands together like Mr. Burns from the Simpsons. "Oh, the joy."

"I do hope your life here becomes easier."

"And I hope that my kids will stay quiet and leave me alone when I'm working," I say. "But it will be easier to do most things from here instead of driving down the road and sitting on a porch. I'm legitimately worried I may have permanent lines on my butt from the boards of your swing."

"I would be willing, as a licensed physician, to check out the area and give an expert opinion." His expression is one hundred percent earnest.

I slap his arm, which is a huge mistake. My fingers curl around his very well defined bicep, and I can't help remembering how he looked without a shirt. My mouth goes completely dry.

His sideways smile tells me he knows my reaction.

I snatch my hand away.

"If for some reason it doesn't work out, or if the kids badger you too much, I've been thinking. I'm willing to do something dramatic."

Dramatic?

"I'd be willing to extend your privileges to indoors. You'd have access to a bathroom and a kitchen where you could store food and snacks."

"Now who's being silly?"

"I was recently told that my swing may have permanent consequences on a very handsome backside. I'm serious about my offer. It would be a huge concession on my part, as I'd have to actually clean said common areas, and maybe even buy a throw pillow for my sofa, but I'd be willing to do it. You impress me, Abigail Brooks. That's not something that happens often."

His voice is light, clearly mocking, but there's an

underlying air of honesty to it that both worries and interests me.

"On that note," he says. "I'd just like to repeat my request."

His request?

He leans against his truck. "Let me take you around to see the real Manila." He straightens and holds his hands up, palm out. "I know, I know, the second I offered, panic set in. Your heart started racing, your blood pressure skyrocketed. I saw your pupils dilate."

Freaking doctors suck.

"But if I give you a tour—remember how small the town is—and you hate it, and you have anything less than a wonderful time, I will never bug you again."

"Steve—"

"Say that again," he says.

"Excuse me?"

His mouth turns up in the corner. "Say my name again."

"Steve?"

He sighs dramatically. "No, don't ask my name. *Say* my name. Like you're thinking about me. Like I've gotten to you. Like I matter."

"Steve." This time it's stern, but I can't help it. He's not listening. "I am not ready to date. All the things you're saying are true, about the heart rate and the blood pressure, but you're assuming it's because I'm scared and need to get over some kind of roadblock." I pause to make sure he's really listening. "That's not it. I'm just not interested in dating right now. It's not personal."

"Alright, alright. I get it. No means no. But it *is* personal." He steps closer. "It's the most personal thing in the world, when someone tells you they *like* you, and they want to spend time with you, and they want to get to know you better, because you're the absolute best part of their day every day. When someone says that on the days they don't see you, they spend all day subconsciously hoping to hear your voice or to catch a glimpse of you." His eyes search my face. "It's very, very personal to me."

And now my heart is freaking galloping. Is he trying to kill me?

"Mom?" Gabe's standing in the doorway.

"Yeah, baby? What?"

"Mom!" Gabe yells louder.

"I'm here," I say. "I heard you."

"Mom! Can you hear me?"

I turn all the way around and wave. "Gabriel Paul Brooks." I exhale. "I am standing twenty feet from you."

"Oh, hey!" He smiles.

"Has he always had trouble hearing?" Steve's words are soft.

They shock me. "Trouble hearing?" I shake my head. "He just doesn't pay attention."

Steve straightens, his doctor face on. "That's more than distraction. He was looking for you, and he didn't hear your response."

I think back on all the times I've been talking to him and he's ignored me. Is it possible he wasn't ignoring me? Have I missed something huge? "Oh my gosh," I say. "I'm a terrible mother."

Steve's hand wraps around my upper arm. "You're one of the best mothers I've met. Maybe *the* best. It's probably nothing, but do you mind if I check it out?"

"Right now?"

"Did you want to wait?"

"Actually, I was thinking of rushing to the ER right now."

He smiles. "No need. The ER came to you." He opens his truck door and rummages around, and when he turns, he's holding a silver thingy.

I've seen them before, but I'm not sure what they're called. "What's that?"

"An otoscope," he says. "It'll give me a great view of the ear canal and the tympanic membrane."

"Great."

"Hey Gabe," Mr. Steve says. "I hear you'd like to learn to ride a horse soon, too."

Gabe grins. "Yes sir. Unless you think I'm too little."

He crouches down on the porch so my seven-year-old son is actually taller than he is. "Not at all. I think I even have a saddle that will fit you. Most of the horses here are on the younger side, or the older ones haven't been used for beginners much, but I have a horse back home you would love. His name is Cromey."

"Cromey?"

He nods. "He's almost *thirty* years old, which for us humans isn't too bad, but for a horse is pretty high up there."

"Are old horses good for little kids?"

Steve smiles at me. "They sure are. You're a bright one."

"Thanks."

"Now, bright kid, did you remember that I'm a doctor?"

Gabe nods. "You fixed Whitney's arm."

"It's not quite fixed yet, but it's much better, and soon, it'll have healed itself thanks to the stabilization we provided. The human body is a really neat thing in many ways."

"Like what?"

"I think there may be something that's keeping you from hearing your mother when she's far away. Do you mind if I check your ears with this thing?"

"What is it?"

Steve hands it to him, and I bounce on my toes a bit.

It looks expensive, and I really don't want Gabe to drop it. "It's just a little flashlight that's attached to a weak microscope. Ears are kind of hard to see into without help, since they're a small space."

"And there's no light," Gabe says.

"Exactly." Steve presses a button and a light comes on at the end of the pointy part.

"Then I guess you can take a look," Gabe says.

"It might tickle," Steve says, "but it won't hurt. Alright?"

Gabe holds really still while Steve pokes around in both ears.

Once he releases Gabe, he smiles. "I have great news. There are a few things that can cause kids to have trouble hearing, and they range from no big deal, like fluid retention, to pretty concerning things, but yours is the easiest fix of all."

"What's that?" Gabe's face is still nervous when he looks at me.

My heart is already lighter. Steve doesn't seem worried in the slightest.

"Your ears are full of something called ear wax."

"Ear wax?" Gabe looks disgusted.

"Think of it like this. A car has oil in its engine, and that keeps it running well. Did you know that?"

Gabe shrugs.

Steve chuckles. "Alright, well my analogy may be a little advanced, but your ear needs something similar. Since it's an opening in your body, where sounds can go to be processed by your brain, and because it has a sensitive little area that captures sound—that's called the eardrum—your body needs to protect it. It creates earwax to keep your ear safe and infection free. But sometimes, especially in tiny ears like yours, that earwax builds up and gets shoved down instead of working its way out."

"What do you have to do?" Gabe's eyes still look very nervous. "Do you have to cut my ear off?"

"What?" Steve laughs full out this time. "No, there will be no cutting of any kind."

Gabe sits down on the step and breathes out. "Oh, good."

Steve looks back at me and mouths the words, "Cut his ear off?" He shakes his head. "Listen, Gabe. I have a little, kind of bendy, stick that will scoop it right out."

"You have it with you?" he asks.

"Not with me, but I have some at my house, and it's close."

Gabe swallows. "Okay."

"Do you want to come with me? Or wait while I go grab it?"

"If I come with you, can I meet Cromey?"

Steve beams. "Yes. That's a great plan. You come with me, and I'll have your mom hold a light while I clean those ears out, and then you can meet Cromey."

Just as he said, it's not painful, and Steve is quick. He pulls out a few small scoops of earwax, and then one huge one from the left side. It only takes three scoops to clean the right side, all of them pretty big. "You're all clear," Steve says.

"That's it?" Gabe asks. Then his eyes widen. "Whoa, I'm talking so loud."

"Yeah, even your own voice will be louder now, since you'll hear it from the outside and the inside."

"That's so cool." Gabe hops off the table and walks toward the door, covering his ear with his hands and then uncovering it, like it's some kind of game.

Now that it's done, and my motherly panic has somewhat subsided, I look around Steve's house. It's spare, practically Spartan, but it's got a few touches that testify that it's been lived in. A photo of Steve when he's quite young with a woman I assume is his mother. There's even a horse head hogging part of the frame behind him.

An old tattered quilt is folded carefully across the back of a new, tan sofa. His television isn't large—especially by today's standards. I would never have guessed this was the house of a doctor. It looks more like a house built by someone's grandpa back in the 50s.

The lamps are unique, and I'm not sure what they're made of—some kind of bumpy, irregular wood that's thick at the base and narrows near the top. I'd ask, but I'm trying *not* to insert myself. "Thanks so much," I say. "We will get out of your hair."

"Wait," Gabe says. "You said I get to meet Cromey, remember?"

"Of course you do." Steve ruffles his hair. "Let's go."

"Can I give him a treat?"

Steve turns around and heads for the kitchen. I grab the back of Gabe's shirt, pulling him up short, to keep him from invading even worse. "Stay here and wait," I say. "It's rude to just wander around someone's house."

"I'm not wandering. I'm following."

When he returns with a handful of carrots, Steve's smiling. "He's right. He could have followed me. My kitchen's not too embarrassing."

I feel my cheeks heat up.

"Ready to meet one of my favorite horses?"

Gabe nods.

As we walk out to the barn, Steve fills us in on his past. "I got him when I was fifteen," he says. "He's the very first horse I ever broke myself."

"You still have him? That's so cool," Gabe says.

"He was four years old then, and he was a real hotrod. He raced and he bucked and he did not want someone to sit on his back."

Gabe listens, enraptured, as Steve tells him how many

times Cromey tossed him off. "And then, the thing that changed it all?"

"What?" Gabe asks, with bated breath.

"I stopped trying to ride him for a whole week."

"You stopped?"

"And when I started again, I strapped a scarecrow to his back. No matter how much he bucked, that thing just kept flopping around. He finally settled down and realized that he was causing the misery for himself. After a week of trying to toss a scarecrow off without any luck, he just gave up."

"That's when you got on?"

"Exactly," Steve says. "Sometimes horses are worried about, or even scared of, something that just isn't that bad." He looks at me then, and I realize he's not just talking about Cromey.

Is he right?

He holds Gabe up so he can reach to give broken-up pieces of carrots to an old bay with white whiskers. "After I broke him, I was supposed to sell him and take the money to buy a few more green horses."

"But you still have him," Gabe says.

"I do." Steve shrugs. "I've always loved things a little too much for my own good. Especially things that require extra patience or a little more work. Those are the ones that are really worth it."

After he drives us back home, and Gabe dashes from the car to show his siblings all the wax that was in his ears —yes, Steve let him keep it, which is super duper gross, but also 100% the coolest thing ever for a seven-year-old boy—I expect him to badger me again.

I brace for it.

But he just leans across me and opens my door. "I'll see you in a few days for the next lesson? Or will you be working?"

"I should be there." I slide across the bench seat and hop out. I close the door, and he starts to drive away. My heart lurches, because I think maybe he's right. Maybe I'm bucking about nothing. Maybe I'm just scared of a scarecrow.

"Wait!" I wave and jog toward the truck where he's backing out the long drive. He probably won't even see me. "Wait, Steve!"

He must hear me, because he stops and turns, his brow furrowed in confusion. He rolls his window down. "Yeah?"

I reach the side of his car and stop, not quite sure what to say.

"You don't need to pay me for Gabe, if that's what you're worried about. I'm happy to help."

He's always happy to help. With horseback lessons. With the cattle drive. With Whitney's arm, which the hospital sent us comped bills for, refusing to even charge our insurance. And now with Gabe's ear. He takes care of things, *and* somehow makes the experience a positive one instead of a terrifying one. For me and for my son.

"I was wrong," I say. "And you were right."

"Huh?" He looks around me, as if something will clue him in to what I'm talking about.

"I won't buck you off," I say. "If you ask again."

He leans forward then, his head coming through the window. "Abigail."

I'm worried he'll mock me. I'm worried he'll gloat. If he does, he'll make me into a liar, because I'll probably run out of habit.

"Abby." He smiles. "I'm working quite a few days over the next week, but would you do me the honor of letting me show you around and introduce you to people at the Fourth of July barbecue and dance?"

A thrill shoots up my spine. My hands shake just a little, so I jam them into my pockets. “Yes, sure.”

His smile broadens, and his one dimple comes out. “Wonderful.”

I think it just might be.

18

AMANDA

I thought things would be simpler, easier, once the ranch hands returned. I was, apparently, wrong.

"It's just that, you literally have to make hay while the sun shines," Abby says.

"I have never understood that phrase. You don't make hay at all," I say. "It just grows."

"We're growing two kinds of hay," Ethan says. "Alfalfa, which is a higher protein content and is good for cows and horses—it's the stuff with the purple flowers. I'm sure you've seen it. We can get two rounds of that grown and baled each summer, if we cut the first right now. Only the second round is really good for horses—it's less rich."

"Horses can't eat rich alfalfa?"

"It gives them terrible diarrhea, apparently. The cows will eat this first round later, and we'll save the second round for the pickier horses."

"You just have a field or two to cut?" I ask.

"Of alfalfa? Yeah, just four of eighteen meadows. But a few of the fields of plain grass hay that got more water are ready to be cut now. Both of them have to be cut when it's dry, and then left to dry for a few days before you can bale them. Weather says we have at least four more dry days ahead, so we're making hay."

"While the sun is shining," Abby says. "See?"

"But why?" I ask. "Why can't you cut it and bundle it up at the same time?"

"It'll mold, I think," Abby says. "And that'll make the cows sick, and it can kill horses. They can't throw up, so they do something called colicking, which is basically where their stomach, like, explodes."

I wish I hadn't asked.

"But surely Kevin and Jeff—"

"Would do what they could if we weren't here," Abby says. "But since we are, we're going to try and learn what to do."

It's like the work literally never ends. I worried all day when they went to check on the cows—which they apparently had a little trouble finding—and then they got lost on their way back. Even Abby looked a little chagrined for not asking for Steve's help. And with the animals, the rain made things harder. Then the second it's dried out, and Jeff and Kevin return, everyone has to leave for long stretches to cut hay, and then bale it, and then cover it.

I don't get why *anyone* would want to run a ranch.

Then again, I make my money from creating photos that highlight products that people might want to buy. So manual labor revolving around animals isn't exactly part of my wheelhouse.

"Well, at least there's a great possibility of things getting horribly dirty, right?"

"Do grass stains count?" Ethan asks. "Because I could probably bring back some impressive stuff if so."

I check the label on the Tide stain treatment. "Yes! That's on here. So, when you get home, especially if you have some really surprising ones—wait." He should wear some of the Lololime stuff that Heather sent for Eddy. I doubt I'll get up the nerve to ask him to wear it, seeing as he doesn't even know what my job is yet. Ethan's cute. I think it could work. I duck into my room and come back with two shirts and a pair of khakis.

"What's that?" He frowns.

"If you wear these—"

Ethan laughs. "I'm not going to church or to an office job. I'm going to work in a field all day."

I put one hand on my hip. "Listen here. I'm not making you pay for these, so stop complaining." I hand them to him.

"These are larges," he says. "I'm not really—"

"Just go put them on."

Ethan throws his hands up in the air, but he does take the clothes and disappear. For all his whining, when he returns, he doesn't look that bad. And with boots and a hat, it'll even look suitable for his task, albeit a little more formal than necessary. "Who are these supposed to be for?" He quirks one eyebrow. "Someone a little bigger than me. . ." His eyes widen. "Dr. Dutton?"

I look around to see whether anyone else is paying attention, and luckily, it doesn't look like it. "Shut your mouth, Ethan Brooks."

"Oh, it's a secret now? Because he's been splashed all over your insta account. I'm shocked it took me this long to figure that out. It must be all the sunshine. It's frying my brain."

"That is why Heather sent it, but—"

"Don't you think she'll be disappointed when it's me wearing it instead?"

"No, I don't. You're quite handsome, and the ladies will love seeing you, too."

"I think they're more interested in hearing and seeing someone else's exciting love life than seeing a good-looking guy." He shrugs. "Which is too bad for me." His cocky smile returns, and I wonder whether he's right.

"It's not like I mind," he says. "Free clothes are free clothes, but I think you should tell Dr. Dog Dreamy what you need and give the people what they want."

"Dog Dreamy?"

Ethan shrugs. "Some show called people Dr. Mac Steamy and Dr. Dreamy and all kinds of stuff. This guy's not a doctor, but he's a dog doctor, right?"

"Vets are most certainly doctors."

Abby has come back into the room, wearing jeans and a t-shirt. "Are we talking about Dutton? Because I think he likes you."

I'm done talking about this. "You two are ridiculous."

Ethan stuffs a few things in a bag and heads for the door.

"I'll catch up," Abby says. "I've got to send an email."

Ethan nods and then he's gone.

"Hello, email," Abby says.

"Wait, are you calling *me* email?" I roll my eyes. "You can just go. I don't need—"

She sits down and pats the table in front of the chair next to her. "Go ahead. Have a seat and tell me how you don't need the super hot vet who's hot for widow."

"I am not—"

"You seem like exactly the kind of person who would be all about having a fun, cowboy fling." She grins. "Yee-haw. I can see the hashtags now." She leans toward me. "Oh, wait. I already have."

I lower my voice. "Says the woman who's actually going on a date with one."

Abby's mouth drops open and she blinks in a very satisfying way. "How do you know about that?"

I shrug.

"Amanda Brooks."

"I might have overheard you on the phone last night."

"What?"

"You were on the home line, since your cell still doesn't work great on the WiFi sometimes, and I picked it up to call—doesn't matter. And you were talking about how Steve was going to be in the rodeo most of the day. You told him, 'I actually like watching you ride.' I did drop the receiver like it was a hot iron, but I'd already put two and two together and come up with four."

She breaths a heavy sigh of relief. "So the kids don't know?"

"I think they might figure it out," I say. "I can't believe that the queen of 'talk to your kids' hasn't told them already."

"I'm going to sit down and ask them about it," she says. "I just haven't had time."

"It's not a democracy. They don't get to decide whether you let the hot doc take you out."

"If it makes them sad or uncomfortable or anxious—"

"Then you'll talk until they're sick of it, and they'll get over it on their own timetable."

If she doesn't stop looking at me in that condescending way, I'm going to stop being supportive.

"You should call Eddy and ask him to go with you to the Fourth of July dinner and dance. I hear it's quite the event for this area."

"Which is exactly why he won't want to go. I'm pretty sure he's the local ladies' man, which is probably hard to do in a town this size. I mean, I imagine he's dated girls from three counties at least."

"Who cares?" Abby shrugs. "You're not looking to marry him."

Definitely not, clearly. "That's true."

"Take him, get some killer photos, and then post one of those bad boys to announce you're dating a hottie-everyman, and then when you breakup, think of the condolences and commiserations you'll get from all your followers. Everyone loves to hate the hot guy when he's broken the heroine's heart." Abby stands up. "Well, I've done my good deed for the day. Now it's time for a little manual labor. Wish me luck."

It's not that I don't wish her luck, but Abby doesn't really seem to need it. She's tanner, fitter, and more energetic right now than she was a few weeks ago, and her kids love it here. For me, on the other hand, I haven't worked out in weeks, one of my girls is flying high and the other is. . .not. And I'm *still* just waiting to find out whether all this soul-crushing (to Maren) time in the country is even going to pay off.

The closer I get to the beginning of July, the more nervous I become.

I've done some digging.

I know they're considering six accounts for just two slots. I don't know exactly who my competition is, but I know I started out in dead last, and I know that we're all posting their content right now as we vie for the best engagement. I have come up with a decent list of seven accounts that *could* be my competition, and two of them are much, much, much larger than mine.

The more I read their feeds, the less I believe I even have a chance. One of them is a yoga instructor. She's always talking about crystals, and shakra, and chi, and she endorses candles and new age music, and a lot of things like yoga mats and incense. I've seen her do some big spreads for things as different as Voltaren for sore muscles, and oils that purport to fix everything. Other than a little inconsistency, her brand is good. She's a heavy lady who promotes healthy body image, so I can't even hope she fails.

Another top contender is a woman who has as many

kids as Abby. She runs a personal weight loss coaching site and generally *only* pushes her own classes, a few protein powder and supplement items aside. I'm sure Lololime would fall all over themselves to pay her if she agreed to partner with them. What I find the most obnoxious about her feed is how much time she spends *saying* that you should give yourself grace and not worry about the scale, all the while posting images of her rock-hard, six-pack abs and her flexed biceps. I mean, it's great she's telling people to chill, but when words and actions conflict, people believe actions.

I close my laptop. It's not healthy to sit around obsessing. The one great thing about having limited internet was that it made me spend less time worrying about likes and shares and follows and tags, and more time worrying about the real world. Now that the real world has caught up, I have trouble closing it down.

"Hey, Mom." Maren sits down at the table across from me, and miracle of miracles, she's already dressed and ready for the day. "I thought maybe I'd work on some of my cheers. I downloaded the videos, but I don't want to annoy anyone."

"That's a great idea," I say. "You can do it in the family room or outside. I think Gabe and Emery and Whitney are outside with Izzy. There's no one you'll annoy."

"I don't really like all the animals," she says. "The chickens are kind of funny, and I don't mind the barn cats, but horses freak me out."

"That's alright."

"Is it?" She sighs. "It makes me feel a little broken, to be honest. Everyone else is out there riding, and petting, and shoveling poop, and I'm just thinking, why does everything have to be about animals here?"

I reach for her hand, but chicken out at the last minute. I slide her a plate with apple slices on it instead.

"Not everyone likes the same things, and thank goodness, or the world would be a very boring place."

"Ethan doesn't even want to go to college," she says. "Do you think that's dumb?"

I have to think this through carefully. "I think it's ill advised."

"What does that mean?"

I tap my lip. "If your cousin was not very bright, if he had limited options, I would encourage him to get right to work. I'd tell him to find a career and start building it. But he's one of the smartest kids I've met, and the best time to get into a good college is right out of high school. If you wait, your options narrow."

"So he should go? Aunt Abby's right?"

"Your aunt is right an irritating amount of the time."

"Yeah."

"But there's also something to be said for people finding joy in the things that they actually like, and not in the things someone else wants for them."

"Like not animals, if that's not what they like."

"Exactly like that," I say. "Or in cheer, even if that's not something I really understand."

"I only like cheer because it's what the popular kids do," she says. "Sometimes I wonder if that's not a good reason."

"What's impressive is that you can identify and admit the real reason," I say. "That kind of honesty is rare." I'm delighted she's actually talking to me.

She eats a single apple slice and then she walks to the front door. She turns just before she ducks out. "Thanks, Mom."

Some days I feel like she's a complete stranger, but occasionally she'll reach out and remind me that she's still my little girl, somewhere down in there. "You're welcome. Anytime, darling. You know that."

The door closes.

I'm scrolling through old photos of Maren and Emery like a crack addict who needs a fix when my phone starts buzzing to announce an incoming call. It's a Utah number. Who would have my number? The only person I can think of is Mrs. Saddler, but I saved her number in my phone. "Hello?"

"Mandy? Can I call you that?"

"Who is this?"

"It's Eddy." He sounds affronted by the fact that I didn't immediately recognize his voice. "Eddy Dutton."

"I don't know so many Eddys that I needed the last name. What's up?"

"Wanna grab lunch?"

"It's barely ten a.m."

"When you wake up at five, it feels like lunchtime, believe me," he says. "We could call it brunch?"

"I don't know," I say. "Is that code for a cup of gas station coffee and a package of powdered sugar donuts? Or a cup of noodles, microwaved at the corner store? Because I'm trying to be positive about the town size, but—"

"There's an actual restaurant I'd like to take you to," he says. "It's called the Gorge Reel and Grill, and right now, every order of tacos comes with a brownie."

"I'd be stupid to miss out on that," I say. "Should I meet you there?"

"Um, if it's a date, I think I ought to pick you up."

"Is it a date?"

"Let's review," he says. "I called you. Check."

"Okay."

"I'm picking you up."

"Check," I say.

"And I plan to wear something nicer than coveralls, even though I have some nasty stuff to do later to a pig."

I chuckle.

"I'll be paying for the meal, even if you *don't* get the free brownie."

"Oh, hey, then it *is* a date."

"See? I'll be there in ten minutes."

"Wait," I say. "What should I wear?"

"Your finest overalls? A pair of rubber boots, in case we go wading for trout later."

"What in the world is wading—"

"Never mind," he says. "I went too far and outed myself as a real redneck. Hopefully you didn't know enough to notice."

After he hangs up, I panic a little. What *do* I wear? I don't own rubber boots. I certainly don't have any overalls. I'm sure he was kidding, but I don't want to look like an idiot at this restaurant. I imagine he actually eats there fairly often. I finally settle for a pair of jeans and a blousy blue top with daisies on the trim. It's about as country as I get. I throw on a pair of Lololime shoes in case there's a photo opportunity.

Almost the second I tie the laces, I hear the growl of a truck engine outside. I dash out there, stopping only long enough to tell Maren I'm running an errand in town. She frowns a bit, but waves as I get into Eddy's truck—it's actually a different car than the white SUV he drives as a vet.

I probably shouldn't have criticized Abby for not telling her kids about her date—I'm actually *going* on a date and lying about where I'm headed.

"Oh, Amanda." He shakes his head. "I hate to tell you this, but those are not overalls, and your shoes are definitely not made of rubber."

"What was the head shake for?"

"I'm having trouble deciding what to call you," he

says. “Mandy felt wrong, like you were my little niece or something, but Amanda sounds too formal.”

“It’s Mrs. Brooks to you, seeing as I’m a client. Don’t you think?”

“Ouch.” He winces. “You’re kind of mean.”

“Honest and mean aren’t the same. I figured the date thing was a joke, and that you take all your valued clients out for food on Free Brownie Wednesdays.”

His hand reaches over the console and wraps around mine. I hadn’t realized how large it was, or quite how rough. It makes my hand look practically dainty by comparison. And something happens that has never happened to me before. The same butterfly-in-the-stomach feeling I always get when I’m watching a romantic comedy, or a really good romance—it happens.

To me.

“I suppose you hold hands with everyone you take on client meals?”

He laughs.

“Is that a no?”

“It’s a definite no.” The butterfly feeling comes back again.

“Did you know that it has never bothered me before, how close Manila is to Jed’s ranch?” Eddy turns sideways and looks at me.

“Does it bother you now?”

He shrugs. “It’s definitely not a long enough ride from one place to the other.” He pulls into the parking lot of the Gorge, parks, and cuts the engine. “It took a lot of gumption for me to hold your hand, and now I just have to let it go again.” His eyes sparkle, but he doesn’t let go. If anything, his fingers tighten around mine.

“Maybe drive in circles next time, like a cab driver in New York with a tourist. I know Manila’s small, but I’m new. I won’t know the difference.”

"Do they really do that?" Eddy asks.

"Oh, all the time," I say. "Not to locals, though. I'll usually get in and tell him where I'm going and my preferred route so he knows he can't overcharge me."

"They do that on television," Eddy says. "The residents telling them where to go, I mean."

"It's not so much that I care which streets he takes, but it's a signal that I'm not lost."

"Fascinating," he says. "I had no idea that an expert navigator of the Big Apple was right here in my car."

He's still holding my hand.

And neither of us is making any move to get out.

"You're going to have to let me go," I say. "At some point. Or we'll starve to death."

He shrugs. "Eating's overrated."

"That's because it's not even ten-thirty yet. Around noon, you'll be shoving me aside in order to sprint to the kitchen."

"You know men pretty well," he says, "for someone with two daughters."

"I have three brothers," I say. "Two biological and a stepbrother."

"Sounds like your brothers needed to learn some manners. I'd never shove you anywhere." He leans a little closer. "I'd drag you along with me."

"How dreamy."

"Speaking of." He releases me, but then he climbs out and circles the truck. I try to open the door, but I can't. He opens it with a grin. "Child locks. I've found them to be just as effective with dates who don't want to let me be the gentleman my mama raised."

"You child locked me in?"

He shrugs. "If you show me you can behave, I'll turn them off."

I lean over and switch it off on the side of the door.

"Nice try, but I'm not an actual child, so I'm onto your wily ways."

"Aw shucks. Outsmarted by the city slicker."

I roll my eyes. "Nice try, Dr. Dutton. You're not a redneck. I can tell."

"Not a fan of hot cowboys?" he asks.

The way he phrased that causes me to freeze. Has he found my insta? I'm easy to find, if you make the slightest effort, and if he knows I've been posting images of him. . . How embarrassing. "So, about that."

He stops. "About what?" He looks totally lost. Maybe I was imagining it.

"Never mind."

The restaurant may be small, like the town, but he's not wrong about the food. It's actually really good. I usually eat half of my meal, tops, as a rule. But I eat both tacos, and most of the beans and rice. When they bring my brownie, I end up eating most of that, too.

"I'm impressed," Eddy says. "Most of the women—"

My eyebrows shoot up. I can't wait to hear the end of that. "Yes?"

He clears his throat. "Nothing."

"Most of the women you bring here. . .don't eat much? Was that what you were going to say?"

My adorable little vet turns bright red.

"Well, I'm old enough to know that it's pointless to eat like a bird around a guy. If I like something, I'll eat it. If I don't, I won't. I look how I look, and pretending I never eat won't change it." I frown. "And how guys can get away with saying something as condescending as 'I like that you have a healthy appetite' is beyond me. Why do you have any opinion on how much I eat?"

He holds his hands up. "I surrender."

I laugh. "Fine, I forgive you, but only because that almost seems sincere."

"Almost?"

I shrug. "I have high standards. What can I say?"

"I've been using my best moves. I went out in the mud and mess and brought your horses back. I helped Ethan fix the fence, and now I'm taking you out for Manila's finest. What more can I do?" He smacks his head. "Order you some custom overalls, that are embroidered? Then you'll feel like I accept you, and like I want you to be comfortable here, in my hometown."

"You really have a shocking amount of insight into women." I can't help smiling. "And what will these custom overalls say?"

"Something about horses," he says. "Maybe Real Men Ride? Or Save a Horse, Ride a—"

"Alright," I say. "I get it."

"But really, in this area, heroes do ride horses."

Now I know he's read my feed. That's the second hashtag he's quoted. I should have gone with my gut before. "So you did find me on insta."

He freezes. "On what?"

"On Instagram. Don't bother playing dumb. You should know, however, that I haven't ever posted a photo of your face. I'd have gotten permission for that. And I'm only playing up the cowboy thing because I'm trying to score a sponsorship contract with Lololime and they have a new Western Living line releasing. Their company is kind of the Cadillac of promo for my brand."

"There were a lot of words I didn't understand in that last statement." He rubs a hand over his eyes. "Is that something you can translate? Did you say you had pictures of me?"

Oh, no. He's not kidding, and this isn't a joke. He had no idea what I was talking about. I've really stuck my foot into it.

Probably best to start at the beginning. "After my

husband died, I found out he'd invested in some bad stuff. Well, it was fine, but I didn't realize he had bought a lot of options. He'd sunk all our money in them, actually, or close enough."

"Options?"

I'm confusing him more. I better get there fast. "The long and short of it was that I was living in New York City with two young girls, and I had no job, and no marketable skills. I had to figure out a way to make money. I put off bill collectors and paid one credit card with another, but it couldn't last."

To his credit, he looks very distressed by the whole thing.

"The one thing I did have was a large and loyal following on my social media account. I'm not proud of this, but I used the fact that I was a widow, and a relatively fashionable one at that, to boost my following even further. And then instead of turning down every offer from companies to promote their products, I started selecting a careful few, cultivating a specific brand for my account."

"I thought you were a photographer," he says. "Like, family photos and stuff."

"My job does require me to take a lot of photos, and I have a great eye for not only what my fans will like, but what will get me the most interaction."

"You're an influencer," he says. "That's your job?"

I nod. "It can be exhausting, always sorting through the promos I'm offered, or sometimes, searching for opportunities myself. Some months are great, while others are quite lean."

"Did you say you put photos of *me* on your account?" His eyes widen and he swallows.

"Well, yes and no. I did put photos of you, from the back or from the side."

He pulls money out of his wallet and puts it on the table. Then he stands. "We better get going. I have an appointment pretty soon."

That was abrupt. Is he upset? What's going on?

He doesn't say much on the way back to Birch Creek, and he makes no move to touch me anywhere, much less try to hold my hand. He answers questions I ask him, but flatly, without much inflection and without any flirting. Clearly he's not impressed with my job—or maybe with me, either.

"Thanks for lunch." He stops in my driveway, but doesn't even put the truck in park. In fact, he puts it in reverse.

What's going on? After one awkward moment, I finally climb out. Thanks to my clever move, turning off the child safety locks, I don't need him to open my door. But that means I have no real excuse to make him look at me or listen to me. But I can't just let him drive off. I don't close the door, however impatient he may be to leave.

"Eddy—why are you so upset?"

His eyes, when he turns toward me, aren't angry. They aren't judgmental, either. They look. . .broken. "I thought that maybe—but it won't work." He shakes his head. "I'm sorry, Amanda."

I realize that's all I'm going to get, and I finally close the door.

But I hate watching him drive away, knowing that was our first and last date. So much for having a fun time—I didn't have a fling.

I got flung.

And it hurts.

19
ABIGAIL

It's a new month, and I feel a little like a new person. I'm still the same old me, obviously. I'm a lawyer. I'm a mother. I'm a lousy sister-in-law and a mediocre aunt. But everything *feels* new.

We have internet. I can work from my tiny bedroom, with my pillows stacked behind me, and my feet kicked out on my twin bed.

The chores and tasks in front of me feel more manageable. Ethan's got the water handled, the guys are showing us how to properly cut and bale hay. We have the first round of alfalfa from one meadow baled and stored under tarps. It's not really much compared to the 700 plus tons that Kevin and Jeff say we'll need for the 180 days the cows need hay, but it's a start.

Most things, once you face them, aren't nearly as scary as you feared.

I need that to be true right now.

Because it's been days since I agreed to let Steve show me around at the 4th of July barbecue and dance, and I still haven't told my kids. Part of the issue is that Amanda and Emery and Maren are always here, so it's hard to get any time alone with my four kids. They can't all fit in my bedroom, nor can we all squeeze into Ethan's and Gabe's, or Izzy's and Whitney's.

But today, Amanda, who seemed really upset last night for some reason, decided to take her girls shopping in Green River. I think they needed a day that more closely resembled normalcy. That, and Amanda says she can't sit around all day, wondering if she'll hear back from Lololime. I always thought what she did was kind of fluffy, that she didn't work very hard to earn her money. Now that we're living in the same place, I can see the amount of time she spends figuring out what products would fit her brand, and coming up with new ideas of fun things to photograph and tips to offer her followers. The churn and burn of coming up with engaging content is probably more stressful in its own way than simply doing legal work that I've grown into over years and years.

I would *hate* doing it myself, but it's not as frivolous a job as I previously thought. It's sort of like inventing the design for and implementing your own organic form of marketing that's tied to your personal image. She always makes it look effortless, somehow.

"Hey guys, we're having dinner together. Isn't that fun?"

"We always have dinner together," Gabe says. "Unless you're working."

"I know," I say, "but it's the first time it's been *only* us for a while."

"You mean, Emery and Maren aren't here," Izzy says. "But I like having them around."

"I do too," I say, and surprisingly, I mean it. "Even so, I like having just my kids sometimes too." I wonder if I overdid it. Am I trying too hard? I can't think the last time I made lasagna, a green salad, a fruit salad, garlic knot rolls, *and* dessert. Will the kids realize how nervous I am? Will they think I'm buttering them up?

If I'm this nervous about telling my kids, maybe I shouldn't be going on this pseudo date at all.

Not that it'll be much of a date, except in word. Steve's actually judging for the rodeo, so for most of the day I'll just be watching, and then at the barbecue, it's not like I'm going to banish my kids, so they'll be with us. Although Gabe, Whitney, and Izzy won't stay for the dance.

Thinking about dancing with Steve makes my stomach a little unsettled. It sends a shiver through my body.

"I'm starving," Ethan says.

And apparently, it makes me forget that the kids are waiting on me to ask one of them to say grace. "Whitney—"

"I'll pray." I can always count on her to volunteer. She loves talking, so it makes sense that she'd love talking to God as well. "Dear God, please bless all this food that Mom made, and also bless our family. Help Dad to know, up in heaven, that we love and miss him. Help us to stay here at the ranch, and don't let the alien people get all the money from it. Amen."

Ethan snickers, but everyone else acts like it was a normal prayer. I suppose it was. And I do hope, if it works this way, that Nate knows we miss him. But part of me hopes he's not watching me *all* the time. That thought only makes me feel more guilty, of course.

The kids have eaten the lasagna, the rolls, the fruit, and a token bite or two of salad by the time I finally get up the nerve to say anything.

"Your dad has been gone for a year now," I say.

"Actually, a year and two months," Ethan says.

"Right." I clear my throat. "And I know that's a long

time in Gabe's life, for instance, but not as long for Ethan and Izzy and me."

"It's the same amount of time for all of us," Whitney says. "Isn't it?"

This is going well.

"Do you want us all to share a memory we have of Dad?" Gabe beams. "Because I thought of one."

How can I say no to that? "Uh, yes. That would be great."

"Once, I was drawing in my room," Gabe says. "I accidentally drew outside of the lines and it made a mark on my nightstand. You know, the wooden one you got made to match the bed?"

I nod.

"I liked making lines on the nightstand. It felt different than paper, and it looked really cool."

"I don't remember—"

He bites his lip. "I knew I shouldn't do it, but I couldn't seem to stop." He looks down at his plate, empty but for the salad. "Dad found me. He was upset, but when I started to cry, he said we could fix it. You were with Izzy at horseback, so we took it to the garage and we sanded the top. We put varnish on it, and he told me I had to be very careful not to touch it until the next night, or you'd find out."

I think about Nate, about the things he did for me, for the kids, without praise or recognition. He did them just because he loved us and wanted us to be happy. It's only been a year. How could I even consider—

"My memory is when I came home in fifth grade, really proud of how good I'd gotten at basketball. Dad was working a lot, and he was getting older, and I told him I knew I could beat him." Ethan laughs. "He destroyed me. Then he told me that if I kept practicing, it wouldn't be too long until I was right. He told me he looked forward to the day I smoked him."

"My turn?" Whitney bounces up and down on her chair. "Mine's a good one. I remember when we were kids and Dad would race around with us on his back."

"Horsey," Izzy says. "That's what he called it. That's why I wanted to learn how to ride."

"I'd never even been on a real horse before he died," Whitney says. "At least he saw you ride for real."

"He can see you now, I think," Ethan says.

It's the first time I've heard him say something hopeful, something that shows he has some kind of faith. I'm happy to hear it.

"But I don't think Mom was going to ask us that," Ethan says. "She made a big, nice dinner, and she looked nervous."

He's too old and far too perceptive. "No, it's fine."

"What did you want to say?" Izzy asks.

I should just tell them something about Nate, a story. But then I'll have to call off my date with Steve and that'll be exhausting and tiring. For all I know, Amanda has already told Maren about it. Suddenly, this exciting, light and fun secret feels heavy and depressing.

"Mom?" Izzy asks. "You can say anything. You know you can."

As a mother and as an adult, I know that's not true. But if I can't bring myself to tell them, I really should cancel. "Mr. Archer asked me to go as his date to the Fourth of July barbecue and dance." My hands tighten into balls in my lap. "I told him no at first."

"But now you're going?" Whitney's eyebrows rise and her mouth opens.

"That's so cool," Izzy says, "because I love Mr. Archer."

Gabe's frowning. "What's a date?"

"It's where two people hold hands and kiss," Whitney says.

I choke.

Ethan pats my back immediately. "That's not what a date is, goofball. It's where two people say, 'I kind of like you. Maybe we should spend some time together and see if we're a good match.'"

I finally stop coughing. "Yes, that's right." I clear my throat. "Good explanation, Ethan."

"And I think it's great, too," Ethan says. "I'm sure Dad would agree. He would want you to be happy, and you look happier when Mr. Archer's around."

Suddenly, I'm fighting back tears.

"Why are you sad?" Gabe asks. "Are you okay?"

I hold out my arms and he walks toward me. I wrap my hands around his back and squeeze. "I'm fine, baby. I have you guys, and that's why I'm fine."

"I hope he gets you ice cream," Whitney says. "Or would that be like cheating? I mean, everyone will want to spend more time with someone who gets them ice cream."

"You should suggest that to him," Ethan says, "the next time you see him."

I kick Ethan under the table.

"I've changed my mind," Ethan says. "I think this is a terrible idea."

"Don't make me kick you again."

Izzy gets up and walks into the kitchen to grab the cake I made. She sets it on the table in front of me. "Was this a bribe? You made the cake so we'd say it's fine for you to go on a date?"

My stomach ties in knots. I wish I'd eaten less, because I'm pretty sure I'm about to puke.

"Don't be stupid," Ethan says. "Mom made us cake

last Sunday. She made brownies last week. And a few nights ago, she made an apple pie."

"Alright." Izzy's still frowning.

"You don't like Mr. Archer?" Whitney asks.

"I like him to teach me about horses," Izzy asks, "but what happens if he and Mom don't like spending time together? What if he doesn't *buy her ice cream* and she never wants to see him again? I doubt there are a lot of great people here who teach horseback lessons."

All the kids' faces turn toward me, because it's not a bad question. "I promise that even if Mr. Archer and I don't have a great date, he will still come teach you lessons."

"How can you promise us something that he would have to do?" Whitney raises one eyebrow. "I think you should ask him."

This is awkward. I pull out my phone and type up a text. TOLD THE KIDS ABOUT OUR DATE. THEY'RE WORRIED THAT IF IT GOES BADLY, YOU'LL STOP TEACHING THEM HORSEBACK LESSONS.

"What did he say?" Gabe asks.

"It takes time for people to text back," Ethan says.

"And he's at work," I say. "He may be really busy."

"Helping fix people's ears," Gabe says.

"Or their arms," Whitney says.

"It would be cool to have a doctor around more," Ethan says. "Especially since our family is apparently accident prone."

TELL THEM IF IT GOES BADLY, AS MY MONEY BACK GUARANTEE, I'LL TEACH THE SAME LESSONS AS I ALWAYS WOULD HAVE. . .FOR FREE.

That makes Izzy laugh. "He must really like you."

"Or maybe he likes you guys," I say. "Maybe he was worried about the same thing."

"We are pretty great," Ethan says.

He's not wrong.

When my phone rings, I answer without thinking. "Hey, Steve," I say.

"How's life in the boondocks?" Robert asks.

I cringe. What do I say, now? *Calm down, Abby. It's not the end of the world—he knows Steve is someone I know. Just keep talking as if nothing's wrong and this isn't awkward at all.* "We're all surviving."

"How was it cutting hay?"

"The cutting was boring," I say. "But the baling was sort of interesting. They have machines for all that stuff, and you know how good Ethan is with mechanical stuff."

"I didn't, actually. I knew he liked dirt bikes."

"He fixed their baler, and he's working on a design for a kind of flow valve that will make watering the meadows much easier and less time consuming."

"Sounds like he's learning, at least, even if it's not really in the cards. Have you heard anything from Gus, yet?"

"No." I turn away from the table and drop my voice. "I'm a little worried. Shouldn't people be dropping off the waitlist by now?"

"Eh, they may still be stringing other schools along."

In July? It feels like wishful thinking.

"And if Ethan doesn't get in, he'll survive. So he goes to community college? That's not a big deal."

"But I'm not sure I can justify refusing him the chance at the ranch so that he can do a year of community college." The kids are so quiet that I know they're listening. "But speaking of the case, I wanted to mention that the brief we talked about is done. I emailed the draft to you."

"Kids are listening, huh?" Robert laughs. "Nice work on that nonexistent brief. Really some exceptional analysis."

"Hush," I whisper.

"Any chance you can fly back for the weekend? It's the Fourth of July."

"It would be fun to go home for a few days, but there's a big barbecue here," I say. "And fireworks."

"There's no way their fireworks will compare to ours. Did I mention I bought a bigger boat? The kids might like to go out on the lake—we could watch the fireworks from there."

"You have a bigger boat, now? It would be fun to go out on the lake. What did you buy?"

"We can't fly back," Whitney yells. "Mom has a *date* on the Fourth of July."

The other end of the line goes dead.

"Robert?"

"Who was that?"

So he did hear her.

"It was Whitney. Sorry, we're around the dinner table, just about to have dessert."

"Did she say you have a date?"

I sigh. "It's just the kids' horse trainer. He asked me to be his date for the barbecue and dance after the rodeo. It's really no big deal, truly."

"I bet the weather there is perfect," Robert says. "Probably the perfect time on the ranch."

"It is pretty gorgeous, especially compared to the sweltering heat of Houston."

He spends the rest of the call asking about the ranch and how things are going, and what our days look like, thankfully. I was worried he would freak out for a minute.

The rest of the evening, and even the next day, are completely normal. None of the kids seem worried or stressed about the upcoming date, not even Gabe. Friday morning rains, which means we're set back again on cutting the second alfalfa field. But the weather says it'll stay dry for a week. That should give it time to dry enough to be cut, and then dry on the ground and be baled. I hope. Although, worst case, the alien fund will have a little less money because the estate will need to buy some hay.

As Amanda pointed out before, not my problem.

Sometimes I forget all of that, probably because Ethan is still holding out hope. I manage to finish all the urgent things on my to do list for work by lunch, and the kids have done their chores, too, all except Ethan. He's out working on something that went wrong with a tractor.

"Who wants to play a game?" I ask.

Everyone's arguing about which game we should play, Emery and Whitney pushing for Monopoly, while Izzy and Maren push for Dominion, when there's a knock at the door. Steve's working, Amanda wouldn't knock, and neither would Ethan.

It's a little pathetic that we don't really know anyone else.

I open the door.

Robert beams at me, a bouquet of lilies and a saran-wrapped pie in his hands. "Surprise!"

"Who is it?" Whitney asks.

Gabe appears at my side, shoving his way around my legs to see. "It's Uncle Robert!"

Robert cringes at the name, but true or not, they've called him that all their lives. "Right. It's me, *Uncle* Robert." He leans toward the doorway. "Is it okay if I come inside?"

I think about closing the door in his face. He didn't ask if he could come—he simply flew out. But then I think about all the things he's done for me. The way he's supported me at work, and come around the house for the past year plus, fixing things that broke, power washing the driveway, replacing light bulbs and changing air filters. All the things Nate did that I never remembered to do.

"Come in." I step backward, opening the door.

"Hey, do you want to play Monopoly?" Whitney asks.

"Or would you rather play Dominion?" Izzy throws him a double thumbs up.

"Uh, maybe I better talk to your mom for a minute first," he says.

"Here, kids." I take the pie. "Why don't you have some cherry pie, and you can play rock paper scissors to pick the game while we chat outside."

I set the flowers on the table and head for the front door, Robert trailing behind me. He looks a little like a puppy that just peed on the floor. Once we get outside, I'm not sure where to go. My porch swing came, but I haven't assembled it yet, so there's just a big box sitting on the front porch. In the end, I perch on the railing. At least it's solid, since Ethan replaced the rotting boards and painted it navy, like I said I wanted.

"Robert."

"Abigail." He smiles.

"What on Earth are you doing here?"

"You don't have to furrow your brow and scowl like that."

"I'm not scowling." I make sure my face is smooth.

"With all the things you said about the ranch, I couldn't stop thinking about it. I wanted to see it. Are you upset?"

"I have a date tomorrow, Robert. Are you sure that's not why you're here?"

He rolls his eyes. "You said it was nothing, just you being nice to the horse trainer."

I mean, I did say that. "But you didn't even ask if you could come visit."

"We're like family—the kids call me Uncle. Do I have to ask?" His eyes are hurt.

He's probably my oldest friend. I may not trust his motivations, but he's right that I can't really ever be mad at him for coming to visit us somewhere. I exhale. "Do not make this stressful for me. Do not make me regret welcoming you inside."

He beams.

"And one more thing." This time I am frowning.

"Yeah?"

"You're sleeping on the couch."

"Wouldn't dream of sleeping anywhere else."

20
AMANDA

I still can't figure out why Eddy just. . .ran like that. Some people don't like social media. I get it. It's exhausting and most of it's fake, but it's not all bad. At least if he told me what bothered him, we could talk about it. But he didn't even explain what upset him.

Eddy just left.

He must not really have liked me much if something like that scared him off entirely.

Even after a day of shopping (not very good shopping, but still, shopping) and pedicures, after going out to eat and getting dessert, I'm still bummed.

Today, thanks to the internet, I've hidden in my room, bingeing romantic comedies. After watching *Someone Like You*, I just can't watch anymore. Who would be so stupid not to want Hugh Jackman from the get-go? Ugh.

I finally force myself to shower and get ready for the day. No one has ever felt great after wallowing in their own filth for two days. I refuse to let stupid, smart, sexy Eddy ruin my entire summer. He may be a jerk, but that's fine. I'm proof against jerks, after all this time. Immune. Unaffected. I am Switzerland.

Actually, that may be more about war or something. I can't remember. But then, I'm Swiss chocolate. Delicious in every circumstance.

I really need to get out of the house.

"Mom," Emery says. "Hey."

Oh, no. My kids are surprised that I've emerged from my room. That's a very bad sign. "I'm going for a walk. Anyone want to come?"

"We just got back inside from playing with the goats," Maren says.

I almost pass out. Maren, playing with goats? "Wait, you did?"

She shrugs. "They're cuter than I thought."

I may die of shock. "Okay."

"Actually, I was thinking about it, and maybe I could take horseback lessons, too. I mean, if everyone else can ride, it wouldn't hurt for me to learn."

Words cannot form properly, and I find myself spluttering. "You—horseback? You?"

"Very funny," she says. "Well, if you think about it and don't think it's a good idea, that's fine. Whatever."

"No," I say. "Emery's loving it, and we have like a dozen horses here, so that's fine."

She smiles—an honest-to-goodness, real smile.

Once I get outside, and I start walking, I feel even better. I can't let my entire life focus on just one thing. It's not healthy. I head for the 'office' out of habit. It's covered with bright yellow flowers, now, and butterflies flit from one to the other. A few bees buzz too, but I avoid them.

When my phone rings, it's actually a little jarring. I swipe talk just to get it to stop making that awful bleating sound. "Hello?"

"Amanda?"

"Heather?"

"I'm calling on an official office line, with my boss, Victoria Davis, on speakerphone with me."

"Okay."

"We wanted to formally notify you that you've been selected as one of Lololime's newest brand sponsors."

The bees keep buzzing and the butterflies keep bobbing around, as though nothing has changed, but I can hardly believe what I'm hearing. "You are? I mean, I have?" I shake my head to try and get my thoughts unjumbled. "That's wonderful news. Thank you so much!"

"It's nice to hear your voice, Amanda," a woman, whom I presume is Mrs. Davis, says. "I can't wait to meet you in person. When will you be returning to New York?"

"My daughter Maren has a cheer camp the two weeks before school starts. Our plan is to head back home the very beginning of August."

"We've loved seeing all the fun, small town posts. I hope you can try to make plans to return next summer. Or if not there, to vacation somewhere similar."

"I'm sure we can work something out," Heather says. "Amanda has been very receptive to all my suggestions."

"That's wonderful to hear," Mrs. Davis says. "I'll look forward to chatting with you. Legal's sending the contract over sometime today."

When I hang up, I expect to uncontrollably dance all over. I figure I'll sing and leap and shout.

But I don't.

I mean, it's nice that I'll have consistent money. I can stop taking almost every opportunity to push things that are on brand and only promote products I love, but otherwise. . .I don't really care. For the last few months, from the time they emailed to let me know that I was on the list of people being considered for a brand sponsor spot, I've almost obsessed about it. And now that I've won—my life hasn't really changed much. It moves along, much as it ever did.

I'm actually more delighted that Maren wants to do an outdoor activity with her cousins and sister than I am that I will now be gushing more often about Lololime than anything else. In my distraction, I've walked nearly back to the house. Bizarrely, there's a strange car there. I wonder who might be visiting. It can't be Eddy or Steve—I know their trucks. And it's not Eddy's work SUV, either.

Maybe it's a friend of Abigail's?

I've nearly reached it when I realize there's someone sitting inside. The driver door opens and the man turns around. It *is* Eddy.

"What are you doing here?" I don't even think before I speak. I really should try doing that at some point.

He nods his head slowly. "I deserve that."

"I'm sorry," I say. "It's been a long couple of days." When his shoulders slump, I'm quick to clarify. "Not because of you—work stuff." What a lie. Work is going better than ever, with the exception of the number of comments demanding more of the hot cowboy.

Oh, no, what if he's gotten on and seen those? How embarrassing. Is that why he's here? Does he want me to take those photos down?

"Can we talk?" He gestures back at the car. "All I had this afternoon were some vaccinations and a few blood draws. My sister's going to do them for me, which is why I have her car. I thought we could, I don't know, go somewhere and chat."

I should tell him no. I should send him packing. I'd feel better, probably. But the part of me that's been licking the wound over and over since he ditched me and peeled out down the driveway wants to know what he has to say. Okay, all of me wants to know. That desire's even stronger than my hurt pride. "Sure." I circle around and climb into the passenger side.

His sister's car has a fuzzy steering wheel cover. Someone painted a landscape on the dashboard, and it's actually quite good. And there are little dreamcatchers hanging on the rearview mirror, the backs of the headrests, and on the door handles. "This car is—"

"I know. Believe me, I know."

"Where are we going?"

He shrugs. "I'm too ashamed to take you to the Gorge again."

"Did I do something embarrassing there?"

His head whips toward me. "No. I did. I mean, not there, but right after."

I put my hand on his, bracing myself for the possibility that he might yank it away. But he doesn't. "Eddy, I'm not angry. I thought *you* were mad at me for posting those photos without getting your permission."

Now he pulls his hand away. "Maybe the Gorge, then. This might be easier with food to pick at."

He doesn't speak on the way, and I don't press. I know he's upset, and I know that things between us are. . .confusing, but I'm just relieved it wasn't *my fault.* I know that's stupid. I should have more self-esteem than that, but it's not like Paul built me up. The intervening years haven't really done a good job of reversing my underlying feelings of inferiority, either. The luck I've had, the career I've built, it's all been just that. Serendipity. Unsustainable, unexplainable, subject to whims outside of my control. People could, at any time, realize that I'm not sophisticated or talented or intelligent. . . or even very pretty.

When we finally reach the Gorge, Eddy jumps out of the car and runs around to open my door. I doubt it's child safety locked, but I'm not going to stress him out any more than he already is. "Thank you."

His half smile looks. . .ashamed, like he said. But what could he have to be embarrassed of? He's smart, successful, and he's very, very good-looking. He must know that, at least.

After we're seated, I order a coffee. He does the same. It *is* almost two in the afternoon, after all.

"We close in half an hour," the waitress says.

"I know," Eddy says. "Thanks, Olivia."

After she walks off, Eddy looks down at his empty hands. "I need to explain something, and it's hard for me to talk about. Can you wait until I'm done to say anything?"

"Sure."

"When I was a teenager, I worked here, in this restaurant. It was open for dinner then, and I came over most days after school, and on Saturday afternoons."

Weird start. "Alright."

"One day, a lady came in. She chatted with me for a while, asking me all kinds of questions. Could I sing? Could I play any instruments?" He rolls his eyes. "I couldn't play anything at all. I figured that would send her packing, but it didn't. Turns out, she and her producer were looking for a front man. They had a band assembled, out in California. This was kind of common back then, apparently. It wasn't the first time they'd kind of hand-crafted a band for a music label."

This is *so* not what I was expecting him to say.

"Anyway, I couldn't believe they wanted me, a nobody whose dad was a park ranger."

It's like he still doesn't realize how ridiculously gorgeous he is. Can that be true?

"I knew it was only because I was good-looking, but I let it get to my head."

So he does know.

"My parents argued at first, but the company offered a lot of money. They thought my parents' concerns were really just a way to negotiate for more money, because by that point, I'd done a sound test. Someone thought I had a nice voice, so they offered even more money. Eventually, they convinced my parents to let me go. They taught me guitar lessons, and they gave me voice lessons, and I met my other band mates." He shrugs. "It was actually really cool. For a while."

Uh-oh. I can hear the 'until' coming from a mile away.

"I liked the other guys in the band. I was the youngest one—by almost three years. Two of them were four years older than I was. I'd barely gotten my driver's license, but they were already twenty. It may sound like I'm making excuses, but I really just want you to know where I was coming from."

Making excuses for what? I'm so confused.

"Our first record did really well—better than anyone thought it would. In fact, we made the record label a killing. It seemed like a no brainer to start working on another one. . .and to go on tour."

I can hear the shoe drop in his voice.

"I didn't even know what most of the stuff the guys were using was called. I told them no a few times, but they made fun of me for being a little kid." He looks up then. "What a stupid reason, right? My name is Eddy Dutton, and I got hooked on cocaine because my friends called me a little kid when I didn't want to try it." He closes his eyes. "My manager covered for us at first. Then the entire record label did. The tour was a success, the second record recorded, and everything was fine." He winces. "Until I was high as a kite, and I hit a pedestrian with my car."

Oh, no.

"He died, immediately."

"I don't remember anything about—"

He drops his head in his hands. "You'd probably remember our band, if I played you a song or two. You might even remember our name. The Shenanigans."

"I'm pretty sure I'd remember a lead singer killing someone with his car."

"I got lucky," he says, bitterly. "The man I killed, the man I *murdered, really*, was out on bail. The evidence against him was overwhelming, from witness testimonies to forensic evidence. He had killed eleven different women. The media decided, with a little incentive from my manager, to drop coverage of his death. I was a minor for another three weeks, and they even managed to get me out of criminal charges." He sighs. "What if I'd hit someone else? And what makes it okay that I took someone's life, just because the person I killed was a terrible person? I robbed all the families whose daughters and wives he killed of their justice, too."

I'm not sure what to say.

"I went to rehab," he says. "Twice. The first time, I graduated—couldn't really even consider drugs after what I'd done. But when I went back out on tour, I felt so *guilty*. I felt like I was worthless, and when someone handed me a way to forget. . .I took it." He sighs. "The second time I graduated from rehab, I broke my contract and went home. The record label threatened me every which way from Sunday. They even filed a suit against me personally, as I was eighteen at that point, for breach of contract. I didn't argue. I let them take everything I still had left in my bank accounts. I let them do whatever they wanted. I knew I could never go back to that life, not if I wanted to find the kid I'd been before it all started."

That was clearly the right call. Look at the life he's made for himself since. "Eddy, I'm not someone who—"

He shakes his head. "You don't get it yet, right? I looked you up."

I blink. He looked me up?

"I saw your insta account—your loyal followers. They love your brand. I did some research into what that means. They're in a frenzy over the photos of me, not because of who I am, but because of how it *looks*, to have a smart, sophisticated widow dating a cowboy. A rugged, good-looking cowboy, but still. I'm the handsome 'every-man' that they want to believe you would fall for if given a chance."

"What's wrong with that?"

"Think for a moment what would happen to your brand if the media saw my full face and discovered who I am. If they look me up and discover that I killed a man. Think what would happen if they discover that it took not one, but two trips to rehab for me to stay straight? I still go to AA meetings regularly, Mandy. Do you think your fans would appreciate your choice of a hot, rugged cowboy, then?"

"You sped away. . .for me? Because you think that's what I need?"

He shrugs. "I thought you were smart and fun and cute. I knew you were only here for a while, but I liked spending time with you. But the thought of inviting the media back into my life? The thought of all that scrutiny and stress and pressure? I did it for both of us. That's why we can't date. That's why I'm not going to be asking you out again. I didn't want to tell you any of this, you know, but the thought of you blaming yourself, or thinking you'd done something wrong—"

The waitress finally shows up with coffee in to-go cups. "Thanks." Eddy throws some cash on the table and stands. The second the waitress is gone, he says, "I did it because I didn't want to hurt anyone else, at least, not any more than I had to."

At least I know it's not me, but like the Lololime news, it doesn't really make me feel any better.

21

ABIGAIL

My initial reservations notwithstanding, Robert acts entirely and completely normal all day—and the morning of the Fourth. He's not flirty. He's not inappropriate.

I think he just missed us.

He spends as much time with the kids as he does with me. I forgot how much they like him. He and Gabe play with an old train set that he finds in the attic. Izzy and Whitney and Emery convince him to play an unknown number of hands of Uno. This morning, when I wake up to help the girls feed and water goats, chickens, cats, and horses, he's already awake and about to head out with Ethan to move the water.

"I didn't realize you'd be up this early," I say.

"It's kind of unfair," he says. "For me, this feels like seven o'clock."

That's true. Different time zones. "You're sure you want to wear those shoes?" I eye his shiny white and black sneakers.

He laughs. "These are almost a year old, but I run on a treadmill mostly, so they don't look it. I've put about twice the miles on them that I was supposed to, so I bought a new pair already. I'm prepared to toss these in the trash before I leave."

"Smart man," Ethan says. "They'll probably be ready for it." He winks at me. "Unless Aunt Amanda gets her hands on them. I wonder what her Tide junk could do with them."

"Her what?"

Robert met Amanda last night. She seemed too tired to stay up and talk when she got back from. . .wherever she went. But at least he knows who she is. "She's a social media influencer," I say. "She's been doing a lot of features for Tide lately, showcasing what kinds of ranch life stains their stuff can successfully eliminate."

"Ah." He turns to Ethan. "Ready?"

"I'm going to watch the saddle bronc riding for the rodeo," I say. "Steve's judging it. I'll be leaving at nine-thirty to make sure I'm there on time, and the girls are pretty excited to watch as well. Barrel racing happens right after it."

"We'll be back by nine," Ethan says.

"Perfect," Robert says. "I'll come with you."

Wonderful.

I keep thinking I should text or call Steve to warn him, but I'm not sure what I'd say. He's already mentioned there was probably a guy who was interested in me back home—someone suitable, someone viable, but that I probably ran here, in part, to escape him.

Stupid Steve and his horse-inspired insight.

I can hardly call him and say, "Hey, you know that guy you predicted existed? Well he's here, visiting, on the one day we were supposed to spend together. Sorry about that." And what if he asks me how I feel about Robert? I don't even know myself.

But I don't put things off. That's not who I am. So

once we're done feeding the animals, and I know Steve might already be at the rodeo, I text him. MY OLDEST FAMILY FRIEND SURPRISED US BY COMING INTO TOWN FOR A VISIT.

CAN'T WAIT TO MEET HER.

I cringe. Of course he assumed it's a female. Is it weird that our oldest family friend is a guy? I can't let that one go. HE'LL PROBABLY COME WITH ME, SO YOU CAN MEET HIM IF YOU HAVE ANY TIME TODAY. I almost send it just like that, but I figure while I'm disclosing information, I may as well get it all out there. HE'S ALSO MY BOSS.

Steve calls.

Of course he does. That's a lot of information to lob at someone you've been flirt-texting and with whom you're supposed to have a not-quite-date tonight. "Hey," I say, going for nonchalant. I'm easy, airy, and totally fine.

"Your boss is here?" I can't tell if he's angry or if he's laughing.

"Uh, yeah. So Robert and Nate and I went to law school together. We met our first year, and we've all been friends ever since."

"So he's *the* guy."

I knew he'd know, but I play dumb anyway. It's a reflex, like an opossum playing dead, an armadillo rolling into a ball, or a turtle sucking into its shell. We're all just hoping we won't be squashed. "What guy? My boss? Yeah, I went part time when I started having kids, and Nate and Robert kept working full time. They both made partner while I changed diapers." Good one, Abby. Toss in a little feminist irritation and maybe that will throw him off the scent.

"The guy who likes you, I mean."

"Robert?" Deny, deny, deny. "I've known him for almost twenty years, remember?"

"Let me guess. Somehow he found out you and I were going to the dance together, and he considers it your first date since Nate passed."

I can't lie and say that's not true.

"And he just happened to be off this weekend and decided to come for a visit. He just misses you and the kids so much."

Is he magical? Can he read minds? "I didn't want you to be shocked, that's all. He'll be there, but it's no big deal. As you mentioned, he knows you and I are hanging out tonight."

"Thanks for the warning," Steve says. "I appreciate it."

"I'll still be there to watch while you judge."

"With your dear old pal sitting next to you, I'm sure."

"And the kids. Is this going to be terribly awkward?"

"Not on my account," Steve says. "Scout's honor, I'll be on my best behavior."

"Thank you."

Now if I could get Robert to make the same promise, maybe we'd actually be fine.

Ethan and Robert finish earlier than usual, which isn't much of a surprise, since Ethan had an extra set of hands with him. I can't help laughing when Robert walks in, barefoot. "Shoes didn't even pass the test to come inside, huh?"

He laughs. "Ethan says you have pretty rigorous standards about what's allowed indoors."

"He's not wrong."

Ethan and Robert take turns using the shower, and by the time they're done, everyone's raring to go.

"Will there be real bucking broncos?" Gabe asks.

"From what I hear, there will be," I say.

"Isn't it kind of awful for the animals?" Robert asks. "I'm asking you now so I don't offend anyone, but to strap the cinch on them seems pretty mean."

"The flank strap is lined with neoprene," Whitney says. "It doesn't hurt them. If it did, they wouldn't buck at all."

"Actually, the rodeo's kind of a good thing for horses," Izzy says. "A lot of the bucking broncos are horses that just refused to settle down for saddle work. This gives them a job they're good at, and a lot of them live to be healthy and strong into their late twenties."

"Some of them compete until they're thirty," Whitney says. "And that's super old for a horse."

"You are all very well informed," Robert says.

"Mr. Archer knows a lot about it," Ethan says. "He's been teaching us."

"So he's going to ride a bucking bronco?" Robert seems genuinely curious.

"He says he's too old for that." Gabe smiles. "But he won a lot when he was younger so they want him to pick the winners."

"You said he was judging—I just forgot." Robert's grin is a little sheepish as we all pile into the minivan.

"I have a bag with snacks, and I have cash. What am I forgetting?"

"Nothing, Mom. Plus, it's not like it's far. I can drive back, or Robert can, if you've forgotten something."

"Absolutely," Robert says. "Let's go."

We arrive in plenty of time to buy tickets and find decent seats, only halfway up in the stands. The whole thing's much closer than I realized it would be. Horses and steers are all over the place. Saddled, haltered, going, coming. It's a lot busier and a lot more. . .legitimate looking than I expected.

"Abby!" Steve's sitting on a beautiful buckskin, wearing dark jeans and a blue button-down shirt that just matches his eyes. "Whitney, Izzy, Ethan, Gabe, welcome." He looks around. "Emery and Maren aren't coming?"

"They're supposed to be," I say. "They'd already left when I did—I wonder if they're lost."

"I'll look for them." Steve wheels around and urges his horse forward. It takes off like a shot, leaving dust behind him.

"So that's the date?" Robert's lips tremble with suppressed laughter.

"The Horse Doc," Gabe says. "That's what people call him."

"He's. . .younger than I imagined." He leans closer and whispers. "And he looks mostly sober."

I forgot that I never corrected my earlier assumption. "Oh, that was a misunderstanding. The beer was for one of his horses."

"Sure it was." Robert winks at me.

I haven't told Robert he's a doctor, either, but I know it will turn into a thing. Better to get it out of the way now, probably. "And it turns out he was sleeping—"

"Aunt Abby!" Emery's carrying an enormous paper dish full of nachos that I'm surprised her mother bought her as she walks up the stadium steps. "We were on the other side. Steve told us you were over here."

"Oh good," Robert says. "You found us."

"Can I have some nachos?" Gabe's eyes practically light up.

"Sure."

"Don't eat them all," I say.

"I can go get him some," Robert says.

"No, you don't have to—"

"I'd love to." He stands up. "Anyone else want anything?"

Ethan, always hungry, wants hot dogs, plural. Whitney wants popcorn, and Izzy, of course, wants cotton candy. "I veto that," I say. "But popcorn or nachos or something super salty that will likely cause an immediate heart attack is fine. I draw the line at starting the day with sticky balls of sugar that inevitably get stuck in my hair."

"No cotton candy consumption before noon," Robert says. "Duly noted."

He's been gone for three seconds when Steve rides around and stops in front of us. "You found them," he says.

"Thanks," Amanda says. "Appreciate the tip."

"Do you need anything?" Steve glances around. "I have a few more minutes before we get started."

"You're riding a horse as a judge?" Ethan asks.

Steve smiles. "I'm judging saddle broncs, but I'm assisting with the calf roping and bull riding. I'll need to be mounted for that. This is just a little warm-up for Moses, here."

"He's a beautiful horse," I say. "Almost as stunning as Farrah."

"I thought you liked my palomino best," he says.

"I do." I smile. "But he's a close second, if he's as sweet as Leo."

"All of mine are good," Steve says, "but Leo's special for sure. Moses is awfully close."

"Maybe I'll have to test them both and see. He could give Leo a run for his money."

"I'd like that." Steve smiles.

Robert shows up a moment later, his arms full of snacks, and starts making his way to our row. Whitney and Izzy jog down the stairs, taking their popcorn and hot dogs. "Thanks."

"I'd better go," Steve says. "I'll come check in later."

The rodeo itself is fascinating. I've never been to one, so it all seems new. The saddle bronc riding looks absolutely horrifying—I'm relieved Steve's only judging. Three out of eight men competing are thrown before the minimum time, and one of them fails to mark up, which means his spurs weren't above the horse's shoulder when his front feet first hit the ground. The broncos are big and shaggy-footed, most of them. I certainly wouldn't get on them for anything.

"You don't have an interest in this, right?" I glare at Ethan, as if I can somehow ensure he doesn't.

"Steve did it," he says. "I bet he could teach me."

"Not if he values his life."

"I'm kidding, Mom. I don't need my brain scrambled. It's hard enough to focus as it is."

Thank goodness.

But when the barrel racing starts, all four of the girls shift to the front of their seats. It's pretty cool to watch the girls fly around the barrels, their reins flipping back and forth, clods of dirt flying up behind their horses' hooves. "Wow." Emery sits back. "I want to do that."

Amanda's mouth drops open.

"I mean, I'd like to one day. I know I probably won't."

"They don't even have rodeos in New York City," Amanda says.

"Actually, I looked it up," Maren says. "They have them in Madison Square Gardens."

Maren looked it up? I don't laugh, but it's kind of hard. She's changed quite a lot in a very short time.

The bull riding's almost too much for me. One guy nearly gets trampled, but Steve rides past and yanks him out of the way just in time.

"That was awesome," Gabe says. "Good job, Mr. Steve!" He claps and cheers as loudly as he can at his size. It's pretty cute to watch.

But eventually, it's time to head back. The kids all whine and complain, but that's how I know they had fun. It took me a while as a parent to discover that truth: if your kids are having a good time, assume there will be a lot of whining later on.

Now, as a seasoned parent, I'm immune.

"Guys, we have chores to do, and I have to make a potato salad for the barbecue."

"Fine, fine." Whitney grumbles, but she stops whining. It's something.

Once we reach the house, Robert says, "I can help with the potato salad. My mom taught me how to make the *best* kind. If you have apples."

"Apples?"

He smiles. "Trust me."

I welcome any and all help in the kitchen, and his mother doesn't let me down. Adding apples to a fairly traditional potato salad really makes it stand out. "Thanks."

"I'm happy to watch the kiddos so you can focus on your date," he says.

The kids are watching *Gravity Falls*, which is a show I do *not* understand at all. But they're entertained, which means I can actually talk for a moment. I lean against the table. "Is that why you came, Robert? Be honest, because Ethan and Izzy can keep an eye on the other two. It's not like I'm a negligent parent."

"I didn't mean to imply that you were at all." He sighs. "And yes. It makes me sound like an idiot, but you know how I feel, and I'm afraid when I heard you had a date, I don't know." He drops his eyes to his shoes. "Maybe I went a little crazy."

"It's hard for me," I say. "I miss Nate every single day. Most days I miss him every minute. I hate being all alone —it's not even about needing to take the trashcans to the curb and do all the laundry alone. The kids have really pitched in, but it's not the same as having someone to talk to about everything, and someone who cares about the little details as much as I do." I laugh. "Or at least someone who pretends to care." Nate never paid much attention to the kids' school stuff or the horseback lessons or the gymnastics lessons. But he did care if one of them was hurting or lonely or upset.

"You can talk to me," Robert says. "Anytime. About anything."

"You're my boss." I sigh. "It's not that simple."

"Fine." He shakes his head. "I didn't want to do this, but I have no choice. You're fired."

"Hilarious." I sink into a chair. "I love working for you, actually. You're an amazing boss. You're brilliant and fair, and you always have my back. It's just that I can't really talk to you about how far my paycheck is stretching or the pair of shoes I want, right? It would sound like I'm asking for money." I shrug. "I don't know, I can't explain it."

"And you can talk to this guy about that stuff?" Robert sits next to me, his eyes almost too earnest.

"Oh please. I barely know him, truly. He's nice, and he's attractive, and he's funny." I sigh. "I want to have someone I can talk to about those things again. I think I realized that out here, in part because I'm in an unfamiliar place so things feel more stressful. In part maybe it's because I feel more isolated. But also, Robert, I won't be here much longer. So if I want to go on a date and not worry that I might break down and start bawling over a plate of ribs and potato salad, well, it's low risk."

He nods. "I get that, actually. But the last time I figured you'd be done dating someone pretty quickly, you married him."

"That's true."

"I know I said I wouldn't bring it up again, but it turns out that was a lie. If you're going to date, I'm going to be throwing my hat into the ring over and over, because Abby?"

"Yeah?"

His intense eyes lock on mine. "You're worth all the effort and then some, and I don't want you to be alone either."

This time, I don't feel uncomfortable. I don't feel uneasy. Maybe talking to Steve helped me somehow. I just feel. . .like I'm waking up after a too-long nap. A little groggy and disoriented, but also ready to stretch and do something active.

"Hey, Abs?" Amanda's standing in the doorway of her bedroom, which opens onto the hall near the kitchen.

"Yeah?"

"You got a second?"

"Sure." I touch Robert's warm hand and squeeze it lightly, then I stand up and head for Amanda's room. After I walk inside, she closes the door. "Whoa, is something wrong?" I've never been invited inside the master before.

She bursts into tears.

"Hey, what's going on?"

"I'm such a loser." I can barely make out what she's saying for all the heaving sobs. "It's been one year and you have two guys chasing you, and I have nothing and no one."

I grab her shoulders to try and snap her out of it, but she takes it as some kind of comforting motion and pulls me in for a hug. I don't think we've hugged in all the time we've known each other. The Brooks aren't really an affectionate family, and I'm only affectionate with my own children. I pat her back as non-awkwardly as possible.

"I'm sorry." She hiccups.

"What's going on?"

She sits me down and tells me about Eddy—how much she likes him even though they just met, and how he basically can't get involved with her because his past could wreck her image, which forms the basis for her entire career. "Lololime could even cancel the contract." She wipes her nose on her sleeve. Ick. "I checked. They have a clause for revelation of past infidelity."

I should probably offer to look over it for her. . .but wait. "You got the deal?" I reach across the bed and pat her knee. "That's amazing! I mean, why aren't you more excited?"

"I don't know!" she wails. "It feels like I can't be happy about anything."

"Was this the first guy since Paul you were really excited about?" I hate prying, but it feels like the only explanation for this kind of reaction.

She freezes. "You think I was excited about Paul?"

"You weren't?"

She laughs. "He was rich. He was tall. He was good-looking. He liked me."

"That's why you married him?" Please say no. Please don't let that be the reason.

She shrugs. "My family had no money, and I was the first child who was attractive. None of us were well educated."

Don't pity her. She'll see that on your face. I open my mouth, but I have no idea what to say.

"I knew it," she mutters. "I knew you and Nate really were happy."

"I think most couples are happy."

She rolls her eyes and groans. "You only think that because you were. It's pretty rare, I think."

I don't point out that her own logic could be applied to prove the reverse assumption. "Is Eddy going to the barbecue tonight?"

"He'll probably have a date who has a real job—who makes something, or *does* something. It's not like it's hard for him—women take one look at his face—"

"He is handsome. Those dimples."

She widens her eyes. "Are you kidding me? You already have *two guys.*"

I laugh. "I have zero interest in Eddy, I can assure you."

"How did you and Nate stay happy?" she asks. "Was it all the hard work people are always talking about?"

I've never really understood all that claptrap. Life with anyone requires a lot of work. I like work. But things between me and Nate were never hard. They were the best part of my life. "I think it helps when you like them at the beginning. Truly like them, I mean."

It was apparently the wrong thing to say. She bursts out crying again.

"I'm so sorry," I say. "But for what it's worth, your biggest problem right now seems to be that you don't know how amazing you are. Eddy would be lucky to date you. You're gorgeous, you're talented—I've seen you run that business. It's not all pretty pictures and clever filters. You're also kind, and you're creative. Don't undervalue yourself."

"Says the Harvard lawyer with the perfect children."

"You mean the one who'll be going to community college this fall? Or do you mean the second grader who kept eating dried glue?"

"What?"

"After Nate died, Gabe started secretly pouring glue into the cubby on his desk, waiting for it to dry, and then *eating* it. I had no idea how to stop him—we took the glue away, but he'd find more. It was like trying to get rid of all the spinning wheels in Sleeping Beauty—it was a plan doomed to failure."

That, inexplicably, *was* the right thing to say. "So you're not one hundred percent perfect."

"Not even close," I say.

"What should I do?"

"You should get dressed," I say. "Look like dynamite. Go to the barbecue, sit by Robert, and flirt outrageously if Eddy comes anywhere near. He may not want to be photographed for your account, but he's a red-blooded male. I bet he'll rise to the occasion if he sees someone else pursuing you."

"Do you really think so?"

"Let's see if Robert will help."

I pitch it perfectly, appealing to Robert's pride by describing him accurately as the hotshot big city lawyer with the pretty face, and giving him something to do while I'm on my date—flirt with another beautiful and age-appropriate woman. "Okay," he says. "I'll do it."

I knew he would. Sometimes dealing with men is like stealing candy from an inattentive grocery checker. (Taking from babies was never a good analogy in my book. First, they eat their candy too fast. And second, there's too much guilt if you take something from them.)

Steve and I agreed we'd meet at the barbecue, since his truck won't fit all my kids comfortably. So we all pile in to the van and minivan, and we head out. Luckily, parking isn't hard. Steve's waiting in front of the city building in faded jeans and a polo shirt.

He looks so different from the Rodeo Steve I saw earlier. This looks more like doctor Steve.

"What?" Robert asks. "No horse?"

Steve frowns.

Robert holds out his hand. "I'm Robert Marwell. I've worked with Abby for a long time. I saw you earlier, but we didn't really meet."

"Is this where you threaten to take me out back and shoot me if I break her heart?" Steve asks.

To my utter shock, Robert actually laughs. "I'm not sure I could shoot you before you punched me. I'm not the most violent person alive, but if I survived whatever you did, I'd be sure to slap a vicious restraining order on you afterward."

Steve laughs too, and I hope that the rest of the night will be just as friendly. "Alright," I say.

The kids disappear faster than a box of name brand cereal in a house with six children.

"Amanda, allow me." Robert opens the door, and she walks in beside him, smiling.

"What's going on there?" Steve asks.

I shrug. "They seem to have hit it off."

Two birds? Welcome to this one stone. It's called Abby the Brilliant. Sic Robert on poor sad Amanda and solve your problems and hopefully hers as well.

"What kind of barbecue do you like best?" Steve asks.

I scrunch my nose. "Is this where I have to confess that I hardly eat meat at all?"

"Excuse me?"

I shrug. "It grosses me out unless it's hidden in stuff. Like, a little meat in a spaghetti sauce is fine as long as it's been simmered long enough so it's tender."

He takes my bowl of potato salad. "I'll try not to take it personally when you don't eat any of my brisket, then."

"You made it?"

"I also brought chili," he says. "It's kind of a tradition at this point."

As we walk inside, every single person we pass smiles and greets Steve, and all of them ask who I am. It's a little. . .embarrassing. It feels like I'm being weighed and judged and found wanting.

"You look absolutely miserable," he whispers. "What's wrong?"

"Is it that obvious?"

"Only to me," he says.

"I don't know any of these people."

Kevin walks by, chatting with a cute brunette, and he stops. "Abby, so glad you came. This is my friend, Rachel."

I feel a little better once I'm acknowledged by someone, even if it's one of only four people here I know. "Food," I say. "I think I need food."

We pass Amanda and Robert, both holding full plates, as we reach the line. I wonder whether Steve delayed bringing us here to minimize the awkward interactions. If he did, mad props to him.

"Is your friend enjoying his trip?" Steve really likes baked beans, judging by the size of his spoonful.

"I think so," I say. "But you were right. He did confess that he came because he heard I had a date."

"No shock there."

I take a generous helping of my own potato salad, and then another spoonful of coleslaw. By the time I add a roll, I only have room for a slice of Steve's brisket, and a little bowl of his chili. "Which one's yours?"

He points.

I scoop. "You're acting like I'm some kind of hot prospect." I can't keep the incredulity from my tone. "I've known Robert for twenty years, and he's an old friend."

"You don't see yourself clearly."

Isn't that what I was just telling Amanda? How can I argue with him now in good faith? "Agree to disagree—I'm pretty objective about most things."

"You okay to sit outside?" He points. "The view over the water is about perfect as the sun sets."

"Sure." As a bonus, Amanda's sitting with Robert inside—and Eddy's watching them like a hawk eyeing chickens. Now that I've actually seen a hawk watching little spring chickens, that phrase has new meaning—like a hawk. Hawks are kind of jerks.

"That seems to be going well."

"What?" Steve asks. "Your friend and your sister-in-law?"

I nod.

"He's just trying to make you jealous."

I didn't intend to tell him, but now I'm kind of stuck. I explain that Amanda likes Eddy and that Robert just happened to be on hand.

"Ah." Steve grins. "Now that's a solid plan."

"Right?"

"I could have come up with that myself. Nice work."

"Hopefully it does work. Amanda's not having the best day—actually, make that the best week."

"But is Eddy really right for her?" Steve pulls a face. "I mean, it's *Eddy*."

"What does that mean?"

"He's. . .got a reputation."

Probably a womanizer. I'm not surprised, with a face and body like he has. "Is this what we're going to talk about all night?"

"No." Steve swivels to look straight at me. "It's not."

"What else did you have in mind?"

"Did you always want to be a lawyer?"

That's not what I expected. "No, not at all."

"What did you want to do?"

"Honestly?" I laugh. "I had those annoying parents who insisted I could do or be anything at all. I really thought I'd be a famous singer."

"Can you sing?"

"I can carry a tune, but I'm no Celine Dion," I say. "I was taking voice lessons, and my singing coach actually said I should be a lawyer some day."

"And just like that, you decided to do it?"

I shake my head. "Heck, no. He was the first, but about half the people I met said that at some point or another."

"What about you made them think that?"

"Beats me. I didn't lie, cheat, or steal, and I never clocked my time, so by my accounting, I did nothing lawyerly."

"You probably just intimidated them with your poise," he says.

"Stop."

"Steve!" A woman with her hair in a bun, surrounded with a halo of greying frizz, rushes up. "Come quick. It's Ron. I think he's having a heart attack."

He leaps to his feet and follows her, pausing only to say, "I'll be back as soon as I can."

I watch as he drops to his knees in front of someone just outside the door. He talks to him, touches him, and asks the man to push on things. After a few moments, he turns back toward me and shakes his head, his lips pursed. His message is pretty clear: not a heart attack. But he can't really just stand up and leave. He's stuck there reassuring everyone and doing doctorly things.

"That was exciting." Robert's leaning against the light post at the edge of the dock a few feet away.

I didn't even see him walk over. "Yeah, never a dull moment, even in this sleepy town."

"Why did they call Steve over to help?" He narrows his eyes. "Is he a nurse or something?"

"Doctor," I say.

"Wait, is he really?"

"Emergency room doc," I say. "That's why they call him the Horse Doc. He doesn't ever talk about it, so I was surprised too when he treated Whitney."

"He put the cast on?"

"Yep. It comes off next week," I say.

"He may not talk about it much, but why didn't you tell me he was a doctor?" Robert's tone isn't recriminating. He just sounds sad.

I walk over to stand next to him. “I don’t know. I thought it might upset you.”

“Because he’s actually a catch?” His smile is wry. “Whereas I’m all mixed up with memories of Nate?”

“It’s not like that.“ But that’s a lie, I realize. Almost all my memories with Robert involve Nate. No matter whom I date eventually, I’ll deal with guilt, but the idea of dating someone whom we knew together? It feels worse, more disloyal, somehow.

Which isn’t rational.

If he could choose, Nate might pick Robert. He’s a known quantity, a good guy. He genuinely loves our kids.

“You sure?” Robert’s staring down at me, his face cast in shadows from the light above us.

Everyone else is gathered around Ron and Steve and the wife.

It’s a strange feeling, being surrounded by people and yet alone. It’s a feeling I’ve felt over and over on repeat ever since Nate died. Except, this time I’m not all alone. Robert’s with me. He’s always with me. “I have memories of you—just you,” I say. “Remember before Nate and I ever started dating? We did our research together for the moot court presentation.”

“You ate an entire package of Red Vines,” Robert says.

“And then I puked.” I shouldn’t find that so funny, but for some reason I do. “I was such an idiot.”

“If you were in a room, you were the only person I even saw.”

I turn to look at him, really look at him. Not as an old friend. Not as Nate’s buddy. As a man. He’s tall. He’s in great shape. He’s smart and kind and successful. And he has always cared for me. As if he can sense my feelings shifting too, his head leans down toward mine.

For one moment, my heart flips over, and I wonder what it would be like to kiss Robert.

But then I remember when we did mock trial together, the three of us. I remember when Ethan was born, and Robert brought Nate cigars. I remember dancing with Nate on New Year's, while Robert danced with Maisie, and I just can't. His lips have nearly reached mine when I stumble backward, my feet saving me from what my heart's not ready to handle.

Except, I forgot I'm standing on a dock.

My foot falls backward, my arms pinwheeling wildly. Robert reaches for me, but he's as shocked as I am. I fall down, down, down, backslapping into the lake. The water is freezing—it hits me like a wall of ice. I'm plunging under, sinking deeper and deeper. It's so dark, I can't even tell which way is up.

Until strong arms wrap around me and drag me upward. When I finally recover enough to open my eyes and make sense of what I'm seeing, I realize it's Steve. He must have taken off at a dead run and dived head first to reach me that fast. "Th-th-thanks." My teeth chatter.

"I'm no expert, but we may need to get you home and dried off." He grabs a wooden ladder. "I'm afraid we may miss the dance."

"You're no expert?" I'm shaking head to toe. "If you're not an expert on stuff like this, who is?"

He leans a little closer, the heat from his body radiating toward me. "It's too bad you had to dive into the lake to avoid an unwanted kiss, because I'm pretty impressive on the dance floor. Maybe for our second date, don't bring your boss."

"I'm not sure my heart can take another."

"Doctor says? It'll be fine."

Tonight certainly went off course, but when he mentioned a second date, I didn't want to escape. I'm going to call that progress.

22

AMANDA

I always knew Abby was dumb, but I had no idea what a monumental idiot she truly was. If I had someone like Robert on the hook, I would never let him go. He does exactly as he promises he will, staying by my side, attentive to me from the moment we walk through the door. He's intelligent *and* witty—many people mistakenly think these are the same thing, but they're really quite different. He's polite and thoughtful. And he's so beautiful that he actually gives Eddy a run for his money.

Where Eddy is all light brown and blonde and grassy green eyes, Robert has more olive skin, golden-brown eyes, and black hair. Where Eddy is longish hair that falls in his face, Robert is perfectly groomed short hair with just a hint of dark stubble. In all honesty, if someone had told me that another such perfect-looking guy existed in real life, in our age bracket, I'd have laughed in their face. If anyone has the power to make me forget Eddy, it's Robert.

But his eyes never stop following her.

As if it wasn't already obvious from the way his body

angles toward her, the way he talks about nothing else—this man is so far gone, it's almost obnoxious. It serves as a reminder that I really am entirely and utterly pathetic. I need my sister-in-law's cast-offs that flew in from another state to be my date.

I am such a loser.

After about fifteen minutes—with no Eddy in sight—I'm ready to throw in the towel and go home. If there was any way Maren and Emery could fit in the car with Abigail, I'd be begging off right now. Sometimes having kids is a real drag. Robert's still talking, and this time he's telling a story about how Abigail had the idea to start working song lyrics and later animals, into their various legal briefs when they were associates. Once, in a crowning achievement, she managed to use the word 'platypus' and the phrase '*The Sun'll Come Out Tomorrow*' in the same legal brief, and it actually improved the argument.

"That might sound silly to you, but among lawyers, this kind of thing, talent meeting whimsy, it's rare. Even in a very boring, very stodgy profession, she brings extra light to every room just by being there," he says with a sigh.

I'm about three inches away from slapping him across the face with my Burberry purse when Eddy walks through the front door. When he sees me, he stops dead, his eyes suitably wide and full of longing. A heartbeat later, he scans to see to whom I'm speaking and catches sight of Robert for the first time.

That phrase, 'a picture's worth a thousand words'? I thought I knew what it meant. After all, it's kind of my job. I take photos that are compelling enough to convince people to purchase products they didn't know they needed. I make sure that I come across as thrifty while also posh. I show my daughters' grace and beauty, while also exposing their underlying vulnerability so that people feel compelled to help me and also want to be like me. That's what makes my brand work.

But I never really *got* it.

When Abigail gave me my pep talk, I heard the words she was saying. How could I not? But deep down, I didn't believe any of it. There's never been a time in my life I couldn't hear my mother saying, "Why can't you sit up straighter? Smile more elegantly. This posture will never get you number one!"

At every single pageant Mom dragged me to, she'd repeat the same thing, over and over, like a crazed mantra. "Shoulders back, head slightly tilted, lips pursed. That's how to win first place, nice and easy. That's where the money is."

That's where the money is.

Except I never did quite measure up. I was lucky to take second place, most of the time. Or worse, I'd win "Miss Personality." I'd shove those plaques so far under my bed that Mom would never find them again. They were worse than taking last place ever could have been.

So Abby's words, while kind, had years and years of stronger, more calculated words to fight with—and lose.

But Eddy's face?

In nearly fifteen years of marriage to Paul, he never once looked at me like Eddy is looking at me now.

In more than three years of dating the most eligible men in New York City, not one of them has reacted in an even somewhat similar way.

Eddy's nostrils flare, his jaw locks, and his eyes, oh, his eyes. They're shocked, and then hurt, and then enraged. If he were a bull in Spain, he'd be charging Robert. If he were a dog in an alley, he'd be lunging at him, snarling, feral.

But he's not either of those things. He's an educated,

civilized man, and his brain reminds him that it's unacceptable to behave in such a way at a community event. And then his date walks through the door after him and takes his arm. I wonder what my face looks like.

Robert says, "Amanda? What's—" He spins around and notices the tall, beautiful couple by the door. "Oh, got it. Game time." No matter what he does, no matter how things go with Abigail, I will be eternally grateful to him. In that moment, he leans closer to me, shifts his arm to the outside of mine, his fingers brushing my forearm, and he whispers in my ear, "Don't worry. He may have been able to find someone else to bring, but she's a dime a dozen. *You're* a rare beauty, and you're an impressive career woman, too. He's wishing he had never come."

"I don't want him to hate me," I say, softly.

Robert chuckles. "Oh, it's not you he hates. It's me he'd like to rip limb from limb. It's me he's boiling to punch." He arches one eyebrow. "Does this job come with hazard pay? If he does boil over?"

"Pretend you need to go to the bathroom," I say.

He tilts his head until our eyes meet. "Excuse me?"

"I want to see what he'll do if you leave for a moment. Go to the bathroom?"

"Where is it?"

"I think it's just outside," I say. "Look, there." I point toward the back door.

"Alright, but I'm not going to be gone long. Tonight's all about making him jealous. It's not about seeming available."

I nod.

The second Robert's gone, the moment his broad shoulders walk through the door, Eddy moves my way—after ditching his date. My mouth goes dry. My hands begin to sweat. Why does that happen? Does my body hate me? It wants me to sound like a raspy grim reaper and to have the hands of a teenage boy? Ugh.

"Amanda."

I had forgotten how deep his voice is and what a beautiful timbre it has. Even knowing how pathetic it makes me, my entire body curls toward him, like a desperate flower toward the sunlight. "Eddy." My only hope is that he can't see the longing in my eyes.

"Who's the guy?"

I should've known he wouldn't tiptoe around it. "He's a lawyer from Houston."

His eyes widen. "He works with Abby?"

How did he figure it out so fast? "He came out to see—"

"At least he's smart," Eddy spits out. "It took him five minutes to attach himself to you, I see." Wait. He *is* jealous? Even knowing that Robert came for Abby? "I bet he can't stay very long, though. What's he here for? Some kind of trial prep thing?"

"Uh. Sure. But their firm has an office in New York City." Where did that come from? I'm not even sure whether it's true.

But Eddy's hand clenches at his side. "How perfect for you." His words are entirely at odds with his tone and his body language.

"Eddy?" I realize where I've seen her before. She's the woman who won the barrels competition today. That must be why her eyes look just a little crazy—like a female version of the leader of a biker gang. "Didn't you say you were going to sing? Everyone's asking."

"Later," he says, not even turning to face her.

"We were so late getting here, that it's already later." I hate the past that phrase indicates. *They were late.* It makes me desperate to know *why* they were late.

"You're like a nagging wife," Eddy says.

She laughs, totally unconcerned that she might be too loud or too much. . . anything. I want to laugh like that, completely secure in my own skin. "Sing now, Edward Dutton, or forever be remembered as the former pop star who reneged on his promise."

Eddy grits his teeth.

Clearly everyone here knows about his past, which makes me feel significantly less special. He came and picked me up and made a big production of telling me the very thing that everyone else already knows. Then again, why wouldn't they? They've probably known him his entire life. Some of them lived through it—probably not this lady who is clearly at least ten years younger than I am, but some of them. The same sense that came over me when we arrived, that I don't *belong* here and never will, washes over me again.

"Fine," he says.

The girl beams and spins around, presumably to tell whoever was bugging them that he'll do it.

"But only on one condition," he whispers, so quietly he must be talking to me. No one else can hear him.

I glance around anyway, just to make sure. I'm the idiot who's always waving back to people when they were waving to the person behind me. Or I'll say 'you're welcome' to someone who was saying thank you to someone on the phone. But no one else is close—he must be talking to me, right?

"What's that?" I finally ask.

"I'll sing for all the people who have loved and hated and been annoyed with me my entire life, like I do at every one of these dumb community events. People who don't really care, but just want something akin to a real celebrity among them." He pauses. "But only if you promise to dance with me once tonight." He's the one looking around this time. "I know you have a date, and I know he's perfect for you, with his boardroom hair and his practiced smile. He probably has no skeletons in his closet, and he can drink a dozen beers at your side instead of clutching his stupid AA chip and avoiding photographs of his face, but you owe me."

"I do?"

"I'm the Sexy Cowboy. I'm Heroes Ride Horses." This time, his smile is sly. "I saved your horses after that storm. I figure the least I'm due is one stupid dance." He searches my eyes, looking for. . .something. "Plus, it's always good to keep them guessing. A little jealousy will only help you."

Heaven help me, he's suggesting the very ploy we're using on him. My laugh is so nervous, it belongs at a speed-dating event. "Right, I mean, okay."

"So you will?" He bites his lip. "Even if I sound off-key and pitchy, you'll still dance with me?"

Somehow, I doubt that will be his problem. "I'll try and look past it." I was talking about his singing, but the way his face brightens, I wonder if he's thinking of something else.

"Will you really?"

I'm not sure what we're talking about anymore.

"And, as always, Eddy Dutton has been badgered into agreeing to perform a few songs for us tonight." A tall man wearing a black cowboy hat at the front of the room gestures. "No matter how many times I've heard this guy, it never gets old."

Eddy stands up and makes his way to the front.

"And I heard a rumor he's even got a few new songs."

As he turns, I can see that Eddy's irritated. I wonder why. "They're definitely not ready to perform." He frowns.

"We don't mind if they're rough." The guy claps him on the back. "We're your biggest fans."

"My only fans." Eddy chuckles. "Maybe by Labor Day."

"We're just happy to hear you're writing new stuff. It's been a hot minute." The guy hands him the mic and walks away, but he's moving with purpose.

"I promised one song," Eddy says. "And that's all you really want, trust me."

A surprising amount of boos and heys rise up from the people in the room.

"Here's your guitar." The brunette barrel racer hands him a beautiful gold and black acoustic, and I have to suppress a twinge of jealousy. That feels like a pretty personal thing for her to be in charge of providing.

"Thanks."

The tall man shows up with a mic stand and sets it up. These people don't mess around. They all want to be able to hear. The sound of chairs being shifted around, the rubber bottoms of their metal legs squeaking on the polished wooden floor, is the only sound that fills the room, my own chair among them.

"This is a song I haven't sung in a while, but I think it fits for the Fourth." I expect it to be a cover—a song I've heard before, but sung by Eddy.

I'm totally wrong.

When his fingers begin moving over the guitar strings, a little thrill runs through me. The chords are strong and sure, as if this is nothing to him. He doesn't look nervous at all. I suppose if he performed in front of thousands and thousands of people, a little meeting room with a hundred people he knows is no big deal.

I've always admired his speaking voice. It's low and easy, rich and full. But his singing voice? I'm not surprised those people scouted him for his face, but he made it sound like that was all he brought to the table. That's clearly not true. They must have known they stumbled upon unmined gold. I wonder how much it's changed since the days he was famous. Even now, as an adult, it's vibrant and thick without being scratchy or heavy.

He's singing about how life rolls along, fast and then slow, boring and nothing new. And then wham, unexpected, it socks you in the face and nothing looks the same anymore. I can certainly relate to that. The chorus, though, he sings more slowly, more forcefully. "Waves and wild wind buffeted me, until I met you. You were the course I didn't know I could find. I'll follow you home to the end. My lighthouse, unexpected and bright. My lighthouse, loving me through the night."

He looks right at me as he sings, and it feels like the entire room falls away.

Am I imagining it? Does everyone feel like he's singing to them? Is that part of his charm? I can't breathe until he takes his last breath, gently strumming the notes one last time. When he smiles at me, I begin to hope. He said he just came to tell me why nothing could happen. He told me he was all wrong for me.

But if that's true, why does this feel so right?

Now that he's not singing, I can hear a huge ruckus outside. I'm near the door, so I rush out to see what has caused it. Everyone's gathered around some man who's lying on the ground, but I notice something else. Abby's standing near the edge of the dock, and my supposed date is right next to her. They look like they're in their own little cocoon. And if Eddy sees that? He'll never believe any part of Robert likes me.

I keep watching the doorway, waiting for the moment Eddy will walk through and find out the truth: I'm a big fat fake. Sometimes it feels like I've been waiting for the world to figure that out for my entire life. Only, just as I see him coming, there's some new hubbub behind me.

It takes a moment for me to process what happened—Abby fell into the lake!

Before I can even take a step, Steve's sprinting across the dock. I watch, completely transfixed, as he leaps off the edge and into the water. I shiver just thinking about it. The night here's always cool—so unlike the City in the summer, where you're lucky if it goes from sweltering to slightly less sweltering. I can't imagine being dumped in all that water. In the dark.

Robert's peering over the side in alarm, and I can tell he's not sure whether to jump in or not, since someone else already has. But his hesitation might be his downfall. When Abby's face crests the edge of the ladder, she's got eyes only for one person, and it's not Robert.

"What happened?" Eddy asks.

"Looks like my sister-in-law miscalculated how close she could stand to the edge."

"Some people stay far from things that are risky." His voice at my back, his breath on my ear, they send shivers up and down my spine. "That's the prudent thing to do, of course, but for some reason, some people skirt the danger, traipsing as close to the edge as they can."

"Probably true." It's hard, but I don't turn around to face him.

"Which are you?"

"What does that mean?" I can't help it this time—I turn.

His grin's at full throttle, both dimples showing, beautifully straight teeth shining. "I've been thinking about our conundrum."

"We have a conundrum?" I'm not entirely sure what that word means. I think it's a dilemma?

"I think we do." His hand brushes against my arm lightly. "At least, on my side there's one."

"Maybe you should explain it," I say, "for your dopey friend."

"Don't." His hand moves to my face, brushing my cheek. "Don't ever say that about yourself."

"I—"

"You're a rockstar in the social realm, with two hundred and fifty thousand followers on Instagram alone. You did that yourself, by posting helpful and beautiful content that people love to read." His eyes drop to my mouth. "And I'm like a ticking time bomb, waiting to go off and ruin everything you've carefully built." He sighs. "I tried to walk away. I should walk away. It's the right thing to do. I've done it for years now, from every drop of alcohol and from every type of drug in the world. No matter how tempting, no matter how desperate I felt, I turned and ran. I know precisely how to do it." His eyes move back up to mine. "But Amanda, this feels harder somehow. I keep circling back around."

"You don't really—"

"I want to punch that shiny, slick lawyer in the face, and I don't even know the man. When he touched your arm—" His nostrils flare again. "And that's not even the worst thing."

"It's not?" Because to me, it sounded like the best.

"No." He licks his lips. "It's not."

"Are you going to share the worst?"

He shakes his head. "I can't. Because I like you too much to blow up your life." His entire face contorts. "This is a big mistake." He turns and takes a step.

I grab his arm, my fingers tightening on his very muscular tricep. "Wait."

He freezes.

"What if we were smart about it?"

He hasn't moved, but I know he's listening. Even with

my heart pounding loudly in my ears, I can tell he's following my every word.

"What if, for my last few weeks here, we saw each other, but I was intentionally careful not to post your face."

"You're saying we can't defuse the bomb, but we tiptoe around it?" When he turns, his eyes are hopeful.

I still can't believe he wants to date me. No matter what he said, I was sure he'd walked away because he hadn't been too interested. Or I worried that he'd realized that he was way out of my league. "My fans like the mystery. And your side profile is good enough to string them along for a few weeks."

"Oh, I'm already getting ideas of ways you could photograph me that wouldn't show my face." His wicked smile heats parts of me that shouldn't be getting hot at a family event.

"Maybe we shouldn't be talking about this right now," I say, glancing over my shoulder at where his date is watching us.

He follows my eyes. "Do you mean because of Rebecca?" He laughs. "She's my manager. I still do gigs occasionally, local stuff only. Birthday parties, weddings, that kind of thing. She takes fifteen percent for setting them all up and collecting payment. I told her I wasn't coming tonight, and she showed up at my place and dragged me here. Her kid's turning two soon and she wants to make enough money to pay for some kind of themed birthday." He shakes his head. "After I sing at one of these things, there's always a little flurry of new bookings."

How did I read that so wrong?

But Rebecca's certainly curious about us. She's looked over here no less than five times. "So she's married, then?"

Eddy pauses. "Actually, she's single. The dad turned out to be a jerk."

Which means I was right. She may want the bookings, but that doesn't mean she's not also hoping for Eddy himself. "Listen."

The music starts up then, and two or three couples walk out onto the middle of the dock. White twinkle lights wound around the handrails and up the light posts click on, and a nice breeze blows across my heated cheeks. "Do I have to listen to whatever lecture you have prepared right now?" His smile is back to being wicked. "Or can I collect on my dance now, and get lectured later?"

"Eddy—"

He wraps his arms around my waist and tugs me toward the dance area. "I learned something, growing up with a sister," he murmurs near my ear.

Rebecca's most definitely watching us now. As we spin around, I notice that Robert is too. He throws me a thumbs up. "What's that?"

"It's easier to beg forgiveness than to get permission most of the time."

I can't imagine ever being able to refuse him anything, not when he looks at me like that.

"And I should confess that I already have plans."

"Plans?"

"You agreed to one dance, but I'm greedy. I always want more."

More of me? "I'm not sure—"

"I know, I know. You have a date. The thing is, I haven't seen him around. He's from the city, so he's probably accustomed to taking his time. We country boys know that you have to make hay while the sun shines."

"A few weeks ago, I had no idea what that meant, but now I know it's cutting the hay at the right time so it can dry and be baled without molding."

Eddy grins. "You're learning."

"But I don't mold when I get wet." Weirdly, that sounded a lot flirtier than I meant for it to sound.

His smile becomes a little wolfish. "Good to know."

"What I mean is, there's no reason to rush with me."

His arms tighten around me, moving our bodies just a hair closer. "Oh, I disagree. You said you only have a few more weeks." His head ducks down lower, until our faces are only inches apart. "I mean to make the most of every moment."

It feels like he *cherishes* me. I've never felt like that in all my life.

The second the dance ends, Robert beelines for us. He looks suitably annoyed that I was dancing with someone else, which makes me all kinds of giddy. I know it's fake, but it's the first time I've ever had two guys fighting over me.

And I love it.

Although, the one person who *really* has two guys interested is sopping wet and on her way home right now. Maybe it's a better fantasy than a real life occurrence.

Without letting Eddy say a word, Robert takes my hand and pulls me back out to dance. "That's going well." He's grinning like a dog with a bone—a little gloaty and slobbery, but probably perfect for my purposes. And he keeps looking at Eddy and grinning wider. "This is more fun than I thought it would be."

"As fun as shoving someone in a lake?"

His hands stiffen. "That was an accident, and I didn't shove her." The muscles in his jaw work, which only makes him look more masculine.

"You accidentally chased her out there?"

He stumbles, almost knocking us both to the ground.

"Whoa."

"I'm sorry," he says. "I wanted to stay and help, but I might need to head back early."

Eddy's already on his way over.

"I think I can take it from here."

Robert's smile returns. "I think maybe you can." He presses an unexpected kiss on my cheek. "I'm going to bail before I get a black eye. Best of luck." He darts away.

Eddy doesn't stop when he reaches me, moving past to follow Robert. I grab his arm. "Slow down there, Cujo."

His eyes are wide when he turns back to me. "Cujo?"

I shrug. "An attack dog? I don't know. That's what came to mind."

"He's not an attack dog." He laughs, his shoulders relaxing and his focus returning to me. "He's bitten by a bat and becomes rabid."

"Maybe."

"Maybe?" He's laughing harder. "I'm a vet. I think I would know."

"Mom?" Maren's voice is not joyful.

I scan until I find her. "Yeah, darling. What's wrong?"

"Izzy and Whitney and Gabe just left. Ethan, too. Can we go?" Her eyes dart to Eddy and then back to me, unapologetically.

"Right." I forgot I had the kids and didn't plan to stay for the dance. "Of course. Grab Emery and meet me at the car."

For once, she doesn't argue with me. It's a miracle.

"About to turn into a pumpkin?" Eddy asks.

"I guess so," I say. "Though I refute the premise that I'm a princess who can't come up with her own ballgown. I own plenty of ballgowns."

"You can't leave quite yet, though, right?"

"Why not?"

He slings an arm around me. "Fourth of July? Your followers will be expecting some kind of fireworks."

A lump forms in my throat. My hands start to sweat again. So stupid. "But—"

"I was thinking." His hands drop to my hips and maneuver us backward, then to the side, then backward again, until we're standing against the rail, near the edge of the water.

"You're not about to toss me in, right? Because that's not something I'm interested in doing."

His laugh comes from deep in his throat. "Not at all."

"That's a relief."

"But I do think that, if I were to hold my camera just right. . ." He angles it and holds it away from us. "I could get a really great profile shot of us."

"Oh, really?"

"Really." His face lowers slowly. So slowly that I'm aware of my heart racing. Of my hands trembling. Of my breath coming more quickly. And still, he's so far away.

When is he going to take the photo? Will it even show up when it's this dark?

His free hand tilts my chin up and his fingers brush against my lips. Then he shifts my hair away from my brow, and his mouth lowers toward mine. There may not be any explosions happening in the sky above us, but there are more than one kind of fireworks. These are the most intense I've ever felt.

His lips are less than a fingertip away from mine when he stops. And then he straightens. "Alright, let's see what I got."

I feel like a puppet with my strings cut. Or a participant in that dumb ice bucket challenge. What just happened to me?

The smile on Eddy's face has never been more devilish. He's an expert at denying himself, and now he's torturing me with the same skillset. He shifts so our shoulders are touching and swipes on his phone. "They're not bad. What do you think?"

He's right. They might be even better than a kissing

photo, because we're both practically quivering with longing. His eyes on mine, his body angled around and over me. I'm leaning toward him, like a desperately cold traveler hovering over a borrowed campfire. I can practically taste what it felt like, yearning for him to kiss me.

"I know you have to go. I'll text them to you." His eyes are staring at my mouth, again.

"You're a little bit evil." My eyebrows pull together. "You know that?"

"Or a little bit brilliant?"

Maybe a perfect mix of the two.

23

ABIGAIL

My first date with Steve, which lasted all of twelve minutes before it was interrupted by, well, sort of by a heart attack that turned out to be a panic attack, ended with a dousing in a freezing river (that looks like a lake to me). Green River's probably never very warm, since it's fed by snow runoff, but at night?

My teeth chattered the whole way home.

Not very romantic.

All in all, I wasn't off to a very good start. Since it was reminiscing with Robert, and then my startled reaction to his attempt at kissing me, that ruined it, I feel obligated to try and fix it.

CAN WE CALL A MULLIGAN?

Steve's at work, I think, so I'm not sure how speedily he'll respond, but I watch the phone for almost an hour anyway. Finally, the second I put it down to formalize some pre-trial paperwork, it bings.

It's Robert, not Steve. I try to manage my disappointment. JUDGE MOVED HIS VACATION AND TWO CASES SETTLED.

WHAT DOES THAT MEAN? I ask.

NOTHING YET. JUST SOMETHING TO WATCH.

Something tells me it's not nothing. It makes me think of hurricane season, when we're all watching the Atlantic, worried over every storm formation, tracking the path of every anomaly until we're safely out of the cone. He wouldn't be warning me if it were really nothing. And I can't very well say, if they move the trial date forward, "Too bad. I'm busy." Nor can I leave my kids here without me. On top of my legal work, I've been supervising all the animals, and riding up at least once a week to check on the cows.

If I'm being honest, it's been nice. Tranquil, even. The things that go wrong are mostly out of my control, which means there's not a lot for me to fret about. Things will either go well or they won't. Ethan's out cutting hay again today, our last alfalfa field, and Kevin says things are looking really promising to get a second cut, which would leave us home free on that front, at least. Alfalfa's apparently the most expensive hay to buy, which means it's great for us to get a second round.

IT'S TAKE A MULLIGAN, NOT CALL A MULLIGAN. AND I LIKED OUR FIRST DATE. BUT I'D BE KEEN ON A SECOND.

My worry about the case evaporates, and I find myself smiling like an idiot. I should want to forget all about Saturday night, but instead, I look back on it in a new light. It's a funny story, at least. Nate and I never had that. We just had a bunch of classes together, flirted a little bit, and then he bought me a drink at one of the law school pub crawls.

I mean, it's not a *bad* story, and certainly not an embarrassing one, but this one's a lot splashier.

Literally.

Amanda said Steve sprinted across the deck and dove headlong into the water the moment he saw me fall.

I've been trying to figure out whether he saw what prompted the fall ever since.

TONIGHT? I'M OFF AT 5.

Tonight? Wow, he really is keen. What a funny word. AMANDA'S TAKING HER GIRLS ON A PICNIC, AND I PROMISED MY KIDS ENCHILADAS.

I LIKE ENCHILADAS. AND I LIKE YOUR KIDS.

Is he implying he'd like our second date to be a meal with my four kids? The ones he teaches horseback lessons to twice a week? He can't be serious. MAYBE TOMORROW'S BETTER.

I'M NOT AFRAID OF JAM HANDS.

Is he quoting *Gilmore Girls*? Because he does have sort of a Luke-like vibe about him, if you replaced Luke's ball cap with a cowboy hat, and if Luke had a six-pack I can't stop thinking about. And if Luke didn't have a receding hairline—so maybe it's not a very strong vibe.

Every time I pause, I relive that moment again and again. His arms went around me, and he dragged me up to the surface. My desperate hands cast around for anything at all, but they found something wide and flat and ridged.

Steve's stomach. They moved upward to his chest. His very hard, very defined chest. I saw it all the day I arrived—but feeling it for myself was different somehow. Now I have a *feeling* to go along with the memory of him, pushing that lawn mower, sweat glistening. . .

I shake my head to clear it, but it's not very effective. In fact, it kind of sends me right back to the beginning of the loop, to when I was plunging underwater, unsure which way was up. And those arms came around me—the strong arms I watch, muscles bunching, each day as he rides. I'm sure he contracts the abs to stabilize himself. Oh, the abs.

On second thought, if we go out tomorrow night without kids, I might leap on him and rub my hands all over his torso. He'd then assume I was rabid or insane and never talk to me again. FINE. I'LL BE SURE TO HAVE PLENTY OF JAM.

THAT'S THE BEAUTY OF KIDS. EVEN WITHOUT JAM IN THE HOUSE, THEY STILL MANAGE TO HAVE JAM HANDS.

He's definitely referencing Luke. HE'S MY FAVORITE CHARACTER.

HE'S MY SPIRIT ANIMAL.

SORRY, BUT I'M PRETTY SURE THAT'S A HORSE.

CRAP, YOU GOT ME.

I am desperate to know what woman made him watch *Gilmore Girls*. . . Not that I have the guts to ask. Not yet, anyway. SEVEN O'CLOCK?

SIX-FIFTEEN? I'M STARVING WHEN I GET OFF WORK.

And that's forty-five minutes sooner. I'm not about to complain. SURE.

WHAT CAN I BRING?

YOUR SPARKLING PERSONALITY? MAYBE SOME WET WIPES.

WET WIPES?

FOR THE STICKY FINGERS.

He sends me a laughing emoji, which makes me kind of proud of him. I dramatically overuse them, even catching myself thinking in emojis sometimes. The fact that he's using them, as a man, gives me hope that mine won't annoy him.

After I relive the water scare one more time, I vow it will be my last. I'm sure I'm making it into a much bigger deal than it is, probably because I'm so starved for affection, like a barn cat. He'll be lucky if I don't purr and rub up against his leg the second we're alone. How embarrassing.

Meanwhile, Robert acted like nothing had happened. He ate French toast, then packed his bag and left Sunday on the flight he had booked from the start. He hasn't mentioned how I dove into a river to avoid kissing him, so I haven't had a chance to even tell him that it wasn't him, it was totally me.

I wish I knew how much of my inexplicable attraction to Steve without the attendant guilt has to do with his location and my finite time here, and how much has to do with our lack of shared history. Unfortunately, I don't know how to unwind those things in my mind.

It's one of those nights where everyone wants to help me make dinner, including Ethan. They're rare, but I cherish them every single time. Ethan's great at making pico, because he never seems to cry no matter how many onions he dices. The only problem is that his taste for jalapeños outstrips everyone else's. I stop him from dumping three full peppers and their seeds just in time.

"We went all the way to Green River to get these," he says. "It would be a shame not to use them."

"Save them for your tacos," I say. "Then they won't go to waste, *and* no one will leave the room crying."

He rolls his eyes. "You guys are such wusses."

"But we're your wusses."

He wraps his arms around my neck and squeezes me. "That's true."

I hate to admit it, but he seems happier here. Much happier than he has for more than a year. Maybe it's working outside. Maybe it's not having the threat of more school hanging over his head. Or maybe it's that we're not in our big, beautiful, perfect home. . .that's chock full of memories.

Better than anyone, I understand that those memories cut both ways. They console when I miss the thought of Nate, but they hurt when I feel his loss most keenly. It's almost like everything around me is mocking me for the light that used to be present.

Gabe nearly slices his finger off, but he successfully dices his first tomato for the salad. Whitney's a pro at baking Rhodes rolls. She always pulls them out when they're perfectly golden. Not doughy, but not a bit overcooked, either. They don't really go with enchiladas, but it's Whitney's thing, and I couldn't tell her no. She's rubbing butter on the tops of them when Izzy whimpers.

"What's wrong?"

"These chips are stale. They're gross."

I text Steve immediately. CHIP EMERGENCY. CAN YOU PICK UP NON-STALE CORN CHIPS?

MANILA'S FINEST. GREAT TIMING. WAS JUST PASSING THROUGH TOWN.

Which means he's close. Will he stop at his house first? Probably.

He arrives right on time, his truck parking out front at 6:14. His hair's still wet when he walks up the steps. The kids may be more excited than I am. Izzy's humming, Whitney's rocking back and forth, a picture she drew of him on top of Farrah, clutched in her hands. Ethan's been asking me rodeo questions all afternoon. Apparently he has some interest in trying some of the events. If Steve can maneuver him away from that, I'll be forever grateful.

Ethan needs a broken hip like I need a bullet to the head.

The kids are almost *too* delighted that we have a visitor. I can't decide whether it's because we're in such a rural location now, or whether it's because they like Steve so much. I suppose it could really be either.

"Mr. Steve!" No matter how many times I've told Gabe that his name is Mr. Archer, he has started calling him Mr. Steve and I can't get him to budge. He races across the room and barrels into Steve, hugging him so tightly, I worry we'll have to scrape him off like a barnacle off the hull of a boat.

Steve meets my eyes over Gabe's little body and makes an "aww" face. At least I know he's not annoyed.

"I made you a picture," Whitney says.

Not to be outdone, Izzy rushes off to grab a drawing she made of Steve's barn and house. I hope he knows he can toss those in the trash when he gets home. I'll be sure to tell him later. Some people might keep them out of obligation, but the sheer volume of precious art generated by my darling children would probably cause any normal person to shudder.

"Hungry?"

"Starving," Steve says. "I usually pick something up on my way home."

"I'm sorry," I say. "You could totally have done that—"

He bumps me with his hip. "I'm way more excited about enchiladas here, made by Texans. I assume you guys really know what you're doing."

"The pico is fresh," Ethan says proudly. "Made it myself. But we usually just buy sauce at H-E-B, so we're all a little nervous about how this will taste."

"Me, the most," Gabe says. "I'm the pickiest."

"That's true," I say.

"I eat the most things," Whitney says. "Other than Ethan, but he doesn't count because he's so old."

"If Ethan's old, what does that make me?" Steve cringes.

"How old are you?" I realize I've never asked him.

"Are you going to answer the same question?" His eyebrows rise.

"My mom's thirty-eight," Gabe says.

"And her birthday's October 5," Izzy says, "the same month as Halloween."

"That's true," Steve says. "And I'm afraid your mother has me beat. I'm thirty-nine as of June 15th."

"You turn forty soon," Whitney says. "When my dad turned 40, my mom threw a huge party for him. Everything was black, and he got a cane, and everyone sang a funeral dirge." She giggles. "It was super funny."

I wonder how he'll deal with the kids talking about Nate. I've been worried about how *I* would take things. I hadn't much considered how much baggage I come with—he's really doing this the hard way. First a "baptism" by water—a dunk in the lake, then one by fire—dinner with all the kids, and discussions about my deceased husband.

"I think that sounds really fun. I bet your Dad felt really loved."

"He did," Izzy says. "He told me that."

"Mom does really cool parties," Whitney says.

"The food is good, but sometimes the decorations aren't that great," Gabe says. "Like one year, I wanted to have a *Last Airbender* party with a sword like Sokka and real boomerangs, but Mom only got *balloon* swords, and the boomerangs were made out of styrofoam."

Ethan snorts. "Mom always makes the best food, though."

"How are you only thirty-eight, with a seventeen-year-old son?" Steve asks.

"She was super duper smart," Izzy says. "She graduated from high school early and finished college at nineteen."

"Of course she did," Steve says. "I should have known."

"Hey, what are we going to do about my birthday?" Whitney asks. "It's in August. We'll still be here, but I don't have any friends."

"You have me," Steve says.

Gabe scrunches his face and looks at Mr. Steve for a moment. I wonder what's going on inside his head. I'd usually ask, but I can't really do that right now. One of the first rules you learn as a litigator is to *never* ask a witness a question to which you don't already know the answer. It's too dangerous. I already feel like this meal is akin to navigating an active minefield.

It kind of zaps some of the excitement. It's like meeting someone's parents on the second date—too much real world, not enough stomach flutters and little thrills. But this is what my life is. I'm not a twenty-two-year-old with nothing on her mind but education and meeting my happily ever after. I've gotten one happily ever after and discovered that nothing is guaranteed to last. Plans change and what makes us who we are is how well we navigate the choppy waters of the unexpected.

"Abby?"

"Let's eat." I wave the kids forward and they stampede, rushing to grab plates and load them with food. Enchiladas, rolls, chips and pico, beans and Spanish rice, and honeydew melon.

"We should tell Mr. Steve the house rules," Whitney says.

He's holding a plate, his hand on the spatula to scoop up an enchilada, but he sets it back down. "Oh, you really should. I'd hate to go to detention on my very first day." He looks at her intently.

"First, you have to eat at least two bites of everything." Whitney looks so serious that I have to suppress a laugh. "Even lima beans, when we have those."

Gabe makes a blech sound.

"Don't worry," Izzy says, "Mom hardly ever makes them. Only if we've been real stinkers."

Steve chuckles.

"Rule two," Gabe says, "if you make your own plate, you have to eat everything you serve, so start small and go back for seconds."

"Very good tip," Steve says.

"And last, no singing at the table." Ethan glares at Whitney, who has a tendency to sing whenever she's happy. Loudly, and sometimes a little off-key.

"I'm not stupid," Whitney says. "I know it's a rule."

"We don't use that word," I say without thinking.

"Sorry," Whitney says, "but I was using it about myself."

"That might be worse," Ethan says.

"Are there any rules about what utensils I use, or how I sit or hold my fork?"

Gabe shakes his head. "No, but once I tried to eat like a dog, and that is not okay."

Steve laughs. "Another gem. Keep lobbing those at me. I'd hate to upset your mother on our first real date."

"Wait, this is a date, and we're here for it?" Ethan pulls a face. "Sorry."

"Don't be," Steve says. "I don't know your mom that well yet, but I've noticed that for her, it's kids first, then work, and then everything else."

"You're smart," Izzy says.

We all sit down, and Izzy insists on pouring everyone lemonade. I suspect Steve might not really have wanted any, but he didn't formally protest, so I let it go. He'll have to learn to speak up if he's not interested in something. The conversation meanders quite a lot, as it usually does, from Pokémon to the fireworks we missed, to the cutting of hay, and then to horses.

"Mom needs to pick a horse," Izzy says. "Because now

Maren's riding Snoopy, and no one else can handle her pulling and kicking at the same time."

Not without bucking her off, it seems.

"Smarty isn't a bad option," Whitney says. "Remember? He's older, but I rode him once, and I liked him."

"I'll take Snoopy tomorrow when we go to check the cows, and he'll be fine for Maren's lesson on Wednesday."

"Still." Izzy huffs. "I'm kinda mad she took him."

"Yeah, it's nice to have your own things," Gabe says. "I really like my Pokémon cards, and I don't like to share."

"What other things do you have that you like?" Steve asks.

Gabe's the world's slowest eater, and even he has finished his food. That's my cue to get dessert. I stand up and walk to the counter in the kitchen.

"At home, I have a really cool train table. And I have shoes with air pockets that make me run super fast. I left them there so they wouldn't get muddy, but I think that was dumb. I'm so much slower without them."

"You still look pretty fast to me," Steve says.

"You're really nice and I like you," Gabe says. "Are you going to be our new dad?"

I drop the plate with the cake on it, but luckily it only falls to the counter. The plate breaks, but the cake doesn't splatter.

"Here." Ethan grabs a spatula. "I'll get that on a new plate."

"I need to go out to the car and grab something from the glove box," I say. "I think there are—" What can I say I need? What excuse can I give? "Wipes. We need wipes."

Whitney stands up. "Can't we just use paper towels—"

Izzy grabs her arm and yanks her back down, watching me carefully. "Not for the frosting. It's not water based—it has oil in it."

"I can go get them," Whitney says.

"Let Mom go." Izzy's eyes are worried. When did she get so big that she knows to cover for me?

I jog to the door. "Be right back." I'm breathing too fast, and my heart's pumping a mile a minute. I don't feel much better by the time I reach the door to my minivan. I realize that I left the key inside the house, anyway. Which doesn't matter. It was just an excuse all along.

Calm down, Abigail. It was a simple question.

But is Steve going to be their new dad? Doesn't ensuring that their new father figure is wonderful, if they end up with one, matter more than whom I like? Isn't it more important than whom I want to kiss or talk to? If I ever remarry, that person will be in their lives forever. They don't have a 'real' dad to go visit or someone else they can call if they're scared or sad. This guy would be it.

"Abby."

Steve followed me. Great. Read the room, dude.

He keeps walking until he's right next to me, but I don't want to see him right now. "It's probably awkward for you to be in there," I say. "I'm sorry. It's just too soon."

"Abby."

I finally meet his gaze. To my surprise, he's smiling like this is a huge joke. "What's funny about this?"

"You're freaking out because a seven-year-old asked a question—a very natural question."

"How am I supposed to answer him?" I drop a hand over my eyes. "I don't know if you will or not. It's way too soon to even think about that, but I can't say no, because what if that's a lie?" I exhale. "I can't really date without them knowing, but I don't want them involved until something's serious. We have this all backward, and I'm—"

His arms wrap around me then, and I curl my face against his chest. "Shhhh," he says.

I bawl against his shoulder like an absolute lunatic. "I'm so sorry," I whisper.

"Let me preface this by saying that you're not a horse, and I know you're not a horse."

This is going somewhere very strange.

"But I know very little about women, and quite a lot about horses."

I close my eyes and relax against his chest, his hand still patting my back gently.

"I've found a lot of horses over the years that were in bad situations. They were being given sugary feed and stuffed into tiny stalls, and they had shoes put on them when they should have been given time off, and they were stressed and tired and abused. I find neglected animals whose feet haven't been trimmed in a year. I find animals that have been lost or abandoned. They're starving, they're wormy, and every single one of them is scared."

His voice, however odd the content, is still comforting. Rumbly and soft and he doesn't require a thing from me. No work, no thought, no analysis.

"When I find these horses, they don't look too great. Some are shaggy, some are patchy, almost all of them have exposed ribs or skinny fat bellies. They're often terrified of humans. It takes time for them to trust me in each circumstance. But some of these horses have become the very best animals I've ever found. All of them have either stayed with me or gone to very good homes. In order to make that happen, I take things one step at a time, understanding that their reaction has more to do with their past than with me or anything I've done."

Their past. The horses'? Or mine?

"You aren't a nag. You're not starving. You haven't been neglected. But you have been dealt a huge trauma recently, and it impacts how you feel, how you hope, and how you plan. It has changed you, probably fundamentally. From what I've seen, I think you're possibly one of the best people I've ever met."

I open my eyes.

"You're embarrassed right now more than anything else, I imagine, but you're also hurting and unsure how to proceed. You know your children better than anyone else. If Gabe just needs to be told, 'don't be silly,' then tell him that. If he needs to be told that 'there's no way this guy will ever replace your father,' then tell him that. One thing you should never do is worry what *I* may think or feel about how you handle anything with your kids. I'm just happy to be along for the ride, and I understand that you're going through something I can't really comprehend."

Like sunlight coming out from behind the clouds, like taking off my boots at the end of a long day, like clicking save and shutting off the computer after finishing a miserable memo, a weight lifts from me. I hadn't realized how much of my stress had to do with trying to say the right thing for both Gabe, the other kids, *and* Steve. "Thank you. For being compassionate, and for being insightful, and for being willing to wait out my past."

"I may not be a spring chicken," Steve says, "but nothing good comes from rushing things, and I don't intend to rush this."

He walks me back inside, and I explain to Gabe that Mr. Steve is a friend of mine, and that I like him a lot. I explain we may be seeing him more, but that no one would ever be a replacement for his father. I also tell him that it's possible that one day I'll remarry. He can choose what he wants to call that new person, if that ever happens.

"If I want to call him Dad, do you think Dad will care?"

"I don't," Ethan says. "The one thing Dad always

wanted more than anything else was for us to be happy."

That night, after Steve leaves, I feel more peaceful than I have in a while. I'm not sure if that means anything, but it's a good feeling. I'm about to plug my phone in for the night when I refresh my email—a compulsion, sadly. I filter through the new ones, deleting the junk, and my finger freezes over one—the sender is Gustav Hopkins.

Abigail,

I'm pleased to be writing with great news. Technically, it's actually terrible news for a lot of people. There was a horrible perpetration of fraud discovered at one of the high schools in Houston—a few hundred kids were caught cheating on the SAT. We've decided that our admission to each of the students who planned to matriculate here should be revoked.

The upshot for you, of course, is that our waitlist has just been updated to reflect an offer of admission to over two dozen new students, including your son, Ethan Brooks. You can expect an admission letter to arrive at your house at any time, but I understand from our earlier communications that you may not be home right now.

I'm attaching a copy of the formal letter via electronic communication in case your travel is ongoing. Please sign and return, with the tuition payment, at your earliest convenience.

Yours truly,

Gus

I should be dancing around the house, shouting and hollering. Singing should be happening. Instead, I decide to wait to share the good news until tomorrow.

Because I know that for him, it probably won't feel like very good news at all.

24
AMANDA

Having lived in New York City for most of my adult life, I never thought much about time zones. I mean, sure, I knew that the West coast was a few hours behind, but it never impacted my day-to-day life. But waking up at six in the morning so I can get ready for a nine a.m. conference call is brutal.

Of course, Abigail and her angel children are already awake, excepting Gabe.

"I'm going to be on an important call," I warn them.

"I'll stick around and make sure Gabe stays quiet," Whitney offers with a smile. I'm not even surprised that she volunteers. It's just what her kids do.

It's not that I've never heard them bicker. They fight and squabble and snap like everyone else. But as soon as their mother notices and quirks her eyebrow, or if they've gotten really out of hand, whips her head around, they start apologizing and backing off. The best thing about coming here, other than the help it provided in landing the Lololime contract, was the time Maren has spent watching siblings who are *kind* to each other. Emery has always wanted that kind of friendship with her and never had it. I've seen a little bit rub off, but we have a long way to go yet.

"Thanks," I say. "I'll let you know when I'm off."

"Great," Whitney says. "Then I'll head out and help feed the animals."

Of course she will. Her kids don't even drag their feet to avoid doing work. Well, maybe Gabe does. He is only a seven-year-old, but he basically does nothing other than play games, follow the bigger kids around, and whine. I'm sure mine were that bad at seven, but I've forgotten—or blocked it. I sit down, the printed list in front of me, my laptop open. Roscoe circles me once and then curls up in a ball near my feet.

I keep expecting him to follow everyone else out the door—chase animals, race around like a dog should, but he only does that when I go outside. If I'm inside, so is he.

My phone rings. "Hello?"

"Amanda?"

"This is Amanda," I say.

"It's Victoria Davis, the Vice President in charge of Social Media with Lololime." As if I didn't already know she was calling today.

"I'm happy to hear from you and excited to be a part of the team."

"Thanks for executing the agreement. From here on out, you can expect my office to schedule a monthly meeting for about an hour at the beginning of each month to discuss our goals and your plans for achieving them."

"Great. I look forward to it."

"I think Heather sent you the list of goals we put together for your account for July."

"She did," I say. "Although, I wanted to sort of clarify expectations." My heart picks up speed.

"I wholeheartedly agree. The best thing we can do on these calls is have you share your ideas for how to specifically boost the products we've assigned, and also how to improve your own brand and following, and then we can provide input on whether our visions align and tweak where necessary."

"Okay." Why does it feel like all the tweaking will be on my part? I suppose they are the ones paying me, so that's likely quite common.

"Heather tells me you plan to stay on the family ranch through the end of July. About four more weeks?"

"That's right. My daughter has a cheerleading camp at the beginning of August that lasts two weeks."

"The reason we sent you a list of products to focus on that include equal parts male and female items is that—"

"Exactly what I wanted to address."

"We think it would be great if you shared images of your mysterious cowboy with a handful of Lolo pieces, worked in organically, of course. I think to keep the followers invested, you can promise that you'll reveal who he is and how you met at the end of the month. Then we can push all of the products in sequence—which will dovetail perfectly with the August release of our Fall lines."

"Here's the thing." I sigh.

"You're not really dating him."

What? Well. "Kind of."

She sighs. "Heather said she pressured you to find a hot cowboy, and we were worried he might not really be suitable—hence the sideways angles. Is he married?"

"No." I splutter. "He—"

"He's too young?"

I think about Kevin and how I considered him. "No, he's about my age. But the thing—"

"Please tell me he's not related to you."

"He's not related to me," I say. "But he has a past that we would not want revealed on social media. It wouldn't reflect well on us or on the brand."

For once, she's deadly quiet. "As long as he's not a murderer," she says, "we can likely play off any flaws that were far in the past."

Not a murderer. It doesn't seem like a high bar, but. . .apparently for me it is. "So the thing is, he—he hit someone with his car while he was high."

The groan she makes into the phone is not good.

"He was kind of a public figure, and the person he hit was a really bad person, a serial killer in fact, so his manager was able to make it all go away. But there's a decent chance of the media finding or remembering the history if he was revealed. . ."

"The media would not let it pass a second time."

"Doubtful."

Her sigh is forceful. "Alright, so much for that plan." She's tapping on something. "I assume you just found out?"

"Absolutely, less than two days ago."

"Because if you'd known when you signed the contract, that would be grounds for termination."

My heart gallops away.

"As it is, this is just the nature of being an influencer. You'll need to cut off contact with him immediately." She covers the phone, based on the muffle of sounds, and asks someone else a few questions. I wish I knew who it was, and whether it was related to me.

"Alright, we have a plan." She's back. "You'll immediately terminate contact with him, and you'll return to New York right away as well. That will help stave off any future speculation. From now on, you'll refer to him as your 'cowboy fling' or your 'mysterious cowboy.'"

Can she really dictate my life like this? I need to talk to Abby. "What products will I—"

"We have to reconfigure your July goals based on this new information." The line's muffled again, briefly. "Is there any chance you could start dating someone in New York? Quickly?"

"I mean, I—"

"It's okay. We'll get back to you." She hangs up.

"You look terribly upset," Abigail says. "Is everything alright?"

"I'm fine." Do not cry, Amanda. *Do not cry!* Of course, my eyeballs don't listen. Tears well up and then run down my face. Is there a more embarrassing way for your body to betray you? I think not.

"I've been 'fine' a lot lately." Abigail sits on a chair in the kitchen. "While you were on your call, Gabe and Whitney followed Emery and Maren outside. Apparently one of the cats just had kittens. They don't seem to be big on spaying and neutering around here." She leans her arms on the tabletop and says, "If you feel like telling me what's totally fine in your life right now, I'd be happy to listen. I'll even promise not to give a single speck of advice." She pretends to zip her lips.

Instead of going away, my tears redouble, and on top of that, I start to hiccup. "This is so embarrassing."

"Something's only embarrassing if you care what people think." Abby smiles. "I'm taking your embarrassment as a compliment. But I should also explain that I've had more than my share of breakdowns in the past year. If something can make that type of thing more likely, it's high stakes situations and changes to your routine. Between your Lolo contract and the move to a cattle ranch, I'd say you've had plenty of both lately."

"Says the woman who lost her husband more recently

and is working a maximum hours job with more kids than me."

Abigail kicks a chair, sliding it almost a foot toward me. Her kind and sweet and light tone is gone. "Sit down."

I obey without thinking.

"Now listen to me." Her entire expression has changed. "I've certainly listened to you enough in the past few weeks to know that you're an excellent mother, that you work hard at your job, and that you are under a great deal of stress. You're a bright woman, but you worry too much about things *looking* perfect. You need to worry more about the real state of things. And you need to stop, and I mean *immediately* stop comparing everything in your life to the lives of people around you. I think that's a hazard of social media in general, but when it's your job, I imagine the comparisons take on lives of their own. All that looking around and judging isn't helping you." She holds up her hand, with two fingers held up. "Two kids can be just as hard or harder than three depending on the time in their life and yours, the personalities involved, and the type of parent you are. As single moms, there is no value in criticizing one another, and there's no point in trying to figure out who has life harder."

I open my mouth, but she forges ahead.

"Never feel you don't have a right to complain or to struggle because someone else may have dealt with 'more.'"

Her entire rant is perfect, and it only makes me sob harder.

After practically yelling at me, I do not expect her to scoot her chair closer and hug me. Suddenly I'm bawling against her shoulder. "I really like Eddy. He's the first guy I've liked this much. . .maybe ever." She stiffens a bit at that, but I forge on. "But he has a past that makes him unsuitable. I know you think I don't really do anything—"

"I was misinformed," she says. "I think what you do is bold and difficult, and I couldn't manage it half as gracefully as you do."

That stops me short for a moment. "Really?"

"Absolutely," she says. "I've always envied your style and your easy grace. I've always admired how you make being a mother look effortless. I, on the other hand, was always lugging around a huge bag of stuff. I could never find what I needed, and I always look sweaty, lost, and scattered."

She's just described a person I've never seen. "You're the most competent mother—no, person—that I know. You are never sweaty, scattered, or lost."

Abby laughs. "Maybe we need magical mirrors in here that show us what other people see in us, not what we do."

"If I could market something like that, I could make a killing," I say.

"I'm sorry about Eddy," she says. "Really sorry." She scrunches her nose. "Are you absolutely positive that his past—"

"My boss just told me to move back to New York immediately, and that I cannot continue to pursue a relationship with him in any way."

"I'm not sure that's legal," Abby says. "But even if your contract would allow them to terminate—"

"I need that revenue," I say. "The last three years have been anxiety-inducing, hope and pray sort of months—where more often than not, I'm crossing my fingers and wishing my posts will be interesting enough to scrape together new sponsors." I shake my head. "Lololime's contract gives me consistent income. Sure, they tell me what they want, but we discuss how to achieve it together. There are no engagement minimums, no specified clicks, nothing like that."

"But they tell you who you can and can't date." Her lips are compressed, signaling her clear disapproval.

"I think it's a fair trade-off," I insist, even though it makes me uneasy too.

"You're the only one who can decide what that deal is worth to you," she says. "And I'll support anything you decide."

For the first time, I'm actually sad at the thought that I won't see Abby anymore. We'll probably end up reverting to how we were before—never talking. The thought should be a relief; living here has been exhausting. But I find that I'm more upset than relieved at the thought of returning home and getting my normal life back.

"This helps," I say. "I felt this bizarre rush of emotion, which makes no sense. In my entire life, I've never been anything but let down by men. There's no reason for me to think that Eddy would be any different, and based on what I've discovered about him, there's every reason for me to believe my rotten luck will hold." I mean, he's admitted that he's an addict and a murderer.

But it was so long ago. And the way I feel around him. . .

"I'd be livid if work told me I couldn't date someone." She shrugs. "Human nature." She lowers her voice. "And I'm so sorry to hear that you've had terrible luck with men. I'm sorry Paul wasn't a good husband. I will say, you only need to find one really good one—so having terrible past luck doesn't really make Eddy less likely to be great." Her eyes widen, and she sucks in a breath.

"What?"

Her eyes well with tears. "I suppose sometimes you

need to have good luck more than once." She swipes at her face, wiping away the errant tear that escaped.

I wonder if it's worse to lose an amazing husband, or to never have had a good husband at all. Then it hits me, what Abby was saying. Why do I have to decide which scenario is worse? Can't they both suck? Why do I make everything into some kind of sick competition? I reach out and place one hand over hers. "I'm so sorry that Nate got sick."

She bobs her head. "I know."

"Thanks for talking to me."

Abby blinks and straightens. "Three plus years out, does it still hit you sometimes, like a Mack truck?"

"I'm not sure what a Mack truck is?" I sigh. "But the grief and the loneliness still hit me, yes."

"I was hoping for a magic solution."

I laugh. "Sorry, no magic here."

"For what it's worth, I'd think long and hard about whether the security of the Lololime contract is worth giving up the right to make my own life decisions."

"It's not—"

"Maybe that's not fair," she says. "But it's how it feels to me. I'm also not saying that it's the wrong thing to do, to let them guide things a bit. I mean, I've met plenty of people who shouldn't be making their own decisions." She tilts her head. "But you, Amanda Brooks? You are not one of them."

Abigail thinks I'm competent and capable? Something swells inside of me, and it's so unfamiliar that it takes a moment to recognize the emotion: pride. "Thanks."

"I'll miss you if you're leaving."

"Maybe we should try talking on the phone now and then," I say.

"Novel idea, yes." She smiles. "But it won't be the same."

"I'm actually kind of glad we got stuffed into this house. And I'm sorry I was such a brat and insisted we get three rooms."

Abby shrugs. "My kids share just fine, and I think it helps them, honestly. When you're in forced proximity, you learn things about the other person." Her knowing smile would have annoyed me a month ago. Now I know she's making a joke about herself and me.

"I should probably have made my girls share for precisely that reason."

"Sounds like you've made up your mind to head back early." She stands up. "That's my cue to move along and let you be."

I don't feel like I ever really had any other choice.

"Mom!" Ethan walks in the door. "You're not working right now." He glances around the room and catches my eye. "Aunt Mandy! You're here too. That's great. You're just the ladies I wanted to see."

"Both of us?" I ask.

"Absolutely. Do you both have ten minutes?"

I shrug.

Abby nods.

"Perfect. I'll be right back. Wait here."

Abby sits down again.

"What do you think this is about?" I ask.

She frowns. "I'm virtually certain he's prepared his big pitch."

"Pitch?"

"We came here to give him a chance to convince me that ranch life was the way to go for him."

"Oh." I can't imagine Maren or Emery putting together any kind of presentation about what they wanted. They simply demand things and argue or cry alternately until I either freak out or they get what they want. "Should I duck into my room?"

"No, please stay," Ethan steps back into the family room.

"Why do you want me around?" I ask.

"To keep Mom honest." Ethan's turned the charm to maximum plus one. His smile's obnoxiously cute, with those double dimples and beautiful teeth.

"Alright," I say. "I'm ready. I'm even thinking honest thoughts."

He chuckles. "It's not that you need to *do* anything, but having you here means she has to really listen and consider."

"Just go ahead already," Abby says.

"Alright, so you know why I'm here." He pulls a stapled stack of paper out of a box and hands one to each of us.

Abby frowns, but peruses the front page.

"This starts with a list of not only the things Uncle Jed specified that needed to be done, but a comprehensive list of tasks from January through December, with a time estimate next to each. I've taken the liberty of going through and assigning each task to either me, or Kevin, or Jeff. Jeff may be attempting to secure financing on his own ranch in the next few years, but he says we have at least one more year with him first. Hopefully by then I'll know enough to hire a replacement or take over his tasks myself. Some times delineated are a very rough ballpark, since I won't really know how much time it will take to mend fences until I see how many are damaged, for instance."

"This is thorough," I say. "And it's easy to read."

"The next page is a spreadsheet that shows the numbers I expect to see. Total expenses and cash flow, and then total income. You'll notice that I factored in waste and injury, as well as replacement inventory for the mother cows that are unable to safely have more calves."

"What's this?" Abby points. "Bull rotation? Why's that an expense?"

"We can't keep breeding the same bulls once we've rolled their daughters into the breeding population." He pulls a face. "So we need to trade or sell a certain number of bulls—tagging and paperwork helps with that—and procure new replacement bulls for the newer herds."

Abby asks a dozen questions, and then a dozen more. I've never seen her in action as a lawyer in court, but she's more terrifying even than I expected her to be.

Ethan fields each question as if he'd prepared his answers over and over.

Finally, Abby nods. "I appreciate the presentation," she says. "And as I promised you I would, I'll consider it. I expect you to consider this as well. I heard from Gus yesterday—and you've been moved from the waitlist to approved status at Rice."

His face falls in much the same way I imagine mine did when Victoria told me I couldn't post more photos of the cowboy if I can't reveal his identity. I actually feel bad for Ethan, because as even-handed as Abby is clearly trying to be, I doubt she's going to let him stay here and manage a ranch alone. He's just too young.

"Aunt Mandy," Ethan says. "If I do manage to convince Mom, are you guys going to insist on being half owners?"

"Isn't that how it works?"

"The terms of the will are a little confusing," Abby says. "It's not clear whether all of the named beneficiaries take if one of them fulfills the terms, or whether only the beneficiaries who work the ranch would receive the full title."

"You and your girls haven't really done anything," he says. "Except for, you know, offering moral support, which I appreciate."

We haven't done anything? I've been here for all the

meals. I've helped clean and cook for all the kids. My girls have helped feed animals.

"I'm not trying to say that you're not welcome here," Ethan says. "But I'm the only one who's done watering and Mom and I have done all the rides out to make sure the cattle are okay and to take more salt and supplements. We've set up the pens and treated the calves and cows that were injured."

Instead of getting upset, I breathe in and out a few times. "I'll have to call Mr. Swift," I say.

"Alright," Ethan says. "Thanks for listening." He ducks back outside, presumably to do more work that none of my family has helped with in the slightest.

"Don't stress about any of that," Abby says. "It's a moot point. We aren't going to stay here—Ethan will be going to school."

I can't help wondering, as she grabs her laptop and starts to work on some kind of legal thing, whether Abby realizes that she's a bit inconsistent. She can't really tell me that I should be able to manage my own life. . .while simultaneously micromanaging her own, very capable child.

25

ABIGAIL

That cliché, "Women: can't live with them, can't live without them," has always bothered me immensely. But the same sentiment does apply well to work. In many ways, I can't live with it, but I also can't live without it.

After Ethan was born, I actually tried staying home. I took a semester off from law school and considered never finishing. I felt so overwhelmed with the baby, and so desperate to be a perfect mother, that I thought the only way I could do it was to do nothing else.

I hated that few months of my life. I've always been the kind of parent who loves being a mom. . .and needs to do other things in addition to mothering. I've learned, over the past few years, that I'm a better version of myself when I have more than one thing on which to focus. Lately, as I've been working extra in order to prove to the partners that I'm qualified and capable, especially from so far away, I've felt this even more keenly. And for the first time in over a year, it's not only my work schedule that's monkeying with my life.

"Wait, you have to work tomorrow?" I exhale into the

phone a little too gustily. "I thought you were off for the next few days." I really wanted to talk to Steve about the whole Ethan at Rice versus on a ranch thing. And also have a real, no kids, no lake date, of course.

"I was supposed to be off." He clears his throat and drops to a whisper, as if he's sharing a government secret. "You didn't hear this from me, but one of the docs at my hospital was recently fired."

"How else would I hear about employment details of a doctor in Wyoming?"

"You're hilarious. But seriously, don't tell anyone I told you."

"I only know you. Who would I tell?"

"You know Jeff and Kevin, and Eddy, sort of."

"You think Kevin's high risk? I had to show him how to set up a Facebook account on his phone."

"It's a small world over here." He sighs. "This guy apparently forced not one, not two, and not even three, but *four* different nurses in the hospital to sleep with him."

"Is his last name Clinton?"

Steve doesn't even laugh. I suppose if someone I knew had turned out to be that horrible, I'd be upset as well. "Sounds like a delightful guy."

"I never liked him," Steve says. "And now I feel justified. The problem isn't that I'm upset about him being a jerk—although I feel really bad for the nurses—but there aren't many docs here, so covering all his scheduled shifts is killer."

"When's your next day off?"

"Eight days away, now." He groans.

Eating dinner after his shift was fine, but between driving and working, he just doesn't have a lot of time. If he teaches the kids a horseback lesson, he basically needs to sleep the rest of the day. "What about Saturday night?" I ask. "After your shift?"

"I'm switching to nights that day," he says. "Could I interest you in a nutritious breakfast?"

"Sure," I say. "Breakfast sounds fine."

"It's a date," he says.

"Since the first one ended with a dunking, does that make this our second date?"

"I hear that's the most important one. Vogue magazine says that's when a girl can decide whether the guy's a creep or a hero."

"Shut up," I say.

"I really should be heading to bed."

I yawn. "Me too."

After he hangs up, I brush my teeth and get ready to sleep. As always, I refresh my inbox one last time, just in case. In case of what? I don't know. Except again, like with Gus earlier, a new message does pop up. This time it's from Robert, and with a header like *Bad News,* I can't help checking it.

Abby,

Just got in from that trip to Atlanta and had this waiting on me (see attached). I'm so sorry—I know you weren't planning to be back yet. I don't think it's wise to refuse the request. Don't want to predispose the judge to rule against us. If you want to skip this one, I can grab Bev to fill in for you. We'll come up with another way to show the partners you're ready. No stress—we can always push the vote.

Robert

. . .

No stress? My success at *this* case was supposed to be the thing that convinced the partners to bring me in. How can I just pass the ball off to Bev at the ten-yard line? I click the attachment and find that the judge had a vacation change and two other cases cancel and can move the trial up to the last week of July. Which means I need to be there for pre-trial prep as soon as possible.

Like, within the week. I doubt I can even stick around long enough to honor our plans for Saturday.

I feel a little bit like Amanda. I shouldn't care about leaving early—I barely know Steve. It's not like I was ever planning to stay permanently, but my feelings of disappointment and alarm are real. For the first time in six weeks, I wonder whether I've been a little bullheaded. Am I wrong not to even consider giving Ethan what he wants?

Could he stay here himself and handle the ranch alone? I haven't even contemplated that option. I'll be sending him off to college alone soon enough. How would coming here be different? A college dorm is much safer than riding on a trail with hundreds of cattle, for one. It's also safer attending classes than working underneath a tractor, trying to drop the transmission, or whatever crazy thing he did yesterday that resulted in him having quarts and quarts of toxic waste dumped on himself.

I'm staring at my phone, debating whether to text Steve, when I hear a tap on my door. I glance at the clock. It's nearly ten o'clock. Pretty late for my early-riser kids.

"Come in."

I expect Ethan—but it's Izzy. "Hey, Mom."

"Is everything okay?"

She nods. "Can I come in?"

"Of course."

She perches on the edge of my bed.

"What's up?"

"I know Ethan just gave his presentation," she says, "and I know he really wants to stay." She drops her eyes to her hands. "I just thought you might want to know what the rest of us thought."

"The animals are a lot of fun," I say. "We could increase the frequency of your lessons back home."

"I just wanted to say that Whitney and I were talking, and she agreed with me."

"Okay."

"For the first time since Dad died, we actually feel like we're a family again."

"With Aunt Mandy and her kids here too?"

"Actually, we wish they'd stay," Izzy says. "Maren was a brat, but even she's getting better, and none of us want to go back to Houston. We like the animals, but we also like the rest. It's not even just the horseback lessons. We've also just been together more."

"Sweetheart, I can't work remotely forever." I'll never make partner from here, either. "And once school starts, you'll be just as busy here as you were back home."

"Maybe."

"I'm sure of it."

Her face turns upward. "Can you just promise me you'll really think about it?"

"Is everything okay?" I brush the hair away from her eyes. "I'm surprised you'd even want to stay. What about all your friends back home?"

"I don't have any," she says. "And neither does Whitney."

Their words barely make sense. "What about Reese and Harper? Liz? Or Shayla?"

"No one knows how to talk around me," she says. "Or at least, that's how it started. When they made some kind of joke, like, 'I'd rather die than drink a pumpkin latte,' they'd all freeze and look at me, as if they'd broken some rule by using the word 'die.' And then they just kind of started hanging out with other people, and there wasn't room for me at the lunch table any more." She shrugs. "I'm fine. It's okay. But we all like the idea that we'd have new schools and a fresh start."

"The new school would be really small," I say. "They probably aren't very academically rigorous, with the limited funding they have and the large geographic area from which they all pull."

"You don't know that," Izzy says. "You're guessing."

I shrug. "It's an educated guess." I grab her by the shoulders and pull her close for a hug. "No matter where we are, no matter what happens, we're always a family. I don't want you to lose that feeling." She doesn't seem to take the encouragement from my words that I hoped she would.

Usually I go right to sleep, but that night, I lie awake for hours.

When my alarm goes off, I want to hit it and roll over. For just one day, I want to pretend that I don't have to tell Ethan he's going to Rice and watch as his face falls and his hopes and dreams are squashed. I want to pretend that my kids will be eager to go home—to the home we were giddy to buy and have lived in happily for years. I want to pretend that I don't have to answer emails, review trial plans, feed animals, make food, clean common areas, and fold laundry.

But most of all, I wish I could close my eyes and get my life back, the one I worked so hard to create. I want my husband back—I want the future to be secure. I want someone else at my side who agrees that the things I'm doing are right. I want someone else to be the bad guy, just for once.

I take five minutes to pretend that I can have all that.

And then when my alarm goes off again, I groan and whine and whimper as I roll out of bed and pull on a pair of jeans. "They want to stay—here—where we're constantly feeding something and scooping poop for something else. Where riding isn't fun, where it's a chore. Where cows are constantly trying to injure themselves just to ruin my entire week." I push my door open and nearly run right into Ethan. "Oh, good morning."

"You seem chipper," he says.

"I'm tired."

His shoulders droop. "I'm sorry." He looks broader than he did before, and bulkier too. His eyes are brighter, and his skin has a healthy glow from being outdoors. All of that will disappear when he's stuck in a classroom all day.

But his future will be safe and secure.

"Ethan—"

He shakes his head. "It's okay, Mom."

"What's okay?"

"I know you want me to go to Rice. I got an email saying they need my tuition deposit soon."

This is when he'll do his final push. He'll argue. He'll plead his case.

"You really pitched in here," he says. "You got us horseback lessons and took them yourself. You made meals and did grocery shopping at a hardware store. You fed animals. You did a trail ride to herd the cattle." He grins. "You held up your end of the bargain. I'm not going to complain or guilt you. And I swear, once school starts, I'll work my hardest at Rice, too. I won't waste your money."

"Whoa, have you changed your mind?" I ask. "Do you want to go?"

He wraps an arm around me, his expression wistful. "I'd way rather stay here. I'm dreading college, to be honest, but if I survived high school, I'm sure I can survive college, too."

"Why aren't you upset?" I ask. "Why aren't you arguing to stay?"

"More than I want to run a ranch, and I do want to run this ranch a lot, I want you to be happy. I realized yesterday that even if you let me stay, you'd all be leaving." His voice becomes very small. "This has been the best summer I could have imagined without Dad, but I don't think I'd have liked it much if you guys hadn't come with me. It was even fun sharing a room with Gabe. He's a funnier little dude than I realized."

Gabe's actually hilarious, with his incessant drawing and his overblown vocabulary.

"I really appreciate you getting me into Rice, by the way. I know it took a lot of work on your part and stressed you out. I'm sorry I put you in that situation to begin with. I should never have thrown out all those applications."

"I'm sorry I haven't had as much time as—"

Ethan says, "Don't apologize for that. It's what makes you the *best* mom. You want what's best for our entire family, and you'll work as hard as it takes to get there—at work, at home, on a ranch. It was actually watching you give 125 percent out here that helped me be okay with going back."

He's giving me more credit than I deserve. "I hope you'll still think that when you hear about the email I got last night. The court changed the docket and now my trial starts at the end of July."

Ethan frowns. "What does that—"

"If we don't leave by the end of this week, my case will go to *Bev*."

"Crazy Bev? The lady with the beehive-mullet? The one who accused you of dressing like a sex-kitten?"

My jaw drops. "How do you know about that?"

"I heard you and Dad talking once. He thought it was the funniest thing in the world, and he said she was unhinged. Would Robert really hand it over to her?"

"If I don't head back, he won't have a choice. Many things can be done remotely these days, but trials still happen in person."

"She seems like the kind of person who's secretly plotting to kill everyone in the office. You can't let her have your case." Ethan forces a smile. "Plus, it'll give us all time to relax before school. Who needs horses and manure when they have an Xbox?" But the light disappears from his eyes.

"Thank you, for supporting me. Izzy came to beg me to stay last night, you know."

"Izzy? Why?"

"She loves it here. I feel like I'm breaking everyone's heart."

"It's alright, Mom." Ethan hugs me, and it almost feels like I'm hugging his dad. "Do you remember how, when I was a little kid, I hated eating broccoli?"

"You called them tiny trees," I say.

"No matter how much I cried, you made me eat them, because they were good for me. I'm sure you're right about this too. I may *want* to work a ranch, but I bet in five or ten years, I'll be thanking you for making me do the work to get a corporate job."

I sure hope so.

"What did Steve say?" He shakes his head. "If you'd told me last year that you'd date again and that I'd actually like him, I'd have called you a liar, but he's a good person."

"I haven't told him yet."

"Oh." He swallows, his Adam's apple bobbing up and down. "It'll probably be fine. I mean, you don't know him that well, and we all knew it probably wouldn't go anywhere."

"How did I get you?" My one desperate hope in coming this summer was that I would get my sweet son back. I didn't give him what he wanted, but my plan worked in spite of that. Even with a bump on the trial date, even telling him no about the ranch, the old Ethan is back. He's worried about his mother, he's comforting me.

All is right with the world.

"You should probably tell Mr. Steve," he says. "I mean, if I were him, I'd want to know sooner, not like, via postcard after you've left."

Guilted by my teenage son. "I'll take it under advisement."

I compose a few different texts while I supervise the kids feeding the horses. Their fuzzy noses and stamping feet soothe me. Even the smell of manure doesn't bother me like it did at first. They predominantly eat grass, after all. Once I let them into the pasture, I expect them to take off in a bunch like they usually do.

But Snoopy sticks around. "You have more than just horse sense, huh?"

"He does," a man says behind me. "He can sense when someone has treats."

I spin around, shocked to hear Steve's voice. "I thought you were working."

"Midday shift today," he says. "Tomorrow we have the morning horseback lesson, remember?"

I shouldn't be smiling, but I can't help it. Anytime I get to see him, I smile. "I'm afraid I have bad news." My smile melts. I want to wait, but I ought to tell him in person. "I won't be able to make it for our Saturday date."

"You hate breakfast?" He tilts his head. "You don't need to try intermittent fasting. You already look great."

If I didn't already know, his half grin tells me he's making a joke to cover his confusion.

"We have to fly back early," I say.

Snoopy gives up on me and jogs toward Steve, bumping him over the fence. Steve pulls out a carrot and breaks it into pieces, giving him the first piece. "Why?"

"The trial date on the big case I'm in charge of moved up."

"Does that happen often?"

I shake my head. "Usually one party would complain." I frown.

"But neither did?"

"The judge sent a request." I consider the language. Robert could have simply signed the bottom, indicating he had commitments that couldn't be changed.

But he didn't.

"We didn't really have a choice." But I wonder whether that's strictly true.

"I'm guessing your friend Robert was all for the shift." He shakes his head. "That guy doesn't play fair."

"He wouldn't have encouraged something that wrecked my plans." But I wish he'd tried a little harder to discourage it.

"Ethan's going back too?"

"He got into Rice," I say. "There was apparently some kind of foul play with an admissions test and a bunch of kids got scratched. It was a lucky break for him."

"Sounds like it." Steve hands the last piece of carrot to Snoopy and stuffs his hands in his pockets.

"I'm sorry to duck out before our breakfast."

"Did I ever tell you that my little sister died?" Steve's not looking at my face. He's staring at Snoopy's hooves.

"No."

He inhales. "I was young—in high school still. She was just a kid. Not even fifteen."

How tragic.

"Before she drowned," he says, "we did everything together. We rode horses. We swam in the creek. Every time we went into town with Mom or Dad, we'd spend every dime we had on baseball cards."

Weird.

"She loved baseball. She'd watch it every chance she got. Her favorite player was Mike Piazza." He shakes his head. "We had Becketts and baseball cards hidden all over our rooms."

"I'm so sorry for your loss," I say.

"After she died, I kept spending every dime I had on baseball cards." He finally meets my eye. "My senior year, my friend Beth came over. She looked around my room and said, 'I had no idea you even like baseball.'"

"Did you?"

He chuckles. "Nope. I actually think it's boring, but I kept right on collecting cards until Beth pointed that out, because that was our dream—to have the biggest baseball card collection on the whole West coast."

"But it wasn't *your* dream."

"I never bought another card, not since that day."

"Do you still have the ones the two of you bought?"

"Even packed up, they take up three boxes, but I still have them all."

It's pretty neat that he's held onto them all this time. "I wonder if any of them are worth anything."

"They're all worth something to me." His hand reaches across the fence and catches mine. "I hope all your dreams come true, Abby. I really do." He pulls my hand toward his mouth and presses his lips to the center of my palm. A thrill races through my entire body and my fingers curl, their tips brushing against the scruff on his face.

Then he turns and walks away.

26

AMANDA

I never liked eggs much. I'd eat them, but only if they were paired with something else. Chickens freaked me right out. Their bizarre, jerky movements. Their beady eyes. Their staccato pecking.

Until we arrived at Birch Creek Ranch.

I'm the first to admit that I was the most useless person who arrived in Utah. I didn't touch a horse the whole time I was there. I never fed the goats—their baaaing grated on my nerves and their little black piles of poo balls gave me the willies.

At first, the chickens strolling around everywhere, and pooping everywhere, made me crazy. But over time, I started to recognize the different hens. Some were red. Some were white. My favorite ones had little beard-looking feathers under their beaks. I called them the Aunties. Some of those chickens laid light brown eggs. Some laid white eggs. But some of them laid light, sky-blue eggs. Initially the bizarre shell color freaked me out, but by the time we board the plane to go home, I'm already missing them.

When a hawk called overhead, or when they dove and

screamed, those chickens would dive under the porch, into the bushes, or underneath a wheelbarrow. The two roosters, one a brilliant rainbow of colors, one a snowy white with long black tail feathers, would fluff up and strut, cawing right back.

It gave me new insight into the phrase 'to chicken out.'

So when I say that I 'chickened out' and texted Eddy my goodbye, I really mean it.

I wanted to go and see him. I wanted to call him and set up a time to meet, but every single time I replayed the way it would go in my head, it came out the same. I looked like a complete jerk, or I sounded like a ninny who lets a company dictate all my actions.

Plus, if I saw his dimples, I might do something stupid, like tell Lololime to jump in a lake. I just got the renewal of the contract on our apartment. Our rent's going up by a hefty amount. The girls' private school tuition is going up again as well—we need the income from that deal.

EMERGENCY BACK HOME. I'M SO SORRY—WE'RE LEAVING TOMORROW MORNING.

That's all I said in my text.

He texted back right away. I HOPE YOU'RE OKAY. I'M SAD YOU HAVE TO LEAVE SO SOON. WISH YOU ALL THE BEST.

Part of me was hoping he'd freak out. If my life was a movie, he'd drive over and interrupt our packing. Then he'd try to convince me to stay. Or he might even demand to know what the emergency is and offer to lend a hand.

But my life would be far too depressing to be a movie or a television show. And in real life, good people respect boundaries. No means no, and when I say I have an emergency and I'm leaving, a guy wishes me luck and lets things go. Maybe that's been my problem all along, wishing that my life would be more like a movie. It's not realistic, which sets up all the wrong expectations.

It hurt almost as much to leave Roscoe as it did to text Eddy my goodbye. The poor little dog was my perfect companion during my time. He followed me everywhere, waiting dejectedly by the front door whenever I left. Sure, I tripped over him, and every time he licked my hand, I cringed a little, knowing all the places his tongue would go, but of all the people who arrived, he chose me to love.

Being chosen and loved is always an honor.

And with the recent loss of Jedediah, I'm worried how he'll handle the fact that I've left again. I even considered bringing him to New York, but in the end, I decided that would be more traumatic for him than the departure of a woman he barely knew.

I'm sitting on the plane, Maren and Emery both plugged into their fully charged iPads, when I get the new proposal from Lololime. I frantically download the attachment, worried they'll make me shut off my phone before I can read it. They want me to push two lines again—the juvenile female line, and the adult one.

More specifically, they want Maren to model the juvenile line, and not only through images I selectively upload to my account. They want posts from her Insta account to interact with and somewhat mirror mine.

I can't articulate why, but the very idea of forcing posts on my teenage daughter enrages me. They signed with *me,* not with her. She only has a few thousand followers. Why would they want me to post the same images she does, and then tag her account? All the proposal says is that it will be 'more interactive and impactful.' What does that even mean? It's almost as bad as the word 'dynamic' was.

"You okay, Mom?" Emery's brow is furrowed. "You look upset."

I smooth my face and force a smile. "I'm fine, darling. Completely fine. I just can't wait to get home." Something brushes against the side of my leg and I reach down automatically to pet Roscoe, only he's not there. It's a kid holding a teddy bear, and I've just grabbed it.

The little boy immediately starts bawling and his mother looks like she's about to report me to Child Protective Services.

"I'm so sorry," I say. "His bear bumped me and it surprised me. That's all."

"Are you saying it's his fault you grabbed him?"

"I didn't grab him," I defend. "I grabbed his toy."

"He's three! What's wrong with you?"

I'd forgotten how crazy most people are. I turn inward, curling my body toward my daughters to avoid any further interactions. But the whole way home, I keep thinking about how I miss Roscoe. How I chickened out with Eddy. And how Lololime sucks. First they want me to build my campaign around a relationship—it's hard enough to date without my success or failure being linked to my performance at work. And now they want me to use my own daughter as some kind of marketing boost.

Of course, when we land in New York, my phone notifies me that the signing bonus for the contract has hit my account, and some of the wind goes out of my sails. They are paying me handsomely for the pleasure of directing my online persona. It's probably to be expected that they'll be annoying and somewhat heavy handed.

The second we arrive, before we even reach baggage claim, Maren's on her phone. At first she's just texting, but within half an hour, she's sending Marco Polos and voice messages to everyone she knows. I forgot how catty she sounds when she's talking to her friends. It sets my teeth on edge.

When we're getting into the cab, I glance at Emery. Her shoulders are hunched, her eyes cast down at her feet, and her fingers are twitching. It's her norm, or it was, before our vacation. I'd forgotten how anxious and unhappy she looked all the time before we reached the ranch.

"You never said anything when I said we were coming home early," I say.

Emery shrugs.

"Are you excited to see your friends again?"

She shrugs.

"Not at all?"

"Mom, I'm fine."

'Fine' is a code word. Abby knew it. I know it. "Emery, you can tell me how you're really feeling."

"No," she says. "I can't tell you, because I already know that you're as 'fine' as I am."

How is my daughter so brilliant?

"It's been a rough week, adjusting to Lololime and the things they expect of me now that I've signed with them."

"It was a rough few weeks trying to make them happy enough to choose you," she says.

She's freaking Gandhi. "Yeah. It was." That makes me wonder how bad the next two years will be—it's not like any part of this process has been fulfilling or particularly joyful.

"Do you like your job?" Her whole body straightens, her eyes brightening as she asks the question.

No one has ever asked me that. They ask what I do. They ask how it works. They ask how much it pays more often than I expected. But no one has ever asked me whether I *like* it. "No." I shake my head. "Sometimes I think I hate it, but I don't know how to do anything else, and I'm good at this."

Her expression's pained, like she just swallowed a bug. "I hope I don't have to spend my whole life doing something I don't like."

Spend her life.

It's a normal word to use in conjunction with time, but it hits me differently today for some reason.

I'm acutely aware that our minutes and hours and days and weeks are a form of currency—they're limited. We can choose how to use them, but then a finite resource of our life is gone.

Time *is* probably the most important currency of my entire life.

That thought hits me like a lightning strike to my brain, and I've been blowing it—every minute I spend at this job, doing something I don't like, is like throwing money away on something stupid. I've gone even one step further. I let the very job I don't like tell me exactly how to spend every bit of time I have—in exchange for money, a currency that is much more available and much less valuable! If I were talking to my own daughter, I'd never hesitate. I'd tell her to quit in a moment.

I whip out my phone and my fingers fly over the keypad as I tell Heather and Victoria that they can't dictate my life choices. They can't demand that I include my daughter in their promotions. I remind them that while I may have signed a contract with them, I'm still a real person living a real life, not a paper doll they can force to dance around. I'm ready to hit send when the panic overtakes me.

I have no idea what else I can do.

With no plan, no ideas, and no place to stay if I can't afford to renew our current apartment, I'm going to what? Burn down the house?

"Do it, Mom." Emery smiles, a real, happy smile, as she peers over my shoulder. "Don't keep doing things you hate for me."

"We need income," I say. "What about your school?"

"Keep the instagram account until you find something else, but ditch the people who order you around and make you feel like a loser." She taps my finger, sending the angry email out into the aether.

My heart races. "Your school tuition's due," I say. "And our apartment rent is going up."

"Then we go to public school," she says. "And we find a smaller place. Maren and I can share a room."

Maren pulls her headphones off. "If we have to share anyway, we may as well live somewhere free." She purses her lips.

"Free?" I blink.

"We could go back to Birch Creek."

"And run a ranch?" I laugh. "You couldn't even—"

"I was taking lessons." Her voice is small. Her eyes are unsure. Her fingers are white across the knuckles where they're gripping the armrest in the cab.

"You're here," the cab driver says in heavily accented English.

I pay him and the girls help me wrangle our luggage out of the trunk. The second our final bag is out, he speeds off, the momentum from the car closing the trunk.

"What a jerk," I say.

"Mom," Maren says.

"Yeah?"

"He was a normal cab driver. You just think he was rude because you've been somewhere that people are mostly nice."

Is she right?

"My friends are all horrible." She tucks her phone in her pocket and hefts both her suitcases. "I didn't realize that I was just like them until I got away from it. . .and then came back."

Could we go back to Birch Creek? We just left.

I imagine the farmhouse with just the three of us. I could turn one of the rooms into an office, and another into a storage room. Maybe I could sell. . .or make. . .or I could. . .surely there's something I'd be good at and also enjoy. I wrack my brain as the doorman helps us drag the mountain of bags inside. I keep flogging it as we unpack.

Could I sell jam? Where? That's probably ill-advised, since I've never made jam. Could I design clothes? I have excellent fashion sense. But I can't sew. I'm guessing that would be an issue. Maybe I could teach. . . What? Social media? Ugh.

I haven't had a single good idea.

A bumping noise outside my door makes me smile. Roscoe wants inside. Except of course, I left him back in Utah. The thought of him curled up against the door, mourning the loss of another owner, breaks my heart. Tears rush to my eyes. "Is someone there?"

Maren pokes her head through the doorway. "I think you used to like your job, when you first started."

It was exciting then, to get contacted by a company, or to be asked to use their products. I tried so many things I'd never have checked out, and I helped people find them too. "But the newer companies, the ones I liked working with, that I enjoyed finding, they can't afford to pay much."

"It would help if your expenses were lower. A paid-off house and free schooling would make that easier." She smiles.

"Are you really interested in going back to Birch Creek? That school's going to be tiny."

"I'm a little nervous about the school," she admits.

"But I could attend an online school if it came to that. There *is* internet there now."

"But what about friends?"

"I was thinking maybe you could call Aunt Abby," she says. "Her kids are kind of the first real friends I've ever had, I think."

"They're your cousins."

"Cousins can be friends, too, right?"

When I call Abby, she emphatically tells me that there's no way they'll go back.

Emery and Maren are *both* disappointed. "I doubt we could run the ranch alone," Maren says.

"With Kevin and Jeff, we can do it," Emery says. "I know we can."

"I can't ride a horse."

"We'll buy a four-wheeler," Emery says. "And I heard Roscoe was awesome at helping on cattle drives."

"There won't be enough of us to bring them home," I say.

"It's easier to get them back—they kind of find their way home for the most part." Emery looks so hopeful. I think about Ethan's face, when he said we hadn't done anything. . . He was right. We hadn't. But if my girls and I have our way, that will change.

"Alright. We'll spend the next few weeks here, packing, wrapping, and shipping. And at the end of July, when our lease is up, we'll get in a truck and move to Birch Creek."

If I wasn't positive before, the girls' whoops and hollers reassure me that it's the right call. It may be scary, but I'm done spending my time on things that don't bring me joy. That night, when I finally pull up my email to send the message to my landlord that I won't be renewing our lease, I notice that Lololime responded.

Twice.

The first email is from Heather, and it's rather heated. She points out, accurately, that her ideas gained me twenty-five percent again as many followers. It mentions the termination clause, which allows voluntary termination on their part for difficulty in communications. I expect the email to upset me more than it does. I have a place to stay. My girls will enroll in the local school system, which costs me nothing. And with what I've got in savings, I can buy a decent car and never have to drive a ridiculous van around again.

When I open the second email, from Victoria, I'm prepared for them to exercise the termination. In fact, I welcome the freedom it will bring.

Mrs. Brooks,

At first, your message upset our entire social media team. We spent many weeks, as you know, selecting the accounts we felt would best showcase our brand and our products, which we all love dearly. We felt that your criticisms of our suggestions and excitement for our partnership were exaggerated and unwarranted attacks.

But then I spoke with my husband. I debated leaving this out, but his words gave me some perspective. I would never allow someone else to dictate whom I dated, or when I moved, or where I lived or how I parented my children. How could I, in good conscience, ask someone to do things I could never do?

I felt it was alright for us to dictate things, given the terms of the agreement and the compensation you're receiving, but he pointed out that you earned that offer by making intelligent and attractive choices up until now. I feel that your honesty, your integrity, and your fire are all things that will serve you well as one of our brand ambassadors.

So if you will accept our apology, moving forward we'd still like to meet once a month to let you know what products we'd like to focus on, but we will leave the method in which you highlight them and the focus of your social media accounts and brand entirely up to you. Thank you for bringing to light a major flaw in our own processes so that we can become the partner you deserve in the future.

Best,

Victoria

"Mom! You're crying." Emery rushes into my room and climbs up on my bed. I'm not sure she would have been bold enough to do that before our summer trip. She wraps her arms around my neck.

"They're happy tears this time," I say. "Look."

I hand her my phone. It takes her a while to work through the email, but a smile engulfs her face once she does. "That's amazing! You'll still have the money."

"And maybe you can like your job again," Maren says.

"I certainly hope so." I pull out my laptop and bring up the Penske truck website. "Now how about we book our moving truck so this whole thing feels real? I'll call Mr. Swift tomorrow morning and tell him that instead of mailing him the keys, we're going to hang on to them."

27

ABIGAIL

I've never taken lead on a case before. My hands shake almost every time I stand up to speak, and I fumble a few things. But every time I do, Robert's there, with sticky notes, with files, with highlighted deposition transcripts, or with a smile and a thumbs up. He's the best second chair lawyer in the history of time. And even so, as I make my closing arguments, I'm not sure how the judge is going to rule.

"You nailed that," Robert says.

"You think?" I sink into the wooden chair and begin gathering our files. "They had a few really good points, and I tried to—"

"No, really." He places his hand over mine.

Instead of making me uncomfortable, it calms me down. Robert really came through with all his promises. He let me run the case, he gave me control over the direction in prep, and he let me do it all remotely. And then, he made me point person for the trial itself. "Thank you."

"Thank *you*," Joey Mayhugh says. "You were brilliant, and we feel confident this is going to go our way."

I hope he's right. "There's always a chance—"

"No one could have done better. If that judge rules against us, he's a blind fool—"

A door creaks, and I realize the judge is already coming back out from his chambers. He has a half smile on his face, his lips twitching. We all stand. He walks across the platform and takes his seat. "I am happy to say that I am neither blind, nor a fool." He motions for us to sit.

Poor Joey looks like he's about to pass out cold.

I pat the chair next to me until he actually sits.

"I've given all of this careful consideration, and not only am I ruling in favor of the Defendant, but I'm also going to order that MiddlePoint Power has to pay a penalty for acting in bad faith. I believe the requested penalty amount was fifty thousand dollars, plus all court costs and legal fees, and that seems more than fair. It's my genuine hope that this case will provide guidance for the other cases like this currently being prosecuted all over Texas, and I have no doubt my reasoning will be upheld if the Plaintiff appeals." He bangs his gavel.

Joey claps.

Robert picks me up and spins me in a circle. I text Ethan and Izzy with the news. Part of me wants to save it and tell them when I get home, but I can't wait. I'm sure they'll be happy enough when we go out to dinner to celebrate.

"This may be a little premature," Robert says. "But I know that you have the balance of Ethan's tuition due soon, and I wanted to make sure you had as much time as possible to work out the finances." A smile steals across his face. "The partners and I met last night about a separate matter, but they all voted, assuming the case turned out the way we hoped, that you would be the next partner at our firm." He hands me a piece of paper. "This is the buy-in information. I know it looks steep, but I can tell you from past years' experience that yours and Nate's shares will pay out enough to replenish the old coffers this coming New Year's."

"Thank you," I say.

"I imagine you'll be having dinner with the kids tonight," he says. "And I don't want to pressure you, but I'd love to take you out to celebrate any time you name."

"I think I'd like that," I say.

This time, his smile doesn't steal over his face. It hijacks it.

The rest of the day feels a bit like walking on a cloud. When Nate passed, after being partner for only three years, I wasn't sure how I'd ever be able to make enough alone to save for retirement and college funds like we planned. Then Ethan tried to bail on college and I wondered what I was doing any of it for in the first place.

But now he's enrolled, and I've made partner, and life will be as close to normal as it can possibly be. It was a lot of work, and I wanted to quit over and over and over. Sometimes I worried I'd collapse from the effort, but I stuck to the plan, and now it has all paid off.

"Take the rest of the day," Robert says. "Ethan starts school soon. Spend time with the ones that matter."

So I do.

My kids and I love Texas Roadhouse. Their hot, buttered rolls are like legal cocaine, and they keep them coming. There are plenty of sides to choose from, and who doesn't like a good steak? But for special occasions? We always go to the same place.

"Yay!" Gabe says when I tell them we're going to Taste of Texas.

"We haven't been in years," Izzy says.

"That may be an exaggeration," I say.

Whitney shakes her head. "We haven't been since before Dad died."

Is she right? I think about it and realize that first he was sick, and then he died, and then I started working, and we've been hanging on by our toenails ever since. Besides, there hasn't been much to celebrate in the past eighteen months. "Well, we're going now."

"I hope they have the same bread," Whitney says.

"I like Texas Roadhouse rolls better," Gabe says.

"Hush," Ethan says. "You don't even remember." He wraps his hand over the top of Gabe's head and tugs him against his hip, giving him a hug the same way you'd hug a bouncy dog.

Which makes me think of Roscoe. That dog barely ate a bite after Amanda left, and he wouldn't move from the door. I should text Kevin and Jeff and see how he's doing.

"What's wrong, Mom?" Izzy asks.

"Nothing. Let's go."

Luckily it's the middle of the week, and we're early enough that we don't need a reservation. They're seating us when my phone rings—and it's the courthouse. "Hang on just a second, kids," I say. "Let me take this."

Ethan gives me a thumbs up, and I know he'll keep an eye on the others and make sure they're not too boisterous. "Hello?"

"Mrs. Brooks?" It's the judge.

I certainly didn't expect him to call. "Is everything okay?"

"Don't worry—I didn't change my mind."

"That's a relief." My laugh is nervous. "What can I do for you?"

"I just realized that the email information I had on file was for the other lawyer on the case, Mr. Robert Marwell. Since you were lead, and you handled things so gracefully, even after he volunteered to take my open slot, I thought I should send it directly to you."

"Wait, volunteered?"

"Mr. Marwell, I mean. When he heard, through the court reporter, that I had a week free on my docket, he called to let me know that you could be ready in time."

He did? Steve was right—Robert wanted me out of Birch Creek and he *lied* to me about having no choice. He used *Bev* to force me back early. The whole win feels tainted, and I'm suddenly far less excited about Taste of Texas. "Is there any strategic reason he would have done that?"

"Strategic?" I can almost hear the frown in the judge's voice. "Not really. I mean, the other side might feel pressured to agree to it, but if they really weren't ready, they could have simply refused." He pauses. "Actually, it might have made it more difficult for you. I know they have at least a dozen of these cases pending, and big companies like that tend to focus heavily on the first in terms of time and resources. So being the first case made it more likely you'd get a fair shake, but their defense would be hitting it harder, too."

"Is there a chance he thought we could catch them unprepared?"

"MiddlePoint Energy?" The judge laughs. "Doubtful."

I give him my email address and thank him for his help, but his words keep bouncing around in my brain all through dinner.

"Is everything okay?" Ethan asks as they're clearing our plates. "You seem. . .deflated. Like an old birthday balloon."

"Gee, you're going to be a hit with the ladies at Rice. You sure know how to turn a phrase."

He rolls his eyes. "You know what I mean."

Sadly, I do. "Robert volunteered to move the case forward."

"Why would he do that?" Izzy asks. "It ruined our summer."

"I wouldn't say it *ruined* it," I say.

"No, it did," Whitney says.

"Oh, yeah," Ethan says.

"Big time." I have trouble taking Gabe seriously when he has butter smeared on his cheek, but his eyes are as earnest as I've ever seen them.

Big time? Coming *home* ruined their summer? "We like living here, though," I say. "You've had pool parties and you've gone back to gymnastics and horseback lessons here."

"Yeah." Izzy nods.

"Uh-huh," Whitney says.

"I miss Roscoe," Gabe says. "I've been praying for him."

That hurts my heart.

"I miss the chickens," Izzy says. "And Kronk and Maggie and Snoopy."

Ethan's utterly silent.

"Are you okay?" I touch his shoulder.

He jumps. "Yeah."

"You sure?"

His eyes are intense when he asks, "Do you like your job?"

"Being a lawyer?" I shrug.

"Did you like winning the case?"

"Everyone likes winning." For some reason, Steve's parting story comes to mind. He collected baseball cards. . .not because he liked them. Because he did it with his sister, and after she died, he mourned her death by continuing the practice. He hadn't even considered whether he actually liked collecting them—he didn't even like baseball.

And now Ethan's asking me whether I like to practice

law, and I realize I haven't considered this since he was a baby.

Do I like legal work?

Nate and I always planned to save enough that our lifestyle didn't need to change at all when we retired. We could spend at our current rate and go right on spending. Our house is already paid off. Our retirement funds are in alright shape—and now that I'll be a partner, we'll be able to keep spending the same thing year in and year out and still save almost the exact amount we planned. The stress that hounded my steps from the diagnosis of Nate's cancer is gone.

But is that what I want?

The same life I had planned with Nate. . .only without him?

Or am I just collecting cards none of us want because it's what we did before? Would Nate even want me to be a partner in his firm? Robert's my only real friend there—and it feels like he manipulated me to get me to come back. I really hope it wasn't so that I would have less time with Steve, but I can't be sure that wasn't his reasoning.

"I'm not saying that I'll do what you all ask, but I'd like to raise something."

The waiter shows up just then, of course, asking about dessert plans. I order the tower of chocolate cake, which is enough for all of us, and a key lime pie, and a Snickers pie.

"Can I get the cinnamon ice cream?" Gabe asks.

How does the kid who didn't remember the bread remember that? "Sure. Add it to the pile." The waiter walks away, beaming. He knows he'll be getting a huge tip.

"We're going to drown in dessert," Whitney says.

"Sometimes it's alright to drown in dessert," I say. "Like when you're hurting or you're sad. Sometimes it's healthy to stick to what you know, or to numb the pain.

But once you're far enough away from the trauma, you need to look around and decide what's healthy for the long term. So I'm going to ask you all something today that I should have asked before. I want to know, if you could pick your dream life, where it would be, and what it would look like."

"I want to run the ranch," Ethan says quietly. "But I want my family close. If you'll be here, I'll stay here too. So I guess what I want is to spend as much time as I can with the people I love."

It's a good thing they're all going to say something, because I can't talk at all right now around the frog in my throat. I bob my head and wipe at my eyes.

"I want to go back to the farm," Gabe says. "And not go to school. I want to play with goats and Roscoe and chickens all day. And I want to learn how to ride a stallion, and I want to fight bad guys with a long sword and wear a mask. And I want people to call me Gabe the Guardian."

Wow, that got specific.

When everyone laughs, he scowls. "I'm serious."

I pat his head. "We know you are, buddy. Your excitement just makes us happy, that's all."

"I want to get Roscoe a girlfriend, and I want to train her," Whitney says. "And I want to live with our cousins, and I want to make a lot of money selling cows, but I don't want anyone to eat them."

Trust Whitney to ask for something even more impossible than Gabe.

Something hits me then. I didn't tell them about this, because I didn't want to upset anyone. "Your Aunt Amanda actually called me," I say. "They're moving back to Birch Creek right now. I think they're actually driving the truck as we speak."

"What?"

"Are you serious?"

"No way!"

"What about you, Izzy? You never went."

"I want to win first place in the rodeo, at barrels," she says. "And I want to learn to make really good cookies and sell them to the Flaming Gorge Resort and the Grill in Manila because they don't have a great bakery. Maybe one day, I'll open a bakery. And I want to go to a small school and have good friends."

I should have known—every single one of them wants to move back to Utah. Every single one of them wants to live on the ranch. None of them want to collect baseball cards with me, in the land called 'Denial: Everything is FINE.'

"Well, then, I suppose I have an email to write," I say. "I hope that the partners won't be too offended when I write them and let them know that instead of becoming the newest partner, I'd like to go back to being Of Counsel and working part time—remotely."

As if it's a sign from Nate, the desserts arrive just then. The waiter totally thinks that's why the kids are all cheering, and that's fine by me. I think our life is about to be a lot sweeter—and not just for the next few minutes while we overdose on pie and cake.

That night, after the other kids are asleep, Ethan asks me, "Do I really not have to go to college?"

I snort. "Check your email, mister. There are plenty of great community colleges that will let you take classes online. I may have had an epiphany: life changes, and some of the best things may not have been part of the plan. But I'm not going to lose my stripes and become a cheetah—you can take a few classes a semester and be the smartest rancher in Utah and Wyoming combined."

He laughs. "Deal."

That next morning, I call Amanda. "How's Manila? Cold yet?"

"I will let you know the second we actually arrive." Her voice is terse—almost angry.

"Oh. I thought you said—"

"Have you ever driven a moving truck?" She swears under her breath.

"Mom! You nearly—"

"Maren, stop telling me what to do!"

"I can let you go," I say. "It sounds like—"

"What did you need, Abigail?"

"Um, well, I know I told you we were definitely not moving back, but we've had a change of plans."

All I hear from the other end is a loud crash, and my heart flies into my throat. My hands tremble. A rushing sound fills my ears. I should never have called her.

There's a whooshing sound, and then a lot more swearing, and then rustling. "Abby?" Amanda sounds. . .happy.

"Are you okay?"

"You surprised me, that's all," Amanda says. "Listen, if you're serious—"

"I am. I mean, we are."

"That's the best news I've heard all month! When will you be coming out?"

"We have a lot of things to do on this end, but I'm hoping to be there a day or two before school starts."

"That's a week," she says. "You think you can get your stuff packed and move out in a week?"

"Probably not," I say. "But we can get enough things ready to fly out. I'll have to go back and forth a few times to sort through things on weekends or something. I just want the kids to have as smooth a transition as possible."

"Let me know what I can do to help. I—I know we didn't get off to the best start."

I wonder whether she means as sisters-in-law or at Birch Creek. I suppose both are equally true. "I'm just relieved you're not upset. It's not a small house, but it's older and two families—"

"We'll remodel it, then," she says. "That could be fun. We can add some space and modernize everything."

To my shock, I'm actually excited by the prospect—of doing it at all—and doing it with her. "I love that idea."

"Okay, I'm going to hang up, but not because I don't want to talk more, or because I'm not excited. It's just that the road is winding and—"

"Of course. See you soon."

Those simple words are surreal to say. 'See you soon,' because Amanda Brooks is about to be a large part of my life for the foreseeable future—and I'm not even dreading it.

As I start making mental checklists in my head, I keep coming back to what she said right before I hung up.

The road is winding.

For the last two decades, ever since I took that pregnancy test and it came up positive, my road has been like a highway. Straight, predictable, and fast. Nate's diagnosis threw a terrible curve into the path of both me and my children, and I worried we'd fly off the road. I've been reassuring people ever since that we're all 'fine.' That the bend in the road didn't flip our entire car and wreck our path.

Of course it wrecked us.

But now we're back in the car, driving again, moving toward the future that lies ahead. I wanted to stick to the highways. Predictable. Straight. Fast. It was what I knew. But when Mr. Swift called, he gave me a choice, and with a little help from Ethan, I exited the highway in favor of a smaller, winding country road.

I had never realized, as I assured everyone I was fine and plowed ahead at 70 miles per hour, how very many things you miss when you don't slow down and look around. I suppose I have Nate to thank for showing me that the winding roads, the forks in the path, and the bends that almost throw us can sometimes bring us to the most stunning vistas.

28

EDDY

Nothing is physically wrong with this dog.

"You can see why we called." Kevin and Jeff are hovering on the steps of the big porch, shifting from foot to foot and hopping around like they're trespassing or something.

"He's listless, and he's definitely losing weight." I sigh. "But I don't think it's a medical issue."

"You mostly see large animals." Jeff frowns. "Maybe we should take him to Green River."

They're questioning my competency. That irritates me. "He did the same thing after Jed died," I remind them.

"He still ate his food though." Kevin climbs a few steps and nudges Roscoe's full bowl. "The only thing eating his food right now is ants."

"Let me have a chat with him," I say. "You two clear out." I slide down the side of the house until my butt hits the wooden slats of the porch floor.

Kevin and Jeff look at me like I just told them I'd be treating Roscoe with a séance and some lavender oil.

"Seriously, give me a minute."

They jump, but they finally leave.

I gently pull Roscoe halfway onto my lap and pet his fluffy head. His eyes don't meet mine, but I can tell he's listening. "You've had a terrible year, my friend."

He sighs.

I pat him. "First, you lost your best and most wonderful person. Jed was a jackhole to most everyone, but he loved you. For a dog, that's enough."

The guys called me out then too, but Roscoe *was* eating—he just wasn't doing much else. He lay by the front door all day and all night.

Until Amanda Brooks arrived.

Something about her brought him back to life. I can't even blame him for that. She did the same for me. I lean a little lower. "I liked her too, although, if you tell anyone I said that, I'll never scratch behind your ears again."

Roscoe closes his eyes.

I have an idea.

I pull out my phone. I have one voicemail from Amanda, one single voicemail. I put it on speaker and press play. The audio on my cell phone isn't perfect, but her voice still floods the surrounding area, loud and clear. "Eddy." She clears her throat. "I don't really have a reason to call, except that I wanted to hear your voice. I had a surprisingly good time last night. I've been thinking about something. I know we can't show your face, and I know you were helping me make a great social media image, which I appreciate, but there's no reason that *off camera* we have to. . ." She pauses. "Ugh. I'm rambling today. Anyway, I thought you might want to, I don't know, eat something today. Or tomorrow. Whatever."

And that's it.

Before I could call her back, she texted me to tell me she was gone.

The moment Roscoe hears her voice, he sits ups, his

ears attentive, his eyes bright. When it stops, he stands up, looking around the porch. He races down the steps and circles the house. Three times. Then he races up the steps to my side, his eyes searching mine. His message is clear. "Where is she?"

I thought it might help, but watching his distress and obvious agitation, maybe what I did was actually mean. "I feel the same way when I listen to it," I admit.

He whines then, sharp and quick at first, and then long and low.

After a few moments, he circles the porch and then drops back down in front of the door, his head far away from me.

"It's worse this time, right?" As I say the words, I realize it's true.

When I was a teenager, all I wanted to do was sing and play. I wanted to make great music, and have fans and friends who liked it. I wanted to impress my parents, and I wanted the shiny, bright future that was shaping up around that surprising talent.

I had no idea that my own flawed nature would wreck it all.

Afterward, I wished desperately that I'd never had that glimpse in the first place. It's much better not to know what you're missing. With my parents and their miserable marriage front and center, I knew the other thing I had to avoid—dating anyone seriously and getting married. Like pursuing success with a musical career, some things are just too risky. The downside is too steep.

I never met a single person who was vibrant enough to make me reconsider my position.

Not until I met Amanda, anyway.

She's hilarious. She's optimistic in the face of misery. She's bright and spunky and when I'm with her, it feels like I'm more alive.

It was a terrible mistake to pursue that kind of joy—to hope for that kind of future. I learned the lesson once, and apparently forgot it.

Now that she's gone, with nothing but a text, I'll never forget it again. "Poor Roscoe." I stroke his back. "You and I are a sorry pair, aren't we? No matter what the guys say, we both know there's nothing I can do for you. The only thing that will help you is to let go." That's probably the one thing he can't do—I know I haven't been able to delete the stupid voicemail either.

I stand up and brush off my jeans. "Maybe a little bit of a distraction will help." I walk to my truck and pull out a can of dog food. I pop the top and pour it over his dry kibble. Roscoe doesn't look very excited, but he's tempted enough by the smell that he eats it.

And sometimes, that's the best-case scenario.

It's not what we *wanted*, but we eat our crappy food and live to see another day. "This time, boy, you and I need to remember: stay away from shiny objects. They may be exciting, but in the long run, they're bad for our health."

29

AMANDA

I've been driving this beast of a truck for four hundred and ninety-three days. Or at least, it feels like I have. We've actually driven more than twenty-one hundred miles.

"Remember when we thought the full size van was bad?" I shake my head. "We had no idea."

"But, Mom! The GPS says we're only five minutes away!" Emery's bouncing up and down on the miserable bench seat, jostling all of us.

"The van was a rental. What're we going to drive when we get there?" Maren asks. "I'm starving right now—we never even stopped for breakfast. Please tell me we aren't going to have to drive *this* around."

I figured we'd buy a car here in Utah—one less thing to transport. But how will I get to the dealership to pick one? Where *is* the closest dealership? Ugh. These are all things Abby would have planned for—things she'd effortlessly navigate.

"This has been the world's worst road trip," Maren says.

She's right. I'm absolutely exhausted. "At least we're

almost there." A terrible thought hits me. "But once we arrive and I park, how will I ever back the dumb truck out again?"

"Mom, the ranch house has a circular drive, remember?" Maren sighs dramatically. "You need more sleep."

She's right, about both things. I toss my phone at her. "Check the Finder app and look for movers, now that we're close enough."

She pokes at my phone for a moment. "Uh. Bad news. There's nothing in range, it says."

"Nothing?" That can't be right. "Nothing at all?"

Out of the corner of my eye, I see Maren swivel the phone toward me. "Nada."

"I can't look at that right now. I'm trying not to crash."

"We can't even unload our stuff from the truck, not until we've cleared out all of Uncle Jed's stuff, right?" Maren asks. "How are we going to do that?"

I try not to panic.

I fail miserably.

"You okay, Mom?" Emery asks. "You're breathing kind of strange."

"I might be a little stressed," I say. "We have a lot of things at the house to disposition."

"Dispowhat?" Maren asks.

"Uncle Jed's things and ours won't all fit," I say.

"Right." Maren's quiet for a moment. "What about Kevin and Jeff? Maybe they can do it. They do work for us."

"They work for the ranch, doing ranch things." We can't really expect them to move a bunch of stuff. "But maybe they can help us find people we can pay." I breathe in and out slowly, and I turn into the driveway—and very nearly plow into a white SUV parked there.

I slam on the brakes and they screech, and thankfully, the enormous, awful truck stops. I shift it into park.

"Whoa!" Maren says. "Isn't that Dr. Dutton's SUV? Telling him we were coming was so smart."

I most certainly didn't tell him anything—but she's right. He's here, standing on the porch, Roscoe lying beside him. Why is he here? Did Mr. Swift tell him I was coming? I figured Eddy'd be too mad at me for the way I left to care.

I open the door and climb down from the ten foot tall platform masquerading as a seat. I toss the keys on the cushion.

Eddy walks down a few porch steps to get a better view. I know it's him, thanks to the familiar SUV and his general shape. But from this distance, he has no way of knowing who I am or what I'm doing here.

"It's me," I say. "Amanda Brooks."

At the sound of my voice, Roscoe leaps to his feet and sprints toward me like a shot. He practically knocks me over in his excitement. I drop to my knees and grit my teeth while he licks me all over my face. "I'm happy to see you too, big guy. Did you miss me?"

"We both did." Eddy didn't bolt toward me, but he moved this way too. He's now only a few feet away. "I thought you were gone for good."

My heart's beating a million miles a second when I look up at him. "That was the plan. Actually, Lololime ordered me to go back to New York, but it turns out I don't take orders very well."

"I'll keep that in mind."

"You should."

"The full size van didn't get you enough attention?" he asks. "Don't tell me the rental place only had moving trucks." His expression is bemused.

"In a small town like this, I need a gimmick, right?

There's already an old lady with a pig. There's an inattentive postal worker. There's a woman who sings to her plants. There just aren't that many good options out there at this point—I decided I'd be the Penske Girl. That has a nice ring to it, right?"

"Actually." Emery climbs out of the passenger side and circles around. "Mom had a meltdown about a mile back. The trip here was hard, and we don't really know anyone. She was kind of panicking about how we're going to unload the truck and clear out the old stuff from Uncle Jed's house by ourselves."

Great. Now he thinks I'm helpless, and worse, hysterical. "I was merely concerned I wouldn't be able to locate movers here," I say. "The app I used in New York turned up no results. I was hoping Kevin and Jeff might know some people—"

Eddy takes another few steps, until he's close enough to reach out and touch me. "You've been in New York City too long."

"We weren't there very long," I say. "It hasn't even been three weeks."

"Roscoe will attest that it felt more than long enough." Eddy crouches down, but Roscoe doesn't so much as shift from my side. "That's why I was here. He's been absolutely miserable without you."

Oh, no. I rub his head again. "I'm sorry you've been sad." It's probably because he lost Jed. I was worried about that—but I figured taking a country dog to New York would be harder on him.

"That's not what I meant when I said you were in New York too long—I meant that you're thinking about things all wrong. You know plenty of people in Birch Creek." Eddy stands up. "We're all your neighbors now, and we'll all lend a hand with whatever you need."

"Hey!" Jeff shouts. He's driving the little utility cart, and Kevin's riding with him. "You're back!"

"I am," I say. "But I'm afraid you'll be wishing I wasn't soon enough."

"She's worried about how she and the girls will get the house cleared out and her stuff moved in," Eddy says.

Jeff and Kevin both whip out their phones. Within fifteen minutes, a dozen neighbors are on site. After introducing myself to three women and seven men, I finally see a familiar face.

"Amanda! You're back." Amanda Saddler's beaming at me, her wrinkled face as animated as ever. "I hear another season of *Bridgerton* will be out soon. I was worried I'd have to watch it by myself."

"You didn't have to drive down here," I say. "It's exhausting work—"

"Oh please," Amanda says. "I may be old, but I'm healthy as a horse."

Another truck pulls up on the side of the road—the driveway is clear full—and Steve climbs out. He jogs over immediately, his eyes scanning the area. Wonder what he's looking for. . .

"I think we should move Jed's stuff into the front of the metal building," Kevin says. "Then you can sort through your things and figure out what to keep before we fill it with the end of the hay crop."

"Good idea," Steve says. "Do you have enough furniture in the truck to fill up all the rooms?"

"I don't," I say, "and I think we ought to leave beds in at least three of the rooms for now. Abigail isn't going to have anything with her when she gets here. Or at least, I don't think she will. She really wants to catch the beginning of the school year."

Steve freezes. "Abby's coming back?"

Looks like I'm not the only chicken in our family. She

clearly didn't tell him about her plans. "She just called me. I think she made the decision very recently."

"Well, we better get going." Steve leads the charge into the house.

Amanda Saddler hefts a huge bag full of cleaning supplies over her shoulder.

"Amanda, really, please don't—"

"You're one of us now, so you should learn this," she says.

"What?" Maren asks.

"City folk stop working when they get old. They *retire*." She cackles. "Out here, we never stop working. Sitting around ain't good for you." She trudges up the steps and into the house. I doubt anyone could stop her.

For hours, as soon as a room's cleared out, Amanda's there, wielding a broom or a vacuum and an armful of cleaning rags and solvents. Every single room we clear is cleaned and ready by the time we're prepared to move boxes and furniture inside.

"Where does this go?" Eddy points at a whitewashed bunk bed.

"That's mine," Emery says. "But me and Maren are going to share the front room. The one with the big bay window."

"If we have to share, it's only fair that we get the best room," Maren says. "Don't you think?"

"Absolutely I do." Eddy hefts the back of the bed and carries it into the house. "But the real question is, who gets the top bunk?"

The girls follow him, both making their case, and for a moment, no one is talking to me or asking me anything.

As I look around at all the people here to lend a hand, most of whom I've just met for the first time, I realize that Eddy's right. I spent far too long in the big city, if this is how life works in a small town. I duck into the pantry for a moment as my eyes well with tears, but unlike the tears I've cried so often in New York, these tears are joyful ones.

THE END

Don't worry—the story isn't over yet. The Vow is out now! So is The Ranch! The Retreat is coming soon!

Are you looking for something you can read right now? If you haven't tried my Finding Home Series yet, you can grab the first book, Finding Faith, in ebook format absolutely free on all platforms. It's got a little narrower focus than the Birch Creek Ranch series, focusing on one standalone love story per book, but the series is already complete.

ACKNOWLEDGMENTS

First and foremost, THANK YOU DOUG BECK! I really can't say enough good things about my dear friend Steve Beck (whose family ranch inspired my idea) and his brother Doug (who runs said ranch). They were tireless in their willingness to answer questions. They were both excited for me, and they never made me feel dumb, even when there were a LOT of things I did not understand. Their family really has a ranch outside of Manila, and they really have owned it since the original land grant. (So cool!) Their father's will inspired my story, and their generosity helped me from inception of the idea through execution of the first book.

Chris Billington and my mother-in-law, Lila Baker, also helped me with ranching questions and helped me to understand the general ideas about ranching and cattle.

While I credit them with helping, I take full responsibility for all errors I made! I'm sure that even after doing as much research as I could, I made quite a few, and I swear none of them are their fault. They did their best to help! I'm a lawyer, and my hubby is an ER doc, and we have a border collie and horses and chickens, but there were SO many things about a working ranch that I just did not understand.

I owe a huge thank you to my dear friend Jenae Niko, and my beloved sister-in-law, Angela Johnson. I love you both. Your lives inspired me to write a story like this in the first place. You've both been so beautifully strong in the midst of trials and adversity. You're a blessing to everyone around you.

I also owe a big thank you to Sissy Wilkinson, one of the "Tried and True Moms" on IG. I knew even less about influencers than I knew about ranches, and she was so KIND to chat with me and help answer my questions. Again, any errors on those things are entirely on me.

One more thank you that needs to come front and center—Steve Archer has got to be the best horse trainer we know. He's been unbelievably patient with all my kids and my horses for years. I figured if there was going to be a horse trainer, he had to be named Steve Archer. I *did* ask permission first. ;)

Thank you, as always, to my husband, to my supportive mother and father, and to my five kiddos. They are always there by my side, cheering me on, and picking up all the slack that happens when I binge draft. Your patience, your understanding, and your cheerleading mean so much. My kids inspired the children in the book—although there are SIX kids in there, so I made one of them up. Maybe one of you can guess which one. :P

Thanks to my cover designer Shaela, for giving my baby a beautiful face. And thanks to my editor, Carrie, for always being willing to squeeze me in and doing such a great job.

And for my fans, you guys already know how much I love you. I appreciate your support, your recommendations, and your patience. THANK YOU!! I love my job, and you make it possible for me to keep doing it.

ABOUT THE AUTHOR

Bridget's a lawyer, but does as little legal work as possible. She has five kids and soooo many animals that she loses count.

Horses, dogs, cats, rabbits, and so many chickens. Animals are her great love, after the hubby, the kids, and the books.

She makes cookies waaaaay too often and believes they should be their own food group. In a (possibly misguided) attempt at balancing the scales, she kickboxes daily. So if you don't like her books, maybe don't tell her in person.

Bridget is active on social media, and has a facebook group she comments in often. (Her husband even gets on there sometimes.) Please feel free to join her there: https://www.facebook.com/groups/750807222376182

ALSO BY B. E. BAKER

The Finding Home Series:

Finding Faith (1)

Finding Cupid (2)

Finding Spring (3)

Finding Liberty (4)

Finding Holly (5)

Finding Home (6)

Finding Balance (7)

Finding Peace (8)

The Finding Home Series Boxset Books 1-3

The Finding Home Series Boxset Books 4-6

The Birch Creek Ranch Series:

The Bequest

The Vow

The Ranch

The Retreat

The Reboot

Children's Picture Book

Yuck! What's for Dinner?

Books by Bridget E. Baker (Same author—still me! But I use a penname for my fantasy and end of the world to keep from confusing Amazon's algorithms!)

The Birthright Series:

Displaced (1)

unForgiven (2)

Disillusioned (3)

misUnderstood (4)

Disavowed (5)

unRepentant (6)

Destroyed (7)

The Birthright Series Collection, Books 1-3

The Sins of Our Ancestors Series:

Marked (1)

Suppressed (2)

Redeemed (3)

Renounced (4)

Reclaimed (5) a novella!

The Anchored Series:

Anchored (1)

Adrift (2)

Awoken (3)

Capsized (4)

A stand alone YA romantic suspense:

Already Gone

Made in the USA
Las Vegas, NV
22 January 2024